Praise for

YOU REALLY GOT ME

"Lovable characters and pulse-pounding chemistry make this one of my favorite reads of the year!"
—Laura Kaye, *New York Times* bestselling author

"A poignant tale about uncompromising love . . . Kelly really brings these multidimensional characters and world alive . . . A no-holds-barred tale of drunken nights, an alpha rockstar, and a charismatic heroine." —HeroesandHeartbreakers.com

"[A] no-nonsense, gritty story line about the uglier side of rock and roll . . . There are destructive moments of anguish and heartbreak followed by intense passion and provocative love. Erika Kelly will captivate your imagination."
—The Reading Cafe

"An entertaining and wild ride as Emmie and Slater learn what's important while fighting their fears. Erika Kelly created an interesting portrayal of the music industry and some lovable characters." —Harlequin Junkie

"A really interesting look at how hard it is to be a whole person, let alone be in a relationship, and also be a celebrity— or an aspiring one . . . This is an author to watch."
—*RT Book Reviews*

TAKE ME HOME TONIGHT

Erika Kelly

BERKLEY SENSATION, NEW YORK

BERKLEY SENSATION

An imprint of Penguin Random House LLC
375 Hudson Street, New York, New York 10014

TAKE ME HOME TONIGHT

A Berkley Sensation Book / published by arrangement with Suzanne Kaufman Kalb

ISBN: 978-1-101-98722-3

PUBLISHING HISTORY
Berkley Sensation mass-market edition / April 2016

PRINTED IN THE UNITED STATES OF AMERICA

10 9 8 7 6 5 4 3 2 1

Cover photos: portrait of a sexy male model © CURA photography / Shutterstock;
piano keyboard © BlueSkyImage / Shutterstock;
electric guitar (tattoo) © Andrei Krauchuk / Thinkstock.
Cover design by Rita Frangie.
Interior text design by Kelly Lipovich.

Penguin
Random
House

This book is dedicated to Sharon,
for talking me down and building me up.

ACKNOWLEDGMENTS

♪ My hero, my best friend, the love of my life . . . .
Superman, I think we're rockin' the empty nest.

♪ Joshua Path, phenomenal singer-songwriter . . . with a
heart full of gratitude, I thank you for being my
consultant on all things music-related in this series.
Your help has been invaluable throughout, but on this
book? I couldn't have written it without you.

♪ I have lucked out with my publishing team. Thank you,
Leis Pederson, for seeing every tree in the forest. Rita
Frangie and the art department, you guys knocked my
covers out of the park. Yvette Grant, Joan Matthews,
and Ryanne Probst, thank you for such great support!

♪ Of all the agents in all the land, I got the best. Thank
you for being so awesome, Kevan.

♪ Sharon, you are the best friend and critique partner a
girl could ask for.

♪ You are always hugely helpful, Olivia, but on this
one . . . you saved the day.

♪ There is no community as supportive and generous as
romance readers and writers. The Dreamweavers, my

chaptermates at CTRWA, COFW, CoLoNY, and WRW, and all the wonderful people I've met along the way—thank you for your friendship, advice, and support. (Like, for example, Laura Kaye, who came up with the title for this book!) And the blogs? Don't get me started. Obsessed with Romance, About That Story, Reading in Pajamas, Herding Cats and Burning Soup, Guilty Pleasures, Cocktails and Books—just to name a few—your passion for stories and support of authors is inspiring. And a special shout-out to Kristy DeBoer and Kathy Page—you ladies rock!

CHAPTER ONE

"I love you, Slater fucking Vaughn!" The zealous fan tossed her panties onstage, and the band launched into its next song.

Oh, I love this one. Closing her eyes, Mimi Romano let herself float away on Slater's sexy, emotional voice and wildly romantic lyrics.

Her phone vibrated in her hand, jerking her back to reality. She whipped it up so fast it leapt into the air, and she scrambled to catch it—it was like trying to wrestle a live fish. Thankfully, she caught it before it hit the ground.

Calm down, you freak! She had to laugh at herself. She'd auditioned, what? Eight hours ago? No way would she get a response so quickly.

Mimi swiped the screen. Even though she knew it was too soon to hear back, her spirits still plummeted when she saw a text from her mom.

Anything?

She'd go out of her mind if people kept bringing it up. I love you but please don't keep asking! It'll make me crazy.

Her mom responded right away. Sorry! Excited for you.

Promise to let you know.

She knew her mom didn't like being on the other side of the world while Mimi pursued this amazing opportunity. But, of course, Mimi hadn't even applied when her mom had decided to spend three months in Australia with her boyfriend—who just happened to be the band's A&R guy.

After dropping her cell phone into her clutch, Mimi looked up to find her friend Violet standing beside her with a hopeful expression. She shook her head. "I'm sure I won't hear for a few days." *Gah.* The wait would kill her. An interview, a debate, pitching a proposal, anything business-related, she could crush. But a cooking competition?

What were you even thinking? Why had she gone after something so outside her wheelhouse?

"What was that?" Violet asked.

"What?"

"That face you just made. Like you just realized you forgot to put on pants."

"Oh, that?" She laughed. "You mean that moment of blind panic?"

Her friend smiled warmly. "Yeah, Meems. That."

"Well, I mean . . . fuck a duck." She let out a huff of breath. "I *really* want to get on this show. I know it's ridiculous. Obviously, I should be looking for a real job instead."

"You've *been* looking for a job. Eleven months, Meems. That's a long time. And you've hit more than your share of dead ends. I think you're amazing for trying something different."

Hope reared its head, but she stomped it back down with the toe of her sling-back sandal. "Half of me's shaking my pom-poms, totally believing what you say, and the other half is like, 'Girl, are you nuts? You don't stand a chance.' I mean, come on, I auditioned for a cooking competition with an MBA."

"You're way more than an MBA. You're the chef for an

up-and-coming rock band, and you're Dino Romano's daughter. You grew up in the restaurant business. And if that still doesn't get them, your amazing personality will."

Her friend was absolutely right. *So* right that hope wriggled back up—and stuck its tongue out at her. A rush of emotion had her enveloping Violet in her arms. "Thank you." She'd needed to hear that.

"Oh, honey, you're shaking."

"I have to get this, V. I have to." Because scoring a spot on a nationally televised cooking show? *That* would fast-track her way onto her dad's payroll. God knows nothing else had.

Okay, really, she had to stop thinking about it. It was out of her hands at this point. She turned around to watch the band.

She'd met Blue Fire while living on Violet's wildflower farm at the tip of Long Island. When one job after another hadn't panned out, she'd wound up helping her mom and Violet develop their wildflower-based products. They sold tea, soap, candles, and potpourri to high-end gourmet and specialty shops in New York.

She loved living with the band, and watching them perform never ceased to thrill her. They were *that* freaking good. Never in her life had she seen a hotter lead singer than Slater Vaughn. With the sculpted physique of an athlete and a striking face that had graced the cover of *GQ*, he'd already hit *People Magazine*'s Sexiest Man Alive issue.

But for all his hotness, she had to admit, her gaze always slipped right past him and onto her favorite distraction: Blue Fire's temporary keyboard player.

Calix Bourbon was a total badass. Dark, tall, brooding. The kind of guy that made a girl think of uninhibited, pull-my-hair-when-he-takes-me-from-behind sex. Not that she wanted him, of course. Calix wasn't the type to have a girlfriend. Just the kind a woman had filthy thoughts about. Harmless.

But filthy.

As he threw his whole body into playing, his dark hair shook, gleaming in the lights, and his thick biceps flexed and bulged. *That man is sexy as fuck.*

Violet bumped her shoulder. "Since when is a rocker dude your type?"

Oh, crap, had she said that out loud? She slapped a hand over her mouth, hiding her smile.

"Unless you're imagining him waiting for the 2 train wearing an Armani suit, a pair of leather cap-toe oxfords, and carrying a Ferragamo briefcase?"

"You think I'd wrap that body up in a suit? But thank you for not cutting his hair off in that scenario."

"Oh, it would be criminal to cut Calix's hair."

Right then the song transitioned to the swoony part. "I *love* this." She held her breath as Slater belted out a note so wrought with emotion it twisted around her heart.

As always, though, her gaze wandered to the keyboard player. At six-four, Calix had the hard, ripped body of a fullback. Add in his mess of shoulder-length hair, facial scruff that framed a generous mouth, and unusual ink all over his body, and the man was pure, smoking-hot badass.

Just then his head tipped back, and it felt almost lurid to watch his intensely sensual expression. As if she'd walked in on him in the throes of sex.

Hot, sweaty, uncivilized sex.

"Why won't he just join the band already?" Concern tightened Violet's brow. "It's not like he has anything else going on. What musician wouldn't want to be with these guys?"

And see? That was why Calix was nothing but a fantasy. A session musician at age twenty-six, he didn't have an ounce of ambition or drive. She didn't know him well—he came to the studio when called and left the moment he was no longer needed—but if she'd met him in college, he'd have been the quintessential frat boy with a cigar in his mouth, a girl's ass cheek in his hand, and a perpetually sloppy grin on his devastatingly handsome face.

Not her type *at all*.

Now, a man in a suit, a sharp watch on his wrist, intelligence in his eyes. Yeah, that.

Her phone buzzed, sending a jolt through her body. Could this be it?

Quickly swiping the screen, she found a text from her dad.

Meeting just ended. Heading back to the city.

Wait, seriously? He'd been out in the Hamptons all weekend, and she hadn't seen him once.

Let's just get a drink before you go.

Better not. Have an early meeting.

She tried to ignore the pinch in her heart. Hey, now. If I can't get those crespelles you promised me, you can at least buy me a drink! She'd planned on sleeping over at his house, but the deal he'd been working on for months had blown up, keeping him in the city until Saturday afternoon.

She knew not to take it personally—of course her dad loved her. He was just super busy.

Tough weekend, tesoro.

One drink with your daughter could be just the thing. ☺

When he didn't immediately respond, her body went tight. He wouldn't blow her off, would he? Not when she'd put herself out there.

But then her phone vibrated, and relief sped through her.

You're right. It will be just the thing. I'm turning onto Main Street. I'll park and we'll get a drink at La Plume.

Let me say good night to Violet. Meet you outside.

But when she turned back to the stage, her gaze caught on Calix. His hair shimmied with his passionate playing.

Completely absorbed in the music, he had no idea how much sex he was having right at that moment. Every woman in the room had to be thinking about dragging him off to the bathroom and licking a path from his pecs to his—

"And I thought rockers weren't your type."

Mimi just smiled at Violet. "I'm just surprised he can play when I'm pulling his hair as hard as I did in my mind just now."

"You dirty girl."

"Listen, my dad's outside. I'm going to go."

A crash of drums hurt her ears. In the following moment of silence, Slater Vaughn pulled up his T-shirt to wipe the perspiration off his handsome face, and women screamed and threw more panties onto the stage. Ben, the drummer, tossed his sticks into the crowd.

Applause broke out, and she allowed herself one last look at Calix. A shock of awareness hit when his gaze met hers across the crowded room. He gave that half smile of his—more a smirk—then disappeared from the stage. Mimi turned to go, when Violet reached for her.

"Let me know if you hear anything."

"Of course. See you at the house."

Making her way through the crowded club, she pushed out the door and stepped into the cool April air. She didn't see her dad's car out front, so she checked for him down the street. Lined with bright blue awnings and black wrought iron benches, the sidewalk was quiet at this late hour.

For eleven months, she'd had nothing to share with him but one failure after another. She'd love more than anything to give him good news tonight.

"Amelia," her dad called from across the median. Typing away on his phone, he stood under an old-fashioned streetlamp.

She'd just give her e-mail a quick check. Pulling her phone from her clutch, she logged into her account and waited for it to load. *Please, please, please let there be an answer.*

Her skin tightened when she saw a message from NBC. She opened the e-mail.

Dear Ms. Romano,

We are happy to welcome you as a contestant on our five-week cooking competition on the Verna Bloom Show. *This is a huge achievement, as over 750 finalists auditioned for the six spots.*

The competition begins in one week, so please show up promptly at 11 A.M. on May 2 for makeup and wardrobe.

Holy crap. Holy freaking crap. Mimi wanted to scream and jump up and down. Instead, she raced across the street and threw herself into her dad's arms.

He laughed, hugging her so tightly her feet lifted off the grass. "Tell me, my love. Tell me the good news." Even though he'd been in America since he was a boy, he still retained a hint of his native Italian accent.

She pulled back, finding it hard to speak through the wild pounding of her heart. "Dad, oh, my God. I made it. I got on the show." She shoved the phone at him.

He pulled his reading glasses out of the pocket of his sport coat to read the screen. His handsome features pulled into a scowl, and he handed the phone back. "Okay."

Confusion—and disappointment—slammed her. "Okay?"

"Come, let's get a drink. We can talk about some ideas for you."

Wait, why was he being so dismissive? "Didn't you read it? I made the *Verna Bloom Show*. Oh, my God, Dad. I made it. There were thousands of applicants, and I made the show."

"Amelia, stop." He looked at her like she'd suggested they do body shots.

"Stop what?"

"You're not doing this show."

"What do you mean I'm not doing it? Of course I'm doing it." Where was this coming from? "You knew I'd auditioned."

"Why would I take it seriously? It's ridiculous."

"There's nothing ridiculous about it. Oh, my God, I can't believe it. I did it. I'm going to be on the show." God, Verna

Bloom was the hottest cooking show host in the country. "Do you know what an amazing opportunity this is?"

"To do what? Make a fool of yourself on national TV?"

She couldn't have been more stunned if he'd shoved her. "I'm not . . . why would I make a fool of myself?"

"Because you're not a chef. You have no training."

"I might not have formal training, but I . . . I cook."

Her dad lowered his chin and raised his eyebrows in a familiar expression that made her feel like the ten-year-old girl who'd told him she could make a *croque-en-bouche* without a recipe. "Standing on a chair beside me as I make *crespelle* is not the kind of training necessary for a career in the culinary arts."

"I'm not looking for a career in the culinary arts." She lifted her arms in a gesture of, *What the hell are you talking about?* "What is the matter with you? You want me to have real-world experience. Well, here it is."

"That's enough. I don't want to talk about this anymore. Come, let's get a drink."

"I don't understand why you're acting this way."

Those dark eyes narrowed on her. "You want me to take you seriously, then take yourself seriously."

Her mind shorted out, and she felt momentarily disoriented. "Of course I take myself seriously. I've spent the last eleven months killing myself to get a job. Why would you say that?"

"Because you're talking to me about reality TV."

"It's a *cooking* show."

"Amelia, for goodness' sake, do you really want to be Verna Bloom's *apprentice*—is that how you see yourself?"

"I see myself as an educated, competent woman who's trying to get the kind of experience that will make her father hire her."

"Why the hell would I hire Verna Bloom's *apprentice*?"

"Because she got chosen out of thousands of applicants to audition. And then she beat out seven hundred and fifty people to land a spot on the show. And then she slammed five other contestants to *win*. You hire winners, right, Dad?"

"I don't hire reality TV imbeciles."

The blow rendered her speechless. She turned away from him so she could calm down enough to think. She wanted to point out the difference between a cooking show and the Kardashians, but that didn't seem the point. Not to her. "I don't know what you want from me. I've done everything you asked. You said Ivy League, and I did it. But you didn't hire me. You said I had to get an MBA first. So I got it. But it still wasn't enough. No, you had to throw out the real-world-experience hoop. I tried to get a job, Dad. You know that. Do you not want me to work for you? Is that the bottom line here? Because that's making a whole lot more sense than anything else right now."

"Amelia Oriana Romano, for God's sake. You think I'm stupid? I'm a stupid man? Is that what you think?"

"No, Dad." She couldn't believe he was getting worked up. She'd just landed an amazing opportunity and instead of being happy he was demeaning her.

"You are not only going to work with me, you're going to take over the company. You think I've built this business just to put it in someone else's hands? Your whole life I've taught you everything I know so that one day you'll step into my shoes."

Yes. That was what she wanted with all her heart.

"But those shoes are too big for you today."

"Too big? I'm sorry, are you saying my magna cum laude degree from Cornell in hotel administration isn't good enough to work at Dino Romano and Associates? My Columbia MBA isn't quite up to snuff? How about my three summer internships with the Hazard Group—your biggest competitor, who, by the way, wouldn't hire me because they thought I would feed deal information to you?"

"Your education is outstanding. But if you came to work in my office, you would be seen as nothing more than my daughter."

"What are you talking about? I'm going to be your daughter no matter when you hire me. And I'll earn their respect. You know I will. I'll do anything. God, Dad, I'll make coffee every day if that's what it takes to get started."

"Did you ever wonder why I have so few people working for me?"

"Uh, because you're frugal? Because you came to America with nothing but the clothes on your back? Because nonno was a tailor and nonna a seamstress, and you grew up in the two rooms in back of the shop? Because you put yourself through college washing dishes? And built this business with your own two hands?"

He chuckled. "Well, yes, all of that. But also because I hire only the best. And the nature of the best means there are very few of them. And, Mimi, my team? They're the major players in the restaurant industry. And they won't have respect for the owner's daughter hired right out of college. Trust me on this. You need to earn your way in this business before you come to them as an equal."

"So does that mean you're not hiring me until I'm forty with fifteen years of experience under my belt?" Because if that were the case, he could forget it.

"Of course not. It means you need to work for a hospitality development company so you can learn all aspects of the business. My firm is small, *tesoro*. Everyone knows a little bit about everything."

"Well, I've run out of job options in New York City. So, I'll earn their respect after my gig on the *Verna Bloom Show*."

"After you've made a fool of yourself on national television, they'll view you as the pampered socialite daughter of Dino Romano."

A prickly heat raced through her body. "Is that what you think of me?"

"Don't be ridiculous. But what do you think the world will think of you?"

"I don't care what the world thinks. I care what you think. You want me to have exposure to every aspect of this business? Well, that's what the winner of this competition gets. As Verna Bloom's sous chef for a season, I'm going to learn about cooking and the management of a kitchen. I'm going to make invaluable connections." She leaned in. "And I think you know better than anybody that the restaurant business in New York is all about connections."

"You should care very much how the world will see you because the show will depict you as a fool. They chose you for ratings." Her dad practically shouted at her. "Because you won't know what you're doing, and you'll cut yourself with a knife, and your sugar won't turn to syrup, and you won't present clean plates, and you'll be shouting *Fuck a duck* every time you get flustered."

Her body sank into a pit of hot, steaming mortification. She could see it. Everything he said, she could see happening.

And so she had to stop listening to him. No matter what, she was doing this show—there were no other options—and she *liked* this one.

His negative thoughts had the power to sink her, so she couldn't be around him right then. Taking out her phone, she turned and headed down the street. She'd call a cab and go home. Or maybe she should go back to the club. Get a ride with the band. No, they'd have to schmooze, do some press. She wanted to go home now.

At the intersection, she searched her contacts for the cab company. But she couldn't see through the blur of tears. More than anyone else's on the planet, she'd wanted his support.

"Amelia, sweetheart." She hadn't even noticed her father had followed her. "I love you, and I want the best for you. And I'm telling you right now this show is a mistake. I'm not trying to upset you. I'm trying to save you."

"Okay, but you *are* upsetting me. I have to do the show, Dad. I have nothing else, and if I don't do it, what then? What other options do I have?"

"We'll come up with something. There are always options." He gave her that determined look of his. The one he got when he tried to bend her to his will. "The kind that won't make you look like a fool."

Hurt pulsed with every beat of her heart. "I've been cooking for the band for four months. I grew up in kitchens. I'm not going to choke."

She was totally going to choke. She didn't know the first thing about culinary arts. But really, screw him.

"You've been making sub sandwiches and spaghetti and

meatballs." He grew serious. "You'll be the laughingstock of the show."

She took a step closer to him. "You're my father. And even if you're worried about me, you should still support me. Do you realize you haven't even said the one word I needed to hear?"

"What word, my angel?"

"How about *congratulations*?"

Just as her finger hovered over the cab company's number, a motorcycle roared down the street. With his long, dark hair fluttering out the half-shell helmet, the unmistakable figure of Calix Bourbon came cruising down the asphalt in a black and chrome Harley.

"I can't say it." Her dad shoved his hands into his pockets. "I can't tell you what you want to hear when I know the truth. And you know why? Because I love you. With all my heart, I love you, and I want the best for you."

"I'm doing this show, and I'm going to win."

"You are so much better than reality TV."

"So much better than the *Verna Bloom Show*, but not good enough to work with you? Cool, but where does that leave me?" She stepped into the intersection, forcing the bike to stop.

"Amelia." The concern in her dad's tone almost made her turn back to him.

Calix's big boot hit the ground. He watched her with those intense, dark eyes.

"Can you give me a ride?"

His heated gaze took a slow, predatory slide from her eyes to her mouth to her breasts, all the way down to her hips.

"Melie." The two syllables fired like pellets out of her dad's mouth. "What the hell are you doing?"

But she ignored him and approached the bike. She'd never ridden on a motorcycle. How could she straddle it in her tight skirt?

Without a word, Calix pulled a combat foldout knife from the pocket of his jeans and flipped it open. The loud flick excited the hell out of her. Leaning in, he looked up, a question in his eyes. Heart pounding, she nodded.

With the tip of the blade he pulled the skirt away from her legs.

"Hey." Her dad charged into the street. "Do *not* touch her."

But Calix didn't even look at him. He kept his inquiring gaze on Mimi.

She gave him a nod. In one swift flick of his wrist, Calix slit her skirt nearly up to her lace boy shorts.

"Are you out of your mind?" her dad shouted.

Instead of answering—and really, maybe she was a little out of her mind—she hitched up the material and threw a leg over the seat. With her hot pink panties exposed for all the world to see, she leaned forward, closing the distance between her and Calix's big body.

"Amelia, I don't know what the hell you're doing, but acting like a rebellious teenager is not going to encourage me to hire you."

"So far nothing I've done has *encouraged* you."

Calix pulled off his helmet and handed it to her. Once she had it on, she wrapped her arms around his incredibly hard, warm waist.

"I told you I'll come up with an idea for you, but if you get on that bike, I won't help you with anything."

"Then I guess it's up to me to take it from here."

Calix's big hand settled on her thigh, giving it a squeeze. She understood the question. "Go."

With a roar, the engine blasted between her thighs.

She never looked back.

CHAPTER TWO

Heavy cloud cover and the speed of the bike made the world around her a blur of shapes and scents. Mimi knew the area well enough to make out scrubby oaks and pines and clusters of small buildings as they passed from one hamlet to the next. Her eyes stung, and she tucked in closely to Calix's back. He smelled good—really good—and the worn leather of his jacket felt soft against her cheek.

He turned off Sunrise Highway, sped down country roads, and all the while Mimi just held on, leaning with him as his bike tore through the black night. And then he eased into a long, winding driveway that led to a sprawling one-story house. He stopped and cut the engine. Her legs felt shaky, and the roar of the machine still vibrated through her body.

"Okay?"

His gruff voice prompted her to actually get off the bike. "Oh, sorry." One foot hit the ground, and she had to hoist the other leg over the seat without kicking him. She stumbled from the awkward angle, but he grabbed her arm, steadying her until she found her balance. "Thanks."

"Give me fifteen, and then I'll get you home." He took the helmet, set it on the seat, and then strode toward the house.

The air smelled amazing. Not sweet like Violet's wildflower farm, but a mix of damp earth, pine, and salty ocean breezes. And those sounds? Tinkling, mixed with deeper notes—an actual clanging. A symphony of wind chimes.

"You coming in?"

His deep voice—with a hint of a growl in it—had her hurrying to join him at the front door. "Yes, of course. Sorry."

Once inside, he flicked on the hall light. His boots thudded across the lightly stained hardwood floors. Framed photographs lined the broad hallway, but she didn't have a chance to look at any of them as she followed him deeper into the house. Too bad, because she really wanted a glimpse into this elusive man's life.

Turning on another light, he entered the kitchen. "You want anything?"

Holy shit, Calix Bourbon had a gorgeous cherry red Aga oven. Where the wood beams on the low ceiling and the tiled island gave the room a cozy feel, the bright blue, red, and grass green pottery displayed in a pie chest made it cheerful.

"Magic," she murmured.

"Excuse me?"

"Your kitchen. It's magical. Do you cook?"

Impatience in such a big man came off a little scary. "Yeah, I cook. You good in here?"

"Of course. Yes. Thanks."

He towered over her, all big, imposing man. His shoulder-length hair was a tousled mess, his black T-shirt looked wrinkled and stretched out, and his jeans probably hadn't hit the spin cycle in weeks. He gave her a chin nod and said, "Fifteen." His deep, slightly raspy voice sparked in her feminine core.

Striding out of the kitchen and across the living room, he punched the handle on the French door, slipping out into the night.

Mimi pulled a chair out from a large barnwood table and collapsed into it. God, she hadn't even had a moment to celebrate tonight's stunning victory. It was huge, right? It totally was. She pulled out her phone and typed a group message to Violet and her mom.

I got it!

A flurry of texts came, making it hard to keep up. But she couldn't stop smiling at their enthusiastic response. She wanted to tell them what her dad had said, but that would let his voice in. And with one week to pull this together, she couldn't afford negativity.

Like hell she'd be the joke of the show.

Her phone rang, and she tensed when she saw her dad's name. She knew him, though. He might have strong ideas about how to do things, but he loved her, and he always came around. He'd apologize, and then he'd help her. Maybe even set her up with lessons from a chef at one of his restaurants. "Hey, Dad."

"What the hell's the matter with you, taking off like that? Who was that man? Where are you?"

"I'm with Calix Bourbon. He's with Blue Fire, and I'm at his house."

"You can't behave like that, Amelia. Can you imagine someone on my team running off like that?"

She got up, headed to the sink, and looked at her reflection in the window. The hair she'd painstakingly blown out and twisted into a tight bun was now an unruly mess. She smoothed the loose pieces behind her ear. "Dad, unless you're going to be happy for me, I'm going to hang up. I love you, but when we don't see eye to eye, you get too pushy. You can't bully me out of this competition."

"Now is not the time to be stubborn. You've been out of school for a year. You must get a job if you're to be taken seriously."

Okay, totally not budging. Which only kicked up her anxiety. Time to come up with a game plan. She'd find a pen and paper and start brainstorming ideas. She'd definitely watch some cooking shows, but she wondered if she knew any chefs she felt comfortable enough with to ask for help.

"I think you know I've exhausted the job opportunities in

Manhattan." In a little enclave by the laundry room, she found a built-in desk. She picked up a pen but didn't see a notepad or Post-its or anything.

"I've got an idea." He sounded pleased with himself. "Over dinner tonight, I was talking to my colleagues about the Camarillo Group. They're doing some exciting work. Monday morning, I'll give Monte Camarillo a call."

Mimi's hand tightened on the pen. "The Camarillo Group . . . aren't they in Miami?"

"That's right."

"You want me to move?" The words came out as weightless as dandelion fluff.

"I want you to gain the kind of experience that will enable you to fit with my team."

She turned, resting her bottom on the edge of the desk. "In Miami?"

"If that's what it takes."

No way. He didn't mean this. He was just bullying her into seeing things his way. She pushed off the desk, tossing the pen down. "Come on, you'd miss me if I moved away. Who would you make *crespelle* for?"

"A few years, Amelia. That's all. It's a two-and-a-half-hour plane ride."

He wasn't provoking her. He meant it.

"Work with Monte's head of development, and I'll hire you." He sounded excited about this brilliant idea to ship her off to another state.

Did he even realize he'd just tossed yet another hoop for her to jump through? "No."

"What do you mean *no*?"

"If I build my relationships in Miami, then I'm building my career there. I want to build it in New York. Where I live." *Where you work.* Besides, what if she went to Miami and he *still* didn't hire her? Forget it.

"Melie . . ."

"Nope. I'm sticking with my plan. And if you can't support me, then I really can't talk to you. Good night, Dad."

"Amelia." She heard the warning in his tone, but she ended the call anyway.

Tossing her phone, she watched it skid across the white tile counter. Panic crawled across her skin. She hated that her dad had given voice to her fears.

But she wouldn't listen. Because she couldn't win with negativity in her head.

And by all that was holy, she was going to kick some TV ass.

All right, enough. Time to get back to the farm and get to work. Mimi glanced out the window. What was taking Calix so long? She should probably call a cab so he didn't have to bother with the long ride back to the farm.

She'd go find him, let him know he didn't have to worry about her. Heading out the same way he'd gone, she found herself in the living room.

Low ceilings and a color palette of cream and pale blues gave the impression of a cozy beach cottage. But she'd seen it from the outside, and this place went on and on.

Eager to learn something about Calix, she stepped closer to the framed family photographs that took up most of the wall space. Looked like four kids, with Calix the oldest. The youngest might have Down syndrome. In every single picture that boy was in the center. An arm hugging him tightly to a broad chest, a hand tousling his dark hair, a kiss pressed to his cheek. So much love in this family.

So . . . Calix Bourbon, badass tatted biker, lived at *home*?

And, boy, what a home. Where the apartment she'd grown up in had modern art pieces placed strategically by a decorator, this one had craft projects the kids had made over many years.

Her heart gave a little pull because she'd have given anything to grow up in a home like this one. As an only child whose parents were rarely around, she didn't have candid pictures. She had professional portraits and yearbook photos. She'd had no siblings to play with, and laughter had been a rare commodity.

Something was off, though. All the joy in these photos didn't make sense against the stillness, the stuffiness of this otherwise beautiful home. It almost felt like time had stopped.

She wanted to throw open the windows, let some fresh air in. Make some noise.

A door creaked, a hushed voice, a wet sob. Mimi stilled. She should make her presence known. A young woman peered into the living room, strappy sandals dangling off a finger, makeup smeared under her eyes. She tucked her phone into a black beaded clutch.

"Who're you?" The girl's eyes widened as she took Mimi in.

Right. Total stranger standing in her living room. *Awkward.* Mimi strode over, extending her hand. "Hi. Mimi Romano."

"Hi, I'm Leonie." She hunched a shoulder adorably. "Lee."

"I'm friends with Calix."

"You are?" Her incredulous tone made Mimi a little self-conscious.

Yeah, okay. With her conservative pencil skirt and silk blouse, she wasn't exactly Calix's type. *I get it.* She laughed. "Not that kind of friend, of course."

She gestured to Mimi's skirt. "Are you okay?"

She'd forgotten about the slit Calix had made, and her hands lowered to cover the gap. "Oh, God. Yes, fine. Your brother had to cut my skirt so I could get on his bike."

"Is he here?" She crept closer, peering around.

"No, he had to do something. He should be back any minute."

"Okay, well." She started to go, but then came back around. "Can I get you something? Water?" And then she smiled, taking in Mimi's skirt. "Leggings?"

"I'm okay, thanks. I'll be leaving soon." Hard to look at a woman with mascara running down her cheek and not want to help. "You all right?"

"Yeah . . . just . . ." She shook her head, like she wasn't too happy with herself. "Bad taste in men."

"You, too, huh?" She hadn't had a ton of relationships. Well, of course, she always chose the competitive, driven guys who put work before girlfriends. Daddy complex much? "I guess we have to wade through the frogs to get to our princes."

She sighed. "But what if we're only attracted to frogs?"

Mimi laughed. "Well, that would suck." Slater's wife, Emmie, had thought she wanted a stable guy, and she'd wound up with a groupie-bait lead singer. And Violet? She looked more like a posh art gallery owner than the future wife of the inked, long-haired bass player in a rock band. Her friend would never have considered dating a guy like Derek if she hadn't worked for the band on their last tour. "I don't know. Maybe we have to change it up. Give a different kind of guy a chance. The kind of guy we didn't think we were attracted to."

Lee didn't look convinced.

"Yeah, okay, maybe not. All I know is we're too young and fabulous to give up. I don't know about you, but I'm holding out for my prince. Let's agree that we won't settle until we find him. Because we totally deserve the best, right?"

"Well, I deserve better than what I've gotten, I'll say that." She drew in a breath, shook her head at Mimi's skirt. "Come on, let's find you something to wear."

The orange glow of the cigar flared in the dark garden.

Calix Bourbon wanted to check on his mom, figuring she'd worked right through dinner, but seeing his dad all alone like that gutted him.

He didn't want to keep Mimi waiting, but he had to spend a little time with his dad.

"Hey." He dragged an Adirondack chair around to face him. The overcast sky did little to illuminate his old man's features, but Calix couldn't miss the tension around his eyes. "How's it going?"

"Just fine." But his dad had never been good at disguising his emotions. Something troubled him. "How'd it go today?" He flicked ash onto the slate patio.

Calix leaned forward, elbows on his knees. "Like every other day. Total cluster fuck." None of his friends were musicians, so he appreciated his dad's insights about what went on in the studio.

"Why don't you guys say somethin' already?" His dad's

gravelly voice rumbled from deep within his chest. "Doesn't sound like he knows what he's doing."

"Irwin hired him, so no one questions him. He's Dak Johnson, a hit maker. And with Irwin off in Australia, no one's checking up on his progress." He ran his fingers through the scruff on his chin. "The guys think they lucked out scoring Irwin, the biggest A&R guy in the business. But what they don't get is that it's *their* band—their name on the album."

"You tell 'em that?"

"Not my place. But I don't know why they give two shits what success Dak's had with other bands—he's not getting *this* one."

"You been with 'em, what, couple months now? Seems like it could be your place."

Eight months, actually. He'd started with Blue Fire last August, when their keyboard player had entered rehab. After finishing out the summer tour, Calix had jammed with them. He'd even cowritten some of the songs they were recording now. Eight months was a long time with one band.

A cool, moist breeze whipped through the garden, giving him chill bumps. "I won't be around much longer."

His dad blew out smoke. "Irwin heard any tracks yet?"

"Nope. And the label thinks Dak's such a genius they give him free rein. But I can tell you this. Four months into this project, and he's changed their sound. Shit we're doing isn't what we worked on in Violet's barn." He glanced to his mom's art studio, imagining her perspiration-dampened T-shirt and the intense concentration on her exhausted features. "Whatever. Not my issue."

His dad dropped the cigar onto the slate and crushed it with the toe of his flip-flop. "They still pushin' you to join?"

He nodded. It didn't look like the original keyboard player would be coming back. The guy had bailed on his second attempt at rehab. And since they'd be hitting the road as soon as this record was done, they'd need a permanent member sooner than later.

Which meant he needed to line up his next gig.

His dad leaned forward, as he lowered his head into his hands.

Damn, but he hated seeing his dad so twisted up. "You sure you're okay?"

He looked up, trying for a smile. "Yeah, sure."

"She all right?"

"Same." But then he turned serious. "You seen your brother today?"

Now they were getting to something. "No. We went straight from the studio to the gig in Southampton. Why? What's up?"

"Nothing. Just . . . he's gettin' restless." Calix could see the strain around his dad's eyes and mouth. "Lee snuck out again tonight."

Calix separated the braided leather band from the other bracelets on his wrist. "She's twenty-two. She doesn't need to sneak."

"That's my point." And the firmness of his tone finally clued Calix in on his dad's concerns. Three grown kids still living at home. Things were starting to pull apart at the seams.

He forced himself to look more relaxed. "Don't worry about it, Dad. We want to be here."

His dad looked at him like he wasn't buying it. But then, by Calix's age, his parents had toured the world and were on their way to accumulating more platinum records than any other punk rock act in history.

"Been thinking. Probably time for you kids to move on."

Well, sure. Gus was twenty-three, Leonie twenty-two. None of them should be living at home. "Nah. We're good."

"That's the thing." His dad scrubbed his face with both hands. "We're not. Nearly three years, and it's not getting better. It's all right for me, she's my girl. But not you guys." He patted his T-shirt pocket, but he wouldn't find any cigarettes. Old habits died hard. "It's all kinds of messed up."

Seeing his dad lost like this tore strips off his heart. It killed him to know his parents—once inseparable and so affectionate it'd almost been uncomfortable to watch—had become distant. His mom had pulled so deeply into her shell of grief she'd flat-out abandoned her husband.

In his gut he knew she'd be healed when she let her husband back in. "It won't be forever. She'll be back to herself soon enough. In the meantime . . ." He fingered the leather band. "We've got it pretty good out here. No complaints."

Too much pain in his dad's eyes. It had to destroy him not to be able to reach his wife.

"Look." Calix stood up. "As long as we're . . ." *Her reason to live.* He dug his hands deep into his pockets, curled his fingers around his keys, looking for the right words. "So what if I'm not in a band and Gus didn't finish college? If it takes another five years—ten—till this family gets back on its feet"—and his mom got back in his dad's bed—"who gives a shit?" A sharp pain in his hand made him realize the teeth had cut into his skin. He dropped the keys. "We're not going anywhere." He wouldn't leave his mom alone. Not yet.

His dad, a giant of a man, got up slowly, and Calix could see pride smoldering in his eyes. He clapped a huge hand on Calix's shoulder. "You're a damn good man." He pulled him in for a bear hug. "Love you, son."

Emotion punched up into his chest. He closed his eyes, drawing in a deep breath. His dad smelled like cigar and the damp earth from his garden.

Clucking had him pulling away. Fifi strutted toward him, her neck muscles working overtime to propel her along. Calix scooped her off the ground, giving her the firm strokes she liked from the top of her head down her back. Her wings flapped, but she settled quickly enough.

"Lookin' just about plump enough for Saturday night dinner," his dad said.

Calix laughed. Family joke. They kept chickens for the eggs.

The sizzle and crackle of his mom's welder cut through the quiet night, and he couldn't take it anymore. "I'm gonna check on her."

His dad nodded, his features turning impassive. "See you inside."

He thought of Mimi, all alone in the house. "Oh, hey, there's a woman in there. Mimi Romano, a friend of the band."

"You got a girl?"

He thought of Mimi, that fiery hair, that lush mouth. The press of her breasts against his back as he'd driven home. "No. She needed a ride. Try not to scare her, okay?"

His dad grinned so widely the deep grooves around his eyes furrowed. "You never let me have any fun."

Opening the coop, Calix dropped his very vocal hen inside, closed the latch, and headed down the path. He entered the refurbished barn slowly, the whine of the welder harsh in his ears. The metal pieces of his mom's found art sculptures filled every corner and table. Wind chimes of all shapes and sizes hung from steel pipes stretched across the ceiling.

Covered in an enormous helmet and thick gloves, his mom stood on a stepladder as she welded together two giant pieces of scrap metal suspended from the ceiling with chains. He came around so he faced her across the worktable and waved to get her attention.

The machine shut off, and she flipped up the plastic eye protector. He should be used to it by now, but her ghostly complexion and the dark circles under her eyes still shook him up.

"Hey, Ma." He scanned for evidence of dinner, and sure enough, on the table closest to the door he found a microwaved bowl of something that might've been macaroni and cheese.

Damn. Now he wished he'd swung by home on the way to the gig.

Of course she hadn't eaten. His vibrant, intelligent, progressive mom loved fresh food. Before Hopper's passing, she'd loved cooking. Every meal was a bounty of the produce from his dad's garden, the eggs from the coop, and the fruit from the orchard.

Of course she wouldn't eat microwaved meals.

Calix gestured to the mac and cheese. "Looks nasty. How about I make you something?"

She rallied with a weak smile. "Thanks, babe. Not hungry. I want to finish this."

He came around the table. "Okay, Mom. I see how it's gonna be." He gently pulled the helmet off.

"I *said* I'm not hungry."

"Easy to say right now. But wait'll you smell my cooking."

"Don't want anything fancy."

"How about some eggs? You can come into the coop with me and choose your own."

Her smile withered for a moment, but she found the strength to agree. "Okay, you little shit. You win. Let's pull some eggs out of Fifi's ass."

Frenetic beats poured out open windows, and laughter rang out into the night. His mom slowed on the patio. "What's going on?"

"No idea." Both hands filled with warm eggs, he used his elbow to pop the handle on the French door and his boot to push it open. "Come on," he said more forcefully. "I'm feeding you." He waited for his mom to pass through, but she stood still, anxious.

He got it. For one terrible moment he'd felt it, too. *Home.*

Music, laughter. This was what his home used to sound like.

And in the center of it all, Hopper. All of it had died with him. So, yeah, it hurt.

Only, unlike his mom, it gave him hope for what they could be again. Because, yes, Hopper had died, but the rest of them—all five of them—were still alive. He just hoped that having her family around her would draw her back out until she was ready to be the heart of it again.

He offered his mom an easy smile. "Stand there much longer, and I'm gonna have a whole litter of Fifi juniors in my arms." Shouts of laughter came from the kitchen. "Grab some basil and tomatoes and whatever you want in your omelet."

When she stood this close, he couldn't miss the way she'd aged so drastically in the past three years. And it cut him to the bone. Not just the random streaks of gray in her hair, but the loss of elasticity in her skin.

When she caught him watching her, she flashed a quick smile. "On it."

He hoped like hell she didn't wind up going back to the studio or her bedroom.

As soon as he got inside, he used the toe of his boot to draw the door shut, and then he stalked into the kitchen.

Calix stopped in the doorway. In front of the stove, Mimi shook her candy-cane-covered ass to the electronic music coming out of his brother's laptop. Her hair, all sleek and straight, whirled like streamers as she spun around. The hanging lights over the island made the normally deep red tones gleam like the orange in the heart of a fire.

His sister held a towel in each hand as she danced around the kitchen, and Gus looked like a DJ in a club, rocking out, while manipulating the buttons and job wheels of the controller attached to his laptop.

Gus. Leonie. Laughter, music.

Fuck.

Fuck.

Swear to God, Calix could feel Hopper as vividly as if he'd been pressed up next to him. *This* was what had made Hopper happy. His family hanging out like this had brought him joy.

And then he remembered his mom's face, the anxiety. He nudged Gus aside and lowered the volume.

Everyone turned to him, wide-eyed and confused.

"Why'd you do that?" Gus reached for the controller.

He lifted his arms to draw attention to the eggs. "Making Mom some dinner."

Gus looked beyond him to the French doors. "She here?"

"She's getting herbs for her omelet."

His brother closed the laptop. "Didn't know that. Sorry."

Calix gave a quick shake of his head, not wanting his brother to feel bad about it.

Leonie threw the dishtowels onto the table. "I got it." She relieved him of four eggs, bringing them to Mimi. "Perfect with sausage."

"Is Calix a sausage eater?" Mimi asked with a strange lilt to her voice.

What the hell? But then Lee and Gus burst out laughing, cluing him in to their private joke.

When Mimi saw Calix wasn't laughing, she sobered. "You in for some eggs and . . . you know?"

Gus tucked his laptop under his arm and said, "*Sausage.*" The three of them broke out laughing again, as his brother headed out of the kitchen.

Hang on. How long had he been outside if Mimi had cooked dinner—and he could see not just the skillet on the stove, but the salad bowl on the table and the plates stacked on the counter—and bonded with his brother and sister?

And look at her. When he'd brought her home, Mimi had been in a tight skirt and silk blouse, something a corporate attorney would wear. Her hair had been wound into a bun.

This woman, with her hair down and wearing his sister's red and white striped leggings and red SUNY Stonington T-shirt, looked like a college girl. With a mouth made for—

Yeah, not going there with Mimi Romano.

She studied him for a moment, and he could read the question in her eyes. *Is this okay?* "There wasn't a whole lot in the fridge, but we defrosted some sausage and got enough vegetables out of your garden to make a salad."

"And now we've got eggs." Lee came up beside him. "Is Ma coming in?" she asked quietly.

"I hope so."

"I brought dinner out to her."

"Yeah, Lee, I saw." His sweet, kind sister gazed up at him with a guilty expression, so he gentled his voice. "Guess she wasn't hungry." Getting to work, he reached for a mixing bowl. "You want to chop an onion?"

"Sure." She pulled a cutting board out of the cabinet under the sink and a knife from the block.

Spatula in hand, Mimi came up beside him. "I feel like I stepped into something here."

He had a good eight inches on her, so he had a view of his sister's T-shirt stretching in places it didn't normally stretch. When she gazed up at him with concern in her green and gold-flecked eyes, something in his chest give a painful kick. "No worries, sweet pants."

"Sweet pants?" She arched a brow.

He tipped his chin down toward her leggings.

"Oh. Right. Your sister loaned them to me."

"Figured that out."

"Look, I obviously don't understand the situation, but if I messed up, please tell me."

"If, by messing up, you mean throwing a party in my kitchen, then yeah, total fuckup." Yanking open the drawer, he pulled out a whisk and started beating the eggs.

As he watched a slow smile spread across her pretty features, warmth spread through him. With one more lingering gaze, Mimi turned back to the stove. Calix added salt and pepper to the batter and then whisked some more.

"So, are you in fashion or something?" he heard Mimi ask Lee.

Reasonable question. Even just hanging around at home, his sister wore a crazy mix of styles that somehow worked on her petite frame.

"I wish." Lee dumped the chopped onion into a skillet. When it sizzled, she lowered the flame.

"A designer? Because you have flair. I mean, your room? God. I don't think I've ever paid attention to the color of my walls or what goes on them."

"Nah," Lee said.

Dumping the sausages onto a plate, Mimi set it on the table. "So, what do you do?"

Lee never looked up from the pan. "I run the philanthropic arm of the family business."

Mimi looked interested, but before she could say more, his dad bustled into the room with an armful of produce from his garden. He looked from person to person, his smile dimming. "Where's your mom?" He set the peppers, onion, and a handful of herbs on the counter.

All the things his mom liked in an omelet.

After a moment of tension, his dad's disappointment palpable, Calix stepped toward him and grabbed some of the vegetables. "This is great, Dad." He set them down.

His dad held Calix's gaze, heavy with the question, *She coming in?*

He hated to let him down, but what could he say? He gave a slight shake of his head. With a pained look of defeat, his dad let out a breath and turned to Mimi.

"Hey." He stuck out his hand. "Terrence Bourbon."

"Hi. Mimi Romano. I hope you don't mind me commandeering your kitchen."

"Not one bit. Calix says you're friends with Blue Fire?"

"She cooks for them." Calix pulled another skillet off the rack, set a low flame under it.

"The band has a chef?" His dad seemed surprised.

"Before you start imagining limos and private jets," Mimi said, "they only hired me as a favor."

"A lot of people coming and going, crazy hours," Calix said. "They need the help."

"True, but I'm not some trained chef. Although—ha!—believe it or not, I just got a gig on the *Verna Bloom Show*."

Leaning into the fridge to grab the butter, Calix shot her a look over his shoulder. She was leaving them?

"Are you serious?" Lee asked.

Mimi's smile lit up the room. "You know it?"

"Duh," Lee said. "Who doesn't?"

"She's running a five-week cooking competition, and the winner gets to apprentice with her next season. Somehow I have to pull off being an actual chef."

"What kind of competition?" his dad asked.

"It's like that show *Chopped*. They give you four random ingredients, and then you get thirty minutes to make something out of it."

"What about seasonings, oil, flour, stuff like that?" Terrence asked.

"We've got access to Verna's pantry and refrigerator."

"But you're not a chef?" Terrence asked.

"I'm not."

"You cook for the band," Calix said.

"I make the food I'm familiar with—my nonna's meatballs, my dad's fettuccine—but basically, I follow recipes, you know? I don't know what flavors work well together, the chemistry of cooking, important stuff like that. And the show starts in a week, so I've got a ton of research to do."

"What kind of research you got planned?" Terrence asked.

"I'll watch *Chopped* to see how the contestants work with what they're given, and then I'll get some cookbooks, learn about measuring and different techniques, cooking times and temperatures. You know, basic stuff like that."

"More recipes, huh?" Lee said with a teasing smile.

Terrence gave Calix a chin nod. "Calix can help you out."

He shot his dad a hard look. *What the hell?*

Mimi must've seen it, because she laughed. "That's okay. I've got it."

"No, seriously, Meems," Lee said. "Calix is a great cook."

"*Cook.*" He gave her a quelling look. "Not a chef."

"You guys, he's got enough on his plate with the band." Mimi waved her hand, as if to dismiss the whole idea. "Dak's driving them nuts with his crazy schedule."

"Oh, my God, let him," Lee said. "I mean, watching shows and reading cookbooks is great, but there's nothing like a teacher. And trust me, we were homeschooled, so *everything* was a learning experience. Cooking was basically our science lab. But Calix took it to a whole other level. He's just, I don't know, intuitive in the kitchen."

As Lee continued to talk to Mimi, Terrence joined him at the stove. "Want this girl in our house."

With a hunch of his shoulders, he gave his dad a look that said, *Why?*

"My bet, you give that girl lessons right here in our kitchen, your ma's gonna get involved."

Calix's hand on the knife stilled. His mom kept strange hours. Insomnia had her sleeping till noon most days. Then, she'd head out for a walk along the beach, regardless of the weather. Since she avoided family meals, she could be counted on to sneak into the kitchen around three, grab a yogurt from the fridge or a granola bar from the pantry, and then hide out in her studio.

The heart of her home didn't beat anymore.

So for three years, he'd tried to get his family to sit down to dinner in the hopes it'd draw her out. It hadn't. Nothing had. But giving Mimi cooking lessons in his mom's kitchen . . . would that work?

"You got time tomorrow?" his dad asked.

Mimi whipped around toward him, startled out of her conversation. "What? No, seriously. You don't have to do that."

He knew Mimi's schedule. Knew she had time between meals. He supposed he could give it a shot. "Be here at two?"

"Calix, I—"

"Two."

"But you have to be in the studio."

Why was she fighting him on this? "Only in the morning."

"You already know that?"

He gave her a hard look, hoping to end the conversation. "He's laying down vocals with Slater in the afternoon."

She bit down on that lush bottom lip, brow tight with concern. "You really don't have—"

"You gonna be here at two?"

A wash of pink covered her clear, smooth complexion. "Okay, sure. Thank you."

Focusing on his mom's dinner, Calix lifted the pan from the flame, shoved the spatula under the omelet, and flipped it. The three of them continued to talk, and Calix couldn't help glancing toward Mimi, who stood with her hip against the counter, one bare foot on top of the other. He did a double-take on her toenails. Tomato red with . . . yellow smiley faces?

In the club tonight, packed with rockers, she'd looked like a businesswoman. He'd had no idea underneath her tight skirt and silk blouse, she had . . . color. Personality. Made him wonder what kind of lingerie she wore.

A flash of Mimi on her back, that deep red mane of hair spread across his pillow, grabbed him by the balls and squeezed.

Oh, hell, no. He shook his head free of the image and grabbed the skillet with sautéed onions and peppers. He spooned the mixture on top of the omelet.

"I think I figured out why there's so little in your fridge,"

Mimi said. "You guys live off the land. Are you, like, Amish or something?"

Lee laughed. "Not at *all*."

"Okay, but all this fresh stuff, I think it would give me a heart attack if I tried to eat it."

"Don't like vegetables?" his dad asked.

"Can't stand them. Total carnivore. Some days I'm just not human until I bite into a thick, juicy steak. I swear, in the zombie apocalypse, I'll have no problem eating the brains of my neighbors."

His dad burst out laughing, and Calix felt a pain lance through his heart. This laughter. If only his mom could be part of this.

"Give me a week," his dad said. "I'll bring you over to our side."

"Like my mom didn't try to get me to eat broccoli? Are you kidding? I remember this one time she pulled the whole *You're not getting up from this table until you eat your broccoli* thing." She pretended to gag. "I mean, seriously, the first person to look at asparagus and think about putting it in his mouth had to have done it on a dare." More gagging faces. "Brussels sprouts? Are you kidding me? Did cavemen try eating rocks, too? Fistfuls of sand? Just because it grows in nature doesn't mean we're meant to eat it. Anyway, I'm stuck at the table, and I'm telling you nothing short of waterboarding would've gotten that stalk in my mouth. But then my mom had some meeting to get to, and my housekeeper tossed me a Twinkie and let me go. And that was the end of the *Let's get Mimi to eat her vegetables* saga."

His dad looked at Mimi with concern. "You an only child?"

Mimi nodded, some of her enthusiasm waning. "Which, of course, meant a lot of broccoli to eat by myself."

"It's all in the preparation," his dad said. "Tell you what. I'll bring some vegetables by the house tomorrow. Give you some tips for cooking with them."

"That would be awesome. Thank you. Just . . . no hurt feelings when I spit them out in a napkin, okay?"

His dad's laughter filled the kitchen, and Calix couldn't keep the smile off his face.

Maybe it would work. Maybe Mimi would draw his mom back into the kitchen. He grabbed the plate. "I'm gonna get this to Mom."

Calix headed down the hall to the guest bedroom. Footsteps had him whipping back around to find Mimi chasing after him with a bowl in one hand and a bottle of salad dressing in the other.

"Would she like salad?"

Alone in the hallway, he got to see that creamy complexion and expressive mouth up close. Her expensive perfume surrounded him. Not heavy, not thick, but rich and perfect for her.

When he realized she was standing there waiting for him to respond, he said, "Sure, thanks." He reached for the bowl. But when she thrust the bottle at him, and he had no other hands to take it, she laughed and shoved it under his arm instead.

She didn't say another word, but there was something in her eyes. An understanding, and that, accompanied by a gentle smile, nearly undid him.

"Thanks." His voice came out gruff. He started to turn when she held a napkin out to him. From the heft, he realized she'd put in a fork and knife. Unnerved, he caught it between two fingers and set off in search of his mom.

My bet, you give that girl lessons right here in our kitchen, your ma's gonna get involved.

Yeah, his dad might be right.

He'd sure as hell give it a try.

CHAPTER THREE

By the time Calix got back to the kitchen, his family had gathered around Gus's laptop, the live version of his parents' hit "Can't Get Enough" playing. He hung back, watching.

Mimi looked over at him, eyes shining with delight. "I can't believe your parents are 100 Proof." She turned to Terrence. "How come no one knows you live out here?"

"No one cares," his dad said.

"They've been here close to thirty years," Gus said. "People're used to us."

Calix needed to get Mimi home. "You want to get going?" Leonie and Gus shot him nasty looks. "What? It's late."

Right then the door opened and Shay breezed in. With her long limbs and straight blond hair, her beckoning eyes and a mouth that had pleased him more times than he could count, she walked right into his arms.

"Hey, babe." As she pressed her lithe body up to his, she got up on her toes to place a kiss on his cheek. She smelled like an ocean breeze, and her skin was cool to the touch.

She headed over to Gus and gave him a fist bump. "S'up, guys?"

"Hey, Shay," Lee said.

"Surf's ridiculous right now." Shay took in the food on the table.

"That's right." His dad shut off the music. "Storm's offshore."

Shay grabbed a fork and speared a sausage. "You guys in?" she asked his brother and sister before biting off the end.

"Hell, yeah." Gus shut down his laptop.

She set the fork down. "Get your wetsuits. Let's go."

As soon as Gus left the room, Shay took in the scene. It seemed to take her a moment to process a table full of food and dirty dishes, the family gathered around at midnight. "What's going on?" And then her gaze settled on Mimi. She pushed away from the table. "Who're you?"

"Mimi Romano." She motioned to him. "A friend of Calix."

The easy smile faded. "How do you know Calix?"

"I'm friends with Blue Fire."

Shay thought about it for a moment, then nodded. "Cool." She snagged a slice of red pepper out of the salad bowl. "You surf?"

"Uh, no. Not at all." Mimi waved a hand. "But don't worry about me. You guys go. I'll call a cab."

"No," Calix said. "I'm taking you."

Gus came back into the room, wearing an unzipped wetsuit, his top half bare. "Let's do this." He jammed his feet into some flip-flops in the mudroom by the back door.

"Is it safe to surf at night?" Mimi asked.

"We've surfed here our whole lives," Gus said. "We know the breaks."

"But it's so cloudy you won't be able to see anything."

Shay's tongue took a slow sweep across her lips. As teenagers, she'd make Calix hard all the time doing shit like that. Every move, every expression, every touch, every damn thing about her used to make him think of sex.

"It's a blast on nights like tonight." She picked a tomato quarter out of the salad and popped it in her mouth.

Lee brought her plate to the sink and turned on the faucet. "You should come down to the beach anyway. There'll be a bonfire, and not everybody will be surfing."

He stepped forward, digging his keys out of his pocket. Mimi hanging out with his friends? He didn't think that'd be her scene. "I'll take her now."

"Where to?" Shay turned her sultry eyes to him.

"Eden's Landing," Mimi said.

"Oh, forget that," Shay said. "That'll take an hour, there and back. You'll miss all the best swells. Let her take a cab." She looked at Mimi. "You okay with that?"

"I just said I was. It's no big deal."

"Come on, Mimi. You really want to go home now?"

The meaningful look his sister gave Mimi made Calix think about the man she'd argued with outside the club. The way they'd acted around each other—the man's concern, and Mimi's defiance—he'd figured it had been Mimi's dad. Dressed in slacks, a sport coat, and a big, fancy watch, the man had a full head of salt-and-pepper hair—not red, like Mimi's—but he had the same expressive features and hands.

"Quit talkin' and let's go," Gus said. "How often do we get swells around here?"

"You in?" Lee asked Mimi.

"Sure. Sounds fun."

"I'll get my wetsuit," Calix said. "Meet you down there."

Shay set a hand on his hip, gave him a lazy look. "I'll come with."

He held her gaze, wishing he had something—anything—to give her. But he just didn't. He turned and left the room, not even looking to see if she followed.

Paddling against a rough current, sea spray pelting his face, Calix angled his board toward the pocket. He popped up to a crouch and held a rail into the wave face, but at the bottom of the trough he got sucked up and over the falls.

The churning water holding him down, he stroked hard until he broke the surface, taking in great gasps of air. With another huge swell approaching, he had to duck under again.

That's it. I'm out. He powered toward shore.

Once his feet hit sand, he bent over and ripped the Velcro

of his ankle leash. He turned back to watch his friends get beat up and battered by the thrashing sea.

Catching his board under his arm, he headed for the bonfire. Gusts of wind battered his exposed skin, making him shiver.

"Fuckin' hard to drop, man." His friend came up beside him.

"Too much blow back." Calix swiped the hair out of his eyes, his body still humming. Setting his board down, he unzipped his wet suit, leaving the top half dangling off his hips.

"That was awesome." Another of the guys jogged up from the ocean. He high-fived Calix. All three of them headed toward the bonfire.

"Calix," someone called.

He looked up to see his friend with one hand digging in a cooler, the other tossing him a beer. He caught it. "Thanks." Standing just beyond the circle gathered around the fire, he grabbed his towel and swiped his face and chest. Pulling his T-shirt over his head, he wondered where Mimi had gone.

Hopefully, Lee was looking out for her. But then he saw his sister with a group of her friends, and Mimi wasn't among them. Had she left on her own? With the competition a week away, he imagined she'd want to get right to work. Probably in her room right then, watching *Chopped* and scouring the Internet for cooking tips. Ambitious woman like her? Yeah, she wouldn't be hanging around when she had a show to do.

Laughter rang out, and Calix looked over to find a group of his buddies clustered together, Mimi right in the middle of them. With her animated expression and gestures, she looked like she'd known these guys for years.

But she didn't know them at all. And while she might be having fun right then, she probably wouldn't want anything to do with them in about an hour. After surfing, they'd smoke some weed and drink beers, and then they'd start hooking up.

He should get her home.

With the next burst of laughter, her gaze caught on his and the smile faded. Something crackled in his chest. It had been a long time since a woman had affected him like that.

Mimi got up, swatted the sand off her ass, and headed toward him. Her brow creased the closer she got. Just before reaching him, she swiped a clean towel off a stack by the cooler.

"Hey," she said softly.

He didn't answer, just took a pull from his beer. Something about her made him go all quiet inside. She didn't look at him the way most women did. Nothing flirty or suggestive about her. She looked like she was trying to figure him out.

Waste of time, really. He wouldn't be around her long enough to matter. He looked toward shore.

But her soft hand cupped his cheek, turning him back to her. When he jerked away, she looked at him in confusion and then laughed. "You've got some blood on your cheek. At least I think it's blood. Here." She took the edge of the towel and wiped.

It stung, so he guessed his board had scraped him on that last dunking. "Leave it."

"Don't be silly. Come here." She wrapped her hand around his wrist and tugged him toward the big white cooler. Leaning over, she dug out a water bottle, and then dropped to her knees. She motioned for him to sit beside her.

He went to rub the scrape but was startled to feel an incision. Before he could give it another thought, her hand grabbed his board shorts and pulled. He settled beside her on the cool sand. "You're making a big deal out of nothing."

"I'm wiping blood off your cheek. Not using urchin spikes and sea grass to stitch you up."

He tried to hold back his laughter and failed—not many people hit that particular spot in him. When the wind whipped her long hair around her face, he surprised himself by pushing it back. The touch of her creamy skin sent a buzz of awareness through him.

He pulled his hand back. "I should get you home."

"Hang on. Let me clean this up first." Uncapping the bottle, she poured some water onto the towel and dabbed the wound. It burned, and he sucked in a breath.

She pulled her hand back. "Okay?"

Her gentle patting, along with the rustle of beach grass, settled him down. For as bold as she could be, Mimi Romano had a surprisingly gentle touch.

"I can't believe I didn't know your parents are 100 Proof. That's crazy." When he didn't respond, she pulled back to look at him. "Why'd they stop playing?"

"They wanted a family."

"They couldn't play and raise a family?"

He didn't want to get into it. "Didn't want to raise kids in that lifestyle. They wanted something more wholesome for us."

"And look at you, all up in the music industry." Gently, she dabbed at the wound, the wind whipping all that sleek hair around her face. "Way to stick it to the 'rents."

"Yeah." She'd meant it as a joke, obviously, but the simple comment sliced across his heart.

"This place is amazing." Her voice was soft, gentle. "You must've loved growing up here."

A cold burst of wind sent sand spattering against his ankles. The next time she reached out to his wound, he noticed goose bumps on her arm. He pulled the towel from her hands, shook it out, and wrapped it around her. "Was that your dad you bailed on tonight?"

She nodded, drawing the towel more tightly around her, like she was snuggling into it.

"Seemed pretty pissed."

"Him or me?"

"You seemed pissed, but your dad . . . looked like he was worried about you."

Her hands settled in her lap. "We disagree on how to run my life."

"Aren't you twenty-four?"

"Exactly. But he's set in his ways. And while I respect his opinion, it's not like his way is the *only* way. I just wish he'd be proud of me when I don't listen to him. You know? I mean, do you sometimes feel like you have to jump through hoops to make your parents happy?"

"No."

"Well, okay, then." She laughed. "In any event, my dad

thinks I'm making a huge mistake by being on the *Verna Bloom Show*."

"Why?"

"Because I'm not a chef, and he thinks I'll make a fool of myself on national television. But I can't let him get in my head. I need to stay positive. I mean, look what happened when I told your dad about it. First thing out of his mouth was, 'What's your plan?' And the second thing? 'Calix can help you.' That's what I wanted my dad to say."

He nodded. His dad was a good guy.

"To be honest, though." She worried the edge of the towel. "It hurt because everything he said was right. I mean, I have an MBA. Why *would* they choose me to be on the show?"

"'Cause you're beautiful. And smart. And you light up a room."

Her eyes widened, her lips softly parted, and she seemed at a loss for words. "Um, thank you. I . . . I didn't know you even noticed me."

"Hard not to."

She kept her gaze on him, as though trying to figure him out.

"What?" he said.

"Nothing. I just . . . I'm surprised to hear you say that." She shook her head. "Whatever. It is what it is. I'm doing the show, and I'm going to kick ass."

"I don't know what your dad was talking about. You're not a ditz. How could you make a fool of yourself?"

"He thinks they chose me—Dino Romano's pampered princess socialite daughter—for the ratings."

"That's harsh." And totally wrong.

"Yeah. But there's truth in it."

"Are you a pampered princess socialite?"

"Of course not. But he's saying they'll spin it that way. He's thinking it's reality TV."

"Okay, even if he's right, which doesn't make sense to me, I still say it can't go down that way. Ten minutes into the first show they'll see the truth about you. No question."

"You're absolutely right. Funny how I let him get into my head like that."

"I can see you on TV." For all the months he'd known her, he'd kept his distance. Something about her made him uncomfortable. But just then, being so close and really noticing her, he got it. She had a natural sensuality that belied her businesswoman demeanor and had him thinking of her in ways he shouldn't. She worked with the band. Off-limits.

"You can?"

"*Fuck a duck.*" He said it in the same exercised tone she used.

She eyed him questioningly, like she thought he was making fun of her.

"First day I met you. *Fuck a duck.*"

She smiled, and even in the moonlight her pale skin flushed sweetly.

"First words that came out of your mouth."

"I'm a delicate flower." She grinned. "What can I say?"

"You'd just quit your job. Said the guy who hired you didn't have any use for you if he couldn't have access to your dad's bank account."

"You remember?"

"Hard not to."

"What does that mean?"

"You make an impression."

"Oh. Yeah, well, believe me, so do you."

He drew back. He hadn't meant to flirt with her—just tell her the truth. He hoped she didn't read into it. Because whatever the attraction, he wouldn't hook up with a friend of the band. "I'm guessing that's why they chose you. You make an impression."

Looking down at her hands, fingers steepled, she blinked a few times. He didn't want her to get all emotional, so he changed the subject. "You gonna stop cooking for the band?"

She snapped up. "Of course not. It's only five competitions. And they tape once a week, so I'll just miss five dinners. And the apprenticeship doesn't start until next season."

"Yeah, but you said you need to get up to speed for the show."

"I do. And I will. But I'm not bailing on the band."

"See? There you go being a pampered princess socialite."
He slowly shook his head.

She threw him a smile so dazzling he had to look away.
"Hey, they were nice enough to give me a job when I didn't
have anything. I'd never bail on them. Besides, they're the
closest thing I've got to a family."

Well, that was just sad. "Your mom lives on the farm.
You've got family."

"Of course. I just meant, you know, outside my mom and
dad." Her gaze drifted to the shoreline, where a bunch of
guys were just coming out of the thrashing sea. She stretched
her legs out, curling her toes.

His gaze tracked from her polished toenails to slim, bare
ankles, and up her nicely shaped candy-cane-covered calves
and thighs.

"Is it okay for me to ask where your mom was tonight?"

Ripped from the low hum of attraction, he let the question
tear through him. Of course she'd want to know. The moment
he'd come in, he'd shut off the music. The mood had changed.
Weird shit from an outsider's perspective. But he wasn't sure
what to say, so he turned to watch his friends laughing and
smoking weed by the fire.

"You don't have to talk about it. It's okay."

He sure as hell didn't want to talk about it. But any
irritation dulled when she touched his arm. And when her
thumb stroked the sensitive skin under his wrist, a slow burn
spread along his nerves.

"You have interesting ink. I've never seen anything like it
before."

"My brother."

Her gaze snapped up to him. "Sorry?"

"He died. Three years ago." *Fuck.* When was the last time
he'd said those words out loud? Or even thought them? It felt
awkward, like putting on a pair of brand-new, unwashed
jeans, stiff and ill-fitting.

She sucked in a breath, forehead crimping in pain. "The
youngest?"

He nodded.

"I wondered . . . he's so obviously missing."

"Yeah. So, when my mom heard the music tonight, she . . . it's hard for her. What our home used to be like . . . the music, laughing, everyone all together . . . she just . . . it's hard."

"I'm so sorry, Calix. I can't even imagine your mom's pain."

"What you did tonight . . . it hasn't been like that since . . . before."

"I'm sorry."

"No, it's a good thing."

"Not for your mom."

"No. Not for her." And then he realized she needed to know the truth. If she was going to be involved, she should be aware. "Full disclosure."

She tilted her head questioningly.

"The cooking lessons? My dad thinks they'll draw my mom out. The kitchen. That's her domain. *Was*. She used to love cooking."

"Ah. I wondered why you'd be so willing."

"I probably wouldn't have."

She pulled the towel around her like a shawl. "No. I didn't think so."

"But I've tried everything and so far nothing's worked. And . . . this seems like it could work."

"Hey, I'm not going to complain. If helping me can help your mom, I'm in."

"Yeah." He tapped his fingers on his knee. "Used to be everyone hung out at our house. My mom was always cooking, music playing. And now it's been three years of silence. No one comes around anymore. Until you showed up tonight. And you . . . well, it made me think."

Her smile, it gave him all the room in the world to just . . . be. Not explain or come up with shit to say. She just . . . gave him space. "I don't want to overwhelm her, but . . ."

"I get it."

Fucking hell, she was beautiful. And patient. And kind. And nothing like what he'd thought.

"Your brother looked like the most loved boy in the world."

Jesus. It was like she'd grabbed hold of his heart and squeezed. "He was."

"Can you tell me how he died?"

His heartbeat kicked up so hard and heavy, it made his head spin. He hadn't talked about it since right after it happened. At all. To anyone. Even his family. They just didn't talk about it.

"You don't have to. I'm sorry I asked."

Strangely, he wanted to. And where the hell did that come from? "We had a gig at a festival in upstate New York. We were playing with some pretty big bands—"

"We? You mean your family?"

"I was in a band."

Her chin snapped up. "Oh. I had no idea. I thought . . ."

"You thought I've always been a session musician?"

"You seem to . . . I don't know. I thought you were just a free spirit, doing what you felt like doing, flitting from one job to another."

"A free spirit?" He barked out a laugh. "Good one."

"So, your band was successful?"

"Getting there. We were playing a big festival, and I'd asked my parents to play, too. Do their own set. Seemed like a great idea at the time. And my dad, he's not like my mom. Not as scarred by the shit that went down over their time in the business."

He flashed her a look, always a little uneasy talking about his family. So why was he? Maybe because she had this patience . . . *no, you know what it is? She's strong.* Mimi Romano had a fuck of a lot of inner strength.

And it fed right into him. "My dad's got a lot of energy. He's one of the most creative guys you'll ever meet, and retirement sucked for him. But what could he do? He'd bought into the whole compound thing, the homeschooling. He was in. But I could see he needed more. I even had him producing some of our songs. And then I suggested they play with us. Just the one event. My mom said she did it for my dad, but I saw her. She loved it, too. They love music. They love performing. It's a rush, you know?"

She smiled warmly, encouraging him to go on.

"Yeah, so, of course, they brought Hopper."

"Did he love music, too?"

"Oh, yeah. Nobody loved music more than him. Whenever we jammed, Hopper was right in the middle of it."

"Did he play?"

"He played everything. He sang. But no. He had some disabilities."

"Down syndrome?"

He nodded.

"I saw the pictures. God, you can feel how happy he was."

Calix tipped his head back. She was killing him. "He was. Happy. He was . . ."

Her warm hand covered his. "He was the luckiest boy in the world."

Oh, fuck. Fuck, fuck, fuck. Why was he having this conversation? Why *her*? "Yeah, until he overdosed."

"Overdosed?"

"While I was getting my ass kissed by the guys from Voltage Records, he wandered off. We spent the whole night looking for him. My mom was . . . she was a mess. We all were." He blew out a breath, pulled on his beard. "They didn't find him till the next morning. OD'd on some band's tour bus."

The bindings around his chest yanked hard, making it hurt to breathe. All his senses narrowed to the whistle of the wind, the roar of the sea, and the thick knot of pain lodged in the center of his chest.

Fuck, what was he thinking bringing this shit up with her? The impulse to run took hold. He needed to ride. Ride until his anxiety—his sorrow—his *guilt*—drained away. So why the fuck couldn't he move? His legs felt weighted down by sandbags.

She got up on her knees, moved behind him, and pressed her soft, warm body into his back. Resting a cheek on his shoulder blade, she didn't say a word. Just held him like that.

Her body heat penetrated his skin, warmed his tissue through to his bones.

And while his mind slowly settled and his thoughts stopped scattering, her warmth was the only sensation getting through.

A few drops of rain splattered on his wetsuit. And he

surprised the hell out of himself by saying, "I was torn." She didn't prod him for more. Didn't move. And for some strange reason, it enabled him to continue. "I wanted to see my parents onstage. It was a big deal, them performing again. And my dad, he's crazy. But the Voltage guys had been coming to our shows, and I knew this was it—they wanted to sign us. So they were kissing my ass. Making me feel like the next Bon Jovi. And I loved it." He fisted a handful of sand so tightly the grains burned in his palm. "I did. I loved the attention."

Her hold tightened around his waist.

"My parents' friend was supposed to be watching Hopper during their set. It's not his fault," he hurried to explain. "It's no one's fault. He just . . . you know, I don't know if the guys from Death Tab thought it'd be funny to invite the Down syndrome kid onto their bus, or if Hopper just followed along. He trusted everyone—why wouldn't he? The guys swear no one offered him anything. But they had drugs and booze all over the place. Hopper didn't know. He was the most trusting kid you'd ever meet."

"I could tell. From the pictures. He didn't know anything but love."

"Fuck." He said it softly, his voice rough and shaky.

Her hand never moved, but her fingers lightly stroked his arm. "I doubt anyone on this earth had a better childhood than he did."

He reached for her hand, gave it a squeeze. "You're right."

The moment he turned to look at her, he knew he shouldn't have. Something about this woman—so vital, so strong, so real—got to him. Dug right down into the man he used to be.

Her features softened, and she licked her lips. And suddenly what he wanted more than anything was to close the distance between them. Get his hands in that silky hair and feel the soft heat of her mouth.

But he wasn't that man anymore. And he didn't have room for anything until his family healed.

So he stopped looking at her mouth and those pretty green eyes that didn't seem to miss a thing. "I'm gonna get you home."

"I appreciate the offer." She pulled away, releasing him. "But I'll take a cab. Stay with your friends."

"Not gonna happen."

Feet pounding on sand caught his attention, but before he could see what was going on, two of his friends flung themselves at him, piling onto his back and laughing.

"Play for us."

"Jax brought his guitar." The smell of reefer clung to their clothes.

Just then lightning split the darkness. The girls shrieked. Thunder rumbled in the distance, and raindrops splattered on his skin.

"Oh, my God," one of them said.

The other took off. "Let's go to Calix's. Come on, you guys."

"Oh, crap." Mimi lifted the towel so it covered her head.

"It's just rain."

"Until you spend forty minutes a day blow-drying your hair straight, you don't get to mock."

"Forty minutes? Who has that much extra time?"

"Women with crazy hair."

"Calix, come on," someone shouted.

A crack of thunder made Mimi jump. The rain turned from steady to a downpour.

"Dude!" someone shouted.

Calix grabbed her hand. "Come on." He led the way to the stairs.

"Calix!" Shay jumped on his back, her knees tucking in against his ribs. "Give me a ride." Letting go of Mimi's hand to grab hold of Shay's legs, he hitched her higher. They all raced up the narrow trail, bracketed by bushes that led to a flat parcel of grass. Climbing the stairs to his cottage, he took a glance at the roiling sea before setting Shay down.

As music and lights flipped on, he did a quick scan for Mimi. Found her pushing the hair out of her eyes and holding the drenched towel. He took it from her. "I'll change into some dry clothes, and then I'll take you home."

"No problem. Take your time."

He dumped the towel on the laundry room floor before

heading down the short hall. Opening the linen closet, he pulled a stack of towels off the shelf.

"Oh, my God, I'm freezing." Shay reached for one, gazing up at him with those hooded eyes and soft lips.

"You want to bring these out there for everyone?"

"Sure, babe." She gave him a lingering look before taking them and heading back out to the living room.

Since Mimi didn't seem to be in a rush, he figured he'd grab a shower. He tossed his wetsuit on the floor of his bedroom as he headed into the bathroom. Turning on the water, he stepped into the warm spray, one hand braced on the tiled wall as his cold skin burned with the hot water.

A rush of cool air had him turning to find Shay, naked, hair streaming down her slender body, stepping into the stall with him.

"I'm so cold." She huddled up to him.

Maybe it was because he'd gotten stirred up from being with Mimi or maybe he just hadn't gotten laid in too long, but his body responded to her in a way it hadn't in a long time.

Her gaze dropped to his semi, and she reached for his hips, pressing kisses to his chest.

Yeah, he was horny, and yeah, he could go for a blow job.

She glanced up at him, eyes hungry and needy, and he took a step back.

But not from Shay.

When she came closer, he reached for her shoulders, tipped her chin. "Shay, no."

She tried to hide it, but there was no mistaking the hurt in her eyes. "You sure about that?"

"Yeah, I am. Let me shower. I'll be out in a minute." He hated hurting her, but he'd hurt her worse by using her. Bracing his hands on the tile, he let the hot water stream down his body.

"I get it, you know."

His muscles tensed, but he kept his head lowered.

"You can't get close to anybody right now. I know. I was there. I saw you shut down. You're not gonna open your heart again, not for a long time. And I love that you don't want to use me or whatever. But it's *me*, Calix. It's me. You *can't* use me."

When she touched his back, he straightened, the heel of his hand slamming on the faucet. "Gotta get Mimi home."

"She said she'd take a cab. Just let her. Stop trying to take care of everyone. Let *me* take care of you."

He got out of the shower and yanked the towel off the rack. Handing it to her, he drew in a breath. "Shay, listen, we've been friends a long time, and I don't want to screw that up."

"You can't screw it up. Nothing can ever mess us up. I'll always be here."

"I don't want you waiting for me."

"Oh, my God, would you stop worrying about it. It's *us*. I don't expect anything from you. I just want to make you feel good."

"Come on, Shay. Of course you expect something from me. Not now, not in a month or maybe even a year, but you do expect me to get back with you. And I don't want that. I don't want any expectations at all. I've got—fuck. I don't want anything from anyone. Don't wait for me, okay? Don't hope. Because it's just not there. It's *not there*."

She ran a palm up his chest. "It'll always be there for us. First love is a powerful thing."

He'd never had to think about it before, but right then he knew he hadn't been in love with Shay. He'd been obsessed with fucking her. She was hot and willing, anytime anywhere. But love? No, he hadn't loved her. "I don't love you like that, Shay. I'm sorry. I don't want to hurt you, but I'm not gonna lie. And I'm not gonna use you just so I can get off. I've known you a long time, and we're always going to be in each other's lives. So, I'm not gonna go there with you again." He hated spelling it out. "That part of our relationship ended a while ago."

Calix turned from her, swiping the towel from the hook on the back of the door.

With a raging hard-on he strode back into his room, his thoughts turning to what T-shirt or sweats he could find that would fit Mimi. He figured he'd find plenty of clothes his friends had left behind in his laundry room, so he'd just grab something for her.

Mimi stood in his doorway, looking between him and Shay, who stood right behind him. "I'm so sorry. I . . ." She gave a little laugh. "Ah. Never mind." Her creamy complexion burning a fiery red, she turned and fled.

CHAPTER FOUR

Hitting the rise in the road, Calix braced for the impact.

A riot of wildflowers exploded onto the scene. Brilliant blues, purples, yellows, oranges, and reds. It went on forever.

Just beyond the fields sat a bar of frothy gray ocean. And above that, a bright blue sky with golden streaks of sunshine lancing through the fat, cotton ball clouds.

This view would never get old.

As he neared the farmhouse where Mimi and half the band lived, he started to regret coming early. He'd wanted to make sure he and Mimi were cool, but he'd picked a bad time. She'd be making breakfast. She wouldn't have time to talk about his dick.

And she'd seen it. In all its glory.

He assumed she'd gotten a cab, because when he'd gone to find her with some clean, dry clothes, she'd already gone.

Pulling his Harley into the gravel driveway, he cut the engine and dropped the kickstand. The earth was wet from last night's rainstorm. A gauzy white curtain pressed against the screen of an open window, and he heard someone shout, "I'm up, asshole." Boots tramped down stairs, and conversation floated from the kitchen. Amid the outdoor scents of damp gravel and sweet wildflowers, he got a whiff of coffee and baking bread.

With a quick rap of his knuckles against the back door, he entered the laundry room.

"Calix." Emmie sounded happy to see him as she reached into a cabinet and pulled down a mug. "Coffee?"

"Sure, thanks."

She poured from the carafe, handed him the mug, and gestured to the creamer and sugar bowl. "I'm so glad you came for breakfast."

At the table, Slater, Ben, and Cooper shoveled eggs into their mouths. Derek had Violet pressed against the counter, standing between her legs. Whatever he said, as he nuzzled her ear, made her fingers curl into fists in his flannel shirt, and she tipped her head against his chest with a shy smile.

"Mimi around?" he asked.

"She's here somewhere." Emmie peered into the oven, an oven mitt covering one hand.

"Got any more biscuits?" Ben called.

"Get 'em yourself," Slater said.

Emmie laughed. "Five more minutes."

Not interested in food, Calix wandered into the living room. Eight months ago, he'd come here for the first time. The place had been filled with old furniture and the kinds of vases and figurines collected over a lifetime. Now, though, with Derek, Ben, and Cooper living here, shoes, clothes, and all kinds of instruments were lying around.

He didn't see Mimi but figured she'd be watching *Chopped* or doing research on her computer. Whatever. He wasn't about to look for her upstairs, so he'd just head outside. Walk down to the beach, while the guys ate breakfast.

The moment he turned, he saw her.

On the covered porch, the early morning sun tipped its light onto her, turning her russet hair a fiery mix of golds, reds, and light browns. She usually wore her hair straight and sleek. This morning it tumbled around her in a bounty of curls.

Huddled over the table, she focused on her project. Wearing a long-sleeve T-shirt and pajama pants, face free of makeup, she looked like an ethereal creature, and it made him want things he couldn't have.

The sound of his boots on the hardwood floor should've snagged her attention, but her intense concentration never broke.

Leaning against the doorway, he watched her use tweezers to carefully place a tiny yellow petal in a pulpy mess of crap covering a screen. The frame of the screen was set over a pan of more of the pulpy stuff immersed in water. Around the room drying racks held sheets of paper the size of notecards. He leaned farther in to get a better look and discovered she'd made scenes out of the delicate and colorful petals.

"This is beautiful." His voice cracked the silence, and she jolted.

Looking up, the palest pink blush spread across her cheeks. "Oh. Hey." And then she smiled before going back to work. "Thanks."

On the face of the card a bride and groom, arms linked, heads tilted toward each other, smiled broadly. The woman held a stunning spray of wildflowers in her hands. It was . . . well, hell. It was remarkable.

"Wedding invitations," she said quietly.

He'd come for a reason, but she was so fucking beautiful he couldn't pull his thoughts together. "I thought you'd be jumping all over that cooking show stuff."

"I've been up since four watching episodes of *Chopped* on YouTube. I needed a break, and I have to finish the invitations anyhow."

"Violet's?"

She nodded. Her loyalty impressed him. A lot about her impressed him. "You left last night."

"Yeah. I called a cab."

"We didn't know. Lee was worried."

"Lee was, huh?" Mischief glittered in her eyes as she perched her wrist on the edge of the table.

"Yeah." Maybe it was the soft morning light or maybe it was her hair all wild like that, but arousal kicked in, strumming his nerves.

"That's a sweet cottage you've got."

"Yeah, it was the original home on the property. My parents didn't want to live so close to the water. They wanted more privacy." Her soft, feminine scent filled the small room, and he needed to get the hell out. "You still coming over at two?"

"I'll be there. But if Dak needs you, just let me know."

He gave her a tight nod, set his mug down, and then darted for the door like a pit bull was at his heels.

"You're leaving?"

"Taking a walk."

"But you just got here."

As he moved behind her, he got a whiff of her shampoo and a glimpse of the pale skin of her slender wrists. His pulse quickened.

"Calix?" Emmie called from the kitchen.

"Yeah?" Hand on the screen door, he waited for more from the disembodied voice.

"You want something to eat before you head into the studio?"

"Nah. I'm good."

"Okay, well, they'll be heading over in about ten minutes."

"Got it." He gave a curt nod to Mimi, his hand twisting the knob.

"You don't like my food?" Mimi asked.

"Your food's fine."

"Then how come you never stay to eat it?" She set the tweezers down, giving him a look that said, *After all we shared last night? You're going to be distant again?*

Well, yeah, last night he'd said too much. He shrugged, gazing out the screen door.

"You know, it's pretty fun around here. How come you never hang out?"

"Got other shit to do."

Again, that knowing look. "You got so much shit to do right this minute you can't have a biscuit with the guys?"

Why was she pushing it?

"Just sit with them. Come on, did you eat breakfast?"

He shook his head.

"Well, lucky you, because I found an awesome recipe for

huevos rancheros. Some chiles, a warm corn tortilla. Splash of sour cream. It's pretty delish, if you ask me."

"I'm good." He opened the door. "Just gonna take a walk before being shut in the studio all day."

She got up. "We should just say it, you know? We're going to be around each other, and we don't want it to be weird."

"Say what?"

"Last night." Her gaze dropped to his package. "I saw your wiener."

For a long moment, they just stared at each other, and then he burst out laughing. "You weren't the first." He stepped through the door. "And you won't be the last." And then he jumped off the stairs and took off across the grass, heading for the ocean.

Rarely did a band work together so well, so perfectly in sync with each other, that it made playing a crystal pure joy. But that was how it was with Blue Fire. Calix closed his eyes, blending into the music, letting it flow into and through him.

The guys had a pretty good gig out here. The studio was right in Slater and Emmie's backyard, their house not even a mile down the road from Violet's.

After the last note faded away, Ben tossed his drumsticks into the air. Everyone looked at each other, faces impassive, and then all of a sudden, they broke into laughter.

This band had a lot of moments like this—they liked each other. Really connected. And, he had to admit, it felt good. Really fucking good.

If he could join a band, it would be this one. But he couldn't. Not yet.

So it wasn't worth thinking about.

"That was great, you guys," Sam, the recording engineer, said into the talkback mic.

Coop pulled off his headphones. "You think he toned down some of that reverb on the backing tracks like we asked?" He lifted his shirt to wipe the perspiration off his face.

"I think we'll just have to *trust* that he *knows* what he's *doing*," Ben said, imitating Dak's patronizing voice, going heavy on the Valley Girl accent. Though Dak didn't sound quite like that, he still placed a strange emphasis on certain *words*.

Calix found Derek watching him. The bass player shook his head.

"What?" Calix asked.

"Dude, you were scorching on keys."

Calix turned to find his water bottle. "Thanks. Yeah, good session."

Slater came out of the isolation booth, the only one not smiling.

"You got a clothespin on your sac, man?" Coop joked.

"It was off, right?" Slater opened the door to the control room. "How'd that sound?"

Dak didn't even look up from the mixing board.

"Dak, man," Slater said. "How'd it sound?"

The guy shoved his messy, dark blond hair out of his eyes and pushed his black glasses up his nose. "Huh? Oh, cool, yeah. I think I want to try it with Calix on vocals."

Derek set his Fender in the stand and joined them in the control room. "What're you talking about?"

"We're going to slow it down. It's not working as a rock song. I want to try it as a ballad, and Calix has perfect pitch."

"So does Slater," Ben said at the same time Coop said, "That song is not a ballad."

"We'll try it that way and see," Dak said.

With a frustrated expression, Coop squared his shoulders. "It's clearly not a ballad."

"I want to hear it with Calix," Dak said.

"Guys." Calix pushed through them to stand in front of Dak. "I'm a session musician. This isn't my band. Not my place to do lead vocals." He brushed past them.

"Hang on. Where you going?" Slater followed him out of the control room and into the lounge.

"I'm gonna let you guys figure it out." He pushed out the door into the bright sun of midmorning.

"Look, I think it's time we have a band meeting," Slater said. "Nothing feels right with this album, and we have to figure out what to do about it."

"Makes sense." Wet grass flattened under his boots. He noticed his dad's truck at the side of Slater's house and couldn't miss his big body in the kitchen with Mimi.

"What're we gonna do about this asshole?" Derek asked, joining them.

Leaving them to discuss it, Calix leapt up the steps to the back porch. They had no fucking idea how hard it was for him to just play keys. No idea. He was used to having total control. As singer for his band, he'd played lead guitar. All his life in his home studio, he'd played and arranged everything.

"Calix, hold up," Slater said. "What do you think of Dak?"

He stopped before opening the door and faced them. "I think if you're not happy with the tracks, you should say something. It's your band. Your sound."

"The problem is that we haven't heard anything," Derek said. "We don't know *what* we've got."

"Guys." Sam stood outside the studio and called from the doorway. "Need you back in here."

"Hang on." Slater's tone had her jaw snapping shut. Turning back to Calix, he said, "You've got more experience at this side of things, so I'm asking for your input. This is important."

"Yeah, it's important. So, like you said, have a meeting. Figure out what you want. You don't want to lose control of your sound."

"Every time we bring it up, we're told we're supposed to trust Dak." Derek looked frustrated.

"Why?" He knew he sounded impatient, but come on. It was their band. Why weren't they fighting for their songs?

"Because he's fuckin' Dak Johnson," Derek said.

"Which worked out great for Pitstop and the other bands he's worked with. But is it working for you?"

Derek and Slater shared a look, some kind of private communication going on. Derek looked uncomfortable. "No."

"Then do something about it."

"You think we haven't?" Slater said. "You see what he does when we challenge him."

"Do you *want* me on lead vocals on that song?" He would

fucking love to sing that damn song. He and Slater had written it together, and he felt that song in his bones.

"No."

"Then talk to him. If he won't back down, get Emmie involved. Let her handle the hard conversations." They needed to make more use of Slater's wife. She was a formidable manager.

"He's right," Derek said. "We've put up with enough of his shit. Let's talk to her right now, before we go back in there."

Slater stopped him before he took off. "She's at a doctor's appointment."

All the anger and frustration fled, and Derek smiled. "Yeah? That's today?"

Slater whacked his arm with the back of his hand, cutting him off. He tried to hide his obvious happiness—but failed. "Yeah." He looked away. "We'll see."

The guys shared a look—both of them unable to contain their smiles.

Calix had no idea what they were talking about, so he went inside. He found his dad and Mimi at the kitchen counter. "Dad."

"Hey, son. Takin' a break?"

He nodded. "What's up?"

Mimi took a step back, a lock of hair falling across her rosy cheek. She pushed it aside with the back of a flour-dusted hand. "Your dad brought me a crate full of the dreaded green matter."

Terrence laughed, pulling a bright yellow squash out of the crate. "She's either color blind or she's not giving me a chance here."

Mimi lifted a thinly sliced wedge of eggplant. "Oh, we're doing it. Lunch *and* dinner." She tried again to push that piece of hair off her face. "But I'm making Terrence stay so when the guys come gunning for me, he'll take the brunt of the blows."

"Violent group you got here." His dad's big grin was infectious.

And goddamn, it felt good to see him happy like that.

Raised voices outside had them all looking out the window.

In the middle of the yard, the band stood in a semicircle facing Dak and Sam. The conversation grew heated.

"Looks like things're coming to a head," his dad said quietly. "You talk to 'em?"

"Yeah."

His dad clapped him on the shoulder to show his approval.

"What's going on?" Mimi asked.

Sam broke from the group, jogging back to the studio. It'd taken months to convert the old barn into a state-of-the-art facility—and Slater had spared no expense. He wasn't just a rock star—he was a musician. He'd be making music the rest of his life.

And that was one of the best things about these guys—it was all about the music for them. Not the fame or rock star lifestyle. Calix hadn't worked with many bands that got it the way these guys did.

"Things aren't working out with Dak," Calix said.

"So why aren't you out there with them?" Mimi asked.

Because he couldn't get more involved. He wrote and arranged songs, played with them . . . He practically lived with them. He had to draw the line somewhere.

He could feel his dad's smile but refused to look. "Not my place."

She made a sound of exasperation. "You've worked with them a long time. They think the world of your talent. Of course it's your place."

He stepped closer to her, counting on his size to quash her attitude. "Not my band."

Didn't work on this one, though. Mimi tipped her chin to look at him. "They need you." That hair slid forward again, and she blew out the side of her mouth to push it away.

He tucked the hair behind her ear, stroking it a few times to secure it. Her eyes widened, her lips softened, parted.

"I said my piece." He spoke quietly. "They'll work it out." She was so fucking beautiful. His body hummed with a desire that was growing harder to tamp down.

"Looks like they're coming in," his dad said.

Stepping back to the counter, Mimi dredged the eggplant in the flour mixture, then dropped it in a skillet of hot oil.

"Better get this in the oven. They'll probably want to eat lunch earlier. How long will it take to cook?"

"Forty minutes," his dad said.

"Oh, that's perfect. I'll put some snacks out in the meantime."

"They're not coming in to eat," Calix said as the door banged open and the whole group stomped inside.

"That's just bullshit, man," Ben said. "It's our fuckin' music."

"You haven't even heard the tracks yet." Sam sounded exasperated. "You know, you're not the first band he's worked with that thinks they know better than him. But until you listen to what he's doing, you really don't know."

"He's trying to change us," Cooper said.

Sam kept her cool. "He's trying to turn good songs into hits. That's what he does. You have to trust him to do that. And before you roll your eyes, why don't you guys give it a listen?" She held up a thumb drive. "Play this, and you'll get it."

"We'll listen," Coop said. "But we're not pulling Slater off lead vocals."

"Listen to the track." Sam offered the disk to Derek.

Movement out the window had Calix turning around to see Dak slamming out of the studio. "Where's he going?"

With his messenger bag slung across his shoulder, Dak stormed down the driveway and disappeared around the side of the house.

"Throwing a tantrum," Ben said. "But at least we're done for the day."

Slater brought a laptop to the table. "Let's give it a go."

Derek inserted the disk. A few moments later, the music started, and Calix felt that same energy returning. It was a great song. Until the vocals kicked in. Slater definitely sounded a little strained.

Over the music, Terrence said, "Song's in the wrong key."

Slater shut off the music. "What's that?"

"This song's in C sharp, right?"

Slater nodded.

"Isn't that too high for you?"

"Yeah," Slater said. "I told him that."

"You should try it in A."

The guys looked at each other. A simple adjustment that Dak hadn't considered.

"Let's change it," Slater said.

"Right now?" Sam pulled out her phone, started texting. "I can see if he'll come back."

"I don't give a shit if he comes back," Derek said. "I want to hear it in A."

Sam looked up from her phone. "You want him back or not?" A text came in, and she opened it. "Oh, wait. That's him." She read it. "Okay, he's just talked to Irwin. He wants a listening party."

Cooper slapped his hand on the counter. "Fuck yeah."

"About time," Ben said. "Let Irwin hear the shit we've been working on."

"How soon?" Derek asked Sam.

"Soon as we can get it together," Sam said.

While the others continued talking, Calix cornered Mimi. "How soon can you pull off a party?"

Those raspberry lips parted, and he wanted to nudge aside her hair with his nose and breathe in her sweet, sexy scent.

"I don't even know what a listening party is."

"This isn't for press or fans, so it's nothing flashy. We're not showing anything off. It'll just be people from the record company. We'll keep it simple." He shrugged. "Like a clambake."

"A clambake? Calix, I've only ever been a guest at one of those. They should hire an event planner."

"The more opportunities you have to cook, the better. Cooking for an event, shit goes wrong, you've got to improvise. Just like during the competition."

The creases in her forehead relaxed, and she grinned. "Wait a second. Are you looking out for me?"

Energy crackled between them. He could feel the pull right in the center of his chest, drawing him to her. "You in or out?"

"I don't know. I'd hate to blow it for you guys."

"I wouldn't have suggested it if I didn't think you could do it."

"You've got a lot of faith in me."

That spark in her eyes? It lit a fuse in him. Something that hadn't happened in years. "We'll help you."

"You're going to help me plan a clambake?"

She sounded a little flirty, and he didn't want her getting the wrong impression, so he shifted gears. "Between me and my mom, yeah. We'll help you."

"My wife's probably done fifty of 'em." Terrence joined them. "You got this."

Mimi looked at them both but settled her gaze on Calix, as though needing his support.

He gave a firm nod.

"Okay. Let's do it."

Careful to keep her fingers away from the flame, Mimi charred the red pepper while watching Calix lean into the refrigerator. The muscles in his biceps bulged as he moved things around, and his jeans cupped the tight, round globes of his ass.

He was so freaking hot, she could barely stand it.

Who would ever have thought the man who'd once played a starring role in her fantasies was now teaching her how to cook? That she'd be standing beside him and breathing in his clean, masculine scent, feeling the heat of his very big, hard body, and gazing into those dark, deeply probing eyes?

A shudder rocked through her. *Lucky bitch.*

Straightening, he removed butcher-paper-wrapped packages from the refrigerator and dumped them on the island. Tearing one of them open, he set a strange clump of meat on a plate.

Reality stripped away her fog of lust. "What is *that*?" A funny smell reminded her to turn the pepper to keep it charring evenly.

"It's a ham hock."

"And things were going so well." In just a few short hours, Calix had taught her that changing up the type of fat used— butter, beef fat, walnut oil—transformed the flavor of a roux. He'd taken a basic recipe for vegetable broth and changed it markedly by adding lemongrass. They'd even tried using roasted vegetables instead of the typical raw carrots, onions, and celery, which had given it a much deeper, richer flavor. "Clearly, they've taken a turn."

He continued opening the other parcels.

"Where on earth did you find that stuff?"

He studied the contents. "I asked the butcher to give me whatever body parts he had left over."

"To freak me out?"

Calix laughed. "I thought you've been watching *Chopped*?"

"I have." But she hadn't believed the *Verna Bloom Show* would use shock-value kinds of ingredients.

"Then you know the kind of shit they give the contestants."

"Wait, did *you* watch it?" When would he have done that? Between having sex with his surfer babe girlfriend and showing up at the farm at 8 a.m.?

Yeah, okay, that was a little bitchy. But if watching him from afar had fueled her nighttime fantasizes, imagine what seeing his massive hard-on had done. That man was *beautiful*.

And Shay was perfect for him. Her easy sensuality to his dark intensity.

"I haven't, but my mom has. She told me what to expect." He held up a package. "You're gonna have to figure out how to incorporate whatever crazy shit they give you." His thick, shoulder-length hair gleamed in the overhead lights.

A woman entered the kitchen. "You talkin' about *Chopped*?" With her height and long dark hair held back in a ponytail, she had to be his mom. She did a quick sweep of Mimi and the kitchen, before heading straight for the refrigerator.

"Yeah. Hey, Ma. This is Mimi Romano."

"Mimi." His mom gave her a nod. "Jo Bourbon." And then she bent low to reach inside a drawer.

"She cooks for the band." The way Calix watched his mom so intently reminded Mimi of the plan to get her interested in the cooking lessons.

"I'm a contestant on a cooking competition. For the *Verna Bloom Show*. Calix is helping me prepare for it."

"It's gonna be like *Chopped*?" She closed the refrigerator, holding a yogurt container and a bag of baby carrots, and then went to the silverware drawer.

"Similar format but not exactly the same." Mimi watched her grab a spoon, then head to the pantry. "It's less about cooking skills and more about our ability to think on our feet. How we handle the pressure of a kitchen. And it's not focused on us the entire time. While we're cooking, Verna's show continues. She just checks in with us now and then. Oh, and also, it's based on points. Three judges giving us points for three different categories."

"What're the categories?" Calix asked.

"Quick thinking, innovation, and presentation."

Jo stopped at the table to peel back the butcher paper. "What're you gonna do with this?"

"Not sure yet." Calix folded his arms across his chest.

"What kinds of dishes are you making each episode?"

The woman was definitely interested. "There're five rounds. Appetizers, soup and salad, side dishes, entrées, and dessert. I've totally got dessert. That's my thing."

Jo nodded. "Got any plans for that offal?"

Jesus God. Offal? *Offal.* "I'm working with organs?" Mimi looked up from the stove, moving the pepper away from the flame. A sick feeling swept over her. "Seriously, I don't think this show is like that. On the application it said we didn't need to be professionally trained. The winner will be her sous chef, so we'll learn everything from her. Giving us weird things . . . I mean, what would be the point?"

"Shock value," Calix said. "Ratings. You should be prepared for it so you don't choke."

"What kind of shit are we talking about?" she asked.

"I don't know. A snail, squirrel guts. Eyeballs."

Panic had her heart pounding. "They're not going to give us stuff like that."

Jo gave her a dull look. "Look, babe, you're not gonna make it past the first round if you get squeamish over guts or eyeballs. You wanna be laughed off the show, be the chick who's freaking out."

Well, that settled her right down. "I don't want to be laughed at."

His mom set the yogurt down before heading into the pantry. "What's the prize? Besides being her sous chef, what do you get if you win?"

"We'll work with her off the show, as well. We get to learn everything there is to know about the food and restaurant business."

"Okay, so they're not looking for chefs. They're looking for an assistant. Someone with personality who can work under pressure." She came out with a granola bar. "That means you gotta be prepared for anything. It's not your culinary skills, but how you react to things. How creative you can be under pressure."

"Yeah, that makes sense. And I can totally do that."

"Then you gotta handle the offal," Calix said.

Jo nodded. "Do it. Touch the offal."

They both looked at her with serious expressions, and she didn't want to let them down. Didn't want to be the joke of the show. Besides, she could do this. She could do anything.

Setting the pepper down on a plate, she headed for the offal. As she peered into the white paper, she forced herself not to make a face, but God, the shiny, dark red—almost black—mass of—"What *is* that?"

Calix snatched it away, and they both burst out laughing.

Great. They were teasing her. "Thanks, guys."

"Looks like you got a challenge here, Calix." With her three items—yogurt, carrots, and granola bar—Jo started out of the kitchen.

When Calix tensed, she plunged her hands into the slimy mess. Just to keep Jo's interest. *Oh, my God, it's disgusting.* "What could I do with this?" She turned to Jo. "What would *you* do with it?"

"Make a broth," Jo answered easily. "If it were me, I wouldn't give a judge anything to eat I wouldn't eat myself. Use it for a sauce or a broth. A gravy—and then strain it. Don't make them eat an eyeball or anything that'll make 'em gag."

"You're so right. I would never have thought of that. Thank you."

Jo looked pretty exhausted, as she gave a nod to Calix, and then headed out of the room.

Worried she'd let him down, she tried again to hold on to Jo's attention. "Can you—" But Calix's hand closed around her arm, and he shook his head.

"That was great," he said quietly. "A good start."

"You're right. I'm an all-or-nothing kind of girl. But you're right. It's our first day, and she definitely showed interest."

He didn't immediately drop her hand, and the warm pressure made her pulse kick up. Slowly, one side of his mouth curled into the most delicious smile. It made her breath go shallow and her heart flutter.

But then he let her go and headed to the French doors. "Hey, Ma?"

Mimi waited, listening.

"The band's gonna have a listening party. Thought we'd do a clambake. You good to show Mimi how to do it?"

Mimi didn't hear his mom's response, but she couldn't miss Calix's deep, sexy voice. "Cool, thanks. Tomorrow?" And then he came back into the kitchen.

Holy mother of God, when Calix smiled, her heart nearly exploded. He came right up to her and gave her a swat on the butt.

"Hey."

"This is good, Meems. Real good. And she won't have to do anything in the kitchen. It's outside, on the beach. That'll make it easier for her."

"I'm glad." She pretended to rub her butt. "Now leave my ass out of it."

Standing beside her, he leaned back, peering down at her ass. "Not possible."

"Calix Bourbon, are you flirting with me?"

And just like that, his good humor switched off. "Nah. Just playin'."

"I know. I've met your girlfriend."

"My what?"

"Uh, Shay?" *The woman you were massively excited about?*

He pressed his lips together, giving her a stern look. "She's not my girlfriend."

"I saw—"

"Not what you thought." He reached for the charred pepper. "Let's get back to work. This is perfect. You want to peel it?"

"Sure." Why'd she have to go and bring up the whole girlfriend thing? She liked playful Calix.

"So, let's talk about what happens when things go wrong. Like when you've got thirty minutes to make a dessert and the cream curdles."

"Oh, I've got desserts down. That's the one thing I know how to cook. Besides, we don't do desserts until the fifth episode."

"I'm not talking about dessert specifically. Just about understanding how things work. The chemistry. I was using dessert to illustrate a point. You with me?"

"Totally." The burned bits peeled off, she set the juicy red pepper back on the plate and rinsed her hands.

"You know why cream curdles?"

"No. But it makes me nervous not knowing when it's going to go from almost perfect to ruined."

"Exactly. You don't want shit like that happening on the show when you've got thirty minutes to get something done and plated. If you understand what's going on, you won't screw it up."

"Okay."

"When you beat the cream, you're creating air bubbles. As it's whipping, the fat's distributed among the bubbles, and that causes them to stick together and create foam. Make sense?"

"Yep."

"Good. So the fat particles need to be cold in order to stick together. So what do you do to make sure you don't ruin the whipped cream? The minute the clock starts, you put the beaters and bowl in the fridge—or freezer, given the time. You put the cream at the back of the fridge."

This was such good information. She wouldn't have known to do that. "Got it."

"Hey, you guys, how's the lesson going?" Lee stood in the doorway. With her platinum hair and petite frame, she looked like a princess who'd gotten kidnapped by a biker gang. Terrence came in behind her, carrying burlap bags.

"Calix?" Terrence's tight expression led Mimi to believe he was less concerned about the lesson than his wife's response to it. When Calix grinned, his dad's features relaxed, and he looked a hundred times less intimidating.

She stepped toward them. "Hey, Lee. Terrence." She gave each one a hug. "This guy's been amazing. You can tell your mom all that homeschooling stuck. And if that's not enough, he convinced her to show me how to do a clambake tomorrow."

Terrence's gaze slid to Calix, and the two of them shared a deeply relieved and hopeful look. It melted her heart to see both of these huge men turn soft over their fervent interest in Jo's recovery.

"You guys wanna beat it so we can finish?" Calix said. "I gotta get Mimi back to the farm so she can make dinner."

"I'm starving," Lee said. "Haven't eaten all day. What do you have here?" She headed to the counter with the butcher paper packages of ham hock and offal.

"Got some real tasty treats for you, Lee." Calix swiped one of the bags up before she could see it.

"I wouldn't trust him as far as I could throw him," Mimi said.

Lee eyed her brother warily. "I think I'm gonna go with Mimi on this one."

"Smart girl." Calix picked up a kidney and waved it in front of Lee's face.

"You're disgusting. Get that away from me." Lee shrieked and took off, Calix chasing after her with the organ.

Mimi turned to find Terrence watching her with an expression filled with warmth—and maybe even gratitude.

She smiled back, hoping very much she didn't let him down.

But, really, what could go wrong? It was just a few cooking lessons.

CHAPTER FIVE

A strong breeze rippled the ocean as Mimi watched the horizon turn from pale yellow to a deep, bruised peach. Cold water rushed around her ankles, catching the fabric of her maxi dress and tugging it.

"Got some more." Lee scooped seaweed from the water and trudged toward shore.

Farther away, Jo worked in silence, scouring the sea.

A shrill whistle had her turning around to find Terrence waving at them from the pit they'd dug. Mimi gathered her kelp and hauled it over to their encampment.

"Good stuff." Terrence relieved her of her load. "Now we're gonna lay it out on top of these stones." His deep, hoarse voice sounded like it hurt to speak. That, and his intimidating size, made a strange contrast to the gentle kindness in his eyes.

Together they stretched the heavy, wet plant out in strips across the steaming stones. She loved that he'd take the time to do this clambake with her. Why hadn't she and her dad done projects together like this?

Fear plucked at her heart. What had she been thinking

rejecting the Miami job? He'd made it clear what she needed to do to get hired, and then she'd refused to even consider it.

Well, she'd been thinking she'd already done everything he'd asked her to do, and after all these years, it still hadn't resulted in a job.

So why wouldn't she try a different path? She didn't believe for a second his team would think less of her for doing the competition. But even more—she wanted to do it. After a lifetime of doing things his way, she wanted to forge her own path.

In her gut, she believed it would lead her to her dad.

"Perfect." Terrence sat back on his heels to examine their work.

"Make sure you get the guys to dig the hole and heat up the stones." Dropping her load of seaweed, Jo wiped her hands on her jeans. "You'll have enough to do with decorating and preparing the food."

As Jo dropped into a beach chair, Mimi studied her. While she could tell the woman had been pretty in her younger days, the map of creases on her skin revealed a life lived hard and fast.

But Mimi knew this project had sparked something in her. Jo's normally dull tone had grown livelier as she'd shown Mimi how to wash the clams and prepare the cheesecloth nests of food. And her husband? Terrence had been there every step of the way, his love for his wife clear in the way he looked at her. And he'd made it fun—cracking them all up as he showed Mimi how to debeard mussels.

"I'm starving." Lee collapsed into a beach chair. "Haven't eaten all day."

Mimi shot her a look over her shoulder. "Grab something from the cooler."

"She never eats," Jo said.

"Uh, you should talk," Lee said right back.

Jo's eyes rounded, clearly ready to get into it with her daughter, but Terrence broke the tension when he burst out laughing. "She got you there."

"I don't even understand not eating," Mimi said. "I'm Italian, and I eat like every meal is Thanksgiving."

"Believe me," Lee said. "I eat."

"I'll tell you why she doesn't eat," Terrence said. "She's waiting for someone to make her something."

"Are you serious?" Mimi asked.

Lee kicked up a little sand with her toes. "What? So I don't cook."

"Spoiled, more like." Terrence grinned at his wife. "Her mom made her breakfast, lunch, and dinner every day of her life."

"Hm, maybe *you* should be the one taking the cooking lessons," Mimi said.

"Forget it." Lee tipped her head back, opening her mouth wide.

"What the hell're you doing?" Jo said.

"I'm a baby bird, waiting for you to feed me."

Jo leaned over, stuck a hand in the basket, and pulled out a baguette. She tore off the end and tossed it to her daughter. "There. You're fed."

"Thanks, Ma." Lee bit into the bread. "Yum. What else you got?"

"See for yourself." Jo slid lower in the chair and closed her eyes.

Reaching into a straw basket, Lee hauled out plastic containers of hummus and sliced vegetables.

"Let's get the food on here now," Terrence said.

Jo pulled a clear plastic bag of Quahog clams out of a cooler. Her long, shaggy hair spilled forward, and she tried to whip it back with a toss of her head. While she took out a bag of mussels, Terrence made his way around the pit to stand behind her, gathering her hair into a ponytail. Jo flinched at his touch, and Terrence froze, hurt momentarily gripping his features.

Mimi looked away, hating to see the man's touch rebuked. But then Lee pulled an elastic off her wrist and tossed it to her dad. He caught it in his huge palm and tied back his wife's hair. Smoothing a hand down the ponytail, Jo thanked him, then got up and brought the bags to the pit.

After spreading out the cheesecloth bundles of potatoes, onions, and carrots, they added another layer of seaweed.

Then, the four of them spread out the shellfish, topping it with more kelp. Finished, they covered the pit with a tarp.

"Shame we don't have corn on the cob," Terrence said.

"Wrong season." Jo sat back in her chair. "Besides, we're just showing her how to do it."

"Looks good," Terrence said in his grumbly voice.

"Hey." Gus came down the stairs, carrying his laptop. "So, listen, I think I got the Zaranov Vodka account today." His bare feet kicked out sand as he headed toward them.

"Good." Terrence's big body landed in a beach chair.

"Oh, yeah, it's awesome." Gus sounded frustrated. "My first contract in months." He wore his dark hair shorter than Calix's but long enough that a lock fell across his eyes. No question he was as handsome as his older brother with those dark eyes and caramel-colored skin, but he didn't have the same intensity. He didn't smolder.

"Good thing we're not looking for the income." Terrence gave his son a hard look, and man, if he'd looked at her like that, she'd have gotten the message to shut the hell up.

"Cool, but I've got to do something other than get turned down." Gus snapped his laptop closed. "I don't know why I waste my time."

"Not wasting time," Terrence said. "There's more to do than merchandising and licensing."

"You know that's the bulk of what I do each day."

"I'm sorry, what exactly do you do, Gus?" Mimi sat cross-legged in the sand, facing the Bourbons. "You're, what, twenty-three? Around my age?"

"Yeah."

"Where'd you go to college?"

She couldn't miss the snap of tension between his parents and Gus. Oh, crap. She'd stepped in it again.

"I didn't."

"He started at Julliard," Terrence said.

"I dropped out."

Three years ago he'd have been twenty—ah, of course. He'd dropped out because of Hopper. And, oh, crap, that would explain why Lee wasn't doing fashion or decorating.

Life had come to a screeching halt for this family.

"So now I run the 100 Proof LLC."

"What does that mean, exactly?"

"I take care of all the business things that still go on from my parent's music. Licensing, merchandising, stuff like that."

"That sounds interesting. I guess you're not a musician?"

"I play, but I like the technical side more. Mixing and spinning."

"And you're good at it. What you played me last night was really cool. Can you do that for a career?"

"There's a lot I could do." Gus leaned forward, his eyes alight with excitement. "I could be a DJ or work in a studio."

Plenty of clubs in the Hamptons used DJs. And, of course, the obvious solution—Slater's studio was half an hour away on the North Fork.

She shot Terrence a questioning look. Seemed *too* obvious, so she should probably keep her mouth shut. Wait, what was she thinking? Calix worked at the studio every day, so it had to be all right. "Why don't you work with Blue Fire?"

He had boyish good looks, but in that moment he looked like a kid holding a present in the shape of what he'd asked for. His excitement leveled, though, and he looked at his laptop. "I'm not trained at anything. I only mess around."

"Don't they already have a recording engineer?" Lee asked.

"Yeah, but she actually works with Dak," Mimi said. "So, once Blue Fire finishes this—"

"They'd never hire me. I don't have the skills they need."

"Would you want to be a gofer? That way you'll learn some skills, get some experience."

"Hell, yeah. You think they'd let me do that?"

"I don't see why not. I can ask them when I go home."

"Will you?" Gus looked so excited she had to smile. Funny, how they were nearly the same age, but he had the exuberance of a much younger man.

"Of course I will." But when she looked to the others to share her amusement, she found nothing but tension. Oh, crap. But Calix worked with the band. He worked in the studio every day. How was Gus doing the same thing bad?

"You got a business to run." Terrence's tone indicated the subject was closed.

Mimi fixed her attention on Jo, who'd gone perfectly still, the beer bottle clutched in both hands.

"I can do both at the same time," Gus said. "I want to do it."

"You wanna get coffee for the guys?" Terrence asked. "Fetch Dak his slippers? From what I hear, the guy's a dick."

"Stop trying to talk me out of it. I want to do it."

"You guys—" Lee began.

"Let him do it." Jo got up.

Terrence watched his wife with concern.

"Let him do it." Jo said it more softly this time. Pain spread like a slow leak across her features. And then she lowered her head. "I need a smoke." She headed down the beach.

"Damn." Gus got up, starting after his mom.

"It's okay. I got it." Terrence gave his son a tired smile and then went after his wife.

"Dad," Gus shouted. Terrence turned to him. "Can I do it?"

His dad drew in a heavy breath and rubbed his chin with a hand. "Yeah, boy. You can do it." He started to go, but he turned back to his son, stabbing a finger at him. "But don't you fuck this up, you get me?"

"Yeah. I get you."

"This isn't about partying. It's about learning. We clear?"

Gus nodded, barely containing his enthusiasm.

Mimi sat there, not quite sure what she'd done but wishing she could take it back.

Ben was in the pocket. From the control room, Calix watched the drummer shred. Perspiration dripped down his face, as his arms stroked, head thrashing, replaying the same beat for the tenth time that day.

Beside him, Derek sorted through a stack of papers, smirking when he found the one he wanted. Pressing it to the laminated glass, he waved to get Ben's attention.

"Let me see it," Cooper said.

"Hey." Dak shifted the headphones off one ear. "Don't interrupt him."

But Calix knew—along with the other guys—that Ben was wasting his time in there. Dak gave too many conflicting instructions. *Try it this way, no, no, try it that way, no, that's not right.* Jesus, how had the guy ever done a successful album?

As soon as Dak had the headphones back on, Derek flashed the sheet of paper to the others. Everyone burst out laughing at the crudely drawn image of a confused face—two oval eyes, a half-circle mouth turned upside down, and a question mark sticking out the top of the head.

Cooper waved to get Ben's attention, as Derek plastered the sheet to the glass again.

Ben halted mid-thrash, as he focused on the paper. Tossing his sticks, he gave the finger, threw off his headphones, and shoved his kit back as he got up.

He burst into the control room. "This sucks."

Dak stood up, shrugging off his headphones. "Grab some water. We'll break for ten then try it again."

"Try *what* again? I don't know what you want me to do. It's all fucked up in my head."

Someone rapped on the door. "Hey." Gus peered into the control room and then entered.

What the hell was his brother doing in the studio?

"Got the screens," Gus said to Dak. "They should be here in about ten days."

Dak barely looked up at him. "I need them now."

Eagerness turned to concern. "Okay. I can rush delivery, but they don't have the five-panel acrylic screen in stock. Rush might get them here in seven days instead of ten."

"Rush."

"It's expensive."

Dak shot him a challenging look.

"On it." Gus fled the control room, and Calix took off after him.

He caught up with his brother in the lounge. "Hey."

"Hey." Gus pulled out the chair and sat down in front of

the computer. He tapped out a few words and then *Acoustic Screens Soundproofing Solutions* filled the screen.

"What's going on?"

"Mimi got me a job here." He looked happier than Calix had seen in a long damn time. "I'm a gofer."

"What're you talking about? How'd that even come up?"

"Mom was doing that clambake yesterday, and Mimi asked why I'm not DJ-ing or something."

"Okay, but what does that have to do with working *here*?"

"Come on." Gus got up so swiftly, the chair shot back. "My job is bullshit, and you know it. What kind of licensing deals do you think I'm getting on a band that broke up twenty years ago?"

"Hey, I get it." Of course it wasn't right that Gus got stuck doing a job he didn't want. That he hadn't gotten to finish college.

"Look, I'm not going anywhere." Gus leaned forward, like he needed Calix to understand. "I'm not bailing on Mom, but how much longer are we supposed to put our lives on hold?"

"I don't know. I don't look at it like that. I just want her to get right in her head and . . . stay with us, you know?" He sought out Hopper's leather bracelet, fingering the bumpy braid. "Until then, I mean, nothing else really matters. It's *Mom*."

"Fuck. I get that, I do. I just . . . Jesus." He ran his hands through his hair. "Think about it. All this time, you're playing. You're keeping up your connections, doing your thing. So when things are better, when Mom's strong enough, you're all set. You start up a band again, and you're back. But me? It's all passing me by."

He couldn't argue with that logic. It was all true. He didn't think any of them had imagined the situation would go on for three years.

"By the time we all decide Mom's strong enough, I'm gonna be too old to do what I really want to do, and I'm gonna be stuck doing this business bullshit when I'm fifty."

Everything his brother said made sense, but that didn't stop the current of anxiety from running through him. Because, well . . . *Mom*.

"And I'm not talking about moving to the city. I'm talking

about working part-time in a studio half an hour from home. Just like you."

"Gus, I get it. You don't have to explain anything to me."

"Really? Because you're the one who makes a family dinner every night. You're the one who comes home to check on Mom. And you're the one who found . . ." With a pained expression, Gus looked away.

But he didn't need to finish the sentence. Calix lived with the image every minute of his life.

Gus turned back to him. "The thing is, man, she hardly ever eats with us."

"Yeah, so? That doesn't mean I'm gonna stop trying."

"No, I know. I don't want you to." Gus let out a rough exhalation. "Look, I don't want you to think I'm giving up on her, but I gotta do something for myself or I'm gonna go out of my mind."

Obviously, he understood. He only knew his mom couldn't handle another son getting hurt by an industry she perceived as debauched and soulless. And even with guys as cool as Blue Fire, the partying got pretty intense. All the hangers-on, the record label parties and club events . . . a hell of a lot of temptation.

"Besides, Mom told me to do it."

"Well, what do you think she'd say? Obviously she doesn't want to hold any of us back." And that was the thing. She'd love it if they all left. She *wanted* to be alone.

And that was the fear that compelled him—every minute of every day—to drive out the terrible desire lying in wait in his mom's heart.

He could see Gus working through it, his frustration turning to resolve. "I'll live at home and run the LLC. I'll eat dinner with you guys when I can, but I'm going to do this job. Because when she's okay, when our lives go back to normal, I need to be ready to DJ or run a studio or whatever the hell works out for me. Okay?"

"Yeah, of course." And he supposed if his brother had to be in the music industry, working at a private studio at the tip of Long Island was the safest place to be. "Just . . . you gotta be cool. You can't get into any bad shit, okay?"

"Yeah, yeah. I already heard it from Dad." He let out a breath, smiling. "Don't worry. I got this."

With the sun in his eyes, Calix strode across the damp grass to Slater and Emmie's house. Knowing what she knew about his family, why would Mimi offer his brother a job without running it by him first?

Leaping up the stairs, he pushed into the kitchen. It smelled of spices—Mexican—but the counters were wiped clean and dishes piled in the drying rack.

In the downtime between breakfast and lunch, Mimi had likely gone back to Violet's farm. Probably for the best. He shouldn't talk to her when he was pissed, but then again, maybe he should. She shouldn't have inserted herself in his family's business.

"Fuckity fuck." *Mimi*. Where was she? "Noooo."

The door to the laundry room was ajar. Water flowed from a tap.

He crossed the kitchen, pushed open the door, ready to confront her, when he found her topless, leaning over a sink and holding a white shirt under the faucet. In her black yoga pants, black patent leather ballet flats, her pale skin practically glowed in the late morning light.

He tried hard not to look, but the skimpy pink lace bra was . . . well, *fuck*. Her breasts wobbled with her exertion, and it ignited a flash of lust in his dick. "Shit. Sorry."

"*Calix*." Her hands jerked the sopping wet shirt to her chest. Water flowed down her stomach and sank into the pants. As if it were on fire, she flung the shirt into the sink, and then stepped back, arms open wide, looking down at the water dripping off her body. "What're you *doing* here?"

Calix swiped a towel out of the laundry basket and tossed it to her.

She mopped her chest—clearly having no idea she was making her luscious breasts jiggle. "Thank you. Crap, what a mess. I got mole sauce all over my shirt, and there's no way it's going to come out."

Making a quick assumption, he opened the cabinet over

the washing machine, scanned the various cleaning supplies, and pulled down a spray bottle of stain removal.

"Oh, good. Thanks."

He also pulled a T-shirt out of the basket and tossed it to her. She caught it, set the bottle down, and pulled the shirt over her head. It hung down to her knees.

And now he had the answer to what lingerie she wore under her business suits.

Hot, feminine, sexy as fuck bras. Did the panties match? All the restraint in the world couldn't have stopped him from checking, and Jesus, he didn't see any panty lines under those stretchy pants. Which meant if he pushed his hand under the elastic waistband, he could cup her bare, round ass.

Desire slammed him hard.

"Sorry, were you looking for me?" She gazed up at him as if she hadn't dropped a bomb into his already vulnerable family.

He'd worked hard to make his mom feel safe again. He didn't like Mimi coming along and threatening it. "Yeah, Mimi. Not sure what you were thinking, getting Gus a job in the studio. I told you how Hopper died."

"I wondered about that. I'm sorry." She stepped toward him, looking remorseful. "I wasn't sure if I should say anything, but then I figured since you worked here, it'd be all right."

"I sure as hell hope it will be."

She seemed genuinely worried. "It just seemed so obvious, you know? The studio's right here. But after I suggested it, I saw how upset your mom got, and I wished I hadn't said anything. I'm really sorry."

He blew out a breath. Hard to stay angry when he saw her point. And maybe it would work out all right. He just . . . the idea of trying something new unnerved him. The risk was too great.

She touched his arm. "You're right. I should've kept my mouth shut." She looked wistful. "You should've seen his face, though. When I suggested it? I mean, he got so excited."

"I'm sure. Trust me, I know how messed up the situation is. Of course Lee should be in fashion. Hopper died the summer before she was going to start at FIT. And Gus? Come on, you don't think I know how talented he is?"

"He needs this." She said it quietly, sweetly, making it impossible to be pissed off.

Unfortunately, their needs didn't come first right then. "There's more at risk than you understand."

"Okay. I'm sorry. I am."

He knew she meant it. He also knew she hadn't done anything wrong. Gus—with all his energy and happiness— who wouldn't want to help him out? Calix had no doubt Mimi had acted out of the kindness of her heart.

And fuck, she had a big heart. And a sexy mouth. And underneath her conservative, expensive designer clothes, the lingerie of a sex kitten.

He had to get out of there. "Just . . . stay out of our business."

Rain hammered the roof of the truck as Calix idled in front of Slater and Emmie's house.

Gus reached for the handle. "Sorry about this, man."

"No problem." He didn't need to come into the studio today, but his brother's truck was in the shop, so Calix had given him a ride. "Text me when you're done."

"Nah, I'll get a ride. Thanks, though." His brother darted out of the cab, slammed the door, and raced toward the studio.

He waited—and not for his brother to get inside. He was thinking about Mimi. Her first show taped today. Hopefully, she'd listened to the weather report and gone into the city last night.

She had to know about the flooding. It was all over the news. Well, *local* news.

Shifting into Drive, he stepped on the accelerator. The wiper blades whipped back and forth across the windshield, giving him brief glimpses of road. Jesus, it was pouring. When a car backed recklessly out of a driveway, Calix slammed on the brakes.

It was just going to nag at him, so he'd text her. Make sure she knew. You in the city?

But as he continued down the road, unable to think about

anything else, he decided to go in and make sure she'd already left.

Turning around, he drove as far up the driveway as he could. He left the engine running as he jumped out and ran up the stairs to the kitchen.

Throwing open the door, he found Mimi alone at the kitchen table, stuffing things into a big black bag. Wearing tight skinny jeans, ridiculously high-heeled sparkling sandals, and a magenta rocker T-shirt, she looked fierce. "You're still here."

In a quick sweep, she took in his rain-soaked body, her gaze lingering at his shoulders. But before he could get the idea she was just noticing the water dripping off the ends of his hair, her lips parted, her eyelids lowered, and a look of pure, erotic heat filled her eyes.

And now he knew what she'd look like on her back, gazing up at him while he fucked her.

Holy hell but she turned him on.

The low thrum of energy in the base of his spine snapped him out of it. Not getting hard for Mimi in Slater and Emmie's kitchen.

Her attention went back to her bag. "Um, yeah, just waiting for Violet to take me to the train."

"You're taping in those shoes?"

Pulling a pair of Chucks out of the bag, she waved them at him. But then her gaze landed on the microwave clock, and her brow furrowed. "I don't want to miss my train."

"LIRR's got delays. I guess you haven't been listening to the news?"

"What? What news?" She looked stricken. "What does that mean?"

"Flooding's shut it down."

"Oh, my God. Are you sure?"

"Heard it on the way over."

"Fuck me with frosting." She pulled her laptop out of the bag, opened it, and hit the power button. "Come on, come on, come on."

"What're you doing?" Calix stood beside her, aware of her perfume, the shine of her hair in tight, very cute braids.

"If I can see where the flooding is, I can figure out which train station to go to."

He watched her bring up the Long Island Railroad's webpage.

"You ready to go, Meems?" Violet came into the kitchen, looking all fresh and sweet.

"Train's down. Flooding."

Her friend glanced at the clock. "Oh, no."

"It's okay. I'll call for a car."

"What time do you have to be there?" Calix asked.

"I've got five hours. I planned to go early, so I should be fine." But he could see by the way she clutched the edge of the table that she wasn't fine at all.

"How long will it take a car to get out here?" Violet said. "Maybe—"

"I'll take her." Calix snapped her laptop shut. "You ready?"

"You don't . . . you can't take me."

He hated the anxiety in her eyes. Even though she had to get into the city, she didn't want to go with him. Because he'd been a dick to her yesterday in the laundry room, telling her to mind her own business. She'd done a nice thing for his brother, and he'd shut her down.

And because he'd always kept his distance, always made her think he didn't give a shit about her. So what if he was attracted to her? It was his problem, not hers. "Look, sweet pants, you want to argue or you want to get to your competition on time?"

She looked up at him, cautious. "You can't take that much time out of your day for me."

Fuck him, those green-gold eyes, that lush pink mouth. How did he crush this attraction?

"Mimi?" Violet's tone let her know she was crazy to argue.

And finally, her features relaxed. "Yeah, okay, thank you."

Sucked for him because truthfully? He wanted to take her. There wasn't anywhere else he'd rather be than with her.

CHAPTER SIX

Sheets of water arced out as his truck practically glided down Route 25.

Mimi pulled her phone out of her bag. Started fiddling with it. "Okay, looks like you can drop me at Hicksville. I can catch the train from there."

He nodded. Wouldn't argue with her.

He was taking her into the city.

She tucked the phone away. "Dak doesn't need you today?" Worrying the piece of paper in her lap, she folded it into neat squares, her fingers smoothing the edge with each fold.

"Dak's having another tantrum. Wants to put things on hold until the listening party."

"You worried about losing him?"

"Not at all. Best thing that could happen."

She rolled the paper into a tube.

He reached out, put his hand over hers. "You're gonna be fine today."

"We don't really know that. I mean, we have absolutely no idea what to expect. But I'm good."

He tugged on the tube.

Stuffing it into her bag, she laughed. "Yeah, okay, I'm a little nervous. So, I probably shouldn't say this, but have you ever considered replacing Dak with your dad?"

A spark flared in his gut, and he tamped it down. "As producer? For Blue Fire?"

"Bad idea?"

"Yeah, sweet pants." His fingers flexed on the wheel. "Bad idea."

"I know. None of my business."

It *was* a bad idea. A terrible idea. But his body vibrated with how great an idea it was. His dad . . . Jesus, his dad would come alive. And he'd be the best damn producer for Blue Fire. No question about it.

"Just seems kind of an obvious fit. Would your dad like that?"

"More than you know."

"So, maybe—"

"No. Not now."

"Okay, sorry." She flipped down the visor, opened the lighted mirror. "It's enough for him, gardening and stuff?" She rolled her lips together, smearing the dark red lipstick.

"No, Mimi. It's not enough for him."

His sharp tone had her snapping around to face him. "I'm not trying to piss you off."

"I'm not pissed. I'm frustrated. Obviously, hiring my dad would be the best thing for him. And for the band."

"But you're worried what it'll do to your mom."

A curt nod was his only answer.

"She'd flip, huh?"

"No. She wouldn't flip at all. She'd shut down, making it impossible to read her." And then how could he look for the signs?

"But maybe she wouldn't. Maybe, since it's pretty safe out in Eden's Landing, it'd make it easier to readjust. I mean, you, Gus, Terrence, this is your life. Music is your passion."

"It isn't the music that worries her. It's everything that goes with it. The decadence. She's seen it all, and she doesn't want it for her kids." It cost her a son.

"Well, obviously you'd know that better than I. Just seems

a shame, you know? I mean, no matter how hard she tried to shield you, you and your brother are both totally into music. It's in your DNA."

"See, now, if we all follow our bliss . . . if my dad becomes a producer, Gus gets a job as a sound engineer, and I form a band again—oh, and Lee? If Lee's at FIT, what happens to my mom? When she's all alone in that big house filled with ghosts, what's gonna happen to her?"

"I don't know, Calix." Her challenging tone surprised him. Thanks to his size, most people backed down from him. "All I know is I'm on the outside looking in, and I can see a lot of frustration in your family. Lee's quiet, and she puts up a good front, but I don't think she's all that different from Gus. Or you."

"What does that mean?"

"You're all really passionate, creative people. And you're suppressing it. Of course, I'm not suggesting everyone abandons your mom. But . . . I don't know, do you ever think maybe she feels pressure when you guys watch her so carefully?"

"I think it reminds her that we're there, and that we need her."

"But what if she's so busy trying to be what you want her to be that she can't grieve in her own way? Do you know what I mean? It's not my family. I'm not saying I know her better than you, but I can't help wondering if you guys got back to your own lives, maybe she'd be able to adapt to the loss. Maybe she'd find her way back to her *own* passions."

"Her passion is her children."

"Was. You're adults now, so I would guess it makes her uncomfortable knowing her adult children are living at home putting off their lives because of her."

"We're not gonna take any chances leaving her alone. Just not gonna do that."

"You know best. But you might want to look a little closer at her reactions."

He wanted to reject everything she was saying. Wanted to say she didn't know the whole truth. The real reason his family kept such vigilant watch over her.

But he couldn't when everything she said made sense. And if it did, what the hell was he supposed to do about it?

Because they'd done it before—gone back to their lives and left her alone.

And look how that had turned out.

Calix double-parked in front of the studio.

He waited as Mimi glanced up at Rockefeller Center, the imposing skyscraper in Midtown Manhattan. Pedestrians raced in both directions, cars honked, and the whine of an emergency vehicle faded into the distance.

She bit down on her bottom lip, before turning to face him. She gave a mock terrified expression. "This is it."

"This is it."

She drew in a deep breath, held it, and then slowly let it out. "I'm really gonna do this."

"And you're gonna kick ass."

"Yeah?" Smiling, she tugged the bag from the floor and dropped it on her lap. "Thank you so much for driving me. I hate that I took so much time out of your day." She started to open the door.

With each movement away from him, his chest tightened. Given the amount of rush-hour traffic, leaving for home at this point would be a waste of time. He should sit it out.

Which meant he could walk her in. Give her some support.

Not that she needed him. She could handle anything.

The door opened, and she slid off the seat.

And it felt like the rope unraveling had run out of length. "You want me to come in with you?"

The hope that lit her beautiful features confirmed he'd made the right call.

Until that hope faded. "No, you've spent enough time on me. Thanks, though. That was nice of you to ask. You should get back to your family."

"I'm gonna be sitting in traffic anyway. Might as well wait it out." No point in arguing when he'd already decided to stay.

She studied him, like she didn't trust that he actually wanted to be with her. "I've taken enough of your time."

"Mimi, what do you want?"

And just like that she cracked, her vulnerability shining through. "I want you to come with me."

The studio was much smaller than Calix had imagined. Not that he'd ever watched the *Verna Bloom Show*. Stadium-style seating held maybe a hundred audience members. Overhead lights crowded the ceiling and boom mics bracketed the rectangular stage.

"You a husband or something?" A woman stood beside him holding a clipboard and wearing a Bluetooth headpiece.

"Just a friend. Am I in the way?"

She went from businesslike to friendly in two seconds flat. "Not at all." She thrust out a hand. "I'm Beth, one of the production assistants. We've got about an hour until we tape, do you want to come to the green room? We've got food, coffee. All kinds of goodies."

Backstage, huh? He'd like to see Mimi, make sure she was holding up. "Sounds good."

The woman talked at him the whole way. Within fifteen minutes, he'd found out she'd gone to Purdue, majored in communications, had always dreamed of being a television producer, and loved living in the city. He scanned each room he passed as he headed down a long hallway, watching for that deep red hair.

"Green room's right down here."

"Where's makeup?"

She came to a stop in the hallway. "You want to see makeup?"

"Yup."

"All righty then. Come on." She stopped again when they came to a brightly lit room. Two people sat in chairs facing the mirrors while stylists with brushes, lipsticks, hair dryers, and eyeliner pencils attended them. No Mimi.

And then that familiar burst of laughter rang out, and

Calix swung around to find her in the room directly across the hall.

Features animated, hands moving, Mimi talked a mile a minute, entertaining the stylists and the guy in the chair next to her.

This was nervous Mimi. He willed her to look at him.

"She your girl?" the woman asked.

"No." It came out too abruptly. "A friend."

"If that's how you look at your friends, where can I sign up?"

Calix kept his focus on Mimi. He wanted to talk to her, reassure her. When she made a big gesture, as if describing a bomb exploding, her gaze snagged on his and she stilled.

He wanted her to feel calm. Wanted her to know she had this. And when she sank back into the chair, when her features relaxed, he knew he'd given that to her.

And then that lush mouth formed a single word, *Hey*, and it ignited a slow burn of intense, powerful awareness.

He wanted to be alone with her, wanted his hands on her. He wanted his mouth on that creamy skin. His heart thundered when he imagined all that hair sliding through his fingers as he kissed her.

"Excuse me." Some guy pushed him aside and entered the room.

"I think your *friend's* going to need a smoke after that," Beth said. "Come on. Let me get you to your seat."

He gave Mimi a chin nod and then followed Beth down the hall.

Calix checked his phone again, waiting for a response from his mom. Still nothing. Probably in the studio. But he wanted to know for sure, so he texted Lee. You got dinner for Mom?

You bet. Me n Dad r making it together. You coming home soon?

Need me? She didn't reply right away, which set off a low buzz of worry.

Finally, his phone vibrated.

Dad seems happy.

She still hadn't answered the question. Yeah? Why?

*Dunno. Think he spent some time with Blue Fire
today. Think it makes him happy to be around music
again.*

Of course it did. For three years, his dad had poured his
creative energy into his gardens, but it couldn't possibly
satisfy. Not the way music did.

Damn Mimi for bringing up the obvious. His dad would
be a great producer for Blue Fire. He had no response for his
sister so just wrote, Yep.

When will you be home?

I can leave right now if you need me. The audience broke
into applause, and the contestants filed out onto the stage.

When she didn't respond right away, Calix grew
uncomfortable. He could've been nearly home by now, and
instead he'd chosen to hang out with Mimi. Suddenly, his
choice seemed pretty stupid, considering he'd had only that
one moment with her backstage.

He texted again. Can be home in two hours.

His phone vibrated. You'd be hitting worst traffic. Just stay.

You're cool?

Totally.

Mom?

In her studio. I'll bring her dinner. No worries.

Yeah, but that was the thing. There were always worries.

Mimi didn't know about them, but they were always
there.

* * *

Standing alongside the other five contestants, Mimi had to wonder what attributes the producers had been looking for since the six of them had absolutely nothing in common.

After meeting and chatting briefly backstage, she'd learned that Pedro ran a popular food truck in the city, making grilled cheese sandwiches. Quiet and intense, he'd hardly interacted with the others, giving only brief responses to their questions. Frazzled Alena worked in her family's Russian bakery in Chicago, and Deborah, who looked scrubbed clean, ran the kitchen at a new age spa in Arizona. Joey, who smelled faintly of weed, owned a beach shack restaurant in Florida, and funky Eleanor ran a tea and coffee café in Missoula, Montana.

Since she was being billed as the chef for a rock band, she'd dressed the part in her rocker heels and T-shirt. If only they knew.

The video introducing each contestant ended, and the audience clapped.

"Great group, right?" Verna Bloom, the petite, dark-haired host of the show, took center stage. "So, let's introduce our judges." She pressed her hands together, talking to the camera. "Our first judge, from the popular New York restaurant of the same name . . ." A drum roll gave way to a crash of cymbals, as the curtain whooshed open and out walked a portly gentleman in a suit.

"Chef Alonso."

The audience clapped wildly—because everyone in New York knew Chef Alonso's popular restaurant on the Lower East Side, featuring classic Italian dishes. Okay, so this judge expected culinary talent. Which, for her, would be a problem.

Verna hugged him. "Chef Alonso is one of the most beloved and innovative chefs not only in the city but in the world. We're thrilled he's able to join us on our show."

The chef smiled, bestowing his warm smile on the audience. "Eating?" He shrugged. "Discovering new talent?" He shrugged again. "How could I refuse?"

The audience laughed.

"Okay, our next panelist is an award-winning teacher at the Institute for Culinary Arts right here in the city."

Oh, hell. Technique would matter to this one. "The lovely, the talented . . . Chef Zoe Burke."

This one didn't get quite as enthusiastic a response. But then she had a very austere and stern presence.

"Isn't she gorgeous, you guys?" Verna hugged the tall, slender woman who wore her hair in a severe bun. "Do you eat? Can I fix you something?" The audience laughed at that one, but Zoe didn't crack a smile.

Mimi suspected winging it wouldn't work with this judge. Palms damp, she swiped them on her chef's jacket. She needed to calm her racing heart. She cut a glance to Calix, third row, first seat off the aisle. He held her gaze with an intense look that beamed pure, high-grade confidence. He was telling her to believe in herself, and it zapped her good and hard in the gut. He was right. If she didn't believe in herself, she'd bomb. It was the whole reason she'd kept contact with her father to a bare minimum this past week.

Zoe took her seat, shaking hands with Chef Alfonso. She sat rigidly, hands clasped on the table.

"And finally, you're not gonna believe who we scored for this show, you guys. I am so darn pleased to introduce our third and final judge. I don't even know how we got so lucky, but ladies and gentlemen, the founder of the Food Channel himself, the incomparable innovator, Mr. Aaron Simmons."

Mimi watched as a white-haired gentleman in black slacks and a gray cardigan strode out. Doubt came roaring back. As the founder of the Food Channel, he'd expect brilliance in the kitchen—why not? He was surrounded by it.

She was so screwed. Her gaze flicked toward the audience, seeking out Calix's. He beamed confidence her way. And she took it. Sucked it in greedily.

You know what? I'm going to own this show.

". . . quick thinking, presentation, and innovation." Verna's tone had a hint of finality, drawing Mimi back to the moment. "Ready, contestants?"

"Ready, Chef," they all murmured.

Mimi repeated the last words. *Quick thinking,*

presentation, and innovation. She said them again, slowly, absorbing each one. It mattered. What they were looking for. It was all about her ability to think on her feet, the presentation on the plate, and using the ingredients in an unusual way. *Got it.*

"Then please reach under the table and bring up your shopping bags."

Mimi hauled up her recyclable bag, dropping the heavy weight on the counter.

"Each bag contains four items. You'll have thirty minutes to make a dish using all four of them. You'll also have the use of items in my pantry and refrigerator. Think you can handle this? Because this is what it'll be like working on my show. We cook fast, with style, and a whole lot of fun."

Mimi couldn't resist one last glance at Calix. His smile radiated assurance.

Warmth suffused her, loosening her, allowing confidence to stream back in. She was smart, she was a quick thinker, she was creative . . . She had this.

"Ladies and gentleman, thirty minutes on the clock. Ready . . . three, two, one . . . open your bags and go."

Verna took her place behind her own kitchen counter and resumed the show, while the contestants worked at a long table on the side of the stage.

As Mimi fumbled with the bag, she couldn't help noticing Pedro had already dumped out his contents. An apple rolled toward her, but he snatched it, even as he tore open the plastic covering the small ham. Yeah, he worked a food truck. The man had skills.

Block it out. Focus.

She reached into her bag and pulled out a tube of crescent rolls, a small cooked ham, an apple, and an unwrapped wedge of cheese. When her attention wandered to Alena on her other side, she remembered Calix's advice to shut out what everyone else was doing. Twenty-seven minutes. *Focus.*

These ingredients seemed more obvious for dessert than appetizers—except for the ham—so she had to shift her thinking. Black pepper. Okay. An image of a tart came to mind. Cheesy. Apples. Oh, caramel drizzle. Could she put pepper in a caramel sauce?

And here's where Calix's training kicks in. Because she had no choice but to rely on her instincts.

Without a recipe in hand, she had to close her eyes, smell the ingredients, and imagine how the flavors would work together.

Pepper with caramel didn't seem right. Maybe some chili powder? Did chili powder work with apples, though? No, not at all. Apples . . . nutmeg, cinnamon. Mint. She associated apples with pork chops . . . so, rosemary.

She was getting it now. She could do this, go on instinct and not second-guess herself. Wait, how long did crescent rolls need to cook? She checked the tube. Fifteen minutes, so that was half the allotted time. They needed to go into the oven immediately.

As she preheated the oven to three-fifty, she visualized the crescent rolls and apples. And then cheese. Oozing out of the crust. *Yes.* Tearing open the tube, she dumped the rolls out, slicing each almost completely in half, but still leaving them connected. If she diced the cheese, it might not melt evenly, so she'd have to grate. She sniffed the cheese—Gouda?

What about the caramel drizzle? She should get that going. But she'd need to whisk it while it cooked, and that would take most of her time. Okay, whatever, just go for it. *Move.* Less thinking, more acting.

Mimi thinly sliced and diced the ham, peeled and chopped the apple, drizzled olive oil on the mixture and added salt, pepper, and thyme leaves. Stuffing the crescent roll crust with shredded Gouda, she pressed her thumb down, making a well. Into it she started to add the ham and apple mixture, but she stopped. Flavor. It was all about flavor. What went with ham, apples, and Gouda? Cloves. Pinch of nutmeg . . . and cinnamon. Yeah. That made sense. And rosemary, right? A good amount of coarse salt. She wasn't going to skimp on the salt. Mixing it well, she pinched an apple and popped it into her mouth. Mm. *Good.*

She spooned the mixture into the wells. Then, just before

setting them in the oven, she sprinkled a few bits of Gouda on each of the three rolls. So, cheese in the crust, cheese on top. Wait, no, she'd cook the tarts first, then put the cheese on top. Otherwise the cheese would burn.

Great. Now, quickly, the drizzle. Racing to the refrigerator, she grabbed butter and a container of half and half, dumped both into a pan, and set a low flame. Measuring brown sugar into it, she started whisking. Oh, salt. *Flavor, Meems.* But just a sprinkle.

No freaking idea what I have here. In all likelihood, they'd call her out for making a dessert, but she had to go with her instincts. It wasn't like she could pull a recipe off her laptop. As she stirred, she glanced at the other contestants. Pedro worked like a machine, in constant motion, attending to multiple stations at once. Impressive. The guy had total command of his workspace.

She shot a look at Calix. Finding his gaze on her so intently delivered a shock to her system. He didn't even smile. Just gave her that intense, steadying look.

She *loved* it. Loved his attention.

"Okay, friends, you've got five minutes on the clock. Five minutes to finish cooking and plating."

Her syrup wasn't thickening. Not going to panic. *You know what? I don't need this much sauce.* She dumped half of it in the sink and set it back on the stove. Better.

With so many scents competing in the kitchen, Mimi couldn't get a sense of her rolls. She didn't want to leave her drizzle—why the hell had she gone with a caramel sauce? It wasn't even necessary. But her gut told her it was, because the tarts alone were too basic.

Time to check the rolls. In a whirl of motion, she swung around, opened the oven, saw the mixture cooked to perfection and the rolls nicely browned, and pulled the cookie sheet out. She sprinkled cheese on top and spun back to the drizzle, which had just started to bubble.

"Two minutes, friends. You've got two minutes on the clock."

Pulling three clean white plates off the stack in the middle of the table, Mimi set a tart on each one, while continuing to whisk.

"One minute. You've got sixty seconds left."

With a spoon, she drizzled her sauce over the tarts. It looked divine, smelled delicious, but . . . crap. They looked plain and boring. What could she do?

She picked up each tart, drizzled sauce on the plates, and set them back down. Herbs littered her work station, so she made a pretty design with the rosemary on either side of the tart. Simple, but pretty.

"Time is up." The timer dinged. "Stand back."

They all threw up their hands and took one step back from the table.

Holy shit. Adrenaline crashed through her system, and perspiration trickled down her spine.

She'd done it. She'd completed the assignment. Whether or not they liked her dish was out of her hands. But she'd done it, and that made her damn proud.

Ten minutes later, the contestants stood before the judges. It was down to Pedro and Mimi. Pedro, standing one step in front of the other contestants, waited for one last judge's assessment.

"Holy cow, buddy, you move like lightning." The audience applauded, and Chef Alonso had a look of disbelief. "Gotta give you a five for quick thinking, and invite you to join my kitchen." Chef Alonso paused while the audience laughed, but he never took his eyes off Pedro. "I give you a three for flavor because brushing the dough with butter and coarse salt just made it taste like a pretzel. I didn't like that. And I give you a two for innovation because, while I think it's clever that you cut the ham into tubes, I just don't find pigs in a blanket all that special."

"Thank you, Chef." Pedro stepped back.

Mimi's turn. Anxiety turned her skin clammy.

"Okay, and now for our last contestant, Mimi Romano," Verna said. "Judges, let's start with Mr. Simmons."

"Let me just say that this tart was absolutely delicious," the older gentleman said. "If I could, I'd give you a five for flavor."

As the audience exploded with applause, she relaxed. This was good. Really good.

"I'm giving you a three for quick thinking, but that might just be an unfortunate comparison to Mr. Speedy over here." Again, they laughed, and Pedro took a bow.

"A four for innovation. It wasn't enormously clever to create a tart, but the way you turned what might've tasted like a dessert into a mouthwatering appetizer was just sensational. And a three for presentation because the drizzle was the same color as the tart, so nothing really popped."

"Thank you so much." It took everything she had not to look for Calix and pump her fist. But she kept her focus on the judges.

"Chef Alonso," Verna said.

"You're a star." The man beamed at her. "Just a star. Calm under pressure. I'm going to disagree with my esteemed colleague on the quick-thinking part, because I watched you make very quick decisions. And in order to pull off these flavors, you had to have relied on your instincts as a chef."

Yeah, so not a chef. But he didn't need to know that. "Thank you."

"So, I give you a five for quick thinking, a five for presentation, and a three for innovation because, as Mr. Simmons mentioned, a tart wasn't enormously clever."

She nodded her thanks. So, that made twenty-five out of thirty. One judge to go.

Please don't be too hard on me. Zoe seemed to relish her role as bad cop. She'd already called out Pedro for making grilled cheese sandwiches. *Do you know what to do with an herb? What, exactly, do you hope to gain from apprenticing with Verna?* And she'd shredded Joey. *Basically, you flip burgers. Do I have that right? You stuff clams into white buns?* And when she'd asked what he hoped to achieve from working on Verna's show, she'd eviscerated him when he'd said he thought a fast-food cooking show would be a hit. Not everyone wants to "cook gourmet," he'd said. And Zoe's lip had curled in disdain. Joey wasn't long for this show.

Mimi girded herself for a tough critique.

But something roiled under Zoe's icy demeanor. "Let me ask you a question."

"Sure."

"Mimi Romano. Any relation to Dino Romano?"

Where was she going with this? "He's my father."

"So, then, I'm curious why you'd choose to be on this show when you've got a world-renown restaurateur for a father. Are you bored? Looking for some attention?"

Looking for attention—what, like Paris Hilton? Okay, hang on. She couldn't let herself get all worked up and jump the gun. She had to stay calm and think.

Alena was keeping her Russian bakery in Chicago afloat in order to support a large, extended family with health issues. Pedro worked his food truck eighteen hours a day seven days a week to send money back to his family in Guatemala.

So, yeah, Zoe *was* painting Mimi with the pampered princess brush.

Oh, it's on, honey. "I love cooking, and I'm excited for the opportunity to work with Verna Bloom."

"Surely you've had the opportunity to work with the finest chefs in the world, given the restaurants your father either owns or invests in?"

"I grew up in and around kitchens, but I've had no formal training, if that's what you're asking."

"And you've got an MBA from Columbia."

Mimi nodded.

"So, no formal training, an MBA . . . are you just playing around with this competition? You've got all the connections you need to follow in your father's footsteps. In fact, looking at your résumé, you've groomed yourself to do just that. You're a businesswoman who doesn't have to knock down any doors. Why cook on national television?"

"I love cooking. I grew up in the kitchen with my grandmother and my dad."

"That's sweet, Ms. Romano. But with all that hard work at Ivy League schools, I'm asking why you'd want to be an apprentice on a cooking show?"

"My grandfather was a tailor, and my grandmother a seamstress. My father put himself through college washing dishes and delivering food. Just like the others in my family, I'm going to forge my own path using my intelligence, my creativity, and my resourcefulness."

"That doesn't answer the question, but all right. Let's get to it." She looked down at Mimi's dish. "I give you a two for quick thinking. Unlike Chef Alonso, I couldn't read your thoughts, so since I could only go with your actions, I found your execution of basic tasks a bit plodding. I give you a two for innovation. I'm just not finding salt, pepper, and a few herbs all that innovative."

Oh, crap. She couldn't afford these low numbers.

"Frankly, it tasted like a dessert that you tried to masquerade as an appetizer with the use of pepper. And I give you a one for presentation because a tart with two sprigs of rosemary?" Zoe remained completely unapologetic, which was so strange since the other judges had the humanity to at least look sorry for delivering a low score.

Five out of fifteen points. Dammit. This could sink her.

"Thank you. I always appreciate constructive criticism." She took a step back, her legs shaky. She'd blown it. Everything Zoe had said was right. A tart was hardly innovative.

"Okay," Verna said. "When we come back, who will stay in the game to be the next Verna Bloom apprentice?"

The moment the show ended, Calix fought his way backstage. A crush of people made it difficult to get to her, but he got a glimpse of those dark red braids and pushed through.

She chatted with the other contestants, her vibrant personality making her stand out among the crowd. He was so damn proud of her. In spite of Zoe's low scores, she'd made it to the next round.

That judge had tried to make her seem undeserving. Like some pampered rich kid who was just playing around, but she'd failed. Because Mimi rocked.

The more he watched, the more he noticed her attention

wasn't really on the conversation. She kept looking away from the group, her gaze scanning. And when she saw him, relief washed over her flushed features.

Calix ploughed through the crowd. As soon as he neared her, he reached out and pulled her into his arms. "You're fucking amazing." It came out a growl.

The way her arms tightened around him, the way she leaned into him, giving him her weight, let him know she'd had enough. He pulled her out of the fray, guiding her down a hallway. His big body shielding her, he tipped her chin. "You did great."

She gave him a wobbly smile. "That was crazy. A total and complete rush."

"You want to get out of here?"

"I want to say good-bye to Pedro. I don't think he deserved to be eliminated, but yeah, I really want to go home."

As the revolving door spilled them out onto Avenue of the Americas, Mimi turned to him, and he knew right away he wasn't going to like what she had to say.

"Hey, thank you so much for bringing me out here and being this huge source of support for me. But I know you need to get back to your family, so . . ." She shrugged.

"You getting rid of me?" She'd given him a good excuse to go. And, yeah, he should take it. But he didn't want to leave her yet.

"I'm totally wired, and at the same time, all I want to do is curl up on my couch, order take-out, and watch movies. I think I'm just going to walk home."

Right. He could head back. "Okay, then."

Both stood awkwardly, tires driving through pools of water the only sound. "You going to your dad's?" he asked.

"No, I kept my apartment in the Village since I'll be back in the city once I get a job. Or, hopefully, this apprenticeship." She blew out a breath, looking down the street, as if contemplating her walk home. "I'm at 12th Street and Second Avenue. Near NYU."

"That's quite a walk."

"Well, if I crap out, I'll catch a cab."

He looked into those green eyes and felt himself tumble into her.

Was it weird that he could feel his skin when he was with her?

All the more reason to get his ass home. "Okay. I'll see you tomorrow."

She didn't smile, didn't respond, just held his gaze. Like they were the only two people in New York City. She gave a sharp intake of breath, and then her tongue peeked out, swiping along her bottom lip. "Right, so, thanks again. You were awesome today. Bye."

He watched her walk away, and he felt it. Every step she took made his pulse spike harder and faster. Until it became unbearable. "Hey. Sweet pants?"

She turned back around, a flare of hope in her eyes.

"Want me to walk you home?" He'd leave his truck in the parking garage. Catch a cab back uptown later.

She drew a sharp breath. "It wouldn't suck."

CHAPTER SEVEN

Calix wasn't sure why he was boarding the elevator in her steel-and-glass high-rise, but he'd come this far. He might as well get her to her apartment.

The moment the doors closed, she leaned against the wall, and a slow bloom of satisfaction spread across her pretty features. "I did it," she said quietly. "I freaking did it."

Somehow standing so close to her in this dimly lit box made him forget all his reasons to stay away from her. He wanted her. Plain and simple. There was something irresistible about this girl. He caught her hand in his, brought it to his mouth, and kissed her open palm. "You did. You were fantastic."

"You helped me."

"Don't think they'll be giving you offal."

"Not that." She touched his arm, like she needed his attention. "You were the voice in my head, reminding me to trust my instincts. You gave me confidence. Every time I started to freak out, I looked at you in the audience, and your badass energy picked me up. Every single time. I needed that." Her smile was filled with affection. "You made me feel like I could do it."

"You could. You did."

She didn't look tired anymore. Her features softened, her lips parted. A crazy energy spun through him, throwing out images—those sultry eyes looking up at him, her mouth wrapped around his cock. He could picture it so vividly, his fingers touching her lips as she sucked him deep, and an explosion of erotic sensation burst in his chest.

The car landed, and the doors opened. Mimi took one step forward and winced.

He stopped her. "You okay?"

"Just a blister."

That was all the invitation he needed. He scooped her off her feet and stepped off the elevator. Lowering his nose into her sweetly scented hair, he breathed her in. Need rocked through him, and he held her more tightly to his chest.

"Calix." But she didn't pack any fight in her tone.

He carried her down the hallway. "Which one?"

Instead of answering, she tucked her face into his neck and clasped her arms around him. "Thank you." Her breath was warm on his skin, and her fingers curled in his hair.

Something hot and alive moved through him. "Gonna run out of carpet in a minute."

"Is it terrible to say I don't care? I think I want to stay like this forever. You feel so good, and I'm so tired."

"Come on, sweet pants."

"Fine." Big, dramatic sigh. "Six twenty-two. See that crystal chandelier?" She didn't even lift her head. "My door's closest to it."

"Key."

She started to pull away from him, but the loss of her touch made him tighten his grip. When he didn't let go, she lifted her head to look at him.

They'd never been this close. Close enough to see the pale nick of a scar right at her cheekbone, that expressive mouth, and the question in her eyes. Need burned through him, sending electrical impulses down his spine and through his dick. He needed her bare, warm skin against his. Needed the wet heat of her mouth, the slick tangle of her tongue. He needed . . . oh, fuck him.

His mouth settled over hers, and sparks fired in his blood. Her body turned toward him, fingers gripping the back of his shirt. The hunger took over, and he swept his tongue across her lips, licking inside her mouth.

With a sharp intake of breath, she was kissing him back. And holy hell, this wasn't some gentle exploration. This was mouth-fucking.

She clutched the back of his neck, her tongue stroking his, and raw desire streaked though him, setting him on fire.

Keeping his arm firmly around her waist, he set her down. But if she thought he was letting her go—not a chance. He just repositioned her so he could lift her against the wall and spread those legs around his hips. Nothing could stop his body from pressing into her and taking that mouth he'd fantasized about for months.

Her tits, her hands, the way she writhed against him, spun him into a frenzy. "Jesus, Mimi." And then she was making noises, hot, hungry purrs deep in her throat. *This feels so fucking good.* He ground his cock against her stomach. Heat blistered through him.

"God." The back of her head hit the wall, and she fought to pull her legs out of his grip.

It took him a moment to shift gears, but he slowly lowered her to the floor. She looked as shaken as he felt. His knees barely supported him, so he braced both arms against the wall to hold himself up.

He needed a moment to cool down. Jesus, he'd never had a kiss like that.

All he could hear were her exhalations as she fought to catch her breath. She fumbled in her big black bag. Her hand shook as she pulled a set of keys out of the inside pocket. After the third attempt to stab the keyhole, he took the key and unlocked the door.

The moment they stepped into the entryway, she dropped her bag and kicked off her sneakers.

His heart still hadn't calmed down. And his dick—his dick needed relief in the worst way. "I'm gonna use the head."

"The what?"

"Bathroom, sweet pants. Gonna take a leak."

"Right. Okay." She moved into the living room of the small but tidy apartment. "It's just right there."

To the left sat a plain galley kitchen. White walls, white cabinets, small stainless steel appliances. To the right, a short hallway—more like a vestibule with two doorways. One went to her bedroom, the other to the bathroom.

Shutting himself inside the good-sized space, all chrome, white, and dark red, he was immediately assailed by her scent. The tiled shower stall held a loofah brush hanging off the faucet by a rope. The corner pockets were wide enough to hold a couple bottles of hair products and one of body wash. Two ruby red bath towels hung neatly over a rack by the door.

Calix caught a look at himself in the spotless mirror. His body was still coming down off the high of that kiss. Sure, he'd had quick and fiery hookups before. Obviously. That was the fun of it. But what had he expected to happen with Mimi?

Fuck. He lowered his head, closing his eyes. This woman brought shit out in him. Not good shit either. As evidenced by the fact he'd driven her to New York City. And stayed.

It was one thing to offer her a ride. A friend would do that. But to stay for the show? To walk her home? What was that?

When he came out, he found her on the couch in a pair of light blue sweats and a white sweatshirt. "I'm gonna head out."

"Okay. Sure." She didn't even get up.

"You good?"

"Great. I'm just going to order take-out and watch a movie."

"Right. See you."

Hand on the door, he felt this strange pull. He didn't want to leave her. And the fuck of it all . . . it wasn't about blowing his nut.

"Calix?"

"Yeah." He didn't turn to face her. Didn't want to see that pretty hair she'd unbraided. The flush in her cheeks from their kiss that hadn't yet subsided.

"It's okay, what just happened. I mean, it's been a crazy day. It just . . . happened. We're okay."

Okay? He couldn't remember the last time a woman had gotten him so worked up. *Go.* He opened the door. "'Night."

He hurried out before he turned back and did something stupid like cuddle with her on the couch.

Sitting on the edge of his chair in the studio's lounge, Calix typed out a text to his dad. You coming to the listening party tonight?

No. And then a second one came in a moment later. Keep an eye on Gus.

Yep. Wasn't much he could do. Gus was his own man. But Calix knew what his dad meant. Other than his two years at Julliard, Gus had lived at home. And he was restless. Anyone could see that.

"I'm just glad Irwin'll get to hear what we've been doing." Cooper lay stretched out on a couch.

"No shit." Ben reached for the water bottle on the table. "None of this would've happened if he'd been in town."

"True," Derek said. "He would've been out here, listening to the tracks. Four fuckin' months, man. What a waste."

"Can't wait to see his face when he listens tonight," Coop said.

Several Amoeba Records executives were coming out to hear the tracks. Irwin would listen at the same time and participate over Skype. *Should be interesting.*

"How long has Slater been in the iso booth, man?" Derek checked his phone.

"We should pull the plug before Dak destroys his vocal chords," Ben said.

Derek got up. "I'll kill the session right now."

"Tell him we're taking a break till Irwin hears the shit," Ben said.

"Don't need to lie." Derek headed into the control room.

Calix got up. "All right, I'm out. See you at the party tonight."

"Check with Dak first, man," Coop said.

"I'm only a half hour away. If he needs me, text." As soon as Calix left the studio, he headed for his bike, unable to resist a glance through the kitchen window.

Disappointment at not seeing Mimi pissed him off. He was getting too caught up in her.

And kissing her like that last night? Not cool. She wasn't just some chick he could bang. Tonight at the party he'd apologize. Get them back on track.

As he neared his bike, he noticed the garage door was open. He heard a growl and then, "Fuck me in a teacup."

Mimi. He smiled at the pure exasperation in her voice and headed toward her.

Sitting on a crate, features beet red, she held a half-inflated palm tree between her legs. She looked up when she saw him. "Is this what it's like to be stoned?" At least a dozen trees surrounded her. Not to mention plastic lobsters and clams and fisherman's netting.

"You've never gotten wasted?"

She shook her head. "Or like I sucked helium. Yeah, that's what it feels like. Does my voice sound funny?"

"Why're you doing this by yourself?"

"I'm sorry, should I have asked my valet to do it?"

"Your what?" He laughed. "No, you should've asked Emmie or Violet. I'm sure Lee would've helped."

"Yeah, no thanks."

"Why not?" He crouched before her and, without even thinking, stroked the hair off her damp forehead.

"I'm trying to stay out of all things Bourbon."

"That's going to be hard to do."

She looked up at him questioningly.

"Cooking lessons?"

"Oh, you know. I'm good." She looked away. "I got this."

"Mimi?" He crouched in front of her. "I'm sorry about last night. I shouldn't have kissed you like that."

"It wasn't the kiss that upset me." Sometimes her sincerity, the pureness in her heart, flipped him out. "It was the way you left. You shut down."

He wasn't used to people being so direct, but he found he liked it with her.

"I hate when you do that. You're all fiery and passionate one minute, and then hard and cold the next."

"Won't happen again." He didn't address which behavior he meant—the kissing or the shutting down. "I still think we should continue the lessons. My dad told me about the clambake. He said my mom was into it. So, if it's good for you and good for her . . ." He shrugged.

"Yeah, okay. I guess so." She lifted the nozzle of the tree to her mouth, essentially dismissing him.

"How're you getting all this shit to the beach?"

She made a strange motion with her hand, and it took a moment to figure out she was pretending to hold a magic wand.

"Mimi."

"Well, obviously, I'm carrying it."

"By yourself?"

"No, the seven dwarves should be here any minute now."

"Someone's feisty today." He got up, knees cracking. "The guys are just sitting around the studio. I'll get them."

"No, no. They're digging the pit and getting the fire going. And I've rented a tent and a bar, so all that's left is decorating. Believe me, I can handle setting tables and hanging lobsters."

She went back to inflating the palm tree.

"How many more of those do you have to blow up?"

She nudged a box toward him with a bare foot, her toenails painted lavender with tiny black treble clefs on them. He pulled out the remaining bags of palm trees. "That's a lot of fuckin' palm trees."

Pinching the base of the nozzle, she pulled her mouth off. "Go big or stay on the porch. That's how I roll."

He looked at her, sweaty, flushed, surrounded by all kinds of decorations, and a rush of affection knocked him on his ass.

"You're a nut." A beautiful, spirited, compassionate nut. He sat down and tore open a plastic bag.

She looked at him, surprised, and he tried to ignore those pink lips wrapped around the clear tube.

Yeah, that was not going to happen.

"Meems!" In a simple but sexy blue and white maxi dress, Violet wrapped Mimi up in a hug, her distinctive soft floral scent floating around her. "You did such a great job."

"You really did." Emmie joined them. While her sundress

appeared basic, it molded to her curves in a fantastically sexy way. Funny thing about Emmie. Her girl-next-door good looks were deceiving. She was a knock-out. "This is amazing."

"Thanks, guys." Standing in the corner of the tent, next to the bar, Mimi took in her work. Burlap-covered metal pails of sand held cardboard cutouts of leaping dolphins. The blue and green glow sticks she'd inserted added a very cool ambiance in the dimly lit space. Calix had helped her hang nets from the ceiling. They'd loaded them with plastic clams, lobsters, and fish.

It did look pretty cool. And she'd surprised herself by enjoying it so much.

"Those desserts?" Emmie said. "To die for."

"They're all her grandma's recipes," Violet said with a note of pride.

"I recognize the tiramisu and the panna cotta, but what was the one sprinkled with confectioner's sugar?" Emmie's hand rested on her lower belly.

"*Torta Barozzi*. That's my family's favorite."

"Well, it's mine now, too. Although I'm going to have to try all of them again just to make sure." Emmie gave a mischievous grin.

"You do realize you're not actually eating for two, right?" Derek threw an arm across both his sister and his fiancée's shoulders.

Emmie gazed up at her brother. "Axl disagrees."

"Axl?" Derek said on a laugh. "That's what we're calling him?"

"We don't know the sex." Slater pushed between Derek and Emmie, tipped his wife's chin, and pressed a kiss on her mouth. "But for the record," he said to Mimi, "we're not announcing anything yet."

"Wait, she's *pregnant*?" Mimi turned fully to her friend. "You're pregnant?"

Emmie's smile was contagious. Slater's too.

"Yeah," Derek said. "But they're waiting until they hit twelve weeks before telling people."

"We're just gonna keep it between us, okay?" When Slater

looked at her like that, all intense and serious, she had to fight the urge to look away. He was just so freaking handsome and charismatic. It was like being around a movie star.

"Thank you for trusting me with the secret. I won't tell a soul." Sometimes she couldn't believe she'd breached the perimeter of this tight group of friends—it filled her with a powerful sense of connection.

"Hey, so how'd it go?" Emmie stroked a hand up his chest, resting it over his heart.

Holy Mother of God, the look that came over him—and it wasn't just the heat in his eyes, it was the utter adoration— like his wife was the keeper of all that was beautiful in the world.

God, she'd never even known love like this existed until she'd moved out to the farm and met these people.

"Irwin's talking to him now."

"Kicked us out," Derek said. "So they could talk privately."

"Dude," Cooper called, waving them over. "Derek? Slater? Come on. Pretty sure Irwin just fired Dak."

"Gotta go, angel." With a brush of his thumb across Emmie's cheek, Slater gave her one more kiss. "You eat for two—or however many people you want." And then he shot Derek a challenging look.

Derek just laughed, then pressed a kiss to the corner of Violet's mouth.

The guys took off, leaving Mimi slightly off-kilter. "Do you two know how lucky you are?"

"Yes," Emmie and Violet said at once. They looked at each other and laughed.

"There isn't a minute during the day that I don't think it," Violet said softly. "How lucky I am. And I can't wait to marry him."

"Do you have a date?" Mimi thought about the invitations—finished except for date, time, and location.

"No, but if Dak's fired, it'll have to be soon. I think we'll probably get married before the new producer starts. Before it gets crazy."

"That's smart," Emmie said. "Once they get back in the studio, it'll be intense. They have to make up for a lot of lost time. And then they'll go on tour. And since you guys aren't doing a big wedding, you might as well do it sooner than later."

Violet turned to Mimi with a concerned expression. "I know you're overwhelmed with the competition, but I was thinking . . . well, do you think . . ."

"Just say it. I'll do anything for you, V. You know that."

"You haven't heard what I'm asking." Violet drew in a breath. "I promise to be actively involved, but I really want your help with the wedding."

"Of course I'll help you. We'll all help you."

"No, I mean planning it." She knew how hard it was for Violet to ask for favors. "I want you to do my wedding. The whole thing."

Mimi's pulse kicked up. "Wait, you want me to plan your wedding?" In her dad's office, he had all kinds of awards and framed certificates. Front and center on the wall hung Mimi's Presidential Achievement Awards, her magna cum laude degree from Cornell, and her Columbia MBA. She was a businesswoman through and through.

Yet here she stood in a tent for a clambake she'd catered. And now her closest friend wanted her to plan her wedding? When had her life taken such a strange and wondrous turn?

Soon she'd be back on track. She'd either apprentice for Verna Bloom or work a full-time job in the restaurant industry. Violet's wedding would fall right before that time—so why not?

"Don't get the wrong idea. I still want it small—just us, our family—and I want it as casual as possible. But seeing what you did here tonight, this"—Violet gestured around the tent—"I want it magical. That's all I really know. Will you do that for me?"

"I would love to." Mimi was gobsmacked. But truly, while waiting for her real life to begin, she couldn't think of anything else she'd rather be doing.

"I wish your mom were here to help," Violet said. "But we'll keep it super simple."

"I just don't know if you should trust *me* with your most special day."

"I want it to be awesome, for sure," Violet said. "But it's not my most special day. Corny as it sounds, every single day is special. Every morning I wake up and realize all over again he's mine. Every time he walks into a room and looks for me and gets that intense look in his eyes as he comes right to me? That's . . ." She turned to Emmie. "Sorry, but your brother's hot."

Emmie just smiled.

"The way he loves you is hot," Mimi said.

"It *is*."

"Sistah, I hear you." Emmie looped her arm around Violet's waist. "We done good."

"You guys make my teeth hurt," Mimi said. "And you suck because you've got the only two hot guys with huge hearts on the whole planet."

"Don't believe that for a second," Emmie said. "You just keep on being all that you are, and he'll find you. You'll find *each other*. Trust me on that. You've got more heart than anyone I know, so you'll attract the same. You'll see."

A tap on her shoulder had her turning away from her friends.

"Excuse me?" One of the teenage servers she'd hired stood there uncomfortably. "That lady over there at the bar, the one glaring at me?"

"Excuse me, guys." Mimi stepped away from her friends, peering over the girl's shoulder to see the woman in question. Ah, she'd seen that groupie many times before. This was a closed party, though, so she had no idea how the nymph had gotten in. "What's she doing here?"

"She says she's someone's girlfriend, and she's pissed because there's no room at the VIP table."

"That's because there is no VIP table. Okay. I'll take care of it. Thanks, Katy. You're doing an awesome job tonight. I appreciate you coming in on so little notice."

"Oh, any time. Not a hardship working an event for these guys." She gave a mischievous shrug of her brows.

Mimi headed for the bar. She'd had plenty of experience with nymphs in the year she'd lived on the farm. Not just at the clubs, but their frequent visits to the studio. Slater and

Derek might be taken, but Cooper and Ben weren't. And those two liked to party.

As she approached the woman—who had to be in her early twenties—she took in her outfit. To a clambake, she'd worn a leather skirt so tight and short it looked like Spanx for the butt and hips. Her halter top was basically a silk scarf that draped over her nipples—gaping on the sides to expose the rest of her large breasts.

"Hi, I'm Mimi Romano. What can I help you with?"

"There's nowhere for me to sit at my boyfriend's table."

"And who's your boyfriend?"

"Dak Johnson."

Had someone just rung the crazy bell? Dak had been holed up in the studio with the band the whole night, which, of course, a girlfriend would've known. "I'm sorry to hear that. It might be best to work out your seating arrangement with Dak. Do you want to give him a call?"

"I'm not going to bother him with something so stupid. I just want to sit down and eat."

"How about I call him? Let him know you're here."

She rolled her eyes. "He obviously knows I'm here."

"Problem?" Calix appeared at her side.

The woman's entire demeanor changed. She went from hard and snarky to soft and seductive. "Hey, there. About time you talked to me."

He ignored her in favor of Mimi. "Everything okay?"

"This is Dak's date . . ." She waited for the woman to share her identity.

"Laney. Laney Morrison." The nymph drew in a deep breath, effectively thrusting out her huge, wobbly breasts.

"Laney." Calix took a step closer to the woman and towered over her. "I don't know what shit you're trying to pull, but this is a private party."

"And I'm invited. Ask Coop. Ask Ben. They know me."

"It's not that kind of party." He waved to one of the servers, a tall, lanky guy Mimi was pretty sure she'd seen at the bonfire at Calix's place. The guy loped over with his easygoing grin.

"Hey, Bones. Need you to make sure this lady gets home

safely." Calix held the guy's gaze a moment too long, until he nodded with understanding.

"You got it, dude."

"I'm not going home," Laney said. "I'm Dak's *date*."

"Come on, babe." With his amiable smile, Bones ushered the nymph away.

Mimi stood beside Calix, watching Laney walk, her hips swaying. The woman cast a seductive glance over her shoulder, mouthing, *Call me.*

"Oh, my God." Why were these women so eager to spend one night with a rocker? When she looked up at Calix, she found him smiling. She swatted his shoulder. "You love this, don't you?"

He laughed. "What's not to love?"

"Skanky women throwing themselves at you . . . they don't even know you."

"What you call skanky, a guy calls hot."

She loved the playful side of him. Too bad she rarely saw it. "And Laney's hot?"

"You're judging her by her clothes. A guy just sees a woman who's gonna get freaky."

"See, that's the difference between us. I'd only get freaky with my boyfriend. Someone I trusted."

He turned so that his body practically caged her in against the tent wall. "You get freaky, Mimi?"

With him standing so close and looking at her so intensely, she heated up. "When I'm comfortable with someone."

His gaze narrowed, his expression turning carnal. "Mimi." His voice sounded rough, demanding, exactly like what she'd want from him in bed.

He leaned into her, eyes filled with fierce heat. God, maybe she was crazy, maybe she was only seeing what she wanted to see, but sometimes it looked like he wanted to eat her up.

After the show, the way he'd come to her backstage, plucking her from the crowd, pulling her aside, he'd looked like he was going to take her right then and there. And holy crap, she'd wanted that.

But just like he'd done after the scorching kiss in her

hallway, his smile faded, and he cleared his throat, breaking whatever lustful thoughts he might've had. He made a move for the bar. "You want something?"

"No, thanks. I'm working."

"Anything left to be done?" He faced the room. Everyone had finished eating, so now they sat at tables or stood in groups drinking. Music played through speakers, but no one danced.

"I guess not."

"You did a good job tonight. Place looks great."

She'd projected images of waves crashing on the beach and then set fans at strategic angles to make the tent walls ripple. It made for a very cool effect. "Yeah, it does, doesn't it? Thanks for your help."

His heated gaze made her breath catch in her throat. See, he was doing it again. Was she crazy? Or was he looking at her like he wanted to flip up her skirt and bend her over the nearest table?

A bolt of electricity ripped through her at the thought. Facedown, her hair wrapped in his fist, those powerful hips slamming into her . . . *damn, girl*.

Well, you know what? He shouldn't look at her like that if he didn't mean it, because she was incredibly attracted to him. *Look at him*. That worn black T-shirt accentuated his broad shoulders and thick biceps. The leather wristbands and all that ink just screamed badass rocker.

And what kind of ink *was* that? She ran a finger over the colorful tattoo on his forearm. "One day you'll have to tell me about these. They're so unusual."

When she glanced up, she found his expression almost feral. She pulled away. God, the way he looked at her made her want to climb him like a tree. *Not even kidding*.

"It's just ink." A minute ago, he'd been playful. Now he was back to Mr. Stoic.

Nuh-uh. She wasn't going to let him shut down. Underneath that hard, impenetrable façade was a deeply sensitive guy. She knew that from the way he cared for his family. And while she doubted many got to see him like that, she had. There was no going back. "Bullshit."

And there it was, that tiny curl of his lip. He liked when she didn't put up with his crap. He turned toward her, giving his back to the party, making her feel like he was sharing a secret. "My brother liked to paint." His voice was low, his words meant only for her. Her heart beat thickly. "He was always making pictures for us. I turned my favorites into ink."

She fought the sting of tears. "Are you serious? God, Calix, that's so beautiful." Talk about sensitive. She reached for his arm. "Can I see them?"

He didn't respond, just held her gaze.

She smoothed her fingers up his forearm, over the colorful ink, but she couldn't make out the images. "It's too dark in here."

He held her gaze for a long moment and then turned away. Dammit, why did he always shut down? But when he got to the edge of the tent, he lifted it and waited for her to pass under.

She hurried over and bent low to slip outside. Fresh ocean air filled her senses, and cloud cover obscured the moon. She followed him to one of the tiki lamps she'd set out to illuminate the path.

Once under the flickering light, she lifted his arm to reveal the watery, colorful designs. "Oh, my God, these are so beautiful." Her fingers skimmed over the ink until the image took form. "It's a guitar."

"It's Hopper's rendition of my Fender."

She traced another image. "This is you?" It was the mess of thick, dark hair, the set of broad shoulders, and curve of a generous mouth that gave it away.

He nodded. And then he lifted his T-shirt to expose his hard, muscular abdomen. "This is my mom."

It took a moment to figure out the spill of hair. The woman had her face turned to the side, head tilting, so her hair flowed down Calix's stomach.

"When she sings, she loses herself. That's what she looks like."

"She tilts her head like that?"

"Exactly like that."

Her fingertips skimmed higher to the frenzy of color and movement. His skin pebbled under her touch.

"That's my dad's garden. Hopper liked to be out there with him. He'd talk my dad's ear off, about nothing really, but my dad liked to say it was a different kind of music."

"Oh, Calix." She let the fabric drop, smoothing it down. "This is the most beautiful thing I've ever seen." She wanted to press against him and hug the pain right out of his body.

"He had some emotional issues. Depression, anger. And my mom tried to help him with it through art. She turned the barn into a studio just for him. She'd sit in there for hours, let him throw paint, smash clay, whatever he wanted. And as he got older, she'd take him to museums and galleries. She tried to channel the feelings he couldn't understand into art."

"She's such a good mom."

"She is."

Her arms slid through his, and she leaned into him. When he remained stiff and unyielding—very unlike the man who'd ravished her outside her apartment the night before—it hit her that he didn't need her to comfort him over a boy she'd never known. That he'd had three years to live with the loss, and more than enough family and friends to share his grief.

He didn't want companionship or friendship outside his small world in Marsapeague. And he certainly didn't want a relationship with her. She pulled back.

But the moment she did, his arms shot up, banding around her. Candlelight flickered on the coarse sand, and she curled her toes in it, all too aware of how much she liked the way his big body felt and the lovely, clean scent of his clothes.

When she turned her head to press more fully against him, her ear to his chest, she heard the rapid beating of his heart. She chanced a look up at him, needing to see his expression. Hoping it reflected the same aching desire she felt for him.

Just the two of them under a tiki lamp, the night awash in sounds—the hum of conversation punctuated with shouts of laughter from inside the tent, the steady crash and drag of the ocean—Mimi felt herself melting against him. Into him.

For one hot, heavy moment, their gazes collided, and her

body tightened at the hunger and need in his eyes. But then his features shuttered, and he took a step back, letting her go.

She shook off the sticky web of desire clinging to her. He made her head spin, and not in a good way. She knew he was attracted to her, but if he wasn't going to act on it, then he needed to stay the hell away. "Hey, so, thanks for helping me today." She spoke too quickly, a current of bitterness in her tone. "Couldn't have done this without you." She stalked up the path, away from the tent.

"Where you going?" he called.

Where *was* she going? She didn't know. She just wanted to get away from him because, frankly, it sucked being attracted to someone who flashed hot and cold. They worked together. It couldn't get complicated.

Then again, maybe she had it all wrong. She'd fantasized about him for nearly a year. It could just all be in her head. And if that were the case, she could imagine how uncomfortable she made him when she looked at him like she wanted to throw him down and mount him. *Awkward.* "I have to get more ice."

Ice? Really, *ice?* She'd hired an event planner to set up the tent and work the bar. So, the ice situation was not on her. Still, she kept going. Where exactly? It wasn't like she was at her house. She was at Emmie and Slater's, so she couldn't lock herself in her bedroom and curl up on her bed and . . . fantasize about running her hands all over that hot, smooth skin.

Grr. That image of her bent over the table, Calix's hand in her hair, hips thrusting into her . . . Jeez, stop already. *Hasn't this gotten you into enough trouble with this guy?*

"You're getting ice?" He caught up with her.

"No, okay? I'm not getting ice. I'm going to . . . do some food prep for tomorrow morning." Yes, that was exactly what she'd do. What was she in the mood to make? Dough. Something she could knead, that yeasty smell in the air. Cinnamon rolls. She could picture the butter oozing out of them as they browned in the oven.

The path narrowed, and beach grass swished and

whispered around her. His heavy footsteps strode right past her. "Where are you going?"

"Home."

"You're leaving?" She watched him stride across the scrubby land like a Viking.

"That's right."

"The band's in crisis, and you're leaving."

"Not my band," he said over his shoulder, leaving her behind.

"Eight months, and it's not your band? What is the matter with you?"

"Not a damn thing. I showed up, did my face time."

She hurried to keep up with him. "That's all these guys are to you? A paycheck?"

"Yeah, Mimi, it's a *job*."

"And you need the money, right? That's why you're doing it. For the cash."

"You got a problem with a man making a living?"

"You know I don't. But you could make a living as a bartender. Or hey, you could own a surf shop. Sell surfboards and sex wax. I'd bet you'd be a pro at selling sex wax."

"How did we go from talking about earning a living to my sex life?"

"We didn't. But I guess that's the extent of what you've got to give. Your rented keyboard skills and your dick. What a wildly fulfilling life you lead."

"Whatever."

Why did he have to be such a jerk?

Worse, why did he have to be such a jerk *and* such a great guy?

Worst of all, why did she care?

CHAPTER EIGHT

As she climbed the steps to the back door, she had to force herself not to chase after him and slap the attitude right off his face. "Have fun skimming over your life." Asshole.

She threw the door open, aware of his boots clattering up the stairs behind her. Awareness burst on her skin.

"What the fuck's that supposed to mean?"

She'd never seen him so angry. "You live at home, you hang out with the same people you've known all your life, you go from one gig to another." She shrugged. "Skimming."

"Okay." His tone said she was crazy. He spun back around. Waving over his shoulder, he said, "See you tomorrow."

Oh, no, he didn't. "You didn't even go to the *listening* part of the listening party."

"I told you. It's not my business."

"That's a stupid thing to say. Of course it's your business. You've been working with these guys for eight months. You're an integral part of their sound. Didn't you even write some of their songs?"

"What's your point?" He stopped at the bottom of the stairs.

"Seems a shame."

He turned to her, looking exasperated. *"What's* a shame?" But the challenge in his eyes told her he wasn't exasperated at all. He was fired up.

"That you're doing something you love, but you don't own it. Sounds pretty lame to me."

"Lame? Are you . . ." He tipped his head back, jamming his hands through his long hair. "I lost my *brother.* I'm trying to rebuild our lives."

"You're not rebuilding anything. You're in a holding pattern." She threw open the door, wanting nothing more than to get busy making the dough for tomorrow's cinnamon buns.

He pounded up the stairs. "You don't know what you're talking about. You've never lost someone, so what gives you the right to get involved in shit that's none of your business?"

"This isn't about rights. It's about caring. It's what people do when they don't skim the surface of their lives. They get involved because they can't just stand there while the people they care about are hurting or screwing up. I don't know, maybe your world is so insular that you get away with skimming and no one calls you out on it. Maybe it takes someone from the outside to throw open the curtains and let some light in."

"Uh-huh. And you're just a beacon of light."

"You go ahead and make me out to be a pushy broad if that makes you feel better, but deep down you know I'm right."

"Right about *what*? You don't know anything about me or my family."

"You know that's not true. You just haven't let anyone else in before. And let's face it, your friends obviously let you get away with skimming." She jerked open a cabinet and pulled out the flour and sugar bins. "And don't lie to yourself about rebuilding your life because that's not what you're doing. You don't want to go back to the world that once made you happy because deep down you think it cost you your brother."

His big hand smacked the counter, rattling the pans in the drying rack. "Are you out of your fucking mind with the shit you say?"

She washed her hands at the sink, looking at his reflection in the window. His nostrils flared, his lips pulled back. She'd never seen him so angry. She should shut her mouth—it truly was none of her business.

But at the same time, he could've continued straight to his motorcycle and gone home. Instead he was here. Of his own volition. She'd hit on something.

Something he needed to hear. And she couldn't help it, but she did care.

Reaching for a towel, she turned to face him. "You loved him with all your heart, and you lost him in the most nonsensical way possible. Come on, Calix. On some level you have to think it's your fault."

"I lost my brother, the heart and soul of my family. We're recovering. That's it. Nothing more, Mrs. Freud."

"And you don't blame yourself? Not one little bit?"

He nodded, jaw muscle popping. "No, I don't. It was no one's fault."

"I don't believe you. I see the look in your eyes right now." He was utterly tormented. "I think you do blame yourself. And instead of dealing with it, feeling anything, you throw yourself into taking care of your family." She watched him carefully. "Have you guys ever talked about it? Have you talked to your friends? Anyone?"

"There's *nothing to say*. We lost him, and now we're trying to keep my mom . . ." He looked away, swallowed. "Trying to get her back."

"You keep talking about your mom. But what about you? Are you grieving? God, Calix, is anyone looking out for you?"

His body practically vibrated with anger. "Am I *grieving*? Are you fucking kidding me? I miss my brother every day. But I can't bring him back. The only thing I can do is keep my family together."

"Okay." She knew it was time to back off. "But you matter, too. And if you can't talk to your family about it, you should at least talk to a friend." She tossed the towel on the counter and came right up to him. "Maybe you should stop pushing it all away and just remember him. Go to the cemetery and sit with him. Remember everything. Let it crash over you, because I just don't think you're ever going to get on with your life until you make peace with that day."

Mouth set tight to the point of quivering, he stood rigidly before her.

She'd upset him enough, so she turned to the counter and reached for her measuring cups.

Bracing himself against the counter with an arm, he looked down at the hardwood floor. "He was *right there*." His words hung heavy and raw in the kitchen. "I don't blame myself. It wasn't my fault, but Jesus Christ, he was right there. If I'd just paid attention . . . fuck."

Oh, God. He totally blamed himself. "I know. If you could just go back for one second, to that one moment when he walked away . . ."

He held her gaze with stark desolation.

His pain sliced her to the bone. "I know."

"You don't know." He lowered his head. "You don't fucking know."

"Calix, everyone has those kinds of regrets. But you can't live your life thinking about the if onlys. You can't go back and fix it. You just can't."

"Fuck."

"And what was there to fix? You have to know it wouldn't have been possible to keep your eyes on Hopper every minute of every day." She stepped closer to him. "It was a crazy night. Your parents were onstage for the first time in years. The record company wanted to sign you." She gave him an imploring look, hoping he could see that, of course, he'd taken his eyes off Hopper.

But he shook his head harshly. "I ate it up. Voltage Records—they were kissing my ass, and I loved it."

Not only did he blame himself, but somehow his ambition had become the reason for his loss.

"They were working me over, making me out to be the shit. And I just fell for it, man. Just totally ate it up."

"Hopper didn't wander off because you let some A&R guy's spiel go to your head. It was a crowded venue. People coming and going. Kids get lost in department stores and malls, at beaches and festivals. Kids wander off. It happens all the time. Hopper wandered off." She stepped closer to him, making him understand through her eyes, her voice, and her heart. "It's not your fault."

He held her gaze, as if weighing her words. "You can say those words as many times as you want, but the fact is that I stopped paying attention to him. I got caught up in the bullshit from Voltage." Despair twisted his features. "It eats me up. It fucking kills me. If I'd just turned around, done something to include him, Hopper would never have left."

"No good will come out of reliving that moment. It's eating you alive. Nothing will change, because it's *out of your control*. It happened, and reliving it, wishing you'd made a different choice in that moment, won't change it. You have to let it go." She gripped his forearms. "Calix, look at me. You can't go back and change that moment. It's over, it's done. Now you have to move forward. There's no other choice."

He straightened, looking at her like she held the answer he'd been desperate for.

She cupped his cheeks. "You're stuck in that moment." God, she needed to get through. "And to get unstuck, you have to forgive yourself. You were a grown man, building a career for yourself. That's normal. You were doing exactly what you should've been doing."

"I can't . . . I . . ." A shock of alertness had him straightening. "I can't get past it. I can't."

"You can. Every time you go to that moment—the one you can't change—replace it with a good memory. Bask in the good. I saw those photos—you have a lot of good memories with your brother."

"I do." His voice sounded shredded.

"So, then let it go."

"I'll never let him go."

"Let *it* go. That moment in time you can't take back. Let it go. There is no do-over. You can't fix it. But you're alive, and you're an amazing musician and the most loyal and devoted son and brother I've ever seen. So let it go. And *live*, dammit."

She didn't know what happened, but suddenly his hands were on her hips, and she was in the air. Her ass landed on the counter, his body shoved between her legs, and he was right in her face. Those eyes—God, those dark, soulful eyes—so filled with emotion. Pain, yearning, confusion. A hand clamped on each of her thighs, and his fingers pressed hard into her flesh.

Her heart pounded. The blood rushed so loudly in her ears, it sounded like a waterfall. His fingers tightened on her thighs. He breathed roughly through his nostrils.

She could see his fight, feel the strain in his muscles, so she softened, letting her hands reach for his face, her fingers stroke the silky scruff of his beard.

And then he leaned in, his breath a sigh against her lips. He kissed her. Tentatively, at first. A sample, a taste. His lips brushed over hers, as if savoring a precious gift.

But she didn't go half-assed at anything, so she parted her lips, let her tongue touch his, and he moaned deep in his throat. And then he was kissing her.

As if the floodgates had burst open, his need crashed over her.

No one had ever kissed her with such wild passion in her life.

His hands slid up her legs, rested right at the juncture, and God, the span of those fingers. His thumb brushed restless strokes on her inner thigh. He pressed forward, his hips flat against the counter, as he devoured her with his mouth and tongue.

He cupped her face, tasting her more deeply. Those big hands on her cheeks, holding her so firmly, gently, like she was precious, only made her heart ache from the tenderness of his touch.

His kisses turned hungrier, dirtier, and she clutched at his shoulders, hands sliding down his back to hold him to her more tightly. And then he caressed her neck down to her collarbone, the heel of his palm pressing into her breasts.

God, she craved him. Wanted to rip off her clothes and climb him, rub her bare skin all over his. Every cell in her body opened to him, letting all his heat, his intensity, sink deep into her. Her legs wrapped around his waist, her heels digging into the hard globes of his ass.

He cupped her breast, kneading it gently, reverently, his

body feverishly hot and his kiss turning ravenous. *Oh, God, oh, God, oh, God.* She pushed harder against him, arching into his touch.

When his thumb flicked over her nipple, electric heat shot straight to her core and she gasped, pulling her mouth off his. "God. We have to . . ." She could barely catch her breath. "What are we *doing*?"

His forehead pressed to hers, his breathing erratic and labored. Slowly, his body twisted away, foreheads still touching, until he pushed back from the counter.

"I think it's pretty obvious." As hard as he tried to hide behind his Mr. Stoic mask, the fine tremble beneath his skin told her he'd been deeply affected.

"God." She pushed him aside and jumped off the counter. "I wasn't going to sleep with you." She went back to the sink to wash her hands again.

"Kind of the natural progression of things, babe."

She slammed the faucet. "Excuse me?"

"You wrap your legs around a man's waist . . . what message did you think you were giving?"

"It was a *kiss*. I wasn't going to have sex with you."

"You make way too big a deal out of sex, sweet pants." He started for the door.

Way too big a— "*I'm* a big deal." Her tone must've startled him, because he stopped abruptly. "And I'm not having sex with someone I haven't even gone on a date with."

She might as well have tossed fresh offal at him for the way his body recoiled. "I don't *date*."

"Yes, I know that. Because you skim. So you just keep right on skimming. But you won't be getting any of *this*." She ran a hand up and down her body like a game show host revealing the contestant's prize.

"Okay, Mimi." His tone let her know that, once again, he thought she was being ridiculous.

"Haven't you ever taken a girl out on a date?"

"No."

"In twenty-six years, not a single date?"

"Nobody dates."

"So your only interaction with women has been hookups."

"Shay and I were together awhile in high school. But we didn't date."

"You took her out, though, right? Before screwing her, you bought her a clam roll? Took her to a movie?"

"Not gonna talk about my relationship with Shay, but I'll repeat. Never taken anyone out on a date."

Drying her hands on a towel, she turned to face him. "You've obviously never wanted anyone enough."

"I've wanted plenty of women enough."

"To bang them, sure. But not enough that you *have* to be with them. And that's what I want. A man who *has* to be with me. Anything less is just a waste of my time."

He sauntered back toward her, looking super pleased with himself. "Sounds like you're holding out for a lot of things."

"What does that mean?"

"You graduated, when? A year ago? And you're still waiting for your dad to hire you. You don't have sex because you're waiting for some guy to fall madly in love with you. Maybe all this talk about skimming has more to do with you than me. Maybe you wish you could go deep, but you can't because you're too scared to go after what you really want."

"What I *really* want is to work for my dad. And if you're trying to talk me into hooking up, you can forget it." She was done talking to him. "In any event, I'm sure you've got a list of go-to girls on your phone right now, so start dialing-for-a-bang. Or go to the beach. Yeah, that's it. Hook up with one of the girls you've grown up with." She looked him in the eye. "We're done here."

Mimi pulled the tray of cinnamon buns from the oven, closing her eyes to breathe in the delicious smell. Since Dak had been fired last night, the guys could sleep in. She'd just leave coffee brewing and the buns out for whenever they got up.

After the way Calix had treated her in the kitchen—like some nymph he could bang at a party—she'd considered bailing on today's cooking lesson. But she needed his help to win this competition, and she wasn't about to let their issues get in her way.

Just . . . no more kissing. It wasn't like it was all *his* fault. She'd gotten just as caught up in their kisses as he had. It just meant something different to her.

Before she headed over for her lesson, though, she'd watch a few episodes of *Chopped*. Maybe talk to her mom about ideas for Violet's wedding. Hard to do that when Australia was fourteen hours ahead of the East Coast, but she'd catch her before she went to bed.

The grumble of an engine cut through the early morning stillness. With the guys sleeping in and no deliveries expected, she had no idea who'd stop by. She peered out the window to see Calix jumping out of a truck and leaping up the stairs.

He punched the screen door open, took a quick sweep of the room. "Gus here?"

"Haven't seen him."

"Fuck." He spun around, trampled down the stairs, and struck off toward the beach. His powerful thighs pumped hard in his worn jeans.

Worried, she ran out the door and took off after him. Racing down the dirt path, she caught up with him just as he headed toward the tent.

"What's going on?"

He pulled up the edge and ducked under it. She followed him in, the heat and fishy scent oppressive. After a quick scan of the place, he turned back around, brushing right past her. "Gus didn't come home last night."

Oh, for crying out loud. "He's twenty-three."

Ignoring her, he strode to the shoreline, long hair flaring out on a breeze. His jeans hugged the hard curves of his ass as he worked his way across the sand.

Again, she traipsed after him. "It can't be all that surprising that a twenty-three-year-old guy wouldn't come home."

Standing on the hard-packed sand, he gazed first in one direction, then the other. Seriously, strip off his dark gray T-shirt, throw a loincloth around his hips, and he could be a warrior leading the charge of a marauding army.

"Fourteen hours." He leveled her with a hard look. "That's how long we had to wait to find out about Hopper. Fourteen hours not having a clue where he was, who he was with, or whether he was breathing. You got any idea the kinds of scenarios we cooked up in all that time? So, yeah, Gus can do whatever *the fuck* he wants. But he's gotta let his mom know so she doesn't go through the same shit she went through three years ago."

Oh, God. "Jo was up all night?" She guessed they'd all been up—looking for Gus, sure, but mostly for Jo. Okay, she'd get right on it. Turning, she headed back to the house. "I'm sure you've checked all the usual places and friends, so I'll wake up the guys and ask them."

"Good idea."

Together, they headed back up the path. When they hit the grass, Mimi said, "When was the last time you saw him?"

"At a table with some of the Amoeba guys. That was about ten, before I left."

"Did you try to get a hold of them? Maybe Emmie can make some calls."

"Already talked to her. She said the Amoeba guys left together. Their drivers came around midnight."

"You know, he could've crashed at a friend's house. It could be that simple."

"I called his friends. He wasn't with them last night."

"Okay, but that doesn't mean he didn't crash at *someone's* house. A friend of a friend. I'm just saying he's probably all right and doing what any other person our age would do."

"Mimi. You don't know. You just . . . don't understand."

"I'm an only child, so if you mean I don't understand losing a sibling, then you're right. I don't. But that doesn't mean I can't understand your worries."

"Worries? You think I'm *worried*? I worry about my mom not getting enough sleep. I worry about her not eating enough. This situation? What we're dealing with right now?" He gripped the back of his neck, rubbed it harshly.

She touched his arm, pulled him back. "What is it? Tell me."

The tortured look in his eyes gutted her.

"What? Just say it. There's obviously more going on here than I understand."

"She tried to kill herself, okay? My mom . . . this isn't just about Gus. It's about . . ."

Shock ripped through her. "Are you . . . *last night*?"

"No, about four months after Hopper died."

Oh, God, this poor family. What they'd gone through. She thought of that house, the photographs, the memories that moved like shadows in every room. And in the short time she'd been around Jo, she'd seen it. A woman who had to fight to stay present, to stay engaged.

Mimi had felt the woman slipping away, retreating into herself, while her family kept trying to draw her out.

And yet . . . she hadn't gotten the sense that Jo was suicidal. More that she couldn't bear the pressure of everyone's expectations for her.

But her perceptions didn't matter. Only Calix's did. And he lived every moment worrying he'd get the call that his mom had . . . *Oh, God*.

"I found her. I was heading out of town with my band, and I just . . . I wanted to see her before I left. My mom told us she needed time alone to grieve, so we'd all gone back to our lives, but I worried about her. I couldn't help . . ." But he shook his head, as though cutting off that train of thought. "I came into the house . . . it was so quiet. And I found her in bed. She'd taken a bottle of pills. I can't . . ." He swallowed, took a breath. "I can't let it happen again."

"No, of course not. But we'll find him. You know we will."

"I've looked everywhere. I've been up and down the beach a dozen times. Every place he might've gone. I've talked to everyone he knows."

And then she remembered the persistent nymph. "Do you know where Laney lives?"

"Why the hell would I know that?"

"Well, if you've had sex with her, you might know."

"*What?* Are you fucking kidding me? Jesus Christ, I am not talking about this right now." He stalked off toward the truck.

"She's slept with everyone else." She picked up her pace across the grass.

"He wouldn't . . ."

But, of course, Gus would. "Let me get my phone. I'll find out where she lives."

"We sent her home last night."

"Yeah, she totally seemed the type to respect our boundaries. Look, you said you talked to everyone he knows, and you've been every place he would go. I don't think we should rule out Laney."

As soon as they got to the house, she ran inside to grab her phone. She could feel his anxiety as he waited for her call to connect.

Coop's call went straight to voice mail. She got luckier with Ben.

"'Lo." He sounded exhausted.

"Hey, Ben. Mimi. When was the last time you saw Gus?"

"Gus?"

"Yeah, Calix's brother. The gofer."

"What?"

"Ben. Wake up. This is important."

"Right. Yeah. Um, Gus. I don't know. Wasn't paying attention."

"Do you have Laney's phone number?"

"Blocked her."

"Ben, listen to me. I need to find her. Do you know where she lives?"

He was quiet for a moment, but then gave a reluctant, "Yeah."

She gave Calix a thumbs-up. "Text me the address, okay?"

"Don't know the address." He cleared his throat. "You know that general store on Manhasset Road in Orient?"

"No. Hang on." She lowered the phone. "You know the general store on Manhasset Road in Orient?"

Calix nodded.

"Yeah, we do."

"Okay, well, her mom runs it. They live in the rooms at the back. If you go along the left side of the building, through the bushes, that's her bedroom. Last window. She leaves it unlocked."

"Great, thanks. By the way, I made cinnamon rolls for you guys. Coffee's brewing. So, whenever you want it, it's here."

"Fuck, Meems. How'm I gonna get back to sleep now?"

"Gotta run." In her leggings and ballet flats, she had nowhere to stow her phone, but before she could give it another thought, Calix took it from her and slid it in his back pocket. "Let's go."

Situated at the very tip of the North Fork, Orient Point wasn't far from Eden's Landing. Mimi watched out the window as Calix drove in silence.

She loved the early morning light out here. It softened the scrubby fields, turned ponds into watercolors, and colored the sand peach.

He cleared his throat. "I'm sorry for last night."

She shot him a look.

"Shouldn't have kissed you."

"I guess this means I should cancel the order for our promise rings?"

She thought she saw a hint of a smile curl his mouth, but it died quickly. He tapped his fingers on the steering wheel.

She turned her attention back out the window. On this lazy Sunday morning in early May, an elderly man ambled down the driveway toward his newspaper, and a trio of cyclists sped by, their forearms resting on the handlebars.

He let out a breath. "I know you're a big deal. Don't want you to think otherwise."

"Can I ask you something?"

He shrugged.

"Would you have followed through? If I'd let you, would you have had sex with me right there on the kitchen counter?"

Tugging on his chin scruff, he said, "Probably not."

"Then why did you treat me like that? Like there was something wrong with me for not being into hookups?"

He stuttered out a laugh. "I don't know. Because I can't keep my hands off you."

Something hot flashed through her, and the part of her that entertained naughty thoughts about him said, *Then don't*. But nothing could come of it, so she let it go. "Okay, well, no harm."

"I respect the hell out of you." He let out a breath. "I'm sorry I made you feel I didn't."

This sweet side of him made her keenly aware of his potential. One day he'd make an awesome boyfriend. "Actually, last night was a good wake-up call for me." She looked down at her hands. The way to really be over him was to say it out loud. "To be honest, I've fantasized about you for a while now. You're really hot and . . . I don't know, you seem like the kind of guy to just take what he wants from a girl in bed."

He shot her a heated, almost feral look. *He likes that.*

But she was over him, so she wasn't about to fan that flame. "And onstage? It's incredibly sexy to watch you get lost in the music. Plus, watching the guys interact with you, that's hot, too."

"How do they interact with me?"

"They respect you. They respect your talent. And that's hot."

"So, just to be clear, what you're saying is, I'm hot?"

She laughed. "I guess if you boil it all down, then, yes, I think you're pretty damn hot. And that's led to some wicked fantasies. But now that I've gotten to know you, I won't be doing that anymore."

"Uh, thanks?"

She could see how that might've sounded offensive. "No, I just mean we're really different. We want different things. You know, reality kills fantasies."

"No, I don't know. But you might want to stop right there."

"Oh, come on, you know exactly what I mean. You see some super-hot girl in a club, and you imagine all the things you want to do to her—or in my case the things I wanted you to do to me—"

"What did you want me to do to you?"

With a smile, she gently swatted his arm. "No, seriously, but then you get to know her and she's dumb or she's, I don't know, materialistic or whatever, and you stop seeing her as the hot girl. Once she opens her mouth, you can't fantasize about her anymore."

"What did you want me to do to you?"

She shook her head. "Stop. We're not going there. I'm saying that I see you as a man now, not some fantasy. Last night our differences became really clear. Like the fact that you don't date. That separates us right there."

"I've got some fantasies of my own."

"You do? About me?"

"No, about a super-hot woman I saw in a club. Yes, of course, you."

"You do not fantasize about me."

He remained quiet, eyes on the road. Fingers tapping the steering wheel.

"What kind of fantasies?"

"I thought we weren't going there?"

She burst out laughing. "Okay, we'll swap. One fantasy. Go."

"Your mouth."

"You like my mouth."

"I really like your mouth."

Automatically, her fingers went to her lips. "I had no idea. But I'm so not your type."

"I don't have a type."

"But I wear business suits to clubs."

"Tight skirts, Mimi. Wrapped around that ass?" He gave a curt nod. "Shit-hot fantasy."

A tingle skittered down her spine. "*Really?* I had no idea. You're always so indifferent around me." Well, not recently. But he had been for the several months before she'd hopped on his bike.

"Your turn."

"Oh." In that moment she realized she couldn't tell him. "This isn't a good idea."

"It was *your* idea."

"Therefore, I have the power to kill it." She shrugged. "I'm killing it."

"You are not killing it. I told you mine, it's only fair you tell me yours."

She gave him a sweet smile. "Didn't your momma teach you life's not fair?"

CHAPTER NINE

"Waiting . . ." He shifted in his seat.

Should she tell him? This was too embarrassing. All he'd mentioned was her mouth and her tight skirts, neither of which was in the same league as *her* fantasies. On the other hand . . . "What the hell, right? We already figured out nothing's going to happen between us."

He pointed toward the sign for Orient Point. "Running out of time here." He turned right down Manhasset Road. The houses on either side of the street looked old and worn-out. Some had untended yards, while others had tidy gardens. The farther they drove, the denser the houses became, until they reached what clearly made up the heart of the town: a cluster of historical buildings with sagging porches and pretty window boxes.

"Okay, fine." But as the image formed in her mind, she knew she couldn't say it out loud. Tell him she imagined him taking her from behind? *Forget it.* "I can't."

"It's that filthy?"

"In general, no. But saying it out loud to you? Yes, it's that filthy."

"Mimi . . ."

"No, I'm sorry. I never should've brought it up. I didn't mean to tease you, but it's way too inappropriate for people who have to work together."

Calix pulled in front of the general store, closed at this early hour. When she opened her door, the air smelled musty.

"Go around back?" she asked as he met her on the sidewalk.

He gave a tight nod. "We're not done with this conversation." And then he led the way along a gravel driveway to the back of the building. A collapsing garage filled with broken bikes and old surfboards sat at the back of the property. In the middle of the small patch of lawn was an umbrella-style laundry dryer that looked like a metal tree.

"Oh, we're done all right."

But he was already at the back door. He knocked, the sound so loud in the early morning stillness that birds flew out of the nearby bushes. Paint peeled from the cedar siding, and the back lawn was a mess of strewn plastic toys that hadn't seen use in decades.

No one answered, so Calix knocked harder.

She pointed to the white lace curtain flapping out of an open window in the corner room. "That's Laney's."

"How do you know?"

"Ben said to walk down the side of the house to the last window. That's the corner room."

"I'm not peeping in her window."

"You want to call home, see if Gus showed up?"

"Yeah." He pulled out his phone and swiped the screen.

What had she been thinking, bringing up her fantasy of him? Like she'd ever tell him what he looked like when he got lost in the music. Or that she wanted to see that same expression when he was with her. More specifically when she watched him over her shoulder. On her knees, his hand fisted in her hair, as he slammed into her from behind.

Sensation flashed across her skin. *Oh, yes.*

Not only was he gorgeous, but he was a really good man. His intense loyalty to his family? His profound love for them? God, whoever won this man's love was going to be one lucky girl. She had a feeling when he did fall for someone, he'd fall hard.

Too bad it wouldn't be her. By the time his family healed, she'd be back in the city working for her dad.

"Okay." Shoving his phone in his pocket, he knocked hard. "Not home, no word from him."

Cupping a hand, he peered through the gauzy curtain covering the pane of glass. "Fuck it." He jumped off the porch, boots squishing in the muddy earth, and strode along the side of the house. "He better not be boning her."

"What if I've got it all wrong, and she's with some other guy? Can you imagine?"

"Thanks for that image, sweet pants. Unfortunately, I gotta check."

She hated what his family had gone through last night, waiting to find out if Gus was lying in a ditch somewhere. God, how awful.

Everything made so much more sense now. *Of course* he didn't commit to a band. Of course he wasn't in a relationship. Every time he left the house, he probably pictured his mom with a bottle of prescription pills. Every time his phone vibrated, he likely dreaded opening the text. He lived on the edge of his seat, waiting for the inevitable news to come.

Her heart ached for him.

At the window, he pushed aside the curtain and peered in. "Gus?" He rapped on the frame. "Gus?" The word came out like a shot.

Voices murmured, and something crashed.

"What the hell?" Gus leaned out the window. "Jesus, Calix. What're you doing here?"

"Need to turn your phone on. Mom's worried."

"Oh." Hair a tangled mess, eyes bloodshot, Gus looked completely hungover. "Sorry, man. I . . ." He scrubbed his face with both hands. "Fuck. I don't know what happened."

"Text Mom. Let her know you're all right."

"How'd you find me?"

"You're not exactly this chick's first Blue Fire conquest."

A wash of color spread across his cheeks. And then he noticed Mimi. "Did you have to bring Mimi?"

"She's the one who found you." Calix checked his brother out. "You stayin', or you want to come back with us?"

"I don't have a ride, so I'll come with you. Hang on a sec." He pulled back inside.

"We'll be in the truck." Calix hadn't even finished his sentence before a black boot flew out the window, followed by its mate.

Then came a jeans-clad leg. Gus landed on the patch of grass, shirt in hand. "Let's go."

Calix started walking, casting his brother a disgusted look. "Put some clothes on."

"Just go."

"You're not even gonna say good-bye?"

Gus snatched up his boots. "I just want to get out of here."

Big, puffy clouds rolled across the sky, taking turns blocking the sun and making the world a patchwork of grays and bright yellows. By the time they hit the truck, Gus had his jeans buttoned and T-shirt on.

Calix fired up the engine and executed a quick turn, heading back toward the main road.

From the backseat, she heard a harsh exhalation. And then, "Sorry, man."

Calix eyed him in the rearview mirror but didn't say anything.

"Mom upset?" Gus's voice sounded rough, unused.

"Yeah, man. She's upset."

"Shit. I don't even have my phone."

"You leave it at her place?"

"I don't know. I don't think so."

"How'd you hook up with her? We sent her packing last night."

"I don't even know who she is. After the party ended, a bunch of us made a bonfire. She was there." He let out a defeated breath. "Guess I got pretty wasted."

"Yeah." Calix tapped his fingers on the wheel. "Look, we got a good thing going with Mom and these cooking lessons. This kind of shit works against us."

Mimi turned around to find Gus's eyes closed, looking pretty miserable.

"Won't happen again."

But if it did, Mimi suspected Calix would take it all on his own shoulders.

He'd never be free until he stopped blaming himself for what happened to his family.

Mimi pulled the tray of scones out of the oven, breathing in the warm, lemony scent. This early time in the kitchen making breakfast, before everyone woke up, was her favorite part of the day.

With the album on hold until they found a new producer, she hadn't seen Calix or Gus since yesterday's rescue operation. What a night that must've been for Jo. She hoped the woman was all right.

The front door slammed. "Meems?" Derek's boots thudded on the hardwood floor.

"Kitchen." She smiled, girding herself, because the rest of the crew wouldn't be far behind.

"Someone's got wedding fever." Derek pointed to the kitchen table strewn with bridal magazines and cookbooks.

"Just getting ideas."

"Smells good." He snatched a scone off the cookie sheet but immediately dropped it. "Fuck, that's hot."

She waved her pot-holder-covered hands at him. "Fresh from the oven."

Derek flipped open a magazine. "You remember she wants simple, right?"

"I've rented out the Eden's Landing country club and sent out invitations to five hundred of your closest friends. I've put a deposit on a man in Arizona famous for making birds out of sugar syrup. Slater's got a call into Katie Perry's people to see if she'll perform. That simple enough?"

When Derek Valencia laughed, the earth moved under her feet. With his tats, shoulder-length hair, and facial scruff, everything about him screamed raw sensuality. He was hot and deep and one hundred percent devoted to his fiancée.

"Since Eden's Landing doesn't have a country club, I'm going to trust you're joking. And since you know my bride better than anyone else, I'm sure you'll give her what she wants." He reached for a scone, tossed it to his other hand. "I, uh, I had an idea, though."

There was nothing hesitant about Derek, so to see him uncomfortable made her feel tender toward him. She motioned for him to sit down. "Tell me."

Instead, he leaned his hip against the table. "I want to build her a gazebo. A big one. Right in the middle of her wildflowers, overlooking the ocean."

A rush of warmth spread through her. "That sounds amazing. Is that where you'll exchange vows?"

He nodded, looking uncertain. "You think she'd like that?"

"I think she could say them in her laundry room and be blissfully happy."

"Yeah. Probably." He gave an almost shy smile. "But what do you think of the gazebo?"

"I think the gazebo's a beautiful idea. Can't you just see her on a glider with her baby in her arms, nursing while looking out at the sea?"

Derek looked utterly stricken. She wondered if she'd said something wrong—maybe he didn't want kids. But then he swallowed, blinked, and said, "Gazebo's a done fuckin' deal."

"Good." She smiled, her heart full, knowing her friend had found such complete happiness. A foster care kid, Violet had never experienced family or real love until she'd crashed into the unrelenting will of Derek Valencia.

The front door slammed again, so hard the windows rattled. Laughter and male voices filled the air.

"What smells so good?" Ben led the troops into the kitchen.

"Scones," Mimi said.

"What kind?" Cooper asked.

"Blueberry lemon. With a crumble top."

Grabby hands made off with more than half of them. "You guys. They're hot."

"No shit." Cooper practically juggled his.

"Someone wanna get the door?" A gruff, deep voice had

everyone spinning around to see the big, hulking figure of
Terrence Bourbon on the back porch, biceps bulging from the
weight of a crate.

"Got it." Ben popped half a scone into his mouth, while
racing to let him in. "Fuck, that's hot."

"Hey, Terrence." Slater slid a thumb drive into the port of
his laptop. Immediately, music began playing.

Terrence set the crate down right next to her. "Brought you
some vegetables from my greenhouse."

"You didn't need to come all the way out here. I'll be at
your place this afternoon."

He started pulling out produce. "You don't have a car, so
I thought I'd deliver the goods myself. Look what I brought.
Know what it is?"

"*Ferns?* You brought me a decorative plant? That's so
sweet, because I know there's no chance you'd ever expect me
to eat something that hangs in a macramé planter."

He burst out laughing.

"Terrence, they look like bugs. Green worms curled up
into little balls. I can't do it."

"You know, just 'cause you said that, I'm gonna make sure
Calix uses fiddleheads in one of your challenges."

"For the love of God, do you hate me?" she said with a
warm smile.

"Jesus, this sucks," Ben shouted over the music.

"We don't have shit to work with," Cooper said. "There's
not one track that's any good."

Terrence glanced over his shoulder. "Get rid of the
auto-tune."

A chair scraped back, and Slater met him at the counter.
"We kept telling him that, but he wanted us to wait till he
finished so we could hear the vibe he was going for."

"He acted like he had this big plan," Ben said. "But Irwin
could tell right away. This album sucks."

"It isn't our sound," Derek said.

"It's Dak's signature sound," Terrence said. "And it
worked with Ten09 and Pitstop, but it's not right for you."

"No, it's not."

"You got someone to replace him?" Terrence asked.

"Emmie's in the city right now talking to the label about finding us a new producer," Slater said.

"But who wants to jump into another guy's project?" Ben said. "We're four months in."

"You should have Terrence do it." The moment the words left Mimi's mouth, she wished she could suck them back in. Especially when the guys jumped out of their seats with excitement.

"Would you?" Cooper asked.

"That would be awesome," Ben said.

She could see Derek and Slater reining in their enthusiasm, giving Terrence the chance to respond.

Even if Terrence wanted to work with these guys, he'd worry about his wife. On the other hand, maybe it would give her peace of mind knowing all her guys worked together in the studio, looking out for each other.

"Let's not put him on the spot," Derek said. "Terrence, I'll tell you straight up, we'd like to work with you. I think you get us. I like your style. But no pressure, man. None at all."

"Let me sit on it for a while. Maybe Irwin's got someone else in mind."

Slater shook his head. "Maybe. But we're taking back control. We're gonna have a say in the next producer, and we'd like to work with you."

"I'll think on it and get back to you." Terrence turned back around and finished unloading his crate.

She watched him, wondering if he was pissed at her for making the suggestion without checking with him first. "I'm sorry," she said quietly. "I shouldn't have said that."

"You got a big heart, Mimi. Nothing wrong with that."

She was one hundred percent positive Calix would disagree.

"**Today's** lesson: Fun with Ferns." Calix held up a fiddlehead.

"I'm not eating it."

Her dead-serious tone made him smile. "It's a plant, sweet pants. Just like a Brussels sprout or asparagus."

"It has *hair*. I don't eat anything with hair." She looked into the colander like it was teeming with beetles.

"It screams, too."

"What?"

"Fiddleheads are bitter, so you gotta blanch 'em. And the minute they hit the boiling water . . ." He paused, just to draw it out. "They scream."

The way she held his gaze, it was like she was trying to figure out whether or not he was joking. "I hope you're enjoying yourself." She stood so close to him that her hair brushed over his arm. Soft, silky, and scented with something extremely feminine. The rise and fall of her breasts in her tight T-shirt sent him back to the other night in the kitchen when he'd had her up on the counter, the weight of her breast in his hand.

The beaded nipple against his palm, her shaky inhalation—fuck, electricity had arced through him at the touch.

"I am." Her heels digging into his back, her fingers pulling his hair? So fucking hot.

Shit. What was the lesson again? "We're talking about techniques, and since my dad brought us the fiddleheads, we're going to blanch them. It kills the enzymes that make them taste bitter. It also seals in the vitamins if you do it right."

"And what's right?"

"With fiddleheads, about four minutes." He gave her the colander and watched as she dumped them into the pot of boiling water.

"Back at it, huh?" His mom came into the kitchen, heading straight for the refrigerator. "Ah, your dad's precious fiddleheads."

"Hey, Jo." Mimi smiled. "Terrence said they're only around for a couple of weeks."

His mom grabbed a yogurt. "When's the next show?"

"Thursday."

"You think they're gonna give you fiddleheads?"

"Not about the fiddleheads, Ma. It's about blanching and what to do with—"

"Decorative plants."

His mom gave Mimi an odd, yet interested, look. "Not a vegetable fan, huh?"

"Oh, God, no."

And then his mom turned her focus on him. "She know the basics?"

Mimi cut in. "You know, to be honest, I really don't. I stick to recipes, and since I won't get to use any during the competition, Calix is teaching me to rely more on my senses and instincts. In my first lesson, he showed me some pretty cool things to add to a basic roux and broth. Last time we worked on cutting, dicing, zesting . . . stuff like that, and today he's teaching me different cooking techniques."

"Sounds good. Just think, given the tight time frame, you ought to learn the basics. Flour, eggs, sugar. So no matter what you're given, you'll have a sense of how things work."

"That's exactly what he said we should do." Mimi gave him an appreciative look, and it shouldn't have made him so damn happy.

So he focused on getting his mom involved. "What do you think we should work on?"

His mom went to the pantry and pulled out tubs of flour and sugar. Then, she grabbed butter and eggs from the fridge. She dropped them all on the island. "Five basics in the kitchen. Flour, sugar, eggs, butter, and leavening. Teach her what they do, so she can always put something together."

"Hang on." With a quick glance to the fiddleheads, Calix shut off the flame. "Let's get them in the ice water."

His mom held up an egg. "See this? This single ingredient will bind, leaven, emulsify, thicken, clarify, and coat. It'll help you set the structure in your baked goods. It'll moisten and add richness. Whip it, and it'll become a leavening agent. Egg whites trap air in the bubbles." She nodded toward her son. "He'll tell you all about it."

After pouring the hot water into the colander, Calix dumped the fiddleheads into the ice bath. By the time he looked up, his mom had gone. "Damn."

"That's okay," Mimi said. "She's definitely interested, so that's good."

"Yeah."

"Small steps."

Calix pulled out a skillet, turned on the burner. "Let's get some butter in there."

Mimi hesitated. "I need to tell you something."

He stilled, waited. She looked anxious, and that got his attention.

"The guys were listening to the tracks to see if they could salvage anything from the last four months."

"Okay." He definitely didn't like her guilty expression, but where could she go with this?

"Your dad told them to cut back on auto-tune. He said Dak was trying to give Blue Fire *his* signature sound. And the guys agreed."

Folding his arms across his chest, he faced her. "Yeah. So?"

"So, I suggested your dad be the producer."

He closed his eyes. His dad would love to get in the studio, work with a band. Especially Blue Fire, a band that was all about the music. "Mimi . . ." He blew out a breath. "Why would you do that?"

"I don't know. It just seemed obvious." And then her tone softened. "Your dad said I had a big heart."

"What you've got is a big mouth." But he didn't pack any heat behind his comment because he knew her intentions were good. And the suggestion made sense.

His gaze dropped to the mouth in question. That sexy, expressive mouth with those raspberry lips that he'd already tasted. Desire stirred in him, and he forced himself to look away.

With butter melting and popping in the pan, Mimi dumped the fiddleheads in. "I'm not eating this. No matter how angry you are at me. No matter how nice Terrence is to me, I'm not eating a spore."

He laughed. "You're crazy."

She kept her focus on the fiddleheads. "I'm sorry for opening my mouth again."

"Why don't you shut it right now?"

Her head snapped up. "That's not a very nice thing to say."

"Remember my fantasy?"

"My mouth?" she whispered.

"Yeah. So, unless you want to stir shit up, you should focus on the damn ferns."

"You're thinking about my mouth, not how I suggested your dad produce Blue Fire's album?"

"That's right, sweet pants."

As she sprinkled salt and pepper over the ferns, he came up behind her. His chest leaning into her back, he squeezed the juice from half a lemon into the mixture. "Still waiting to hear yours."

"My fantasy?" She tipped her head up to look at him. "Yeah, that's not going to happen."

"You know what else you need?" His mom barreled into the kitchen, heading straight for the pantry. "Baking soda." She set the tub on the counter. "I think you should make a quick bread." Picking a fiddlehead out of the pan, she popped it in her mouth. "Perfect. Take it off the flame now or it'll turn mushy."

Mimi turned off the stove and dumped the fiddleheads onto a plate.

"Try one." His mom grabbed a clean fork out of the dishwasher and stabbed one.

"I'd rather blanch my eyeballs."

His mom looked between the plate and Mimi. Then between Mimi and Calix. "She serious?"

"Oh, she's very serious," Mimi said.

"You're scared of a fiddlehead?"

"You see how tightly it's coiled?"

"Yeah." His mom's tone held a challenge.

"How many bugs do you think are lodged in there?"

His mom stared at Mimi. "Are you fucking with me?"

"I am in no way fucking with you. I'm not eating that. If an alien spacecraft slammed into Earth destroying the ecosystems, leaving us with nothing but fiddleheads to eat, I'd go all-out cannibal. No remorse."

For one strange moment, his mom seemed to take in all that Mimi had just said. And then she threw her head back and laughed. A deep, throaty laugh.

A sound he hadn't heard in three long, painful years.

"You're a riot." She shook her head. "All right, screw the fiddleheads." She picked up the baking soda and slammed it back down on the counter. "Focus on this. The point of making a quick bread is so you get the chemistry of what's happening here. Baking soda combined with an acid—and that could be cream of tartar or buttermilk, yogurt, or vinegar—creates bubbles from the carbon dioxide gas that the two produce."

Calix smiled. His mom had loved homeschooling them.

"So, that's why the bread rises," Mimi said.

"That's right. And since the baking soda reacts as soon as it hits the liquid, you're going to add it to the dry ingredients first. Okay, so let's talk about what goes into a quick bread."

Calix leaned back against the counter, pulled his phone out of his pocket, and texted his dad. Mom's giving Mimi a cooking lesson.

His dad responded right away. Yeah?

Mimi told me what she said. You as producer.

Thinking on it.

You think Mom can handle it?

I'll talk to her tonight.

But do you think she can handle it?

Think she can handle anything.

He didn't know about that, but he did think his dad should take the gig with Blue Fire.

Because Calix would be around. He wasn't going anywhere.

In their home studio, Calix and his brother jammed to Robert Johnson's *Crossroads*. The pads of his fingers hurt from not having played guitar in too damn long, but he hadn't had this much fun with Gus in years.

Watching him, Calix realized Mimi was right. Gus

belonged in the music industry. Nothing made him happier. And what better way to give him exposure and experience than a studio that was half an hour from home? There *wasn't* a better opportunity.

The door opened. For some reason, he'd expected to see his dad, ready to jam with them. Which would've been awesome—another thing that hadn't happened in years.

But it was Mimi. Her mouth moved, but he couldn't hear her. When he lowered the volume, he heard his brother singing in a strained and raspy voice. Fuck, man, it felt good to see Gus lost in the music.

He gave Mimi a chin nod. "What's up?"

"Hey, sorry to bother you. I—"

"Oh, hey, Meems." Gus swiped the hair out of his eyes.

"You don't have any dark rum, so I wonder if I could borrow your truck to go to the store?"

"You drive?" Gus's tone was teasing.

"I drive a little. I just don't have a car because I live in the city."

"You've been living on the farm for a year." Calix had always wondered about that.

"Yeah, but it's temporary. Just until I get a job. So, can I borrow your truck?"

"What do you need rum for? Isn't your lesson over?" He'd told his mom he had shit to do, so she could take over. But the lesson should've ended a while ago.

With a proud smile, she said, "I'm showing your mom how to make my nonna's *tiramisu*. Without a recipe, I might add."

"Don't you have to cook dinner for the band?"

"What's your problem?" Gus smacked him on the arm.

"What? She's got a job." He knew how seriously Mimi took her cooking gig.

"She's working with *Mom*."

"Yeah, I know that." But Mimi mattered, too. Whatever. He dug into his pocket for his keys. "Here."

"She doesn't drive." Gus got up.

"No, I *do* drive." She sounded tentative.

"When was the last time you got behind the wheel?" But Gus just laughed. "It's cool. I'll go. You need anything else?"

"No, just rum. You don't mind?"

"Nah. I got plans anyhow, so I'll just pick up the rum and drop it back here real quick."

"Okay, thanks." Mimi gave him a warm smile.

Calix set his Les Paul on the stand. "What plans?"

His brother gave him a defiant look. "With Laney."

"Laney? Thought you couldn't wait to get away from her."

"Yeah, well. I've been talking to her. I like her."

"You can't be serious. She's been with everyone."

"Fuck you." His features flushed, and he set his guitar in the stand.

Calix grabbed his arm and pulled him back. "She's trouble. You know that."

"She's fun." Muscles strained in his neck, Gus gave him a challenging look. "And she lets me do anything to her." He shot a sheepish look to Mimi. "Sorry, Mimi."

"No, don't be. I'll leave you two."

"Don't bother." Gus stalked toward the door. "I'm out of here."

"Gus, come on. You can have any girl you want."

"Yeah? That's great. Because I want *her*. And another thing you should know. She's got a friend in a band, and they need my help. I'm going to do some mixing for them."

"As soon as Blue Fire finds another producer, you'll get your job back."

"Yeah, okay, cool, but until that happens, I'm gonna help this band out." Gus reached the door.

"Gus." Frustration had him snapping. "Hang on."

"For what?"

In that moment, he could see his brother's resolve to break out on his own. Long overdue, but still. Worrisome. Because, frankly, it was one thing to work with Blue Fire, another entirely to work with the kinds of guys Laney would hang out with.

"I love you, bro. I love Mom," Gus said. "But whatever we're doing here? It isn't working. And I'm gonna fuckin' blow my brains out if I don't start doin' something that matters to me." He gave Mimi an apologetic look. She rubbed his arm, gave it a squeeze, and then he was gone.

With an uncomfortable sense of foreboding, Calix shut down the stereo. Arms wrapped around him from behind. And just that simple gesture made him want to lean into her, share some of this terrible weight he carried. Because he was torn.

His brother was wrong. It *was* working. Their mom was alive, wasn't she? Every night he found her working in the studio was a victory.

But Gus was also indisputably right. Because in three years nothing had changed. She still avoided family time. Still slept in the guest bedroom.

So what the hell was he supposed to do?

Mimi's scent floated around him, and it made him want to lose himself in her.

"Calix," she whispered.

That voice . . . Jesus, he wanted nothing more than to turn in her arms, strip off her clothes, and fuck her until they both collasped.

And as long as he was being honest, no one else would do.

"I was wrong." She tightened her hold. "You don't skim at all. You go deeper than anyone I know."

She was treading on dangerous ground. He tried to pry her arms off him, but she wouldn't let go.

"You're so deep into your family, there's nothing left to give. Not to your friends, or women, or even to music."

"Nothing else matters."

"Yeah, it does. You don't see it because you're so consumed with blaming yourself. But you have to know shutting down your lives isn't helping your mom. It's not giving her a reason to live. How *could* it?" She pulled back—not letting him go, but shifting to face him—and cupped his jaw. "Calix, please listen to me. It's not your fault."

She didn't get it. "We've already talked about this. I don't blame myself."

She tapped his temple. "In here you don't." Then, she patted his heart. "But in here you do. Look, I can only tell you what I see. And I see a man who's doing penance for destroying his family. You think it's on you to single-handedly keep everyone together because you took your eyes off Hopper. But it's not working, because there *is no penance to do*. He didn't die because you were talking to a record company executive. He didn't die because you brought your parents to that music festival. He died because bad things happen."

He turned away from her. "Yeah, I got that. We all get that."

But she grabbed him back. "No, you don't. Because if you did, you'd be living. You're stuck in that one moment you can't take back."

"You don't know what you're talking about. If we all go back to our lives, then what's my mom's reason to get out of bed?"

"No offense, but you're not the reason she gets out of bed. She can barely stand to be around any of you. And not because she doesn't love you, but because she's in pain. She wants to crawl into a cool, dark cave and just grieve."

Yes. The truth in her words stripped him raw. Sleeping in the guest bedroom was his mom's cave. How had he never seen it like that before?

"But she can't. Not while you're constantly coaxing her out."

"If you think I can walk away . . . I'm telling you right now you can forget it. If anything happened, I couldn't live with myself."

She took a deep breath, gave him a serious look. "Hopper would hate the silence in this house. He'd hate the way everyone stopped living. Do right by your brother and live your life. If you believe in heaven or an afterlife or any kind of enduring soul, live the life that would bring that beautiful smile to his face."

She started out the door, and damn it all to hell but he could not let her go.

Swinging around, he lunged to catch up with her and caught her arm. "Why won't you just mind your own damn business?"

"I don't know." Her tone sounded pleading. "I know I should, but it hurts me to see you like this." She took in a shaky breath, the tips of her fingers touching her mouth.

"Goddamn that mouth." No matter how hard he tried to keep his distance, this woman had gotten in. In a way no one else ever had. He hauled her against him and kissed her.

And fuck, did he need her. That mouth, so warm, so soft, Jesus, he wanted to sink inside her and never come out. She tasted like vanilla, and she smelled like elegance. He had to have more. Had to. His hands slid down her back, curving over her ass and squeezing. She gasped as his cock pressed into her stomach.

But he couldn't stop. He needed more, so he lifted her and pressed her back against the wall. Her legs wrapped around his hips, and she ground against him. Mimi Romano. Fuck him, she made him wild.

Desire spiked so hard and fast, he got swept under. Their hips rocked in a rhythm that worked him into a frenzy of need. And that lush mouth, so soft and warm and wet, turned his bones to liquid.

When he thrust up high and hard, striking right at her core, she pulled her mouth off his. "Okay, okay." She struggled to get out of his hold. "Stop. Calix, God. We have to stop doing this."

Stop? Yeah, he'd tried that. But he couldn't. He just couldn't get enough of her. "Date me."

"What?"

"Date me."

"You don't date."

"I want to date *you*." He pressed another hot kiss on her mouth. "I need more."

She gazed up at him with a wary expression, but his resolve never wavered. Her hands slid into his hair, cupping the sides of his head. "Yes."

CHAPTER TEN

Every time Mimi remembered the kiss, a zing shot through her. God, he was so intense. He kissed her like he couldn't get close enough, deep enough. And she loved it.

As she walked along the side of the road, careful to mind the ruts in the grass, she kept thinking about what he'd said. *I need more.* He had no idea how happy that had made her.

She just didn't know what this date meant to him. Nothing between them had been casual—each kiss had ripped her wide open, each conversation had been deep and rich and real. But what if a date just meant sex?

Would she have sex with him? Knowing he didn't want a relationship, knowing he had nothing to give beyond one single hookup—or even a couple hookups—would she be okay with that? She'd have to look at it as fulfilling a fantasy.

Yeah, no, that wouldn't work for her. Sex to grow closer . . . definitely. But Calix didn't want to explore feelings. Sex was a distraction for him. She didn't want to be someone's distraction.

A truck roared past, music blaring, girls laughing, and she moved farther onto the grass. She loved her walk to work. In this second week of May, the air had grown warmer, which meant more people were out jogging and riding bikes.

In Eden's Landing the pier and the small town around it were the hub of the neighborhood, so all traffic tended to move in that direction. A very cool coffeehouse, an old school grocer, an artist's co-op, and an appliance repair shop made up the bulk of businesses on Main Street. In warmer weather, local vendors sold their wares on the pier.

What would a date with Calix look like? An uneasy feeling snaked through her when she imagined hanging out with his friends at the beach. That wasn't really her idea of fun—drinking, getting high, hooking up. But then he wouldn't enjoy her idea of fun, now would he?

Only, what was her idea of fun these days? Her days of clubbing and dining out had ended months ago. And funny thing, she hadn't missed them at all. She loved living out here with the band. They hung out, jammed, had dinners on the beach. They liked each other and didn't need much more than their instruments to have fun.

Imagine if Calix joined Blue Fire. Him, his dad, Gus—if both worlds merged. That would be awesome.

As she headed up Slater and Emmie's driveway, she wondered about the trucks parked in front of the house. A bunch of people jammed on aluminum lawn chairs outside the open garage.

She saw Gus among them and waved. He handed his guitar off to the woman next to him and headed toward her with a huge grin. "Hey, Meems."

"You guys are back at work?" she asked.

"Just for a few days."

"Who're those people?"

"My dad thought it'd be cool to add a tumbao drum pattern to a couple of the songs, so they're trying it out."

"Tumbao?"

"It's an Afro-Cuban drumset groove."

"How fun is that?"

"Very. Actually, it was Calix's idea. He suggested my dad step in for a few days, record some tracks. See if he fits with the band."

"That's a great idea." Damn, Calix kept surprising her. "Well, you have fun. I'll see you at lunch."

She loved that Calix sincerely wanted what was best for his family. He didn't have some hidden agenda, wasn't some kind of control freak. His sole focus was on healing his family, and he'd do whatever it took.

As she climbed the steps to the back door, she felt a pinch in her heart. She was in trouble. She was falling for him—hard—but all those qualities she loved about him? They were reserved for his family. She got to witness all that intense loyalty and devotion, his kindness and generosity—his deep, powerful love—but she didn't think he'd ever shine it on her. Yeah, he couldn't keep his hands off her when they were in the same room, but the moment he got away from her, he cooled. He had time to remember what mattered to him.

Would she ever matter to him? She hadn't even turned on her phone this morning for fear she'd find a text telling her about some plans he'd "forgotten about," blowing off their date.

She opened the back door, kicked off her flats, and tossed her jacket on the table. The kitchen smelled . . . well, like a flower shop. She stepped into it and *Oh, my God*, there were flowers everywhere.

Maybe Emmie and Slater had announced their pregnancy. Slater was such a sweetheart to do this for her. God, he loved his woman.

She needed to get cooking, but she didn't want to disturb the flowers. What if Emmie hadn't seen them yet? She pulled out her phone to take a picture. *Holy cow, look at this.* It was fantastic. Wildflowers in all kinds of blues, purples, and pinks were scattered on counters, on the island, all over the kitchen table. It was gorgeous—and the display was incredibly artistic. Slater had obviously taken time to arrange them just so.

Setting her phone on the bay window behind the sink, Mimi turned her thoughts to the day's agenda. Since she had another lesson with Calix that afternoon, she thought she'd make a boeuf bourguignon in the slow cooker. She hoped they had a nice Bordeaux around.

As she plugged in the Crock-Pot, she noticed a vase with

a spray of fragrant beach roses. A white card propped up against it.

Mimi

Wait a minute. Someone had done this for *her*? Before opening it, she held it to her chest, taking in the flowers covering every surface. She dared to hope . . . Calix? She unfolded the card.

When I wake up I'm wondering when I'll see you
When I'm working I picture your smile
When I'm with you I can feel my heart beating
And before I fall asleep I wish like hell I hadn't skimmed
over you
I don't want to skim. Not with you.
I want more.
Will you give me more?

Mimi closed her eyes, letting the words sink in. She got swept back into the hunger of his kiss and the urgency of his hands pulling her closer.

Now that she knew him—that he was locked down, heart, mind, and soul, from that one single moment when Hopper wandered away from him backstage at the concert—this date—this gesture—meant everything to her.

As hard as it was for him, he was opening, letting her in. And she wanted to honor that. To be so good for him.

Yanking open the desk drawer, she pulled out a pen, tore a yellow Post-it off the stack, and wrote,

Yes, yes, yes!

Could he do it, though? Stick with her and not shut down? Because she'd give him everything she had—she just didn't know how much he could give in return.

Time spent with her tripped his anxiety. Made him feel like he was taking his attention off his family—leaving his mom vulnerable.

As much as she wanted to throw herself in, she had to hold back. Because Calix Bourbon—he was a risk to her heart. A big one.

But *come on*. He was a risk she had to take.

Mimi wound up getting to the Bourbon house early so she and Lee could brainstorm ideas for the wedding. All she'd had to do was mention the event for Lee to jump right in and offer to help. Which was a big relief, given the short time frame.

Laptop open on the table, they sat side by side searching for menus.

"Okay, magical food to go with magical decor." Lee typed the words.

"Really? We're putting *magical food* into a search engine?" When Lee shot her a look, Mimi said, "What do you think is going to come up, exactly?"

"Well, see right here." Lee tapped the screen. "Anchovies, artichoke, asparagus—all these ingredients draw on magical elements to make your wishes come true."

"Uh, yeah, Lee. Look a little closer. Those ingredients draw lust." That was something she most definitely didn't need to know how to draw—she had loads of it. No, she needed to find actual menus. She was doing double-duty here. Planning the menu all while learning as much as she could for the competition.

"Exactly. And lust is totally magical."

"At a wedding reception? Wouldn't that be called an orgy?"

"Oh, look, bananas draw sex."

"Really?" Mimi reached for the fruit basket. She pulled a banana off the bunch and peeled it, taking a huge bite. She chomped loudly, openmouthed, and moaning. "Oh, mm, yes, yes, yes!" She slapped her palm on the table.

"See? It works." Lee laughed, grabbed it from her. "Told ya. Let's eat everything on the list so we can get lucky tonight."

Actually, she might be getting lucky anyway. But she wouldn't tell Lee about her date. Not yet anyway.

"Okay." She dragged the computer toward her. "I think we're done with magical foods."

Lee stabbed a finger at the screen. "Wait. Look, whipped cream is joy and celebration. We're totally serving pears and bananas with whipped cream. It's like Utopia in a bowl."

"Give me the computer. You've lost any tech cred you might have had." Mimi typed in *wedding reception menus*.

Lee made a snoring sound. "There's nothing magical about a garden salad and chicken marsala. Bo-ring."

"We can take a basic dish and turn it into something amazing. Besides, Violet's not talking about the menu. She wants the décor to be magical."

The creak of a door let her know Jo was back from her walk.

"Okay, forget menus for the moment." Lee pushed the laptop aside. "Let's start with the basics. Do you want a sit-down meal?"

"That seems too fussy, don't you think?"

"Not if we put Hobbit ears on the waitstaff."

"Oh, my God, you think maybe you're taking this whole magical idea too far?"

"It's literally the only thing you gave me to work with." Lee bumped shoulders with her. "You're doing Italian desserts, why not just do Italian food? Make it the theme."

"Okay," Mimi said in a fake happy voice. "And everyone will wear togas and gladiator sandals."

Lee pinched her. "You don't have to be a brat. It's a wedding. Shouldn't weddings have themes? Color schemes?"

"That's horseshit." Jo stood behind them.

"Say what you really think, Mom." Lee sat back in her chair.

"Just because you're doing Italian desserts doesn't mean you have to serve Italian food. What do they like? The bride and groom?"

"The only information we have from Mimi is that the bride wants a magical wedding."

Jo headed for the refrigerator. "Well, that narrows the field."

"If we show you some menus, will you give us suggestions?" Lee asked.

"No." She sounded bored, yet she grabbed her yogurt and came right back to them.

"Come on, Mom. You're good at this stuff."

"I've never planned a wedding in my life. Your dad and I eloped." She grabbed a spoon out of the silverware drawer. "You don't need to look at menus. Keep it simple. Good, clean food."

"Like what?" Lee asked.

Jo sighed, like she was put out, but she dragged a chair closer. Mimi and Lee scooted over, making room for her. Once seated, Jo angled the computer in her direction. "You got pictures of them?"

"The bride and groom? Yep." As Mimi logged into her Facebook account, the front door banged shut. Boots pounded on the hardwood floor.

"Ma?" Calix called.

A wave of excitement rolled through her, but Mimi stayed focused on her laptop.

"Kitchen," Jo said.

Keeping her cool, Mimi pulled up pictures of the band at a picnic dinner last September. Jo leaned closer as Mimi clicked through them. "Anything else?" Jo asked.

"Yeah, sure." Mimi opened an album from last Christmas when Derek had proposed to Violet. The band had gathered around to sing her a song. It was the most romantic proposal Mimi had ever seen.

Calix came into the kitchen. "Hey, Ma." He squeezed her shoulder. When his gaze landed on Mimi, heat unfurled from her core, spreading in a slow climb up her chest.

That big, dark-eyed man leaned forward, right across his mom, and brushed a soft kiss on Mimi's cheek. Holy hell. Mimi thought she'd go up in flames.

Lee's eyebrows lifted practically to her hairline, and she pushed the half-eaten banana toward Mimi, who laughed, shaking her head. But her cheeks still felt heated. She couldn't believe Calix would show her affection in front of his family.

Her heart fluttered wildly. More than anything, she wanted this kind of intimacy with him. To be *his*.

But did he want that?

He'd made it clear he *didn't*. So what was he doing?

Hang on. Just because she went all in didn't mean everyone did. She had to give him a chance. Reaching into the back pocket of her jeans, she pulled out the note she'd written him.

"Ready for your cooking lesson?" he asked.

"In a minute," Jo said. "She's working on a menu for the wedding."

"Did they set a date yet?" he asked.

"May twenty-second."

"That's in two weeks," Jo said. "Is that enough time to get everything done?"

"We're going to keep it simple," Mimi said. "Violet doesn't want a big production."

"No, she only wants magic." Lee gave Mimi a teasing look.

Calix stared into the refrigerator. While he looked like he was deciding what he wanted, she suspected his attention was trained on his mom and her interest in the conversation.

"Then we'll have to keep the ceremony short and sweet."

Mimi cut a glance to Calix at his mom's use of the word *we*. He turned at the exact same moment. A hint of a smile on his beautiful mouth made her soar.

She wanted so much more than sex with him. She wanted love.

Her skin tightened at the thought of Calix letting her in all the way. Pouring all that devotion and loyalty on her. That love. She wanted that so much.

Calix pulled out a glass container of the leftover gnocchi she'd made for dinner the night before.

"Hey, that's mine." Lee got up and tried to snatch it out of her brother's hands. He just laughed and held it over her head. "She brought that over for me."

"Uh-huh." He shoved it in the microwave.

"You make that from scratch?" Jo asked.

Mimi nodded. "It's one of my nonna's recipes."

Calix popped the door open before the gnocchi could heat through. Stabbing one with a fork, he shoved it in his mouth. "Damn, this is good." He leaned against the counter, long legs crossed in front of him.

Done with the computer, Jo sat back in her chair. "So, here's my suggestion. I'd have comfort food. That's what I get from looking at those pictures and hearing you talk about them. Make it a homemade kind of event, a buffet. Mac and cheese, brioche rolls, slow-cooked tenderloin, stuff like that."

"I like it."

"Where's the magic in mac and cheese?" Lee said.

"The magic's in the mood, babe." Jo's chair scraped back as she got up. "The décor. And that's what you should be thinking about. Let Mimi take care of the food—that's what she's good at."

She was? Mimi felt ridiculously happy to hear Jo's confidence in her.

But at the same time she couldn't help thinking about her dad. It was so easy for this family to jump in and support her. Spend all this time helping her. But her own father couldn't?

"Hey, Ma. Got a question." Calix set the gnocchi down. "Since we went over the five ingredients yesterday, I thought today we'd give her a challenge that'll make her use them."

"Okay. You got any ideas?" Jo asked.

"Not really. Do you?" Calix seemed to hold his breath, all his hope for his family tied up in his mom's interest in coming back to the kitchen.

And Mimi could see how much Jo wanted to please her children. But she could also see a woman who desperately needed to be left alone. And unless Mimi was reading this all wrong, no one was letting Jo grieve in her own way, in her own time. Trying to please her family was possibly draining her of whatever energy she had left.

And suddenly this whole plan felt very wrong.

"Yeah, sure," Jo said. "I can help."

For one moment, Calix just stood there, his vulnerability as clear as a little boy's. "Great. Let's do this." He stepped aside as his mom leaned into the refrigerator and started pulling out ingredients.

He came up behind Mimi, giving her hip a hard squeeze. She smiled, refusing to take away from his moment of victory.

And that's when she remembered the note. She handed it to him.

He opened it, read it, and then his features bloomed into a genuine and unfettered smile. It was beautiful.

Needing to help Jo, she started to pull away, but he took both her shoulders, turned her toward him, and planted a hard kiss on her mouth.

"Tonight."

"Tonight," she whispered.

Lying side by side, gazing up at a sky full of glittering stars, they held hands.

He makes it so damn hard for me to hold back.

He'd shown up at the farm with his hair still damp from a shower and a box of homemade truffles and driven her out to the lighthouse in Montauk. Since the park closed at four thirty in May, they'd parked along the side of the dark road and walked in with their blanket and picnic basket.

For a guy who didn't date, Calix had created an award-winning one.

But hope was a dangerously compelling drug. The naïve girl in her was jumping up and down on her bed, screaming into a pillow. *He's totally into me!* But the experienced woman warned her that he could only give so much before turning back into Mr. Stoic.

She didn't come first.

Unless . . . maybe this date meant they were past that now? *Stop worrying about it and just be here now.*

With the taste of dark chocolate still on her tongue and the steady crash of waves as background music, Mimi rolled to her side to face him.

"So, why homeschooling? Why not public school?" His family seemed isolated enough on all that land. She'd think his parents would want to socialize their kids.

He turned toward her with a mischievous smile. "Oh, I started out in public school. It lasted until second grade."

"Ah, so the deviant behavior started way back then, huh?"

"How do you know it wasn't my superpowers that set me apart?"

"Ooh, I love a man with superpowers. Especially if he's like Captain Marvel. I always wanted to date a dude with the wisdom of Solomon, the strength of Hercules, the stamina of Atlas, the power of Zeus, the courage of Achilles, and the speed of Mercury. Please tell me that's your real identity?"

"Thanks, Meems. Way to emasculate a guy."

"Oh, don't worry. You've got a superpower. Believe me, I've seen it."

"Yeah?" He made a show of adjusting his dick. "Is that why you went out with me? To get some of this superpower?"

When he smiled like that, the dimples bracketing his mouth came out. And made her go all gooey inside.

Can I kiss him yet?

"Okay, Shazam. Settle down. Back to the homeschooling story."

"I think you can guess why. Shit my parents saw." He paused. "They lived hard and fast, and bad things happened. They wanted a safer world for us."

"By bad things, do you mean sex, drugs, and rock 'n' roll?"

"Sure, but it's easy to put that stamp on it. The reality, though . . . the reality's they lost their friends to overdoses, AIDS, all kinds of shit. I think the worst, though, was the bus crash." He looked at her, as if asking whether she knew about it.

She didn't.

"Happened back in 'ninety-two. One of their tour buses ran off the road. Four roadies and their manager died."

"Oh, God."

"Yeah. Up until that, they'd had bad experiences. Accountants taking advantage of them, betrayals, a close friend OD'ing. But the crash, that was it for my mom. She wanted out. A clean slate. They moved out here and basically reinvented themselves."

"And created this world for their children to grow up in."

"Exactly."

God, and then she'd lost her boy. But Mimi didn't want to darken their date, so she steered the conversation in a different direction. "I wanted a big family like yours. You know how when you're little and you blow out the candles on your birthday cake? And your parents are all, 'Make it a good one, make it matter'?"

He grabbed her hand and brought it to his thigh. "No. In my family we don't make wishes. We make shit happen."

"Is that on the Bourbon family crest?"

"If we had one, it would be." Another of his toe-curling smiles. "So what was your wish? Unless you can't tell me because if you do, it won't happen."

"It's too late for that. It already didn't happen."

"What'd you wish for?" He rolled onto his side, tucking an arm under his head.

"I'd close my eyes and wish with all my might for a big, happy family. That's all I wanted. Every time I went to the playground, I'd spend more time watching other families than playing. Or at the beach, I'd be building a sandcastle with my mom or my nanny, and all around me kids were playing together, fighting, crying. But they had each other, you know?"

"Yeah. I know." His voice whispered across her skin like a caress.

"I remember being on my perfectly clean beach blanket with my little take-out containers from Mirabelle's. And next to us was this huge encampment, a couple of moms and all their kids. One kid cried because he had sand in his sandwich, another squirted her juice box at everyone, making kids scatter and moms yell. And I was so freaking jealous. I just wanted to be in the middle of that chaos, because I imagined that when they got home, they'd curl up on the couch together and watch a movie, sharing popcorn, getting into bed with each other and telling secrets. I hated going to bed. Hated it. I'd be all alone in my bedroom with a head full of thoughts I was dying to share."

"You seem tight with your mom."

"We're close now. But I think she spent too many years trying to figure out her place in the world. She married my dad right out of college and got pregnant right away. She never got a career going. As soon as I started school, she had all this time to fill. Lunches and tennis, that wasn't her thing. So she joined boards and committees, trying to fill the void. But I guess she didn't figure out until later that, once you get locked into those roles, they become all-consuming. And I think she felt pretty crappy about it since she'd wanted to be a stay-at-home mom. She was just all kinds of unhappy. And, you know, she wasn't home much. My dad wasn't either, so it was just really, incredibly lonely."

The pity in his eyes made her regret going off like that. "Am I an awesome date or what?" She smiled. "I think I'm supposed to show you how I can tie a knot in the stem of a cherry with my tongue."

"I never got that one. Is the message that she can do the same thing with my dick?"

"Nobody ties Shazam's dick in a knot."

"See, right there? You give good date conversation." He reached for a lock of hair that spilled across her cheek and tucked it back behind her ear, his fingertips lingering on the shell. "I like talking to you."

Her skin hummed under his gentle touch. "Yeah. Me, too."

"I like you."

She could not get over how gorgeous this man was. "Yeah?"

Eyes bright and intense, he looked as if his whole body vibrated with emotion. "It's been a hard three years, and I've been holding on so tight. But then you come along and give me a different spin on things. Part of me wants to stick with what I've been doing because I'm so fucking scared my mom's gonna knock back another bottle of sleeping pills. But the other part of me . . ." He let out a breath. "I know it's not working. I see her face when I make her come inside for dinner." He closed his eyes. "I didn't get it before, but you're right. It's *not* working. Family dinners and all that aren't making her feel loved. It's making her sneak around. I've been going about it all wrong."

"No, you haven't. You've tried one thing, and it's not working. So now you can try something different." She cupped his cheek, caressing his chin with her thumb. "She knows you love her."

"What if I try something different and it doesn't work?"

"Have you guys seen a therapist? Maybe it would help to talk to someone."

One side of his mouth curled into a wry smile. "Bourbons don't roll like that."

"Okay, then, have you at least talked to your mom?"

He had this dismissive expression, like she was crazy, and it made her laugh. "It never once occurred to you to ask your mom how she feels?"

"She doesn't want to talk about it."

"Men." She made a show of rolling her eyes. "All your worries could be put to rest if you just talked to her. Ask her what she wants. Tell her your concerns, and let her address them."

"You're so beautiful, Mimi Romano."

"Are we talking about my mouth again?"

"No. I meant in here." He pressed his palm to her heart. "So fucking beautiful."

The heated look he gave her filled her with want. And then he hooked his hand around the back of her neck and drew her close, giving her the softest, sweetest kiss. The slow tangle of his tongue, the wet heat of his mouth . . . it was beautiful.

She ran her fingers through his chin whiskers and up his jaw until they sifted through his long, silky hair. He pushed closer to her, his body hot and hard, his kiss voluptuous.

His hand slipped under her shirt, gliding up her stomach to her breast, and he gave it a gentle squeeze. With a thrust of his hips, his erection hit her stomach. Lust speared through her, and she hooked a leg over his, binding their bodies together.

His hand pulled out of her shirt, slid around to her ass, and cupped it hard. "Jesus, Mimi." His deep voice sounded rough as he squeezed her. "I gotta have you."

When he came to the button of her jeans, he looked at her, asking permission, and she found his mouth again, giving it to him. The moment he had her jeans unzipped, his hand pushed down, cupping between her legs. She moaned, rocking into him. His finger stroked lightly over her underpants, and when he touched her clit, she gasped at the shower of fiery sparks.

With each flick over her sensitive nub, electricity pulsed through her. She needed more. She kissed him with her whole body, hands in his hair, leg hooked around his thigh, drawing him against her, tongue slow dancing with his. God, she was burning up, her legs trembling. His arm between them kept his erection from her, and she was going out of her mind with the need to feel him.

She pushed between their straining bodies, running the heel of her palm up his very hard length. He pulled his mouth off hers. "Fuck." He dove back in for a kiss, taking her bottom lip into his mouth and sucking on it, as his hand shoved under the elastic of her panties and his finger found her slick heat.

Her back arched, and she gasped as he swirled around her nub. God, oh, God, she was writhing against him, the pleasure so intense. She couldn't—oh, God—"Calix." Her body clenched and then a moment later burst in pure sensual release. His strokes didn't let up, and she kept cresting and peaking—*oh, yes*—until she shuddered and collapsed against him. "Oh, my God." She'd need a moment to catch her breath after that.

And, God, he smelled so good. She breathed in the distinctive scent of his skin and clean cotton of his T-shirt. She started to pull away, but he tightened his hold, grinding his erection into her stomach. She smiled into his neck when she remembered his fantasy.

She stroked the hair off his forehead. "Didn't you have some kind of fantasy about my mouth?"

The look on his face, hungry but hesitant—as if he didn't expect her to do anything but holy shit did he want her to—got her pulse spiking. "Did you picture it here?" She pressed a kiss to the corner of his mouth, his scruff tickling her cheek. "Or here?" Another to his jaw. "Maybe here?" She kissed his neck, right at the curve of his shoulder, and because he smelled so good, she sank her teeth into the muscle.

He sucked in a breath, his dick so hard it throbbed against her. She reached down and gripped him through his jeans, and he pushed into her hand.

Lifting his shirt all the way up to his collarbone, she kissed each pec, then licked his nipple, biting down on it.

"Fuck, Mimi."

"Not there? Sorry, maybe you meant here instead." More kisses down his chest, following the thin line of silky hair that led to the waistband of his jeans. She gave his erection another squeeze, and he shuddered.

Popping the stud open, she kissed until she reached the head of his cock. Holy crap, he went commando. Why was that so hot? She peeled back the material, exposing his jutting masculinity.

A hunger so intense it stole her breath gripped her. She closed her hand around him, so hard, so perfect. But instead of taking him in her mouth, she licked underneath the ridge. "Right here? Is this where you wanted my mouth?"

She glanced up at him, and he let out a choked sound.

"Don't fuck with me, Mimi." His fingers curled around the back of her neck.

"Can I fuck with you just a little?" She shoved his pants down. He lifted his hips, and she pushed them down to his knees.

"Mouth, Mimi."

"Oh, did you . . ." Her tongue swirled around the head of his cock. His eyes closed, and his ass muscles clenched. "You must want it right . . . here." And then she took him all the way in.

His eyes rolled back in his head. She could feel the tremble in her legs as he let out a shaky breath. His hand tightened on her neck. "Fuuuck."

She licked all around the head, breathing in the smell of soap fresh from the shower he'd taken right before picking her up. Stretching out on her side, her bare feet hitting cool sand, she gripped his ass as she drew him deeper into her mouth.

"Ah, Jesus, Mimi, so good."

She sucked hard, flicking her tongue across the vein on the underside of his dick.

"Gotta see you." As he rolled onto his back, his hand at her neck urged her to stay with him. She got up on her knees, not releasing him, and he hitched up on his elbows. His gaze turned crazy with lust. "Look at you." He grew even thicker, harder.

She loved having him in her mouth. Loved it. Loved the sounds he made, the impatient thrust of his hips, the restraint she felt in his body. Because he cared. He didn't want to hurt her.

She pulled off him. "Don't you dare hold back with me, Calix Bourbon. If this is a fantasy, then you let go." They might never have this kind of intimacy again. "Take it."

He drew in a deep breath, desire softening his tense features. She sucked him in, deep, all the way to the back of her throat. Her hand slid around his thigh, holding him tightly to her.

Collapsing onto his back, he let out a moan of ecstasy, his fingers curling into her hair as he guided her movements on his cock, and it thrilled her. Thrilled her that he'd let go.

She wanted him to give her everything he had to give. His neck arched, and his hand fisted her hair as his hips pumped. "Holy shit, Mimi." His vein thickened under her tongue, and she knew he was close. So she sucked him harder, flicked her tongue faster.

And when his hand pressed down, holding her against him, when his hips jerked up and his cock swelled, she knew he was there.

He started to pull out, but she wouldn't let him. She clamped her hand on his thigh and held him to her. "I'm coming. Fuck. Jesus, I'm coming."

His body went rigid, and with a roar he exploded into her mouth. She loved it. Loved that he finally let himself go. His pumps slowed, and his dick softened. When his fingers relaxed in her hair, she eased back. He lunged forward, his hands catching under her arms and hauling her up to him. His body still shaking from his explosive release, he kissed her. So much passion and hope in that joining of their mouths.

But when she settled against him, her ear pressed to his

chest so she could hear his thundering heart, she couldn't help facing the truth.

She'd crossed a line.

Calix wanted to date her. But she wanted more.

She wanted everything.

CHAPTER ELEVEN

Calix parked his bike in the driveway of Slater and Emmie's house.

Yesterday, his dad had agreed to produce Blue Fire's album. So he'd called a brief meeting this morning to talk about his plans. Since work wouldn't start until contracts came in, Emmie was on her way into the city right then to take care of it.

His boots crunched gravel as he walked along the side of the house. Each step that brought him closer to the kitchen wound him up tighter.

Mimi. Every time he closed his eyes, he saw her face, that lush mouth wrapped around his cock. Her sexy expression when she'd looked up at him. Jesus, he'd never come so hard in his life.

Honestly? Most girls treated sex like an audition. They wanted to give him the best time of his life so he'd come back for more. But Mimi, she'd been in it with him—and that was what undid him. He'd felt so damn connected to her.

Fuck. He had to stop thinking about her.

This is what you do. You get carried away with shit.

Finding out his dad had taken this job had thrown

everything into a tailspin. Of course, his mom had given him the green light, but what was she supposed to say? *No, stay home so I can continue to avoid you?*

What Mimi said struck a chord. His mom *wanted* them to leave her alone. Having her husband out of the house—having all of them gone—she'd welcome that.

But what would she do with all that time alone? If all three guys were off working on the album—and no doubt the hours would be long and grueling—what would the loneliness do to her? If Mimi was right, it would give her time to grieve and figure out a new kind of life for herself. One without children to care for.

But what if Mimi was wrong? What if being alone in her grief proved unbearable? What if she couldn't see a future—and the only relief she could imagine came from joining Hopper?

A shock of fear skidded along his nerves. He couldn't take that risk.

Voices in the backyard tore him out of his thoughts.

The band stood around the table, backs to him, as they ate the breakfast Mimi had set out on this warm, sunny day. All kinds of baked goods, a couple carafes of coffee, some jugs of orange juice, and tableware covered a folding table.

Mimi stood talking to Violet, using her hands to tell a story. She was just a woman standing in the sunshine on a clear May morning, but she made his heart expand so swiftly, it hurt. Her dark red curls gleamed in the morning sun, and her round ass in the black yoga pants made his cock go hard. Because he'd held it in his hands last night. He'd squeezed it, and she'd gone wild in his arms.

As she threw her head back in laughter, her gaze caught on him. Joy burst from inside her and shone right through her skin. She turned toward him, the smile so fucking glorious it snapped the bindings, catapulting him head over ass. She started toward him, and he just knew what she'd do. Knew she'd rush him, throw herself into his arms, wrap her legs around him, and kiss the motherfucking daylights out of him. Right there in front of everyone.

Because Mimi Romano didn't hold back.

She gave everything—and in turn she wanted everything. But he couldn't give it to her. He wanted to more than he could breathe, but he couldn't.

Could. Not.

Abruptly, he looked away. Kept walking. Went right into the studio. He gave her no acknowledgment whatsoever. With every step he took, he expected her to approach him, call out, do something to get his attention. So he moved faster. Had to get away, because if she so much as touched him, smiled up at him, he'd lose it.

He flung the door open so hard it jerked on its hinges.

Once inside the quiet, dark lounge of the studio, he quickly shut the door.

Sweat popped out on his forehead, and he tugged on the leather band, separating it from the others. He was such an *asshole*. Running from her like that?

Look, he was obviously into her, so he had to figure out a way to keep himself in check. He wasn't the selfish, reckless bastard he'd been three years ago. Hopper's death had made sure of that.

He could keep himself from getting carried away. He'd *have* to do that, because he wasn't giving her up.

Sounds from the control room snagged his attention. Low murmurs and a muted, "Fuck, yeah. Oh, yeah."

Opening the door, he found his brother's back against the wall, Laney on her knees in front of him. "Are you fucking kidding me?"

Laney didn't even pull off. She just turned, giving him seductive eyes, and then continued sucking Gus's cock. Gus pushed her head back. "Lane, stop."

Kissing the tip, Laney got up, licking her lips, while Gus pulled up his pants.

"Get *the fuck* out of here." Calix held the door open. "You don't come back to this studio, you hear me?"

"I'm his girlfriend." Her eyes fired with defiance. She snatched her bag off the chair and strode to the door. Before she left, she said, "See you at home, baby." And then she was gone.

"*Home?*" Anger burned so hot in his veins, Calix kicked the chair into the console. "What *the hell* is she talking about?"

"Nothing. I'm going to her place after work, that's all." He had a hard time articulating and reeked of pot.

"You're high." Calix could not believe this.

Gus buckled his belt with fumbling fingers.

"You show up for work high . . . you get a blow job in the control room? Jesus, Gus, the band's right outside."

"Like you'd turn down a blow job?"

"Yeah, asshole, I'd turn down a blow job by that skank any day, but I sure as hell wouldn't get one in the control room on a job. The whole point of this gig is to help you build a career. How's that gonna happen when you get fired from your first job?"

"I didn't get caught. Jesus. Calm down."

"*I* caught you."

"You're not with the band."

Why Calix felt that remark so harshly, he didn't know. Of course he wasn't with the band. He knew that. "I'm taking you home before Dad or any of the guys sees you. You need to sober up and come back when you're ready to work." He stepped closer, leaning in to make his point. "You get one pass. The next time you come to work high or have sex with that girl on Slater's property, you're out. Do you understand? And if you don't think I'll do it, think about this. I'm a session musician. This is my livelihood. You don't mess with my reputation. Now, get out of here."

"No. Laney left. I don't want to miss the meeting."

"You either get out of here now or you're fired. Don't test me."

"You're an asshole." As Gus passed him, he rammed his shoulder into Calix. But he saw his brother's expression. He wasn't angry. He was scared.

As Calix followed him out, Gus turned and said, "I'm going. You don't have to follow me."

"You think I'm letting you drive home when you're high?" He held out his hand. "Give me the keys."

"Fuck you." But there was no heat behind his words.

"Give me the fucking keys." Calix shouted it so loudly, Gus flinched.

His brother dug into his pocket and tossed the keys at Calix, then headed out the door.

Goddammit. He'd have to deal with Mimi later.

As soon as they got home, Calix steered Gus toward his room. Then he headed into the kitchen to grab something to eat while he waited for his brother to shower and change his clothes.

At the table, Lee hovered over a bowl of cereal. "S'up." She straightened, brow furrowed in confusion. "Where's Meems?"

Dammit. He'd forgotten about her lesson. Since she had her competition that afternoon, she'd wanted to do it earlier in the day. He'd planned on bringing her home with him after the meeting. "Forgot."

So not only had he hurt her, but he'd bailed on her. *Well done.*

And this was why he didn't do relationships. Not now anyway.

He closed his eyes, remembering how happy she'd been—how beautiful she'd looked standing there in all that sunshine. And he'd blown her off.

"You forgot Mimi." Lee's flat, challenging tone put him back in motion.

He aimed for the refrigerator. "Yeah, Lee. I forgot."

"Okay, that makes absolutely no sense. You were just at the house. Aren't you supposed to be in a meeting with Dad?"

As he leaned in, the cool air hit him in the face. But he didn't see food. Since he hadn't looked at Mimi, he'd never seen the hurt he'd caused by ignoring her. He imagined it right then. "Forgot something. Had to come back home." The image crushed his heart like an empty Coke can.

"Baloney. Last night you left the house with a picnic basket. And don't think I didn't hear about the flowers all over Slater and Emmie's kitchen. And then you forget about her the very next morning? Something happened. Spill it."

"Nothing happened. Leave it alone."

"No, I want to know. How did you forget her?"

He gave her a hard look.

"Shouldn't mess with Mimi." His mom came in from the garden carrying a basket full of herbs. Since when did she get up so early?

Ah. She'd gotten up for Mimi's lesson.

"I agree," Lee said.

"It's not that big a deal. I'll go back and get her."

"The whole point of the early lesson was so Mimi could get it in before she has to catch the train into the city," Lee said. "Going back to get her will waste an hour. That's shitty."

"Jesus, we had one date. That's it."

Lee came up behind them. "So the date sucked? She was boring? Her touch repulsed you?"

The back door opened, and his dad walked in. "Hey." He shot a look to Calix. "Where'd you go? We had a meeting."

Well, he wasn't about to tell his dad what he'd found in the control room. "Sorry, didn't think I was needed."

Disapproval tightened his dad's features. "You in the band?"

Calix shrugged. Technically no, he wasn't *in* the band.

His dad gave him a look that said, *You can't be serious.* "You were needed."

"Hey, Dad, you didn't bring Mimi with you, did you?" Lee asked.

"No, should I have?" Terrence asked.

"She's got a lesson this morning, but apparently Calix *forgot* to bring her over."

"Oh, hey, how'd the date go last night?" his dad asked.

He should never have made such a big deal about it. "It was fine."

His dad held his gaze a little too long, before giving a nod of understanding. "Got it."

What did that mean? "Got what?"

"No sparks. It's cool."

Sparks? Just looking at Mimi set his heart pounding. But touching her? She made him burn. "It's not like that. We're just dating."

"Sure." His dad looked indifferent.

"Just dating?" Lee pulled his arm so he faced her. "A, since when do you date? B, you don't spread flowers around her kitchen, make her truffles and a picnic dinner if you don't want her to *think* it's a date, and C, you're full of shit. I know you, Calix, and right now? You're full of shit."

He shrugged, trying to play it cool when his insides felt like curdled milk. "You're making this thing way bigger than it is. We want different things. She knows that."

"What exactly does she want?" Lee asked.

"A serious relationship."

"And you want, what, a hookup?" Lee planted herself right in his path.

"Leave it alone."

Now was not the time to point out the facts to her. That she was going to be alone with their mom all day, every day. She should be begging him not to get involved with anyone.

"Lee." His dad gave her a shake of his head. "Doesn't work like that. When a man wants a woman, nothing stops him from going after her." He watched his wife. "Trust me, we can screw around all we want, talk about how we're never gonna get tied down, but when we find her, it's done."

"Is that how it was for you and Mom?" Lee asked.

"Hell, yeah." He kept his gaze on his wife, who looked as if Terrence were standing on a landmine and shouldn't dare make a move. He came around the table and crouched beside her. "You're the love of my life, you know that, right?"

Every muscle in Calix's body tightened. He couldn't take his eyes off the private moment between his parents. For three years his mom had given Terrence nothing. But right then, when he'd put his heart on the line? Publicly? She *had* to give him something back.

If his mom rejected Terrence again, Calix thought a piece of his heart would die.

She let out an uncomfortable laugh and shoved a hand through Terrence's long hair. "Yeah, I suckered you in all right."

His dad looked like a weight had been lifted off his shoulders. He didn't smile, just brushed a kiss on her cheek and pulled out a chair. "Trying to convince a guy to date a woman's useless. Believe me, when Calix falls, you'll know."

"Then don't play with Mimi," Lee said. "She's way more sensitive than she lets on."

"What's that mean?"

"Nothing. Forget it. It's not like you're interested in her, so what does it matter?" Lee brought her bowl to the sink and dumped the leftover cereal down the drain.

Calix got up and stood beside her. "Tell me."

"Tell you what? What it feels like to get flowers and truffles, to have the guy you're into make a big deal about a date, and then have him kick you to the curb the next day? Do I really have to explain how that feels?"

"I'm not kicking her to the curb. I wouldn't do that." But, of course, he'd done exactly that. And what Lee said was right. He'd made a big deal out of the date. And worst of all? Mimi had trusted him—trusted his intentions—enough to be totally open and uninhibited around him.

And then he'd ignored her as if the gift she'd given him had meant nothing.

It had meant *too* much. More than he could handle right then.

"He likes her, just not that way," his dad said. "I get it. You'll go through a lot of those kinds of girls before you meet the one you can't stay away from. And believe me, you'll know. It'll hit you right between the eyes."

"Why'd you lead her on if you knew you didn't want a relationship?" Lee asked. "You know Mimi's not the girl you hook up with. She deserves a guy who loves her, appreciates her, just . . . gobbles her up."

"I don't know what you think is going to happen. Soon as Dad signs that contract, we're back in the studio. I'm not gonna have time to be anyone's boyfriend." But he couldn't get his dad's words out of his head. *Those kinds of girls.* Mimi wasn't one of them. She was . . . different. Unique. She fit him in a way he didn't completely understand.

He did want her. He appreciated the hell out of her. And damn straight he wanted to gobble her up.

"My point right there," his dad said. "When it's the right

girl, a guy doesn't talk about timing or any of that crap. He just takes her."

"Hello?" That familiar voice gutted him. Tentatively, Mimi entered the kitchen. With her hair in braids and her skintight jeans and tight tank top, she looked like a hot biker chick. "I wasn't sure if you guys remembered I was coming early today."

"We remembered," Jo said.

"Hey, Meems." Lee gave her a hug. "How'd you get here?"

"Violet gave me a ride."

Mimi dropped her messenger bag and went to the sink to wash her hands. "Is this okay? That I came early?"

Calix had to fix it. He snatched the hand towel off the counter and stood beside her. "Hey, sorry I left without you."

She gazed up at him, confusion, hurt, plain in her eyes.

"I had a situation." He lowered his voice. "With Gus."

She took the towel from him. "Let's just get to work, okay?" She joined his mom at the island.

"We'll let you get to it." His dad motioned to Lee, and they left.

Calix hadn't noticed all the prep work his mom had done, but she'd laid out little bowls, each with a different herb inside.

Drying her hands, Mimi sniffed the thyme. "Oh, good. I really wanted to work with seasonings. I only know the basics."

She was shutting him out. Just like her dad. She only wanted to surround herself with positivity.

"Calix?" His mom's voice carried a note of impatience.

"Right. Okay." The last thing he wanted to do was mess with her the day of her competition, but he had to fix it. After the lesson, he'd talk to her.

Don't you hold back with me, Calix Bourbon. He'd never forget those words. And the look in her eyes when she'd said it?

He would never get enough of that. Of her.

He could have her. He just needed to slow the hell down. *Date* her. Not get so damn carried away.

Quickly, he washed his hands and got down to business.

"Remember to taste everything. Every ingredient you get, taste it before you use it. It'll give you a sense of how it works with the other ingredients. Second thing is to use salt. Don't be afraid of salt."

"Got it." Still not looking at him.

Dammit. Maybe he should talk to her now. Clear the air.

His mom nudged him. "You want to pick up the pace? She's got a train to catch."

Right. He looked down at the counter, each bowl filled with a different herb. "If you're using fresh herbs, you want to add them later. Dry spices, early. The more a seasoning cooks, the deeper the flavor. The less time it has to cook, the sharper the flavor." He got a whiff of her perfume, and it sent him back to the beach. Their bodies grinding together with the frantic need to get closer.

Fuck.

"I should be writing this down," Mimi said.

"Nah," his mom said. "It'll make sense once you do it."

Focus. "And if you're going to used dried herbs, make sure to crush them before you add them." He wanted her to look at him, give him one of her smiles. The one she reserved for him—because she trusted him.

"It releases the flavor." Jo elbowed him, making him realize he just stood there.

"Generally, you can use a teaspoon of dried herbs for a tablespoon of fresh."

She held up a sprig of parsley, addressing his mom. "Do I want to tear, chop, or use a mortar and pestle?"

The French doors opened, and Shay breezed in. "Hey, you guys. What's all this?"

"Hey," Jo said, preoccupied at the island with Mimi.

"Can I borrow Calix?"

"You can have him later." Jo focused on the mortar and pestle. "He's working right now." Then, she looked up. "Shouldn't you be at work?"

"We don't start till Memorial Day weekend." She and some of their friends were lifeguards. "Besides, it won't take long. Bones got his Jeep stuck on the beach. We need a few beasts to give him a push."

The best thing he could do for Mimi would be to leave her alone. She needed her focus on the competition, not on the shit he'd thrown at her. "Sure."

His mom shot him a look.

"You got this?" Besides, he needed a break. Needed to clear his head. He'd come back ready to talk to her long before she had to leave for the train.

"No, Calix," his mom said. "I don't got this."

"Swear it won't take long at all. Please?" Shay gave her little girl smile.

He walked away. "Yeah, sure thing."

At the French door, he jerked it open. He shouldn't have done it—should've walked right out—but he couldn't help himself. He cast a glance over his shoulder.

The hurt was blatantly scrawled all over Mimi's features. What was he supposed to do? Yes, he wanted to go back in there, carry her off to his cottage, and fuck the living daylights out of her. Yes, he wanted her. Of course he wanted her.

Look at her. Those dark red braids, the flush of color in her creamy cheeks, that fiery spirit. He'd been locked in his own head for three fucking years. Of course he wanted Mimi Romano.

But he couldn't have her.

His dad was wrong. Maybe timing didn't matter for normal people. But it did for people trying to keep their moms from walking into the goddamn ocean with rocks in their pockets.

Shay's hand reached for his, clasped it, and tugged. "Come on."

And so he followed her out of the house.

Because he needed to figure out what the hell he was doing.

Even before he hit the sand, he heard the engine gunning.

Calix jogged the rest of the way and then slammed his palm on the hood. "Don't hammer the throttle."

Bones immediately jerked his foot off the accelerator. "What?"

"Come on. You start letting some air out of your tires, and I'll shovel."

"Cool." The door opened, and Bones hopped out. "Thanks, man."

Laughter had him glancing toward Shay as she pulled off her T-shirt and shorts, stripping down to her bright yellow bikini. She saw him watching and shook her hips to the beat from someone's boom box. With a lazy look in her eyes and a sway of her slender hips, she blew him a kiss.

He bent over and got to work digging out the sand in front of the wheels. At the other end of the Jeep, Bones squatted with his tire gauge. "Not workin' today?"

"The producer quit. My dad's gonna take over, but not for a few days."

Bone shot him a look. "Your dad?"

"Yeah."

"So things're going good then?"

"No change."

Bones nodded, looking back to the tire. "Cool."

Finished, Calix tossed his shovel to the sand. "I'll grab some branches."

As he headed toward the path that led back up to his property, he turned to watch his friends. Mimi was right. They let him stay the same, never challenged him. It wasn't their fault—he didn't invite their input. Because it was his problem to handle. And, of course, he thought he'd had it under control.

But Mimi didn't wait for invitations. When she cared passionately about something, she threw herself in. His skin tightened at the idea he'd lost that. Her passion. He wanted her to pour it all over him. He wanted it to sink into his every crevice. He wanted to feel it in his aching bones—like water, bringing him back to life.

Because that's what she was doing. Bringing him back to life.

Awareness pinched his nerves, sending a stinging sensation throughout his body. "Bones?"

His friend looked up from the tire.

He motioned to the others. "Have them grab some branches, okay? You should be good to go."

"Yeah, sure, man. What's up?"

"I gotta get back. I was right in the middle of something."

Bones nodded. "Thanks for the help."

Calix raced up the path. With each step he took, one thought pounded through him. *I can have her.* He could have Mimi *and* be there for his mom. How had the two become mutually exclusive?

As if his own happiness would cost him his mom.

And the kicker of it all? Mimi was right about something else. Hopper would *hate* to see his family so unhappy. No music, no laughter? What kind of way was that to live?

He burst into the house, expecting to hear their voices, but it was dead quiet.

"Ma? Mimi?"

"They left." His sister appeared in the doorway, holding her sketch pad.

"What do you mean they left?" Where would they go?

"Mom took her to the train station. Mimi couldn't concentrate. She just wanted to get to the city early. Get her head on right."

Because of him. Because he'd acted like a pussy and treated her like shit after she'd given him everything last night. "I'm such an asshole."

"Nah. An asshole wouldn't see that he'd messed up. And he definitely wouldn't care."

As he hurried down the hall, he fished his keys out of his pocket.

"Where you going?"

"Gotta get her back."

CHAPTER TWELVE

He'd gotten the train schedule off his phone, so he knew he could get to Hicksville before Mimi. The moment he pulled into the parking lot, he called her.

The call went straight to voice mail, which meant she'd likely hit Ignore.

He texted her. I was a dick. But I'm at the Hicksville train station, and I need you to get off.

She responded instantly. Do NOT mess with me right now. The only thing on my mind is the competition.

Done messing with you. I'm taking you to the competition.

Oh, fun, you and Shay?

She turned him on. Everything about her. No, saucy girl. You and me. The horn blared, signaling the arrival of the train. You're here. Get off.

I did get off. Wasn't all that rewarding.

Seriously, she could make him smile like nobody else. Before he could respond, another text came in.

What say we let your mood swing a few more times, see where it settles?

I deserved that, sweet pants. Can admit I freaked out. Now give me a chance to make it right.

The train pulled into the station, wheels clacking, brakes squealing. He got out of the truck, leaned against the hood, and folded his arms across his chest.

He had no idea if his feisty girl would forgive him so easily.

So he sent her one more text. Wanna be with you.

When the train came to a complete stop, the conductor announced the next station and reminded passengers to mind the gap.

The moment the doors opened, Calix straightened. The odds were against him, especially when he considered the way she'd distanced herself from her dad.

But damn, he really needed her to get off that train.

He needed to make it right.

He needed *her.*

He hadn't taken a full breath since the night he'd walked in on his mom unconscious in her bed. Mimi had changed him. Changed everything.

Passengers poured out the doors, hurrying down the stairs to get into taxis or waiting cars. He looked for those dark red braids. The doors closed, and the train pulled away from the tracks.

Fuck.

He deserved that. She needed to focus on the competition. Not on his bullshit.

"You better know what you're doing."

He swung around to find her opening the passenger side door. "I do."

As he got into the cab, he breathed in that familiar scent.

Funny thing about Mimi, she could wear her hair in braids, dress down in yoga pants and T-shirts, but she still exuded refinement and grace. "I'm—"

"Don't want to hear it. You punked out." She jammed her bag on the floor between her feet. "You got your shit together?"

"I do."

"Then drive."

As he pulled out of the parking lot, he put his hand on her thigh and squeezed. She didn't even look at him, just kept her gaze out the window.

"You want to talk about spices?"

"Yeah. I do." After a moment, the muscles in her leg relaxed.

"So, today it's either gonna be soup or salad."

She didn't respond.

"I think you're best off going with a theme. And don't try to get too inventive because you'll muddy the flavors."

"But what if I get weird ingredients that don't work together in a theme?"

"Then you put together the things that will go together and find a way to add the weird thing creatively. Let's say they give you kale, and it doesn't go with your potato leek soup. What can you do with it?"

"Puree it and put just a little in the soup?"

"Well, kale's pretty bitter. So, if you're going to work with kale, you might want to blanch it first."

"To get rid of the bitterness. Like the decorative plant we tried to make edible."

"Yeah, like that. But another way to go is to use it as a garnish."

"Like parsley?"

"Like those fried onion things people put in green bean casseroles."

"So, you mean slice it up and put it in a fryer?"

"Even simpler. Make thin strips, drizzle some olive oil on them. Make sure they're dry, by the way. Stick 'em in the oven—three twenty-five for fifteen minutes or so—and then salt 'em. Just use a little."

"I love that idea." She shook her head. "You're so funny."

"I know." He flipped on his blinker, changed lanes. "My riffs on kale are worldwide."

"That would be funny, as in surprising. I mean, no one who looks at you would figure you'd know how to make a garnish out of kale."

"Wait, so you're saying I'm *not* a badass?"

"Brace—this is going to suck to hear this—but you're an incredibly creative and sensitive man." Her phone rang, and she leaned over to pull it out of her messenger bag. "You're so much deeper than you let on. And don't worry. I'm not talking about your feelings for me." She hit Ignore. "Let's talk about salads."

He'd done that. Made her think he didn't care about her. "Let's do talk about them."

"Salads?"

"My feelings for you."

"Nope. Salads or nothing."

"You want to concentrate on the competition? Let's get it out in the open so it won't be a worm in your brain."

"There are no worms in my brain."

"You think I don't have real feelings for you. That's a worm in your brain." He tapped the brakes when a sea of red lights appeared on the highway before him. They'd left early enough, though, so she wouldn't be late. "Look, it's a pretty strange time in my life, and I'm doing the best I can, but the truth is the only time I'm actually happy is when I'm with you." She deserved everything, but he wasn't offering much of anything. He felt pretty shitty about that. "I don't have a lot to give right now, but I do want to . . . date you." He chanced a look at her. "Is that enough for you?"

Those big eyes, filled with so much emotion, made him feel reckless, hungry. Like he could press his foot to the pedal and keep driving west. Just her and his truck.

The temptation was overwhelming.

She watched him for a moment. "Yeah. That's enough."

And just like that the bands around his chest snapped.

* * *

With figs, butter lettuce, a ball of fresh mozzarella, and beef flank, Mimi knew she should've gone with soup. Salad was too obvious. But she'd only had thirty minutes, and if she'd tried for a soup with those ingredients, she'd have failed.

She'd never made soup before, though her nonna had made an amazing pasta *fagioli*.

Alena had made *botvinia*, a cold Russian soup made of greens and fish, only she'd used the beef flank instead. According to the judges, she'd needed some kind of sweet-sour liquid that required five days to ferment, which of course, she didn't have. Plus, the butter lettuce didn't have the same texture, color, or weight as spinach or sorrel, so she'd gotten the lowest scores of anyone so far.

"Ms. Romano," Verna said in her upbeat tone. "Please tell us what you've made."

"I've prepared a *Caprese* salad with grilled steak flanks and a fig and balsamic vinaigrette."

"Thank you. Chef Alonso?"

"I like it. I thought everything worked well together. Pureeing the fig into the dressing was inspired. And while my colleagues might disagree because it is, after all, a basic salad, I'm going to give you a five for quick thinking. First, I like that you pan-fried the steak because I'm assuming you knew you didn't have time to marinate."

"That's correct, Chef." Well, actually, her nonna had always pan-fried steak flanks, so she'd done what she knew.

"And, secondly, you handled all the ingredients and preparation, including charring the pepper, and still managed to cook a perfect steak. I also liked how you stabbed it before preparing it and inserted fresh herbs. That gave it a sharper, more flavorful taste."

"Thank you, Chef." She couldn't help cutting a quick glance to Calix, who sat in the same spot as last time, third row, right on the aisle. His smile burst with pride. Affection for him slammed her. He'd done so much for her in so little time.

"I'm going to give you a five for presentation because, come on . . ." He tipped his plate, though he'd eaten more than half the salad. "Isn't that the prettiest salad you've ever seen? The green, the red, the white. It's the Italian flag. Gorgeous. But I'm going to have to give you a three for innovation because, well, you used the ingredients in your bag in exactly the manner they were presented."

She nodded in agreement. He'd been more than generous.

"Chef Zoe?" Vern said.

Aaaand the judge who'd tip the balance in the other direction.

Mimi dug her short fingernails into her palms behind her back. She may have made a freaking salad, but she only had to get one more point than Alena, the lowest scorer.

"To be honest," Chef Zoe said, "I didn't see any quick thinking. You charred a pepper, pureed a fig." Her expression said, *Big whoopty-doo.* "So I'm giving you a two."

Oh, fuckity fuckity fuck.

"Actually, I'll give you a three because you do handle situations calmly."

I'll take that point.

"I saw you having trouble with the consistency of the dressing. You could've just added more olive oil, but you stayed calm, did a lot of tasting, and managed to pull off a beautifully balanced salad dressing. So, sure, I'll bump it to a three. And for innovation? While this is a beautiful presentation, I see nothing innovative whatsoever. Given your Italian heritage and your father's obvious preference for Italian restaurants, I'm going to guess this dish was a no-brainer for you. I give you a one. And a three for presentation."

Okay, seriously? Using her Italian heritage against her? She hadn't brought up Alena's Russian heritage when discussing that soup. "Thank you, Chef."

"I notice your father in the audience today." Zoe nodded to the front row.

Like losing her footing on a staircase, a spikey tingle raced along her limbs. Shielding her eyes from the lights with a hand, she canvassed the audience. Only when her dad waved did she spot him.

She slapped a hand over her mouth. Holy shit. Her dad had come to the taping?

And then regret rushed in hard and fast. She'd been so focused on staying positive, she'd iced him out. "Hi, Dad."

The audience laughed, so she guessed she might've sounded a little weepy.

After the initial surprise wore off, though, insecurity tumbled in. It was a good thing she hadn't known he was coming. She'd have been too self-conscious, too worried about making a fool out of herself.

"I'm sure he's pleased with your classically Italian dish," Chef Zoe said.

Classic *Caprese* salad didn't have roasted peppers. No, it wasn't exactly innovative, but it still wasn't *classic*. "I'm sure he is."

"Okay, hang on one second," Verna said. "Dino Romano is in the house. How cool is that? Not to put you on the spot or anything . . ." The host pointed at him. "But you have got to be a judge on our next cooking competition." Verna faced the camera. "I don't know if you're familiar with the name, but Dino Romano's responsible for some of our finest restaurants here in New York City." She ticked names off on her fingers. "La Terrazza dell'Eden, Taverna Romano, Cielo, and so many more." She approached him. "Do you cook?"

Her father flicked his hand back and forth several times. "Not so much."

"That's not true." Should she have kept her mouth shut? "My dad's a great cook. We've been cooking together since I was little."

The audience gave a collective, "Aw," and Verna flashed her bright smile to the camera. "You *guys*. Isn't that sweet? What kinds of things do you cook together?"

"My daughter's specialty is desserts. You've not lived until you've tasted her *torta Barozzi*."

"Do you know I've never made that before?" Verna said. "I've tasted it, and it's one sinfully delicious chocolate cake. She better make that on the final show, right? And if not, I'm inviting myself over to the Romanos for the next special occasion. I want one of those." She clapped her hands, turning sideways to face the judges. "Okay, back to the competition. Let's finish up today's judging. So, Mr. Simmons? What scores do you have for Dino Romano's daughter?"

With one last glance at her dad, she tried to read his expression. Was he proud of her? Or disgusted that his daughter demeaned herself on reality TV? But the lights were too bright, and the Food Channel founder had begun his evaluation.

She would just die if she got booted off the show with her dad in the audience.

"Ms. Romano, this salad is not only delicious, but it's beautiful. And I love the dressing. I'm going to have to respectfully disagree with Chef Zoe on the innovation angle, because classic *Caprese*—and Mr. Romano can correct me if I'm wrong—does not employ peppers. And in this dish they not only add flavor but color. The toasted pine nuts gave it texture, which was nice since everything else was soft. So I'll give you a four for quick thinking—because like Chef Alonso, I was impressed with the number of projects you had going at once that you managed to complete to perfection, and a five, as always, for presentation because that is a beautiful plate. And a four, also, for innovation—I dropped one point because it is true that you didn't repurpose the ingredients you had in your bag."

Relief swept through her, making her knees weak.

She'd made it. God, she'd made it past round two. "Thank you, sir."

Thank God she hadn't failed in front of her dad.

"Dad." Mimi wove through the crowd backstage and ran straight into his arms. "I can't believe you came." She breathed in the cologne he'd worn her whole life and sank into his tight embrace. Just around his shoulder, she caught sight of Calix, watching her with a smile.

Her dad pulled back. "Well, this guy made sure I did."

Calix came to her side, and she gazed up at him. "You invited my dad?"

He gave the slightest shrug, as if to dismiss the effort.

"I can't believe you did that. *How* did you do that?"

"I had Violet ask your mom for me." He reached his hand out to her dad. "Glad to meet you in person, Mr. Romano."

As they shook hands, her heart filled to overflowing. She was just so happy to have Calix with her. Happy that he'd shown up at the train station and chosen to be with her, and happy that he'd cared enough to get her dad to come to the show.

"Calix is an unusual name." Her dad was six feet tall and had a solid build, but he was dwarfed by Calix.

She looped an arm through Calix's. "He has unusual parents."

"It's Greek, and it means 'very handsome.'" Calix smiled. "We're not Greek, and no one would call the Bourbons handsome, so I have no explanation for the name."

"I see. Well, Calix, it's nice to meet you." He had his gaze fixed on where their arms joined. "You never did say how you knew my daughter."

"He's with Blue Fire, Dad. He's the guy on the motorcycle."

Her dad's eyes narrowed on Calix. "You brought my daughter into the city on a motorcycle?"

Mimi burst out laughing. "No, Dad."

"I took the truck. This time."

Not many people stood up to her dad, and Mimi found it hot that Calix had.

Her dad rocked back on his heels, clearly not too happy with her taste in friends. "I see."

Calix might not know it, but he'd just been deleted from Dino Romano's files. She knew without a doubt the next time she mentioned Calix's name, her dad would say, "And who is that?"

"So." Her dad rubbed his hands together. "We'll have dinner." Her dad said it to Mimi, as though Calix no longer existed.

Mimi drew Calix closer. "You hungry, sweet cheeks?"

Calix gazed at her with mischief in his eyes. "I could eat, sweet pants."

"Good." Her dad turned, heading toward the exit. "We'll

celebrate tonight's victory, and I'll share my good news with you."

"News?"

He pulled her closer to the wall, away from the chaos. "I've made some calls." He shrugged, like it was no big deal. "I spoke with Monte Camarillo."

Mimi crashed. All the adrenaline from the day—Calix icing her out, the high stress of the show, the shock of seeing her dad in the audience—just knocked her on her ass. "Dad."

"Send him a résumé. He's looking forward to meeting you." Her dad gave her a knowing smile. "Their specialty is franchise equity investments, which is a great place for you to be. And he said their director of investor relations could use some help."

Bringing up Miami now? Really? "No, thank you."

He looked like she'd refused the winnings from a lottery ticket. "Excuse me?"

"Dad, I'm in the middle of a competition."

"I'm aware of that. You did a wonderful job today. I'm so proud of you." He clapped a hand on her shoulder. "You're doing great, but when it's over . . ." He shrugged again, still smiling. "You'll take this very good opportunity with the boys in Florida." He grew serious. "And it's a necessary path to work with me."

Necessary path? "You know something, Dad? I'm going to take a rain check on that dinner. I've got a splitting headache. It's been a really rough twelve hours, and I just need to crash."

"That's fine. I'll take you home. You'll stay with me tonight, and I'll make you fettuccine."

A strong arm wrapped around her shoulders, drawing her tight to Calix's warm, hard body. "We've got plans, Mr. Romano, but thank you."

Her dad's jaw hardened, and he gave Calix a challenging look. Then, he softened when he looked at Mimi. "Melie, my love. We'll have dinner. You'll watch a movie." He said it with so much affection she found it hard to stay angry.

"I don't think so, Dad. Honestly the last thing I want to talk about is a job opportunity in Miami—or Paris or Hong

Kong. Because I'm going to win this competition, and to do that, I have to keep my head in the game."

"Amelia. Stop this right now. You can't think . . ." He gestured impatiently. "You made a *salad*. You can't think my team will take you seriously for what you're doing here."

The cut burned, but she did her best to ignore it. She got up on her toes and planted a kiss on his after-shave-scented cheek. "Of course they'll take me seriously. This show's going to open doors that'll not only be new to you but otherwise unavailable to an unemployed twenty-four-year-old." She couldn't keep the exhaustion from her voice. "This isn't a reality TV show. It's a cooking show. And people will want to feed off the celebrity that will flow from it. I'll be known as the Ivy League MBA chef who gets shit done." She gazed up at him. "Come on, Dad. I've trusted your judgment for years. Don't you think it's time you returned the favor?"

As she and Calix made their way down the crowded corridor, she called over her shoulder, "Thanks for coming, though. I really appreciate it."

Mimi hadn't even pulled her keys out of the lock before Calix had her up against the wall inside her apartment, his big hands cupping her ass, his mouth hot and hungry over hers. He kissed her slowly, deeply, and so sensuously she lost herself in him completely.

When he tried to push closer and met with her messenger bag, he pulled away. Eyes glazed, mouth wet and lips swollen, he let her down like he couldn't bear to take his hands off her.

Lifting her braids, he pulled off the bag and immediately had her back up against the wall. His tongue stroked inside her mouth, and his hips rocked into her. "Need you naked."

She was so hot, so wildly submersed in sensation, she could barely force her lips to form words. "Shower."

"The best kind of naked."

She grinned against his mouth. "You have to set me down first."

"Not letting you go." He carried her across the small living room and kneed the bathroom door open. She had to tighten her legs and arms around him when he leaned into the shower stall to turn on the faucet. The moment he set her down, he reached behind his neck and pulled his shirt off. "Naked, sweet pants. Now."

With all this energy racing through her, her fingers didn't have the strength to manipulate the stud of her jeans. He batted her hands away, popping the button and unzipping them. He yanked them down, and she kicked off her Converse so he could pull them off her legs.

As he shoved off his own jeans, she started to work the elastics in her hair.

"Leave the braids."

A sharp sting of awareness sizzled through her, and she shuddered.

His eyes flared. "Does that have something to do with your fantasy?"

She nodded, trying for a mischievous smile, but she was too worked up to pull it off. "That's for you to find out."

Gripping her hips, he pulled her up against him. "Tell me."

God, she loved his possessive hold on her. "You'll know. When you do it to me, you'll definitely know."

"Fuck, Mimi." He drew her T-shirt over her head. She lifted her arms, but before he could pull the shirt off, his hands covered her breasts, plumping them together in the lacy bra. He lowered his face into her cleavage and licked.

She moaned as a fiery wash of sensation swept through her. Needing to see him, she tore the shirt off and then reached behind to unhook her bra.

Calix dropped to his knees, pressing his nose to her lacy boy shorts. He clutched her ass, drawing her to his face. The moment he licked her clit through her panties, electricity flashed through her.

Her hips rocked, and he pushed the lace aside. And then his tongue was inside her, making a delicious sweep that forced her up on her toes. Her fingers dug into his silky hair as she tried to keep her knees from buckling.

His tongue flicked over her clit, his hands gripping her ass, spreading her cheeks. She wanted to see him, his whole body, his expression, but honest to God, he had her in a state of arousal so wild she couldn't move a muscle.

Her legs shook, and her fingers fisted in his hair. The burn spread along her limbs, tingling to the soles of her feet, and her head tipped back as all her senses narrowed to the rising climax that rose so powerfully it threatened to obliterate her. "Mother of God."

Sliding two fingers inside, he rubbed her inner walls, making her feverish with desire. The tension churned through her, tightening until—Oh, God—ecstasy burst free, sending her soaring, toppling through the air.

His licks turned more languid, more sensual, sparking one climax after another.

When her fingers relaxed in his hair, he sat back on his heels, eyeing her with fierce hunger.

Hands on his knees, he stood up. "Naked."

The moment she skimmed off her panties, he grabbed her arm and practically shoved her into the tub, rolling the door so hard it slammed and the glass rattled. Angling her under the spray, he tipped her head back, letting the warm water spread across her scalp.

His mouth opened on her neck, his tongue flicking gently, sensuously, as his hands caressed from her shoulders down to her hands. "Mimi." He whispered her name like a blessing.

She reached for the body wash, popped the top, and poured some in her palm. Then she rubbed her hands together, spreading the lather across his muscular chest. His rock-hard erection at her stomach demanded attention, so she caressed down his torso.

When she wrapped her soapy hands around him, he hissed in a breath, reaching behind to clutch her ass and give it a squeeze. Swirling her hands in opposite directions, she tugged on him, watching his expression turn wild with pleasure.

When she started to lower herself to her knees, he reached under her arms and dragged her up his body. "As much as I want your mouth on me, I need to be inside you. Need to make you mine."

Make you mine. Didn't he know? She was his. She'd give him everything she had if only he wanted it.

He reached for the body wash, lathered up, and then soaped the back of her neck, his strong fingers kneading the tense muscles down to her shoulders, where he massaged with firm, delicious strokes.

"That feels so good." She couldn't help eyeing that erection, so hard it knocked against his belly. Without thinking, she reached for him.

He jerked his hips back. "Mimi."

"Need you." She wanted him so badly. She knew the feel of him in her mouth, the ridge on her tongue. The taste of him at the back of her throat.

"It'll be over too fast." His features hardened as he made slow, soapy circles down her chest until he found her breasts.

She moaned as those big hands slid over her, cupping and pushing them together. His fingers circled her nipples, gentle, soft strokes. So good. Between her legs, she pulsed and ached with need. And then his hands glided down her stomach until one finger parted her curls and stroked inside. Sensation tore through her, and she arched into him. One hand skimmed her ass, fingers teasing between the cheeks, while the other swept through her sensitive folds.

"Calix." Her heart thundered, and a flash flood of desire threatened to knock her knees out.

"Rinse." He turned her to the spray, washing the soap off. By the time she'd finished, he was waiting by the sink, one towel wrapped around his waist, the other open for her.

Holy Mother of God, that bare chest. Broad shoulders, tan skin, a smattering of silky soft hair, and that mouthwatering expanse of ripped torso that tapered to powerful hips. The man had the body of a warrior.

She walked into his arms, pressing her mouth to his warm, damp skin, and he quickly toweled her off.

"Bed. Now."

"My hair." She started to turn to the mirror when he lifted her, delivering her to the neatly made bed and gently setting her down.

Thighs pressed to the edge of the mattress, he watched her

for a moment, feral hunger so clear on his features she squirmed. She cupped her breasts, pushing them together, and pinched her nipples.

He got on his knees and stalked toward her, his intention so carnal, so wicked, her thighs clamped together and her hips lifted off the bed. But those big hands gripped her knees and pushed her legs apart. His face went between her legs, and just as he got close enough to lick, he pulled back. His finger stroked the ink between her hips and pelvis. "Mimi."

She smiled because he'd found it. Only two other guys had ever gotten to see it.

Slowly, he looked up at her. "Who did this to you?"

Not when or why, but who. She loved his possessiveness. "A tattoo artist in the East Village."

His thumb stroked across it.

"Do you like it?" Her voice shook.

"It's fucking hot." His tongue traced the path of bluebirds holding a string of tiny red hearts from her hip bone to just below her bikini line. "Really fucking hot." With a big hand on each thigh, holding her wide open, he looked up at her. "Why'd you get it?"

"I want the men I let inside me to know they mean something. That I only let them in because they've touched my heart."

A shadow crossed his features, and he turned harsh. "How many men have seen it?"

"Are you going to tell me how many women you've been with?"

He made a sound at the back of his throat that voiced his displeasure, and then he licked inside her. Long, sensuous caresses that made her burn. When his tongue swirled around her clit, she grabbed his head to keep him *right there*. "God, oh, God."

Fire lashed through her core. She grabbed fistfuls of his hair as his tongue flicked faster and harder over her nub. "Calix, I—" And then it hit. Sensation whisked her right out of her mind, sent her spinning and tumbling, and God, it just kept rolling through her in waves.

As her senses slowly returned, she relaxed her fingers and

let out a rush of breath. Her entire body quaked. "That was . . . God."

He let go of her legs, rising over her, and she reached for his cock.

His eyes closed, and his head tipped back, the corded muscles in his neck straining. She gave him a few pumps. "Okay. Fuck. Jesus." He grabbed the base of his dick. "Condom."

Funny how she felt so close to this man, their intimacy so intense, she'd forgotten they hadn't been together in this way before. She leaned toward the nightstand, but it was just out of her reach.

"Top drawer?" He yanked it open and pulled one out. Tearing it open with his teeth, he quickly sheathed himself. His fingers went between her legs, stroking her overly sensitive flesh. "You're so fucking wet." Again, he gripped his cock, found her throbbing center, and then gently eased himself in. A rush of color spread across his cheeks, and his biceps strained with his effort to go slowly. "You on birth control?"

She nodded. With each gentle thrust, he eased deeper and deeper inside. She loved that he was letting her body adjust to him, even when she knew how desperate he was for relief.

"Yes." He was so close to bottoming out, and she was so wet for him. "Do it." She lifted her hips, grabbed his ass, and pulled him hard against her.

His eyes closed, and he made a growl of deep satisfaction as he pushed all the way in. "You good?"

"So good."

"Can't hold back anymore."

"Don't hold back. Never hold back."

"Love when you say that, Meems." He dropped his head into the curve of her neck and started thrusting. Hard, fast. His hand shifted under her ass, lifting her, and she wrapped her legs around him. "Wanna watch you come." His elbows locked as he powered into her, eyes glazed with lust. "Fantasy number one." His words came out rough, gravelly. "Looking at you like this. Under me. Your hair on the pillow." He squeezed his eyes shut, lust seizing his features. And then they slowly opened, and he gazed at her with pure, unabashed desire. "Fantasy number two, that fucking mouth." He lowered for a kiss, claiming his prize with a brutal hunger. His thrusts turned more desperate, and he tore his mouth away.

When he got up on his knees, he grabbed her hips, dragging her toward him and spreading her thighs wide. He eased back in—slowly, lusciously—watching her expression, and when her eyelids lowered and her back arched, he slammed back into her. Each deep thrust stroked over the sensitive spot of her inner wall, sparking pleasure, driving her higher, closer, to a deliciously unbearable pressure. Again and again he pounded into her, leaning forward so his pelvis scraped against her clit. A flash flood of desire engulfed her, and she came with a gasp as she planted her feet on the mattress and slammed her hips up to meet his thrusts.

"Gonna come now, Meems. Gonna come so fucking hard." He lost his rhythm, slamming into her with quick, hard punches of his hips. And then his head snapped back. "Fuck." His eyes closed, jaw tightened, as he came long and hard.

And then he collapsed on top of her, his face in her neck. "Beautiful."

Holy shit. That had been the most intense sex she'd ever had. And not only did she love the way he handled her body—considerate but aggressive—but she'd never felt more cherished.

He rolled off her, falling onto his side, one arm cinching around her waist, as his breathing slowed.

She couldn't believe it. Calix Bourbon in her bed. Hottest sex of her life.

And *feelings*. Oh, the feelings.

Please, please, please, don't bail on me again.

She turned to look at him, a fervent wish taking hold of her.

Please be mine.

CHAPTER THIRTEEN

The smell of Chinese food lingered in the apartment. Maybe it was the roller coaster of emotions—or maybe it was Calix's sexy bare chest beside her in bed—but Mimi just couldn't seem to muster up an appetite.

"You okay?" Using chopsticks, he picked up a piece of his kung pao chicken.

"Sure, why?"

"You're not eating."

"I'm not all that hungry." She jammed the chopsticks into the rice.

"Your dad?"

"Yeah. Now you see why I've kept my distance."

"I do."

"I can't believe you got him to come to the competition. You never said a word."

He shrugged. "Wasn't sure if he'd show."

"That was incredibly sweet of you. Seriously, Calix, thank you."

"Kind of wish I hadn't. I didn't think . . . I don't know why he had to bring up Miami."

A hint of color seeped into his cheeks, and he focused intensely on his chopsticks.

But she wouldn't let him feel bad for her father's stupidity. "I love that he came. Even more, I love that you invited him. It's not your fault he ruined it." Feeling a little sick to her stomach, she set the carton on the nightstand. "Honestly, though, it wasn't the job in Miami that got me. It was the way he said, *You made a salad.* That just . . . wow."

"Yeah, but what you told him? About why you're doing the competition? That was badass."

"Yeah?"

"Oh, yeah." He squeezed her thigh. "He's gonna think on that."

"I hope so, but I'm afraid he'll be so stubborn, he won't give me a job unless I follow the exact path he sets out."

"You happy doing what you're doing?"

When she thought about it, she realized she had so much more going on in her life than just the show. She loved cooking for the band, and to her great surprise, she'd loved planning the clambake. And the wedding? "I *am*." She smiled. "I totally am. Maybe it's because it's temporary, though. I think I've been so fixated on the end goal that I've never done anything just for fun. It's like I've felt these hands at my back, pushing, prodding, hurrying me along. Get an A on the test, a perfect score on the SAT, the right summer internship. I've never done something on a whim."

"Well, you look good doing it."

"What does that mean?"

"I've seen you in your business suits with your hair all straight and shiny and—don't get me wrong, you're on fire—but you're stressed. The woman at the farm? With her curls and her pajama bottoms? Her hands all covered in dough?" He shrugged. "She's warm. Fun. Happy." He gave her thigh another squeeze. "Sexy as fuck."

The sweetest rush of pleasure spread through her, and she leaned into him, pressing a kiss right over his heart. "I am happy." Lowering her head to the pillow, she lifted the sheet and covered her face.

"What're you doing?" He sounded amused.

"I'm hiding."

"I see that. Why?"

"Because I'm happy goofing off when I know I should be taking my life seriously. It's like taking a gap year before you start college. Before I know it, I'll be back on track, but I'll have this awesome memory of the year I played hooky." And had *amazing* sex with Calix Bourbon.

He whipped off the sheet. "You do realize you don't have to jump through hoops, right?"

"What's that mean?"

"Sweet pants, you've got it all. You can do anything you want with your life." He leaned in close. "The world's your oyster."

"I want to work for my dad."

"Yeah? 'Cause I admire your tenacity and all, but at some point you gotta wonder if you're so focused on getting hired by your dad that you're ignoring other possibilities that might make you even happier."

She sat up. "No, no, it's like cake. I'm having a few slices of fun right now, but it'll get old soon enough, and I'm going to want something better for me. I do want to work for my dad."

"Okay. It just seems like the moment you stop jumping through his hoops . . ." He shrugged. "World's gonna crack wide open for you."

World's gonna crack wide open for you. Was she so single-minded, she'd shut out other possibilities? She didn't like to see herself in that light. She saw herself as driven, ambitious, the kind of woman who knocks down walls to get what she wants.

But she hadn't knocked anything down. She was more like a windup toy banging into the same wall over and over.

Oh, she didn't like that image one bit. "Fuck-a-rama." She threw back the covers, swung her legs off the bed, and headed for her closet.

Yanking the silk robe off the hook, she jabbed an arm into it. God, she'd never even considered what she wanted to do with her life. She'd bypassed the whole doctor, lawyer, CEO discussion because she'd been so intent on working with her dad.

On *being* with him.

An arm belted around her waist and pulled her back onto the bed. Calix's strong hands turned her to face him. "What just happened?" That deep, rough voice warmed her blood.

"I think I'm just really tired."

"Sweet pants." His tone held a warning. He wasn't going to put up with evasion, and she *loved* that. Loved that he wanted to know her, cared enough to listen to her.

"It was the idea that I'd *limit* myself. Shut myself down. Because I did. I totally did that. And I know why. God, I can even tell you the exact moment it happened."

Calix tipped her chin, forcing her to look into those dark, intense eyes. "Tell me."

"I was eight, and my mom went on this four-day cruise with her friends. She'd made it very clear to my dad that he couldn't work. This was his chance to spend quality time with his daughter. I can't even tell you how excited I was. Time alone with my dad? No interruptions? He couldn't cut me off mid-sentence to read an e-mail or text. He couldn't leave the table to take a call. He was all mine. I was beyond happy."

"I'll bet."

"I made a list in my head of all the things I wanted to do." She could actually see that piece of notebook paper—the edges torn from the binding—and the grape-scented ink she'd used to write it. "I wanted a tea party. I wanted him to play Barbies with me. I wanted to finally put together the Lego motorcycle set I'd gotten for Christmas."

Calix smiled. "I got that same one. Spent one whole morning putting that fucker together, and then Gus comes running into the room to tell me we were going for ice cream, and he slammed right into it. Never played with Legos again."

"I don't blame you. That's terrible."

He smiled warmly. "Go on."

"Okay, so tea party, dolls, Legos." She tried to recall what else she'd had on that list. "Oh, I wanted to go to the Central Park Zoo and the carousel. And number one on my list, I wanted to go to Serendipity."

"Sounds like a good plan for four days."

"We didn't make it through the first day. During the tea party, he got up from the table so fast he knocked everything over." Watching that brown liquid drip off the plastic table onto the fluffy white rug had made her cry. The stain had looked so ugly in her otherwise pristine room.

"Why'd he get up?"

"He got a call. And when we were on the floor playing Barbies, he was shouting so angrily at whoever was on the phone that I actually felt bad for my dolls. I remember tucking them back in their cases so they wouldn't have to hear it, because they'd only ever known quiet play with me." She glanced up at him. "I can't believe I just told you that."

"Tell me more."

Her heart squeezed with so much warmth for him. "So, we did go to the zoo, and that was fun. We got to see them feeding the sea lions, and we probably watched the puffins for three days." She shot him a look. "That's in kid time."

He smiled at her like she utterly delighted him. He couldn't know what that meant to her—*she* hadn't known until she'd received such unadulterated interest from a man who mattered so much to her.

But she hadn't finished yet. "And then we got to Serendipity. When the hostess told him the wait would be an hour and a half, he lost it. He grabbed my hand and pushed through the crowd, shoving me in the car. Oh, my God, I was mortified. Everyone was staring at me—not at him, but me." She glanced up at him again. "You know what's funny? I remember touching my ears. They felt so hot, and I imagined them all red, like your skin after a hot shower."

He kissed the shell of her ear, and her hand came up to cup his cheek.

"Anyway, that was the last I saw of him. The rest of the weekend I hung out with my nanny because my mom wasn't around to arrange playdates."

He shifted lower, tipped her chin, and pressed a kiss to her mouth. "I'm sorry."

That had been the turning point. When she'd started doing

things that would involve her dad in her life. "You know why I joined Future Business Leaders of America?"

"No fucking idea."

She laughed. A rush of affection made her turn in his arms, wrap her arms around his neck. She'd never shared this story with anyone, and she was glad she'd done it with him. "Because I could get my dad to come as a speaker. To work on projects with us. I applied to all the schools he wanted me to because I knew it'd get him involved. He'd research the programs, take me on college visits. And it worked. He did all of that."

"Is it still working for you?"

"Well, it's not like I'm going to give up everything I've worked so hard for. And I do think I'll kick ass as a restaurateur. This competition, cooking for the band? Knowing all aspects of the business will only make me even stronger."

"But maybe remembering that weekend will free you a little, in case he doesn't wind up hiring you for some reason."

For a moment the world came to a screeching halt. *Was* there a possibility her dad wouldn't hire her? No, he wouldn't do that. He'd told her he wanted her to take over the business. *Of course he'll hire me.*

Right?

He ran his fingers through her hair. "You okay?"

She nodded. "Yeah." And then she turned into him, chest to chest. "Though I'm thinking . . . you could probably make it even better."

"Might take some time." He rolled her onto her back, his warm hand sliding under her silk robe and sweeping up her chest to gently palm her breast.

Heat flared across her skin. She leaned into his touch. "Oh, I've got time. For you, sweet cheeks, I've got all the time in the world."

And then he kissed her, his tongue stroking into her mouth, his hand gently squeezing her breast. She wrapped her arms around his back, wanting to feel all that smooth, warm skin. Her legs shifted restlessly. She wanted him between them, wanted to feel his weight on her, the silky strands of his hair on her skin.

He pushed the robe off her shoulders. "Want all of you."

She sat up just enough for him to pull it off and toss it. And then he shifted on top of her, and she got the skin-on-skin contact she craved. His hand found her breast again, and he lowered to lick her nipple. When his mouth closed over her, the warm wet suction sent her body into a state of pure, hot arousal.

The trill of a phone tore her out of her sensual haze. He got up, leaving her cold, naked, and stunned.

"Yeah?"

Shaken, Mimi drew the sheet up to cover herself. If her phone had rung, she'd have ignored it. Whoever it was . . . it could wait.

"Dammit." The muscles across his broad back tensed as he hunched over, tugging hard on one of his leather bands. "Yeah, okay. Make some calls. See if someone knows where they are." He got up, stalking into the bathroom and swiping his boxers off the floor. With the phone cradled between his shoulder and chin, he stepped into them, hauled them up and over his hips. "I can be home in an hour and a half." He snatched his shirt off the vanity. "Hey. Lee? Keep me updated." Coming back out of the bathroom, he tossed his phone on the chair as he pulled his shirt on and then scooped his jeans off the floor. "I gotta get back."

"What's going on?"

"Gus just loaded up his truck."

He stuffed his phone in his pocket and then snagged his keys off the dresser.

"And?"

Finally, he looked at her. "Says he's moving in with Laney. Got their own place."

"Okay."

Finally, he seemed to realize he was leaving a naked woman in bed. He stopped, taking her in. "I've gotta get home."

"Why?"

"What do you mean why? I just told you. Gus's moving out."

"What can you do about it tonight?"

"Find out where he's going."

"How?" She'd never seen him like this. Like a SWAT team leader in the middle of a call-out.

"Ask around."

"And then what?"

He let out an impatient breath. "And then I talk to him."

"You're going to force him to move back home?"

"He can't live with that girl."

"Isn't that what he's doing?"

"Okay." He dismissed her, working his foot into a boot.

"He's twenty-three. Exactly how are you going to get him to come home?"

"I don't have time for this."

As he gave her that same *You don't understand* tone, it struck her that Calix wasn't an unreasonable man. It wasn't worry about his brother moving out that compelled him.

He was panicked. Fear had a grip on him, and he'd gone into take-charge mode.

He needed to get back to base so he could get a handle on the situation.

And get his eyes on his mom.

She totally got it. Everything in her softened as she called up an image of Calix pacing the house with his mom for fourteen hours as they waited to find out what had happened to Hopper. That sick feeling in the pit of his stomach, the helplessness.

And of him waiting in the hospital to find out whether or not she'd survive her overdose.

He'd given up his apartment, his band, and his life to make sure she didn't try to take her life again.

She threw back the covers and got up. "I'll get dressed."

Relief flashed through him. And that was when she got something else. For as much as he was surrounded by his family and all those childhood friends, Calix was essentially alone. He shouldered the burden of his family's well-being by himself.

Walking right up to him, she wrapped her arms around his waist and held him close.

His body stiffened. "We need to get going."

But she ignored him, burrowing deeper. If she had any doubts about whether or not he wanted her comfort, they were dispelled when his arms wrapped loosely around her.

She slid a leg between his, getting even closer, and his hands shifted slowly across her back until his arms banded around her. And then he was holding her tightly, resting his chin on top of her head. They stood like that for several long moments until she leaned back. "Give me five minutes."

She gazed up into his eyes, watching the anxiety recede just slightly.

And then she got ready to go.

The band was on fire. Calix's fingers flew over the keyboard; everyone was in perfect sync. His dad had hired the tumbao group for a few days, which made the sound richer, fuller. And a hell of a lot more fun.

Movement behind the glass caught his eye, and when he looked up, he saw Gus entering the control room. A moment later, the door opened and Laney stumbled in, laughing.

No one had heard from Gus all weekend—not since he'd packed up his truck and moved out. And now, Monday morning, he showed up late and with *her*?

Calix stopped playing. Shit was about to get ugly.

Gus made a grab for Laney, but she flew out of his hold and slammed into Terrence, who whipped off his headphones and shoved his chair back.

Calix took off. As soon as he opened the door, he caught his dad's angry tone.

"Not discussing it with you. Don't have the time. Told you not to fuck up. You did."

Taking in his brother's bedhead, the dirty, wrinkled clothes, and the bloodshot eyes, Calix caught hold of his upper arm and ushered him and Laney out the door, through the lounge, and into the bright sunlight of a May afternoon.

He stepped right up to Laney. "I told you not to come here."

"I'm just dropping him off." Underneath that thick black

eyeliner and cheaply dyed blond hair, she was probably a pretty girl. But she looked harsh and worn-out, and he couldn't miss the wary look in her eyes. This girl had been wounded, and she wasn't done fighting back.

He didn't want to add to her hurt, but he couldn't let her cause trouble around here. "Next time you drop him off, don't get out of your truck."

Gus pushed between him and Laney. "You don't have to talk to her like that."

"She's not welcome here, and you know that. So does she."

"I'm *with* him." She reached for Gus's hand. "Come on, baby, let's go."

Gus gently peeled her off. "Lane, wait in the truck. I want to talk to my brother."

"You're gonna stand up for me, right?"

His brother looked supremely uncomfortable. "Go. I'll be right there."

She bit down on her bottom lip, watching him carefully. "Your family sucks."

Calix gave her a hard look. "His family cares about him."

"So do I."

"Really? Because you might've just gotten him fired."

"It's his *dad*. His dad's not going to fire him." Pressing up to Gus, she gave him a long, wet kiss. Gus set his hands on her hips and pushed her back. "You know why he likes me?" she asked over her shoulder. "'Cause I'm a hell of a lot more fun than you assholes." She sashayed back down the driveway.

Gus ran a hand through his hair. "We had to get furniture for the new place. We don't have any."

"You get it after work. You don't bail on your job."

"Can you get off my back? You and I both know this isn't about furniture. It's about me moving out. Look, I get it. I know you think I'm bailing on Mom, but I'm not. I'm gonna be over as often as I can. But come on, I gotta have a life."

"You want a life with Laney Morrison?" He shook his head. "That girl is trouble."

"Only when you treat her like shit. She gets defensive and turns bitchy, I know that. But when I'm alone with her, she's different. She's pretty cool. And you know what? She's fun.

And wild. And I *need* that." He looked off toward the ocean, obviously deeply conflicted. "You don't know how much I need that."

"Did you know she fucked with Slater and Emmie?"

His eyes went wide.

"Slater didn't want anything to do with her, so she got naked and waited for him in bed. *Emmie's* bed. After Ben scraped her off, she tried to hook up with Cooper. He brought her to a bonfire one night, and she took a swing at Violet."

Gus's features tightened, and he looked away.

"That's why she's not allowed here."

"She's not like that anymore."

"Because she has you?"

"Yeah, man. Because I make her feel worthwhile."

"Okay." He pulled on his scruff. He wasn't going to get him to give up the girl. "You do what you gotta do, but the band's not gonna tolerate you showing up hungover or high. And they're definitely not gonna put up with you making your own hours. These guys are serious about their music, and the only people they let in are on their level."

Gus kicked at the gravel, blowing out a shaky breath.

"You want this?" Calix asked.

His head snapped up, squinting in the sunlight. "You know I do."

"I think you know Dad's not gonna tolerate this shit. I'll talk to him, but it might be too late." He rubbed the back of his neck. "Hear me on this one, though. You don't want to be associated with the woman who fucked with Emmie and Violet."

"Yeah, I get it. Just . . . it means a lot to her to be part of this."

"She's not, and she never will be."

"Yeah, okay."

He drew his brother in for a hug. "Come by the house tonight and talk to Dad. Let him know you've got your head on right, and that you're not gonna fuck up again."

Gus nodded tersely, then turned to go.

"Oh, and text me your address, okay?"

His brother just gave a half-hearted wave over his shoulder as he headed down the driveway.

He could see his brother's struggle, and he didn't have a clue how to make things right. Like everyone else, Gus needed to find his legs in the world, and Calix guessed this thing with Laney had to run its course.

But at what cost?

I'm here. ♥

Happiness shot through him, and he shoved the phone into his back pocket. It'd take her a few minutes to get from the main house to his cottage, so maybe he'd toss his laundry in the dryer. Clean up a little.

On his way, though, he stopped at the window, peering out into the darkness.

Impatience had him bursting out of his skin. He needed a beer, calm his shit. Stalking off to the kitchen, he yanked open the refrigerator, nabbed a bottle off the shelf. Popped the top.

Tipping his head back and letting the cold liquid slide down his throat, he closed his eyes. *Mimi.* Her neck arched, breasts thrust high, as he licked her soft, slick folds.

Fuck. She was so responsive. It made him wild for her. He palmed his dick, willing it to calm the fuck down.

He'd hardly seen her this week. Since his dad had signed the contract, the band was back in the studio full force. And that meant he'd had to miss her third competition—which she'd rocked. And Joey from Florida had failed.

He was used to seeing her every day—so that was probably why he was all worked up.

Eagerness coiled through him, making him edgy. It took all his discipline not to go out there, meet her halfway.

Are you fucking kidding me? He could wait. He'd wait.

Laundry. He headed into the small room that smelled strongly of detergent. Lifting the lid of the washing machine, he transferred the wet clothes to the dryer.

That night in her apartment . . . fuck, it had been good. Just thinking about her mouth, the slam and swivel of her hips, dammit. He squeezed his cock. It fucking ached.

Where was she? He started the machine, let the lid slam shut. As the walls closed in on him, he stalked back into the living room and threw open the front door, started down the stairs. He'd—

"Calix?" Her excitement hit him hard in the chest.

He curled his toes in his boots to keep from going after her.

And then he saw her. Racing toward him, all those curls sailing behind her, a smile so wide it made his heart thunder.

She ran, and he forced himself to stay put. This wasn't some movie scene. He wasn't going to catch her and spin her around or some shit.

And then she flew at him. Knocked him so hard he had to take a step back to keep from losing his balance. Her perfume swirled around him, and her hair brushed over his skin.

That's it. He was done. Grabbing a fistful of hair at the back of her neck, he tilted her head and found her mouth. Licking into the soft, wet heat made him go dizzy with want.

The moment he lifted her, her legs wrapped around him and her hands scraped into his hair. She kissed him with a hunger that sent him spinning. Lost in her, he was aware of nothing but the velvety stroke of her tongue and the press of her breasts against his chest.

He carried her up the steps and tumbled into the house, kissing her with all the pent-up need he'd shoved down all day.

Fuck. She tasted good, smelled good, and her hands—clutching, pulling, grabbing—edged him to that frantic place where he had to have her. His thigh slammed into the end table, but he didn't pull away. Just clutched her ass and stumbled to the couch.

Dropping onto the cushion, he draped her legs on either side of him. She rolled over his cock, hands digging into his hair, kissing him with fierce desire.

He pulled up her shirt, and she whisked it over her head. Even while kissing him, she reached around to unhook her bra and fling it aside. His hands glided up all the smooth skin of her back, until they hooked over her shoulders, pressing her harder to him.

"Take this off." She tugged on his shirt, before scrambling off him to peel down her jeans.

When she stood before him in just her panties, he grabbed her around the waist. "Come here." Drawing her closer, he yanked them down, and he couldn't help himself from taking a lick of that string of pretty red hearts. She honored him with this—giving herself to him—and he loved it. Fucking loved it. His tongue trailed the short path from the last heart to her clit, and then he gave it a luxurious swirl.

Her fingers curled into his hair. "Oh, Calix." She said it softly, sweetly, and it streamed through him like a melody.

He licked inside her, so slick and hot. Her fingers drove through his hair, pressing on his scalp, urging him on.

More. He needed more. Catching her hips, he tipped her onto the couch. He fell to his knees on the floor, burying his face between her legs, so fucking turned on when her hips rose and she slammed against his mouth, fingers fisting in his hair. His tongue stroked her, long licks with a circle over her clit with each pass. Each time she cried out, thrusting harder, pulling on his hair.

He loved that she lost herself, let herself go so completely with him. It turned him on like nothing else.

Fuck, his cock ached. He popped the buttons on his jeans, reached into his boxers, and gave himself a hard squeeze. And when she lurched forward, when she curled over him, chanting, "Yes, yes, oh, God, yes," he focused his tongue on her clit, licking her through an orgasm that had her body convulsing with pleasure.

"Oh, my God." She collapsed onto her back, breathing heavily. "I missed you."

But he couldn't talk. He needed to be inside her. Now. He pushed her back on the couch, lowering himself on top of her, pressing his dick hard against her stomach. He fucking ached. Caressing her breast, he sucked the nipple into his mouth, and she arched up into him.

"God. *God.*"

She clutched at him, ground against his cock. He was going out of his mind, but he had to get a condom.

"I'm clean, Calix. You know I am."

"Yeah, me, too." But he didn't want to go bare. He'd never done it before, and . . . *you don't go bare with someone you're just dating.* "Hang on a second."

He tore himself off her, feeling his skin cool as he walked down the dark hallway to his bedroom. Good to have a moment alone. Pull himself together. He hated how carried away he got with her.

Bare feet slapped on the wood floor, and her laughter filled the cottage as she whipped past him, flinging herself onto his bed. Rolling onto her back, she rose up on her elbows and watched him with a mischievous smile.

Grabbing a condom out of his nightstand, his hands shook as he tore open the packet.

She lunged for him. "I want to do it." Eyes gleaming, she clasped his dick with her warm hands.

Sensation shot through him. "Shit, Mimi."

"Oh, my God, look at you. You're so hot, you make me crazy." When her hair spilled forward, need bore down on him and fucking her became an imperative. But her mouth closed over the head of his dick, and he shouted from the overwhelming pleasure of warm, wet suction.

Her hands gripped him, and her tongue swirled around his head, raw desire ripping through him. She licked him like he was dessert. Like she loved his cock. And then she sucked him in, that wicked tongue flicking up and down his length.

"Stop. Jesus, Mimi." He pulled her off his dick because, dammit, he had to have her *right fucking now.* He pushed her back, her head landing on the soft pillow, the look in her eyes so mischievous, so hungry, so fucking pornographic, he barely gave her a moment to settle in. His arms went under her knees, and he lifted her legs, pushing inside, watching that graceful neck arch, that lush mouth fall open, and her eyes turn lusty.

And then he was fucking her. Her breasts bounced, her neck strained, and her hips pitched up, meeting his thrusts. Fuck, she felt good. *So good.*

Pleasure spread like fire, crackling and sparking. He was close. "Fuck."

She pushed her breasts together, fingers digging into the plump flesh and rubbing her pretty pink nipples.

"Holy fuck, Mimi." He wanted it to last, so he slowed his strokes. Savoring every pass through her tight, slick-as-fuck channel. He knocked her hand aside, so he could grasp her breast and lick her nipple. And then he pulled out. "Roll over."

Her expression turned carnal, and recognition snapped. Was this her fantasy? Him taking her from behind? Quickly, she flipped onto her stomach, hoisting her ass in the air. Her face turned into the bedding, and he could see the raw desire. This was absolutely her fantasy.

Gripping her hips, he slid slowly inside. Her eyes closed, and she gave a rapturous sigh.

Oh, fuck, yes.

He started pumping, taking his time, not wanting to lose it too soon, not when she was so obviously turned on. He leaned forward, reaching for her tits, squeezing them gently at first, but then, when her ass rammed back into him, he palmed her more roughly.

Fuck, she liked it. She liked it a lot. Screw taking his time. Need beat an urgent tattoo in his bloodstream. His balls tightened, and electricity pulsed down his spine right into his cock. "Mimi." Up on his knees, he gripped her hips and drew her back hard against him. Her arms stretched out in front of her, fingers fisting in the pillow.

He needed her to come. Right fucking now. Slipping a hand between her legs, he found her clit, rubbed, and that was it. Her back bowed, and she cried out. He'd never heard a purer sound of ecstasy in his life.

With her face pressed into the sheets, he slammed into her again and again, harder and harder. She whimpered, moaned, knuckles white with tension.

Oh, Christ. His legs trembled, his spine tingled, and then sensation blew up so hot and wild he clamped on to her hips, held on tight, and ground his cock into her. He came in scalding hot bursts of pleasure. "Fuck." It kept coming, wave after wave of euphoria. Jesus, it wouldn't stop. "Fuck!"

His thrusts slowed, each slide lighting up his still-sensitive cock.

He collapsed on top of her, then immediately rolled to the side. So intense.

Too intense. His body quaked with his explosive release. The moment she reached for him, he pulled away. Got out of bed. "Be right back."

In the bathroom, he snagged a few sheets of toilet paper, wadded up the condom, and tossed it. Resting his hands on the counter, he leaned forward, needing a moment to get his shit together.

What was happening? What the motherlovingfuck was he doing?

Was it all the stress—Gus moving in with Laney, and his dad working for Blue Fire?

Too much shit threatening his mom?

Because he was completely out of control.

He splashed some cold water on his face. He'd head out to the living room, grab their clothes, and pull his shit together. But when he came out, he found her sprawled on her back, that luscious body naked, those curls spilling all over his white pillowcase. Emotion flared and then tightened in his chest.

She was so fucking beautiful. His heart . . . He thought it might explode.

He quickly turned from her, grabbing a pair of boxers from the top drawer of his dresser. "You want something to drink?" Stepping into them, he shot her a quick look, waiting for an answer.

She was up on her knees, crooking a finger and patting the bed. "I want to tell you something."

The need to get away warred with the pull to be near her, please her, make her happy—no, that was bullshit, she made *him* happy. She was fucking irresistible. He came back, sat on the edge of the bed, and she walked toward him on her knees, draping her arms around him, pressing her breasts just under his chin. "You almost got it."

He breathed her in, the faint scent of perfume on her skin, the gardenias in her shampoo. "Got what?"

She ran the tip of her nose up his cheek, nudging his hair back, and then whispered in his ear. "My fantasy."

Lust turned his body rigid. So, it *had* been taking her from behind. But . . . "What do you mean *almost*?"

"Close . . ." She slowly licked his earlobe. "But no cigar."

"Tell me."

"Where's the fun in that?" Her hands stroked down his chest and back. She pinched his nipple.

He grabbed her wrist. "It's taking you from behind, but what else? Just tell me."

"Why? Are we never having sex again? You done with me?"

He twisted around, grabbing her by the waist, and toppling her onto her back. "No fucking way am I done with you." Her legs immediately came around him, and he kissed her. Oh, fuck him, she tasted so good. This woman was passionate. She loved with all her heart.

And he needed it. Everything she had to give, he was starved for.

"Are you into spanking?" he asked. "Is that it?"

"You slap my ass, and I throat-punch you."

"Good. 'Cause I'm not into that shit."

"What are you into?"

"You." He said it too quickly, and he wished he could take it back. He was rushing ahead, and he had to slow down. Get a hold of himself.

But her smile told him it was too late. And since when did he think he could hide anything from her?

"I'm gonna grab a water. You want anything?"

This time he didn't wait for an answer.

CHAPTER FOURTEEN

When he got back to his room with the water bottles, he found her standing at his dresser, top drawer open, staring at a framed photograph.

She turned to him. "You keep Hopper in a drawer?"

A riot of energy whipped through him, and he snatched it out of her hands. Shoving it back under his T-shirts, he slammed the drawer shut.

The shirt she'd borrowed reached her knees. "Why don't you hang it on the wall?"

Handing her the water bottle, he gave a curt shake of his head, letting her know the conversation was done.

"What?" She tossed the bottle onto the bed. "It's been three years."

"Yeah, and I don't need that reminder every day."

She gave him a frustrated look. "It's not a reminder that he died, dummy. It's a celebration of his life. What he meant to you. The good memories."

"You don't understand." Dammit, he'd forgotten to bring back their clothes.

"All you can think about are the bad ones?"

Well, okay. Maybe she did understand.

"Tell me about them." She started for him.

But he went to the bed. Sat on the edge of the mattress. "Them what?"

"The bad ones. Tell me." She reached back into the drawer and pulled out the picture. Adjusting the brace at the back of the frame, she set it on top of the dresser.

Hopper smiled, his brown eyes trained on something just over Calix's shoulder, as if refusing to acknowledge him.

"Why would I do that?"

"So you can get rid of them and make room for the good ones."

He liked the sound of that, but he didn't believe for a second it would work.

Besides, he should get her home. No one had heard from Gus since his dad had fired him several days ago. And Gus still hadn't given anyone his new address, so there was no way to get in touch, see how he was doing.

He needed to find his brother. Gus showing up at work wasted, moving in with a groupie, getting fired? Shit was out of control, and it was time Calix did something about it.

"Calix?" That soft, sweet voice.

Sometimes he felt like he had his finger on the fast forward button, his heart racing as the world sped by in a blur. But she calmed him right down.

Even when she pushed, making him face shit he didn't want to deal with, it eased the pressure in his chest.

And the bad memories? Well, there was only one, really, that burned so bright in his gut. He *needed* to get it out.

Maybe even more than he needed to go on a wild-goose chase to find Gus in the middle of the night.

He looked at Hopper's picture—the most familiar face in the world. "My brother . . ." The muscle in his throat hardened into a knot.

Mimi reached for him, drawing him back so that they lay side by side on the big bed. With her head on his chest, not looking at him, she made it easier to continue.

Swallowing hurt like a bitch, so he waited for the knot to ease. He sifted her hair through his fingers until it did. "Hopper was a moody fucker. The older and more independent we got, the harder it was on him. Gus and I . . . we were pretty wild. It was all about music, girls, and hanging out with our friends. I mean, we spent time with Hopper, don't get me wrong. We loved him. But we were full of piss and vinegar. And that was tough on him."

Her hair tickled his chin, and he smoothed the silky, springy curls.

The next words balled up on his tongue. The hardest memory. The one he hadn't shared with anyone. She gazed up at him, and the look of kindness just tore him open.

"He didn't like to be alone. Especially at night. And for some reason, he only wanted to sleep in my bed."

She waited for him to say more, and when he didn't, she said, "He loved you the most."

Ice-cold pain lanced through him. "Yeah. Probably. I didn't mind it so much when we were younger, but as I got older, it pissed me off. And I . . ." These memories pelted him like hard, icy balls of hail. "I'd kick him out. Literally, I'd kick him until he fell out of my bed."

Her hand gripped his biceps. She got it.

Fuck me. Why had he done that? If he could take back anything in his life, it would be kicking his brother like that. The sound of his soft body hitting the floor was just as vivid today as it had been back then. "But he'd always climb right back in. Stubborn as fuck." He shifted, sitting straighter, as the worst memory clawed through him. "I loved my brother, I did. But I didn't want him in my bed. I wanted to be left alone."

"Of course you did. That's totally normal."

"One night I screamed at him. I . . ." *Fuck me.* "I grabbed him by his shirt and dragged him out of my bedroom." He would never forget the feel of those doughy shoulders in his hands, the heat coming off Hopper's overwrought body. The look in his brother's eyes as he waited for Calix to change his mind. Because, of course, he'd change his mind. Everyone always gave in to Hopper. "I shoved him out the door. And . . . *fuck.*"

Her fingers brushed his chest, a soothing stroke.

"The way he looked at me." That forlorn expression

haunted him. "I felt like a dick, but I wasn't going to back down. I was going to teach him that he couldn't sleep in my bed anymore. I was too old for that." Perspiration beaded over his lip, and he swiped it away. "I got back into bed, watching my door. Because I *knew*. I knew he'd come back in. And I was ready."

She pressed her face into his chest. He could tell she didn't want to hear this.

"And, of course, the door opened. I launched the first weapon, but it was a pillow so it just hit him and fell to the floor. Hopper just stared at me, like I hadn't just thrown something at him. Like he was waiting for me to break and pull back the blanket to let him in. So I threw the book that was on my nightstand. It hit him right in the face, and I shouted for him to get the fuck out."

She burrowed deeper into his chest, her warm breath on his skin.

"It took me forever to fall asleep that night." That panicky feeling started up in his chest. "The next morning I was disgusted with myself. I stared up at the ceiling remembering his face, the way I'd shouted at him, and I was sick to my stomach. I had to fix it, you know? I was gonna make him his favorite pancakes."

"What were his favorite pancakes?"

Calix smiled, running his fingers through her hair. "Buttermilk. With a smiley face. Strawberry slices for the mouth, chocolate chips for the eyes, the tip of the banana for the nose, and whipped cream hair."

"I want that."

"Not gonna make it for you, Meems."

"You totally are."

He stroked her hair, lifting the curls and letting them fall through his fingers.

Yeah, he totally was.

"You ready to tell me what happened when you woke up?"

No. Dammit. "Got out of bed, and there he was. On the floor, right next to me. My sweatshirt balled up under his head, the little crocheted blanket my mom made him covering his shoulders." He could see it in his mind as vividly as the day it'd happened. "I think that's what killed me the most, seeing that baby blanket on him. It just drove it home. I was growing up, maturing, but Hopper wasn't. Not in the same way. And he never would. He'd never have the full life I was gonna have."

"What'd you do?"

"Left him sleeping. Made his breakfast. Then I woke him up, showed him his treat, and it was like nothing had happened. Like I hadn't broken his heart."

"How old were you?"

"Thirteen."

"Oh, come on. All thirteen-year-old boys are smelly, selfish jerks."

He smiled. "How would you know?"

"Trying to make you feel better here." She looked up at him. "Is it working?"

"Yeah. It is."

Only when she placed her hand over his did he realize he'd been rubbing his leather bracelet. "What is that?" She pushed his fingers away and stroked the braid.

"A bracelet."

She gave him an impatient expression. "I'm asking what it means to you."

"I've got a lot of them."

"Okay, but that's the one you're always touching."

He watched her thumb the leather, darkened by water and wear. "Hopper made it."

"Oh." She sounded like she understood.

But she didn't. "In the hospital, they were gonna cut off my mom's bracelets. But she freaked out. Even all drugged up, she fought like a tiger. Wouldn't let them cut this one. She only calmed down when I promised her I'd take care of it." He let out a tight breath. "She watched me tie it around my wrist, and then she let go. Like she'd found some peace."

"You haven't given it back?"

"She hasn't asked for it yet."

"Calix," someone shouted. Multiple voices spilled into the cottage. He didn't know why their intrusion brought him so much relief.

At the sound of bare feet padding down the hallway, Mimi sat up.

"Calix," Shay called.

He threw off the covers and snatched the pajama pants off the back of a chair. "I'll grab your clothes."

He blocked the door the same moment Shay reached it. "Hey." He rested his forearms on either side.

"We saw your lights on." She tried to see past him, but he didn't budge.

She tried to duck under his arm. "You got someone in there?"

"Yeah, Shay. I do." And she was wearing nothing but a T-shirt.

She tried for a playful expression, but it just came across as confused and hurt. She mouthed, *Who is she?*

He nudged her back, stepped out of the room, and closed the door behind him.

This was good, his friends coming over. He'd get everyone in on finding Gus.

Someone turned the music on. "Wait up." Shay tugged at the waistband of his pajama pants.

He stopped so abruptly she slammed into him. Her cool hands landed on his chest.

He'd start with her. "You hear anything about where Gus moved?"

"Of course not. You know I'd tell you."

"Yeah." He continued on into the living room. He fist-bumped his buddies, hugged some of the women, and then picked his and Mimi's clothing off the floor.

Shay stepped in front of him, a pair of lacy pale pink underpants dangling off a finger. "You gonna tell me who these belong to?"

This was not going to go well. "Mimi."

Her eyes widened, her mouth gaping open. "That girl you're giving cooking lessons to?"

He nodded, balling the panties and shoving them in his pocket. "Yeah. Let me bring these to her."

"You're such a player." She tried for a teasing tone.

"Not playing."

Shock hit her features hard. "She's not your type at all."

"It's not—" He stopped himself from saying it wasn't serious. First of all, it was none of her business, but second—fuck him—the words didn't fit his heart. He didn't know what he had with Mimi, but he sure as hell knew it had to be some kind of serious if he couldn't stop seeing her. "I gotta find Bones."

Scanning the crowd, he found his friend in the kitchen. A head taller than everyone else, Bones stood out. Calix greeted him. "Dude."

With his lanky frame, lazy eyes, and easy smile, his friend always looked stoned. And maybe he was, but he was the nicest guy around. "Hey, man. How's it goin'?"

"Listen, still haven't heard from Gus." He'd known Bones so long he didn't have to even ask a question.

"Gotcha. I'll make some more calls. We'll get him."

"Appreciate it." Without a doubt Bones would come through for him. He lifted the pile of clothes in his arms. "Let me take care of these, and I'll be right back."

"You okay with us crashing here? It started to rain, and we saw your bedroom light on from the beach."

He thought about Mimi, waiting for him in bed. "Sure, man." It was pouring out there. His friends needed a place to wait out the storm.

Besides, this was good. Normal. They got too heavy all the time. Needed to lighten up and just *date*.

It was fine.

Mimi watched out the window as the guys finished up work on the gazebo for the day. "It's like an episode of *The Bachelor*. Look at them—their skin's actually glistening." They all had their shirts off, their muscular bodies on display in the twilight. Slater even wore a tool belt around his waist.

Emmie came up beside her, drying her hands on a towel. "And to think I'm carrying that man's child."

"Do you want a boy or a girl?"

"I don't care. I just want to see Slater hold his baby." And then Emmie turned toward her. "You know what? I totally want a girl. More than anything in the whole world, I want a daddy's girl." Tears glittered in her eyes.

Mimi reached for her friend's hand and gaze it a squeeze. "He'll be an awesome dad."

"He will."

Violet came up from the basement. "What're we looking at?"

"Shirtless, hot men."

"Ooh, can I see?" Violet edged between them, smelling like fragrant tea leaves. Her gaze went straight for Derek, who jumped off the ledge of the gazebo. She sucked in a breath. "That one's mine."

"Oh, he's yours all right," Emmie said. "I don't know what kind of voodoo you practice, but you've changed him. That is not the boy I grew up with."

"Speaking of boys," Violet said. "You came home early last night, Meems. How'd your date go?"

"It wasn't much of a date. We had about an hour before his friends showed up."

"He invited his friends over during your date?" Emmie looked confused.

"He didn't invite them. They just showed up. We were in bed, all cozy and intimate, and they just let themselves into his house and took it over like they owned it. He left me alone in his bedroom, while he went out to get my clothes—"

"Is she about to skip over the part where her clothes wound up somewhere other than the bedroom?" Violet asked Emmie.

"I'm picturing panties hanging off ceiling fans and shirts covering lamps," Emmie said. "You?"

"A can of whipped cream on the coffee table?" Violet said.

"Chocolate syrup dribbled all over the floor?" Emmie looked totally serious.

"Yes, and don't forget the stripper pole in the living room 'cause I totally rocked it. Now, can we get back to my humiliation?" She noted their twinge of pity, so she forged ahead. "Anyhow, it took him forever to come back with my clothes. And by the time he did, and I got dressed and went out there, there was a party in full swing. Music, bongs, couples making out in corners." He'd said something about wanting her to get to know his friends, but then he'd just left her alone. She was pretty sure he'd been avoiding her.

Of course she *had* pushed him to talk about things that made him uncomfortable. Again.

Note: You suck at dating.

"Is that why you took a cab home?"

Okay, this was embarrassing. "You saw?" Made it look like she'd thrown a tantrum.

"We heard the car door slam. Derek looked out the window and saw a cab."

"Why didn't Calix drive you home?" Emmie tore lettuce leaves in a big bowl.

"He didn't know I'd left." Yeah, okay? She'd thrown a tantrum.

"You bailed on him?"

"Yup." And she didn't regret it. "Look, he's not . . . he doesn't want a relationship. And I forget that sometimes." She thought about the flowers and the truffles, meeting her at the train in Hicksville. Inviting her dad to her show? God, that was . . . that was the sweetest thing ever. "He can be incredibly romantic. But at the end of the day, we're just dating." She looked at each of them. "And he makes sure to remind me of that every time we get close. Because, of course, I'm always thinking there's so much more going on."

Mimi glanced out the window. The other guys were heading to the house, but Calix hung back with his dad. She envied their comfortable rapport. She wished she had that with her dad. But she didn't because she was always trying so hard to be smart, witty—someone he'd want to be around.

Why *didn't* he want to be around her? He had enough money to last several lifetimes, so why did work still come first?

"Meems?" Violet nudged her.

"Where'd you go?" Emmie asked.

"Uh, out to the gazebo where one very hot man is standing shirtless."

They all looked out to see Calix and Terrence. Violet laughed.

The screen door slapped shut and boots pounded into the kitchen. "What's so funny?" Derek headed straight for his woman.

A soft smile spread across Violet's pretty features. "Your face." The woman glowed from within.

"Well, then you're gonna have a lot to laugh about since you'll be seeing it the rest of your life." Derek wrapped her in his arms and nuzzled her neck. "You smell good."

"Long-ass day." Ben kicked a chair out with his boot. "What's for dinner? I'm starving."

"How 'bout washing your hands, asswipe?" Cooper flicked him with a kitchen towel.

"I'm getting there. Can I sit down first? I've been working all day."

"Dinner's ready, so you might want to go ahead and wash up." Mimi headed to the oven and pulled out the first tray of baked ziti. Setting it down on a trivet in the middle of the table, she turned to find Slater and Emmie in a clutch by the counter. He towered over her, swallowing her up in his muscular arms, so that all Mimi could see was the top of her head at his shoulder.

Her heart caught in her throat, and she just stood there for the longest time. Letting it sink in. *This is what love looks like.* If the band had walked into Slater and Emmie's home while they were in bed, Slater would've kicked everyone out. No question. And not because he didn't want to hang out with his bandmates, but because he cherished Emmie. He coveted his time with her.

No matter how much Calix wanted her, he still held himself back. He wasn't all in—and he'd been very clear that he couldn't be. He couldn't see a future beyond getting his family back on track. Which was why he was a session musician. *Hello.*

She got a little sick realizing she was falling for a guy who couldn't be hers.

Mimi reached around Slater and Emmie and grabbed the salad bowl. After putting it on the table, she headed to the fridge to grab the dressing.

Violet intercepted her. "You okay?"

Mimi handed off the dressing to Emmie. "I guess so. As the saying goes, he's just not that into me."

"Or maybe his life is too complicated right now."

"Yeah, whatever. I just wish I hadn't been so pushy. Making him talk about his brother, getting Gus and his dad jobs with Blue Fire . . . God. I don't know why I can't keep my nose out of his business."

"Because you care. That's one of the best things about you. You care so much. God, Meems, when Derek and I were broken up, you're the one who kept me sane. If it wasn't for you, I wouldn't be with him." She shot her fiancé a fierce look. "I would have missed out on *this*."

"That's not true. You two would've found your way back to each other. And that's kind of my point. I want what you and Derek have. I want a man who loves me that much."

"That takes time. It took a while for Derek to fall for me."

"Please. Who did the chasing in that relationship?"

Violet smiled, but her brow creased. "I tortured him. I tortured us. Don't do that, Meems. When you find love, grab it. Hold on to it. Don't be afraid of it."

She agreed. *But what if the one you love doesn't grab you back?*

"You got the dressing?" Cooper called.

"Get it yourself," Slater said.

"It's in Emmie's hand. You want me to tackle her to the ground and pry it out of her fingers?"

"No, I want you to get off your ass so my pregnant wife doesn't have to come to you." A chair scraped back, and Slater strode over to Emmie, kissing her cheek and placing a huge hand on her belly. And it was adorable because she wasn't even showing yet. "Sit with me. Haven't seen you all day."

"You're gonna see her all night," Ben said. "If you know what I mean."

"Oh, he knows," Coop said. "Must be tough for you, Benny. After a whole day of beating the skins, last thing you must want to do is beat—" Derek cuffed the back of his head. "Hey."

"Watch your mouth around my bride."

"Bride," Ben said. "Jesus Christ, what's happened to you guys? We're supposed to be having fun."

"Yeah, man, we're rock stars. Rock stars don't get *married*." Coop made a face. "They don't have *babies*."

"Oh, we have fun." Derek gave Violet a very hot and wicked grin. "We have lots of fun."

"Babies are fun," Emmie said.

"No, angel, making babies is fun," Slater said.

"Our baby will be fun," Emmie said. "You'll see."

Chairs scraped back as Emmie and Slater sat down at the table.

"Christ, what're you gonna do when we tour? Don't tell me you're gonna bring that squalling, red-faced—" Again, Derek cuffed the back of Coop's head. "Would you cut it out?"

"You're talking about my nephew."

"You know it's a boy?" Mimi asked.

Emmie smiled. "Still too soon. Twelve weeks, remember?"

"Speaking of weeks," Derek said. "Our wedding's *next* week. Do we even have a guest list yet?"

Ben shook his head. "Never thought I'd hear shit like that come out of your mouth."

"Word." Offering Ben a fist bump, Cooper grabbed a slice of garlic bread.

"We don't really need one," Violet said. "It's just us."

"Mimi's gonna need a headcount, though, right?" Derek asked. "She'll need to know how much food to make."

"You can always elope," Cooper said helpfully.

"We're not eloping." Derek's chair shot back, and he crossed the kitchen to lift Violet and set her on the counter. "We're exchanging our vows in front of all you fuckers." He turned to Mimi. "Okay, we've got what, nine people?"

Nine? He must've been including Calix and Terrence. "No, Francesca and Irwin are coming back for it."

"Cool. Eleven."

"Mom," Emmie said.

Derek shrugged. "Under twenty."

Violet shot Mimi a concerned look. "I don't even have a dress."

"We'll go shopping this weekend," Mimi said.

"Don't care what you wear." Derek pressed a kiss to his bride's mouth. "Wanna marry you."

Violet's expression turned all sweet and soft. She threaded her fingers through Derek's shoulder-length hair and said, "Oh, that's gonna happen. Fancy dress or not."

The moment Derek and Violet started making out, it was time for Mimi to move on. To keep things simple, Violet had decided to skip a formal wedding cake and just go with Nonna's desserts, so that was easy enough. She'd get the invitations finished tonight. Given the guest list—just bandmates and close family, she didn't need to send them, but Violet saw them more as a keepsake, so Mimi would get them in the mail tomorrow.

She thought about sending one to the Bourbons. Would Calix even come? A wedding seemed a little too chummy. Without even thinking, she glanced out the window to see him.

But he wasn't there. He wasn't in the backyard. Or the wildflower fields.

Calix had left.

He'd left.

She hadn't heard from him since the text he'd sent her last night after she'd bailed on his impromptu party, asking where she'd gone.

Tonight, he'd been right there, in her backyard, and he hadn't bothered to come in and see her.

Wow. Talk about a wake-up call. He wasn't kidding when he said they were just dating.

Too bad she'd passed dating weeks ago.

CHAPTER FIFTEEN

"Nothing could keep me away, my love."

Mimi hunkered under the covers, phone at her ear, unreasonably happy that her mom would be home for Violet's wedding. "Even if you can only stay such a short time?"

"I wouldn't miss it for anything."

"Is Irwin still coming with you?"

"Of course. Between you and me, I think he'll welcome the break. He says he rues the day he ever signed this band. They're absolute ruffians." Her mom exhaled harshly. "I'm talking about bar brawls, naked women wandering hotel hallways, estranged relatives showing up with demands. It's like a soap opera, which is what he hates most about working with bands. This one's so talented, it makes it doubly frustrating for him."

"Are you enjoying yourself?" Her mom talked a lot about Irwin's business. She worried her mom wasn't seeing to her own interests.

"Enormously. He joins me on my travels whenever he can, but I'm quite content to explore on my own. We had a lovely week in Fiji, and when I get back from Violet's wedding, I've got a trip planned to New Zealand."

"Sounds wonderful."

"How's Violet handling running things without me?"

"With the help you guys hired, she's doing okay. She misses you, though. You guys have a rhythm together."

"Oh, I know. I miss it. Do you know I dream of wildflowers? Tea leaves? As much as I'm enjoying my travels, I do miss the farm. And you. You, most of all."

"I miss you, too, Mom."

After a pause her mom said, "Sweetheart, when are you going to talk to me?"

"I am talking to you."

"Do you think anyone on this earth knows your voice better than I do?"

Rolling onto her side, she drew her knees up, curling into a little pillbug. "Probably not. I'm kind of a mess right now. I mean, I should be one year into my career, and instead I'm in this crazy cooking competition that Dad thinks is stupid and a huge waste of my time. I guess I'm scared I'm going to win, apprentice for Verna, and then find out he still won't hire me. And then what will I do? I'll be more than two years out from graduation with nothing to show for it."

"Nothing? After appearing on the *Verna Bloom Show*, how can you think you'll have nothing? You'll have a whole new world of opportunities. Television production, culinary arts—those seem like exciting possibilities. And so what if your dad doesn't hire you? Can you imagine no other career that will make you happy?"

"I worked damn hard for this career, and there's not a chance I'm giving up." It was more than just working with her dad. It was carrying on his legacy.

Oh, get real. She knew that wasn't the issue. Not by a longshot. "I just want to work with my dad. Why . . ."

"Go on."

"Do you think maybe he just doesn't *like* me? I've done everything he's asked, and he still doesn't hire me. He barely spends any time with me. Do you think—"

"Stop right there. Your father adores you. But I know exactly what you're feeling, because I felt the same way. And unfortunately, I didn't figure out what was really going on until I divorced him. Sweetheart, your father's been working since he was eleven years old. And here's a secret. No amount of money in his bank account will make him feel safe."

She'd kind of suspected that.

"You have to remember that every time his family got evicted, they had to find somewhere to live until they could save up enough money to rent a new place. That meant barely anything to eat, no school supplies or new clothes. You think this is about you—about some inadequacy he sees in *you*, but you're wrong. Fear drives him. Fear from a deprived and insecure childhood. If he's pushing you, it's because he never wants you to know what it's like to go without. Perhaps he's going about it the wrong way, but he believes the path he's building for you will ensure you're never without a job or money or a roof over your head."

"I didn't . . . I mean, I knew that stuff about him. His childhood. But I guess I never saw it like that. I'm so preoccupied with him not hiring me that I wasn't looking at it from his perspective." She rolled onto her back, stretching her legs out. It hadn't made sense before. Her dad loved her—she'd never doubted that—but he just didn't have time for her. But now she understood why. And it had nothing to do with her. "Good talk, Ma."

Her mom laughed. "Glad it helped. Listen, my love, it's late. Get some sleep, and plan on seeing us next Thursday. We'll likely head back on Sunday."

"Love you, Mom."

"I love you, sweetheart."

Mimi set her phone on the nightstand and reached for the body lotion. Pouring some into her palm, she rubbed her hands together and then spread it up her arms and around her elbows.

Hearing her mom's perspective of her dad opened something up inside her. The restaurant world saw him as this all-powerful, supremely successful restaurateur, but deep down he was the little boy with an empty stomach delivering bread for the bakery next door to help his parents pay the rent.

Turning off the lamp, she shifted lower and pulled the quilt up, rolling onto her side.

A rap at her door put her senses on alert. "Yeah?" Maybe Violet needed to talk about the wedding.

"Meems?" That was definitely not Violet's voice.

She sat up, covering her chest with the sheet. What was he doing here? "Come in."

The door slowly pushed open and six feet four inches of hard-bodied man blocked the yellow light of the hallway. "What's up?"

Intense energy rolled off him. "I fucked up last night."

She had about a second of relief and happiness before a sharp stroke of clarity hit her. "You made a choice, that's all." *You didn't choose me.*

She couldn't see his expression, but he didn't move and he didn't offer a response.

Not being able to see his reaction empowered her. So she continued. "But that choice made me feel pretty shitty. So I left." The sheet dropped. "And I don't want to feel shitty. I don't want to constantly have to hold back my feelings and question myself. I don't like it." She liked him so much, but she didn't like the way he made her feel.

She had to do this. "Calix?"

"Yeah?"

"I don't want to date you anymore."

He took a few more steps toward the bed. "I don't blame you." He didn't sound too broken up over it.

And that *hurt.*

His thighs hit the mattress. "I'm not so great at this dating thing."

"No, you are, actually. It's me." She could see it so clearly now. "You've been incredible. Flowers, truffles, a picnic. Getting my dad to come to the show, the cooking lessons . . . you've been better than great. When people date, they don't have to see each other every day. They don't have to text and call and check in. *Couples* do that. I'm the one jumping ahead. And that's not your fault. It's mine. I'm just . . ." Emboldened, she charged forward. "I'm crazy about you. I want more. I want everything." And she realized right then she couldn't have it with him. "But you don't. I get it. That's fine. But I just can't date you anymore."

"Fuck that." Fingers on the duvet, he loomed over her. "This isn't dating. It's never been dating. I've been calling it that to keep myself in check because I'm falling so fast and hard I can't get my damn bearings. I want you, Mimi. I want every fucking part of you that I can wrap my hands around. And don't tell me you don't get that when we're in bed, because I don't think I've ever come undone the way I do with you."

Her pulse spiked, and she wanted to pause this moment until each sexy, gorgeous word sank in, so she could actually feel them underneath her skin. "Well, you're a good lover. You like sex."

"Fuck, yeah, I like sex." His knees hit the mattress, and he climbed over her. "But what we do isn't sex. You take me to a place I've never been. And I'm telling you right now I am not leaving it anytime soon. Not a fucking chance."

A dangerous heat shot through her as she looked into his fiery eyes.

"For three years I've been running on a damn treadmill. Not getting anywhere but hustling just the same. And then you come along and knock me off my stride. And, no, that has not gone down smoothly. I keep telling myself all kinds of bullshit just so I can get back on and keep doing what I've been doing. Because if I get off? If I get off and things go bad? I will not handle that well. But last night I was lying in bed missing the fuck out of you, and all that bullshit I like to tell myself to keep you at arm's length did not ring true. Not anymore. And I had to face the truth. This—" His hand flicked back and forth between them. "*Us* is freaking me the fuck out."

She wanted to say something but knew he wasn't done.

Tugging on his scruff, he turned slightly away from her. "Losing my brother was the hardest thing I've ever had to deal with. I *loved* him."

His Adam's apple jumped as he rubbed his thighs. "I loved my brother. I know there was a lot mixed in with that. Frustration and guilt. Anger. He drove me crazy. But I loved him. And . . ." He cautiously looked back at her. "I don't know if I can do that again. Open up to all that . . ." He let out a breath. "I don't know."

She nodded. He couldn't love that wholly again. She got it. What could she say? She appreciated his honesty. But did it mean he couldn't love her? And if so . . . could she really stay with him?

"And last night, talking about him? Truth is, I haven't talked about Hopper in three years." He leaned back on an arm, twisting to face her. "That was tough. And that memory in particular? Fuck. That one sucks."

"I'm sorry. I keep doing that, pushing you too hard."

"Thing is, I don't think . . . if you didn't push . . ." He sighed. "I felt better after telling you. I've held on to it so long, and talking about it? The guilt . . . it eased up a little. You know?"

She nodded, too aware of the warmth in his eyes, the heat from his skin. She'd resigned herself to moving on, but the connection between them crackled like always. It wasn't over.

"I missed you." He finally looked up at her. "All my friends were there, but I didn't want to be with them. I wanted to be with you. And then you didn't answer my text, and I knew I'd fucked up." Bringing her palm to his mouth, he kissed her. "I don't think I have it in me to love again."

The pain slammed her hard. God, what was her problem? She'd *known* that.

"But I can't *not* do it. I can tell myself all kinds of shit to justify keeping a distance between us, but it's not working. It's not fucking working, Meems. I can't stay away from you."

Hope crashed through her. "I don't want you to stay away from me."

"I gotta have you, sweet pants." Threading his fingers through her hair, he brushed it off her shoulder. "I suck at it, but . . ." He shrugged. "You gonna bear with me?"

"I'm gonna bear with you."

His smile was slow to bloom, but as it spread his hard features turned soft and warm. And she found him utterly irresistible.

He leaned into her, cupping her cheek. "Now can I kiss that mouth?"

She nestled into his hand. "Sweet cheeks, when you're all sweet like this, you can do just about anything you want."

"Good." A hint of a smile curved his lips as he stroked her jaw. "Because it's mine." And then he kissed her.

Doubt floated away as she sank into the warmth and indescribable softness of his mouth. Happiness, pure and clean, flowed through her. He was falling for her just as hard—his journey would be different, but that was okay. Because he couldn't stop himself. She might be rushing headlong into him, and he might be bobbing and weaving, but they would meet. Eventually, soon, they would collide in a fiery crack of love.

His hand pushed under her tank top, sweeping up her stomach to cup her breast. "I'm sorry I didn't take care of you last night."

Yeah. She would so bear with him. "Calix." She said it on a sigh because his hands felt so good, caressing her body with such reverence. And she understood his struggle. He'd done a really good job of keeping himself cut off from relationships with any depth—but with her? He was pushing himself out of his comfort zone, and she was the lucky girl who got to unearth all the treasures he kept hidden.

He brushed his lips over the sensitive skin of her neck. "You smell so good."

"It's my lotion. I just put it on."

"Got any more?"

As she reached for it, he grabbed his T-shirt behind his neck and yanked it off.

Instantly, heat suffused her. All that strength and musculature wrapped up in warm caramel-colored skin had her aching for his touch.

He stood up to unbutton and pull off his jeans, and when he turned to toss them on a chair, she got a good look at his tight, round ass in black boxer briefs. *This man is mine. Holy cow. Calix Bourbon is mine.*

"Shirt off, Mimi."

Oh, Lordy. Heat streamed through her as she pulled off her shirt, tossing it onto the floor.

Calix climbed onto the bed, leaning over her. He kissed the spot just under her ear. "I want to make you feel good."

Settling back on her pillow, she handed him the bottle and watched the scented white liquid spill into his hand. Then, tipping it over, he let the cool lotion drizzle onto her collarbone, her cleavage, and down her stomach. Each strike against her skin was a little shock of cold that instantly warmed, but it was the hungry look in his eyes that made her burn.

Those powerful thighs straddled hers as he caressed her collarbone, spreading the lotion across her chest. Gentle pressure and the sensuous glide relaxed her muscles, but looking into those dark eyes and seeing the desire, the barely leashed hunger, kept electricity buzzing through her system.

"You're so beautiful, Mimi." His fingers swept up and around her neck, kneading the muscles. When he leaned forward, his erection slid into the pool of creamy lotion and glided across her stomach. The sizzle of awareness had her squirming.

She reached for him, desperate to feel him in her hand, but he pushed back with a shake of his head and a tortured smile.

"I want you, Calix." Oh, God, the man drove her wild. With creamy lotion on her hand, she covered his erection, stroked, and watched him burn with passion. God, she loved the hot, hard feel of him, the way his nostrils flared as his hips flexed, pumping his cock into her fist.

His fingers worked the muscles of her arms, inciting a riot of goose bumps, then moved slowly back up to her shoulders. The pleasure of his touch made her body sing and thrum. Those big hands massaged her slowly, sensuously, making her feel like she was floating.

Until the bastard reached her breasts. He pushed them together, his thumbs flicking her nipples. An arrow of lust shot straight to her core, making her arch into his touch. His expression turned feral as he watched his hands move in slow, sensuous circles, plumping them, her nipples peeking through his fingers.

Her arousal blazed out of control. Callused fingers slid over the sensitive beads, making her throb between her legs. "Okay, sweet cheeks." She could barely get the words out. "You're killing me here."

She gave his cock a lusty squeeze, and he shuddered. As she stroked him with both hands, his breathing turned choppy. He lowered his head, eyes closing.

He made the sexiest sounds as he supported his weight on both arms, hovering over her as she stroked his length.

She rose off the pillow, never taking her hands off him. "I want you in my mouth."

The look of surprise softened into a pained smile. And then he swooped in for a kiss. "You're so fucking hot."

Pushing him onto his back, she slid down the bed. Gripping the base, she licked the head of his cock, glided the flat of her tongue down that hot, throbbing length, and then sucked him to the back of her throat. Everything about this man lit her up.

His eyes rolled back in his head as his hips punched up. "Fuck."

We'll get to that next.

The next morning, when Calix entered the studio, he found the guys sitting in the lounge, tuning instruments. It pissed him off that Gus wasn't there, that he hadn't given up Laney and fought to get his job back. Both times he'd talked to his brother over the phone this past week, he'd barely been able to hear him over the party noises in the background.

Part of Calix understood. Gus was making up for the college years he'd missed out on. The other, bigger part, though, worried for the kind of trouble his brother could get into. Because it wouldn't just impact Gus.

And the uncertainty of what might happen was stressing Calix the hell out.

"Since when do I give a shit about mansions?" Ben said. "I'd buy a boat."

"A boat?" Cooper said. "The only boat you've ever seen was in your bathtub when you were two."

"Hello? Lake Austin? I lived there for eleven years."

"How 'bout you, Calix?" Derek said. "These guys're spending the money they haven't made yet."

"Coop's gonna buy a Maserati," Ben said.

"I *said* I'm going to buy my mom a house first."

Calix remembered that Coop's mom was an addict. He had the impression she'd been sober a few years now, though. A house seemed like a good choice.

"Yeah," Ben said. "But that's so you can have a garage to park your sweet ride."

Coop smiled. "Thanks for listening. You get me, you really get me." He fell on top of Ben, and the two wound up on the floor wrestling.

His dad came out of the control room. "Calix."

"Hey, Dad. Listen, I need to leave early today."

"What's up?" Slater said.

"Mimi's fourth show. I missed the third, and I'm not gonna do that again."

Derek sent a look to Slater. "I'll bet Violet would like to see that."

Slater nodded. "Let's do it."

"Bet your mom would like it, too." His dad pulled out his cell phone. "You think we can get tickets for this many people?"

He had no idea how getting a block of tickets worked, but Mimi would like the support so he'd find out. "Let me look into it." Then again, it was all about ratings, right? Blue Fire and 100 Proof in the audience? Yeah, he figured they'd find enough seats.

As he opened up the search engine on his phone, he heard the guys talking about seeing Mimi. It wasn't about sitting in the audience of a television show. It was about Mimi. And that hit him hard. That these guys cared enough about her to take time off work. She'd said they were like her family, and now he could see why she felt that way. They acted like one.

These were good guys. Really good guys. A yearning tore through him—to dig deep into the music, become part of the creation, the words, instrumentation, vocalization, just immerse completely—fuck, he missed that. He *needed* it. And these guys—

An image of his mom in her art studio jolted him. Sweaty, exhausted, deep grooves around her mouth and eyes.

Yeah, just . . . not the right time.

"Okay." Terrence clapped his big paws together. "Let's talk about what we're gonna do today."

Calix swiped it out of his mind and focused on what mattered right then. Gathering everyone around Mimi.

Calix kept his eyes on the monitor. He couldn't even say what the other two contestants had made. He'd focused on Mimi the whole time. And she was a star.

Now, the three remaining contestants faced the panel of judges, with Deborah, the spa cook, standing in front of the line-up.

"I don't know what to tell you." Zoe, the spike-haired, severe woman who'd rarely found a nice thing to say to any of them, looked like she'd swallowed a bug. "Your food is simply bland. I know you work for a spa, but we're not looking for clean, healthy food here. This is your chance to experiment, have some fun, but you're not. I'm not seeing you adapting. And for that reason I'm giving you a one for innovation. But since you always pull together a very pretty plate, I'll give you a four for presentation. And quick thinking?" She shrugged. *Whatever.* "A three."

"That was harsh." Cooper elbowed him. "She gonna shred Mimi, too?"

Calix nodded. "Count on it."

Leaning across Violet, Emmie tapped his knee and nodded toward the stage.

Mimi had stepped forward, hands clasped at the small of her back.

"Okay, Ms. Romano," Verna said. "Tell us what you've prepared."

"I've made a caramelized cod on a bed of *ciambotta* with crispy polenta strips."

"Sounds awesome." Verna gestured to the first judge. "Chef Alonso, what do you think?"

The chef looked at Mimi as if she were his daughter and had just finished her dance recital. *Too bad her dad didn't give her that.* "I saw the way you looked at that fennel bulb, Ms. Romano, and I wasn't sure how this was going to go." He looked to the other judges. "She wears it all on her sleeve, doesn't she?"

The severe woman gave no response, but the older gentleman smiled warmly.

Calix agreed with the judge. And that was one of the things he liked best about Mimi. She was straight up. He always knew where he stood. That gave him a comfort he didn't fully understand.

"But I have to say when I saw you making, essentially, a ratatouille, I was worried. Fennel in a ratatouille? My palette revolted. But then you caramelized the fish, and it started to come together for me. The fennel with carrots, potatoes, and sage was magnificent and the dish paired beautifully with the cod. But the crispy polenta?" He clapped his hands together. "With a slightly sweet and soft main course, you were clever to add something savory and crispy. I didn't see you add much more than salt, pepper, and parmigiana to the polenta, but it was sensational. I give you three fives. Well done."

The audience exploded with applause. So far no one had scored fives across the board.

"Thank you, Chef," Mimi said. "And it's the wine."

"Excuse me?" the chef asked.

"In my family, we add a little Merlot."

"Ah." The chef took another bite of the polenta and closed his eyes. "Yes. Oh, excellent." When he opened them, he turned to his colleague. "Isn't that fabulous?"

"Well, I'd say Ms. Romano knocked this one out of the park," Verna said. "Mr. Simmons?"

"Correct me if I'm wrong, but classic *ciambotta* is tomatoes, zucchini, potatoes, onions . . . maybe eggplant?" Mr. Simmons asked.

Chef Alonso nodded.

"So, then using the fennel to create the dish is quite

innovative," he continued. "I'm not a fennel fan, but I quite enjoyed it here." His lips pressed together, eyebrows lifted, and he said, "I liked everything about it. I'll give you a four for quick thinking, a five for innovation, and a five for presentation."

"Thank you, sir."

"Yes!" Violet pumped her fist a few times.

Cooper let out a wolf whistle, and Ben shouted, "Go, Mimi!"

Laughter moved like a wave across the audience, and the male judges nodded their approval.

But not Zoe.

"Chef Zoe?" Verna said.

"Your fan base keeps growing with each show. And who did you bring with you today?"

"That's Blue Fire, the band I cook for."

"We love you, Mimi," Cooper called.

She flushed prettily. "Love you, too, Coop."

"Since you're not being judged by the company you keep," Zoe said, "let's get on with your dish." She spat the last word out like a husk in her oatmeal.

"What a bitch," Coop said.

Zoe sneered at the white plate. "Let's just say you saved this dish by adding the crispy polenta. Otherwise, between the fish and the soggy ratatouille, I could've gummed it. But, and here I'm going to respectfully disagree with my *very* agreeable colleagues, I don't see any innovation. You fall back on your Italian heritage every time. I'd almost rather have your father on the show than his protégée daughter."

"Oh, no, she didn't," Violet said a little too loudly.

"She's so insulting," Emmie said.

"So, I'm going to give you a three for quick thinking because you did pull together quite a few dishes in the limited time frame. As for presentation, why is it that you always seem to forget about it until the last moment? And then, in your haste, you simply toss a sprig of some herb and a splash of color? I'm afraid I can only give you a two for that. And a one for innovation because, like I said, you can't seem to break out of your Italian comfort zone."

"I'm no chef, but crispy polenta strips?" Violet whispered to him. "That's pretty innovative."

"Thank you, Chef Zoe." Mimi nodded, looking deceptively relaxed. "I appreciate the feedback."

Mimi stepped back into the line-up, her gaze immediately seeking Calix out. He knew the lights made it hard for her to see him, but he always knew when it happened. The moment their gazes connected, static electricity flashed across his skin.

Derek leaned across Violet. "Mimi rocks."

He couldn't keep the smile off his face because she did.

And when the voice in his head whispered, *Mine*, not a single part of him rebelled.

Mimi's father gave them a private room in one of his Upper West Side restaurants. The eleven of them sat around one long table in a dimly lit room with stone walls.

Calix sat back in his chair, enjoying the conversations around him. Across from him, Slater and Derek were arguing over bass players.

"Wooten might be funkier than Pastorious," Slater said. "But he's still a fuckin' master."

"Can't touch Pastorious," Derek said.

"You haven't seen him live," Slater said.

"He's good. I'm just saying he's no Pastorious."

Huddled together at one end of the table, his sister and Ben nearly touched foreheads as they talked quietly to each other. *Where did that come from?* Then again, Lee seemed to like bad boys—rockers, in particular. Although Ben didn't strike him as all that bad.

When Mimi's hand squeezed his thigh, he tuned into her conversation with his parents.

"Doesn't matter what you think." His mom's exercised tone surprised him. "It's about points. It's down to the two of you, and you can't afford any deductions."

"She's got thirty minutes," his dad said. "She's gotta make a good dish, not worry about impressing a hard-ass judge. She should focus on getting high scores from the other two judges, and to do that, she needs to knock it out of the park."

"I'm telling you, anything Italian is out." His mom had that stubborn look. It made Calix happy to see her so engaged.

"Yeah, but I know I can pull off a good Italian dessert," Mimi said. "It's what I know best."

"You do what you want," his mom said. "But if you want to win this thing, you're gonna have to mix it up, get creative. Because Eleanor may run a tea and coffee house, but she's inventive and clever."

"She is." Mimi shot him a glance, looking for confirmation.

"You've got all week to work on desserts." Calix kissed her. "You've got this."

Her eyes rounded in surprise, and her fingertips touched her lips. Made him realize he'd never given her that. A public declaration. Which, from her perspective, meant he hadn't fully committed, could bail at any moment, and no one would be the wiser.

She deserved so much better.

And fuck him, but he wanted to claim her.

He leaned in and kissed her again, giving a gentle brush of his tongue. Everything about her softened. He took advantage of the intimacy and cupped the back of her head to give her an openmouthed kiss.

So sweet. So fucking sweet.

When she pulled back, she kept her forehead tipped against his. "Wow."

He gave a soft laugh as his heart settled down. "You did great tonight, sweet pants."

"Thank you. Thank you for bringing everybody. It made it a thousand times more fun." Her tongue peeked out, moistening her lips, and he couldn't stop himself from going in for more. She tasted like tiramisu, a hint of coffee and sweet cream, and when she slid a hand up this thigh, he fell into her mouth, her scent, the pressure of her grip. He kissed her softly, gently, but deeply, wanting her to know how much she meant to him.

"*Calix.*" It took the snap of a linen napkin to the back of his head for him to realize his dad was trying to get his attention. Terrence gave a chin nod to the other end of the table.

Calix turned to find the band watching him, cracking up. "Sorry, what?"

"Happy to clear the room for ya," Cooper said.

Derek ignored him. "Listen, Em says the label's setting up our tour dates."

Automatically, Calix looked to his mom. She sat still as a stone.

"You know we need a permanent keyboard player," Slater said. "And we're not gonna find a better fit than you."

Mimi squeezed his knee. He knew she wanted him to consider the offer.

He looked to his mom, who sat still as a statue.

"Thing is, man," Derek said, "you're more than a keyboard player to us. Sure, we can find someone on keys, but you write with us. You get where we're coming from. Like Slater said, it's a good fit. You keep telling us no, but before we start a search, we gotta ask one more time."

"I like working with you guys." One more glance at his mom had the ravioli hardening in his stomach. "But I think you're best off looking for someone else."

Mimi's fingers pressed into his thigh muscles. But when he turned to her, he caught his dad's expression instead. Brows pitched up, lips pressed together, he looked like he wanted Calix to take the job.

His dad leaned in close to his mom, gave her shoulder a squeeze as he spoke quietly in her ear. She gave no reaction.

"Calix." Mimi's soft voice jolted him out of his thoughts. "It'll suck as much for them to hire someone else as it will for you when they do. Can you imagine a better gig? Please just think about it."

Of course he wouldn't find a better gig. He'd give his left nut to join Blue Fire. Experience told him this kind of connection didn't come along all that often—if ever—in a musician's life.

But as he watched his mom's stony expression, his gut told him it just wasn't the right time.

And he was starting to wonder if it would ever be.

CHAPTER SIXTEEN

When her ass pitched higher, when her hips slammed back on him, Calix thrust deep and hard. "Fuck." Jesus, look at her, up on her knees on his bed, so wet, so slick, so tight around him. Each time her ass hit his groin, she'd swivel, the movement sandwiching his cock tighter between her slick walls. The intense pressure sent him out of his mind.

A moan ripped from his throat at the sight of all that smooth skin, the shake of her ass cheeks as he pounded into her. Leaning over, one hand sliding up her stomach, he caught her breast in his palm, pinched her nipple. "Give me that mouth."

But she was gasping, head lowered, and she just rammed harder back onto him.

"Mouth, Mimi."

"I . . . God, I can't . . . oh, my God." Lowering her head to the pillow, she made desperate sounds. She was close. One stroke of her clit, and he knew she'd explode. But he wasn't ready yet. He didn't want this to ever end. And he needed that fucking mouth.

He grabbed her braids, wound them around his fingers, and tugged her head back.

She cried out, her expression turning frenzied with lust. When she slammed back, grinding on him, he realized he'd found it. "*Fuck*." This was her fantasy. Holy fuck. Electricity tripped down his spine, and his balls tightened.

One hand on her hip holding her tightly against him, the other pulling on her braids, his orgasm ripped through him. He came so hard, lights flashed behind his eyelids. Wild pleasure gripped him. Waves of it roared through him, the ecstasy unrelenting. Nothing had ever felt so good.

His thrusts turned more languid, each stroke offering a fiery rush of sensation.

When he calmed down, he released her hair, and she collapsed onto the bed, breathing heavily.

Holding the edge of the condom, he pulled out of her, then rolled it up in a tissue and tossed it in the trash bin.

"Shazam." She'd turned onto her side, giving him a glimpse of her rosy cheeks, those plump breasts, and a look of utter satisfaction.

He burst out laughing, emotion spilling into his every crack and crevice, until it flooded him. She inched closer, hitching a leg over his, settling a hand over his heart, and he watched her drift off to sleep.

Moments ticked by. His body cooled. But sleep didn't come. How could he be wired after coming that hard?

That good feeling started to curl at the edges. Mimi had work in the morning, so he should probably get her home. Except she looked so peaceful, and she'd had a rough day, so he'd let her sleep a little.

But the restlessness only got worse. He reached for his cell phone on the nightstand.

He texted Lee. Mom okay?

When she didn't respond, he carefully shifted Mimi off him and got out of bed.

He started to send another text, this one to his dad, when his phone rang. *Lee*. "What's up?"

"Why are you texting me about Mom at one in the morning?" Her voice was sleep-roughened.

"Is she still in the studio?"

"I don't know. I'm sleeping." She let out an exhalation that let him know she felt put out. "I'll go check."

"Thanks."

"Hang on."

As he stood in the living room, staring out the window into the darkness, he remembered Mimi's braids in his hand, the look in her eyes as he'd pulled on them while he'd pounded into her. The small of his back warmed. His cock wanted more.

Mimi's fantasy. Fucking hell, that woman slayed him.

"Lights off in the studio," Lee said.

"Check her room."

"I know. Give me a second. What's the problem?"

"Nothing. No problem."

"You worried about her?"

"Can't sleep till I know she's okay."

"Yeah." She sounded softer. "Give me a second. If she's sleeping, I don't want to wake her."

He heard a door creak, and then his sister said, "She's not in her room."

Cold flushed across his skin. "Where the hell is she?" He stalked into the kitchen. Should he head up to the house?

"Hang on. Give me a second. All the lights are out."

"Maybe she's on the beach?" Kind of late, but maybe she was taking a walk to help her fall asleep. "I'll head out right now." He had the door open when he heard Lee suck in a breath. And then a whispered, "Oh, my God."

Oh, fuck. Fuck fuck fuck. One hand at the back of his neck, the other clutching the phone, Calix leaned his forehead against the cool wood of the door frame. In his mind's eye he saw his mom in bed, head flopped to one side, skin ashen.

"You won't believe this."

"What? Tell me."

"She's with Dad. She's in his bed."

Calix let out a huff of breath, and it felt like someone had pried the lid off his brain, releasing all the pressure.

"Can you believe it? She's back in his bed. This is so awesome. This is the best thing ever."

His body felt stuck with needles and pins, like it had fallen asleep and he was just getting sensation back in it.

"You there?"

"Yeah, Lee. I'm here. I'm just . . ." The cool air dried the perspiration off his skin, and his mind cleared.

"Me, too. She's okay. Ma's okay."

"Thanks for checking."

"Best reason ever to wake a girl up."

"See you in the morning."

"See you."

All he wanted was to get back in bed with Mimi. The clambake, the cooking lessons, the wedding . . . she'd done this. She'd brought his mom back.

He thought of Blue Fire. And it brought a jolt of excitement to the center of his chest.

Because . . . well, what if the timing worked out after all?

The sound of his ringtone had him jackknifing up in bed. His hand shot out, knocking the bottle of water off the nightstand. Finding the cell phone, he snatched it up. Didn't recognize the number.

"Hello?" Beside him, Mimi got up on an elbow.

"Calix?" *Gus.*

"Where are you?" Calix couldn't identify the strange noises in the background.

"Suffolk County Jail. In Riverhead."

A powerful mix of fear and anger made him sick to his stomach. "What happened?"

"Calm down. It's not a big deal. I got into a fight. But you need to come get me."

"Suffolk County Jail?"

"Yeah."

"*Goddammit.*"

"Yeah, I know. Just . . . come bail me out."

"What did you do?"

"I'll talk to you when I see you."

"On my way." As he tossed the phone on the bed, he found

it empty. Mimi sat at his desk, face lit up from the screen of his laptop.

Her finger traced the thick blue line on Google Maps. "We take 48 to 25." She wrote down the directions on a scrap of paper. "Got it."

As he pulled on his boxers and jeans, he watched her getting dressed. "Just crash here. I don't have time to take you home."

"What? No. I'm going with you."

Like hell he'd take her to a jail at three in the morning. "No, you're not."

She ignored him, continuing to get dressed.

"You need your sleep."

Tugging on the elastics, she pulled her fingers through the braids, loosening them, as she headed into the bathroom. "Do you have an extra toothbrush?"

He hooked an arm around her waist. "Go back to bed. I'll get you home in time to make breakfast for the guys."

When those beautiful green-brown eyes gazed up at him, the hard edges of the world softened. "You're not alone anymore, you big dummy. Now, can I have a damn toothbrush?"

He yanked open the bottom drawer of his vanity and rooted around for a new toothbrush. Handing it to her, he cupped the back of her neck and squeezed gently. "Mimi?"

"Yeah?"

His chest tightened with emotion. Having her with him . . . it made a difference. "Thanks."

"What the fuck, Gus?" At nearly four in the morning, the streets in Riverhead were deserted. Calix gripped the steering wheel as he eyed his brother in the rearview mirror.

"Sorry."

Gus looked like shit. His hair was a mess, and he had a livid cut under his eye and a swollen lip. "Gonna need a little more than that."

"Got in a fight."

"Dammit, Gus, don't make me pull it out of you."

"Fine. Laney's friends played in some shitty club tonight. She was pissed at me because I didn't want to go. They suck, man. Truly suck. I didn't want to go out—" He looked out the window, two fingers rubbing his temple. "She's *always* going out. Next thing I know she's gone. She calls me later, drunk off her ass, so I go get her. I'm already pissed because she doesn't listen to a damn thing I say. She just does what she wants when she wants, and if I have an opinion about anything, she gets in my face. So I find her at this club. Minute she sees me, she starts making out with the drummer. I knew she was doing it to get a reaction, so I pulled her off him and tried to get her to come home with me. But she got all crazy, started fighting and screaming. And that's when the shithead sucker-punched me." Gus let out a breath, looking utterly defeated. "The whole thing was so fucking stupid. *I'm* so fucking stupid."

Calix watched him in the mirror. This was the first time in weeks his brother didn't sound defiant.

"She's crazy," Gus said.

Calix didn't say a word, but Mimi reached for his thigh and gave it a rub. Yeah, his brother was snapping out of it.

"I'm sorry, man." Gus's voice sounded gravelly.

"You done with her?"

"Done. Seriously, man, done. I should've listened to you."

"You want to get your stuff now?" Calix wanted to get this shit behind him.

"Nah, I'm beat. I'll get it tomorrow."

"I'll come with you."

"Might be best. She'll go nuts."

"We'll take care of it." He was so damn relieved to have his brother back. "Come back to my place. I want to get you cleaned up before Mom sees you."

Challenge flashed in his eyes. "She can handle more than you think."

"Let me tell you something. She's doing great right now, and I don't want anything to mess with that. You get me?"

He watched Gus struggle with the question. "Yeah, of

course." And then he scrubbed his face with both hands. "I need to sleep for, like, a week."

"Let me get Mimi home first."

She turned toward him. "No, you don't have to do that."

"You've got to be up in two hours to make breakfast. I'm taking you home."

"Calix."

But he wasn't discussing it with her. He needed to deal with his family, and she had a job to do.

With a vegetable peeler, Mimi scraped beautiful curls off a chilled block of chocolate.

"What in the world is going on in here?" Lee came in and surveyed the kitchen. The two bright spots of pink on her cheeks and her windblown hair revealed the blustery spring weather that Mimi had missed since she'd been holed up in the Bourbon kitchen all day.

"Girl's been busy," Jo said.

"I see that." Approaching the island, Lee picked up a parfait glass. "Can I taste?"

"Are you kidding?" Mimi said. "You can set up a roadside farm stand. We've got enough to feed the whole county."

The counters, the island, even the chairs had cookies, scones, muffins, cupcakes, layer cakes, mousses, and various quick breads. Yeah, they'd baked a lot. A glance at the microwave clock made her realize she'd been cooking nearly eight hours.

Thank goodness she'd left sub sandwiches in the fridge for the guys because she'd blown right through dinner.

Lee spooned some of the mango mousse into her mouth. "Oh, my God." Her eyes went wide. "Oh, my flipping God. This is so good."

"We've been working off basic recipes, substituting, adding, tweaking. At first I just did boring stuff like using applesauce instead of oil—"

"But then she got more confident," Jo said. "That one's got pureed mango instead of butter, and it's damn good, if a little dry."

"Try that one." Mimi pointed to the variation of *tiramisu* she'd made with cream cheese and Meyer lemons. "It's to die for."

Lee sank a spoon into it, and the moment she tasted it, her features softened with a rapturous expression. "This is unbelievable."

Jo fought a smile. "Never seen you look like that with my food."

"Maybe because your desserts always had wheat germ and bran in them."

Jo grabbed something out of the fruit basket and lobbed it at her, but Lee ducked. "Hey." She gaped at her mom. "You threw a *fig* at me."

Jo shrugged with a smile. "You make MVP on your volleyball team three years in a row?"

"Possibly." With a huge grin, Lee grabbed a muffin and tossed it at her mom. Jo caught it handily.

"You can thank the wheat germ and bran for that." Just as Jo reached for a scone, Mimi stepped between them.

"Okay, before we get into an all-out food fight here, it's time to decorate." She indicated an unfrosted chocolate cake. "It's one thing to have a tasty cake, but it's got to look pretty. And now that the Queen of Style's in the house, talk to me."

Lee's smile dazzled with anticipation. "Oh, how fun. I'd love to do that. So, what're we talking about? Frosting? Sprinkles?"

"Sprinkles?" Mimi rolled her eyes. "I am not working with sprinkles." But even as the words left her mouth, images popped into her mind. She saw vintage cake stands with fluffy white-frosted cakes. Some with flecks of shredded coconut, others with polka-dot sprinkles. She saw an antique pie chest with cookie sandwiches, the frosting in pastel blue, pink, and lavender. "I totally want sprinkles."

"You're not impressing those judges with sprinkles on your cakes," Jo said.

"Not the grocery store kind. The ones you have to special order. Pastel disks and polka dots. Sanding sugar in lavender and pink, white and pale blue." She spun around to Jo. "Can you teach me how to make fluffy white frosting? Not butter-cream, but something fluffy?"

"Sure. You make it like a meringue. Sugar, water, egg whites." Jo looked to Lee with an expression that said, *Any idea where she's going with this?*

But Lee just smiled and headed for the refrigerator. "This is going to be so much fun."

In her mind she saw bay window seats with blue and white toile cushions. Walls painted the palest peach, like the inside of a shell. Tin ceiling tiles. Wrought iron café tables and pink and white striped paper straws. Old-fashioned milkshake glasses.

This would be an awesome bakery.

A clatter had her turning to find Jo setting down a copper bowl and a whisk. Lee came out of the pantry with a dusty storage container. When she set it on the counter, she pulled off the top and revealed the most amazing array of toppings and sprinkles.

Lee tipped the box so Mimi could see inside. "Like these?"

She couldn't believe the variety. Sprinkles in orange and black, red and green, pink, red, and white, every holiday represented. But then she saw the pastel-colored ones. Just like she'd imagined. She pulled those out. "This is it. We've hit the motherlode."

"Oh, honey, you have no idea. My mom and I love baking." Her features twisted with sadness—but it was more reminiscent than tortured. "We used to do this with Hopper."

Jo froze. The slightest tremble in her hands made Mimi look to Lee, but her gaze was trained on her mom. The room went dead silent as Jo pulled in a shuddery breath and reached for a glass jar of polka dot sprinkles. For a long moment she just stared at it, and Mimi could only imagine the crush of memories bearing down on her. Then Jo lifted it, stared at it for a moment, and said, "To Hopper." She blinked a couple times, her features pulling in tight. "My baby boy."

The sharp bite of tears stung her eyes, but Mimi found her voice. "To Hopper."

Lee picked up a jar of sprinkles shaped like bats. Her eyes glittered. "To Hopper."

Jo reached for her daughter, belted her arms around her, and tucked her faced into Lee's neck. When Mimi turned away to give them privacy, Lee grabbed her shirt, tugging her toward them. Jo's arms went around her, bringing her into the circle. She smelled of vanilla and warm butter.

"Love you, Mommy."

"Love you, too, my sweet girl."

Mimi was so deeply sorry for their loss. At the same time, her heart had never felt so full. What a gift to be welcomed into this incredibly loving and loyal family.

She'd questioned her involvement with them so many times, but it was all right.

Thankfully, it had turned out all right.

Day four of Bake-a-palooza, Mimi pulled the salted caramel *pots de crème* out of the oven and looked for counter space in Slater and Emmie's kitchen. But she couldn't find any. She'd have to move into the dining room.

"Mimi?" The front door slammed and heels click-clacked on the wood floor.

"Kitchen."

Violet appeared, wearing a pretty sundress and kitten heels and carrying a garment bag. Pausing for a moment, she took in the mess. "What the . . ." Then she moved into the room, her gaze going from one counter to another, to the table and then the chairs. "Have I died and gone to heaven?" She hung the bag off the laundry room door.

Heading to the nearest counter, Violet lifted a dark chocolate cupcake with fluffy white frosting and polka dot sprinkles in the watery colors of dyed Easter eggs. Meringue-covered tarts sat next to parfaits of rum-soaked lady fingers and whipped cream. "I've never seen anything so beautiful in my life. It's like I walked onto a movie set."

"I'm trying as many variations as I can."

"Yeah, but the way you decorated them." She showed her the cupcake. "Can I eat this?"

"Of course. Help yourself. What the guys don't eat, I thought I'd bring to the shelter."

Violet moaned. "Oh, my God. It tastes as good as it looks."

Mimi had given herself odd challenges, working with ingredients that wouldn't normally go together. And then she'd had a blast decorating, thanks to Lee and Jo. After hours of experimenting the other day, the three of them had come up with gorgeous, fanciful presentations with polka dots, stripes, and pastel-colored stars. Today she'd added wildflowers.

"It's so . . . whimsical." Violet reached for a sugar cookie with glittering lavender sugar crystals on top. "Can I have this for my wedding?"

"Sugar cookies?"

"No. This." She gestured around the room, every counter and table. "This . . . whimsy." Then, she set the cookie down, wiped her hands on a kitchen towel, and reached for her dress. "You won't believe this."

She unzipped the bag to reveal a wedding gown. Pushing the edges of the bag off the hanger, she exposed the dress fully. A strapless beaded bodice gave way to a fluffy full skirt made of tulle cut petals.

It was stunning and fanciful and, yes, totally whimsical.

"Oh, my God." Mimi ran her fingers over the pearlescent beads on the top. "It's perfectly you."

"I know." She said it reverently in a whisper, before turning to the counters. "And this? This just fits so perfectly."

"So, that's our theme? Whimsy?"

"That's our theme."

A bark of laughter drew their attention outside as the guys spilled out of the studio, striding across the grass with all their masculine swagger. Cleaned up and bright-eyed, Gus looked happy to be back at work.

"Did you make dinner?" Violet quickly tucked the dress back into the garment bag.

"We're grilling tonight. Burgers, dogs. Keeping it simple . . . and out of the kitchen."

The guys approached the house, talking, laughing, so clearly enjoying each other. And even though Calix walked a few feet away from them, he laughed, too.

She hated the distance he kept. While the others would come into the house, wash up, and eat dinner, he'd go home to gather his family around a table. She understood. It gave him breathing room to remind his mom she was loved and needed.

At least Mimi knew she'd get him for a few hours at night.

Just as Gus, Terrence, and Calix broke away from the others and started off down the driveway, Calix glanced up to the window. A pulse fluttered in her throat when his steps faltered. And then he stopped, turning fully to her.

When Terrence realized his son wasn't with him, he swung around, called out to him. But Calix didn't take his gaze off her. She could see the conflict flicker across his features—the part of him that felt compelled to go home, make sure his family sat together for dinner—and the part that wanted to be with her.

Why *couldn't* he choose her? It didn't have to be all the time. She didn't want to be petty, but why couldn't he spend a whole night with her every now and then?

And then one half of his mouth curled into a wicked smile. Her heart beat faster as he waved off his dad and brother. "Go on without me," she thought he said as he headed for the house.

He took the stairs in a leap, pushed open the door, and came right to her. Scooping her off the ground, he burrowed his face in her neck.

She clung to him, feet dangling, arms clasped around his shoulders. Was he shaking?

He pulled back to look at her, dark eyes sparkling with happiness. "Hey." She was unused to seeing her big, fierce guy so easy in his heart.

She kissed him sweetly, warmly. "Hungry?"

"What'd you make?"

She wriggled free. "Really? You'll stay if I've made something you like?"

"I'll stay 'cause this is where I want to be."

Oh. Oh, yes. That was what she wanted to hear.

"Wait a damn second." Ben stuffed a muffin into his mouth,

his fingers tipped with frosting to indicate he'd sampled other treats. "What the hell kind of voodoo you got?"

"What?" Mimi stuttered out a laugh.

"Since when's Calix such a pussy?"

Calix nabbed a cookie, shoved it in his mouth. As he chewed, he took in the baked goods all around him. "What's this?"

"She baked." Violet sat on Derek's lap, his arms around her, his big hand cupping her hip. "Isn't it the prettiest stuff you've ever seen?" she asked her fiancé.

Derek kissed her like he didn't have a crowd around him. "Beautiful."

"Good. Because we're doing this for the wedding."

"Doing what?" Derek sounded confused. "Dessert?"

"No. Whimsy." Violet waved a hand with a flourish, indicating all that Mimi had made.

"Cool."

"You couldn't care less."

"I care." He stroked the hair off her face. "About marrying you. The rest . . ." He shrugged. "I just want you happy."

"I'm happy." Violet smiled sweetly.

Calix reached for a cookie, brushed the sugar crystals off, and popped it in his mouth. After a few chews, he cocked his head.

Mimi smiled. "Instead of shortening I used a paste of coconut milk, banana, and applesauce with cinnamon, nutmeg, and allspice. What do you think?"

"I think you're going to win this thing."

She loved his total belief in her. "You want me to pack up some goodies to take home with you?" She started piling her treats on a plate, but he slid his arms through hers and wrapped them around her waist, pulling her back to him.

He nuzzled her neck. "Don't need dessert, sweet pants."

Head nestled under his chin, hands pressed to his warm forearms, she whispered, "What do you need?"

"Got everything right here."

Emotion rose like a tide, overflowing the banks of her heart. Her senses swam with all that was Calix—his scent, his heat, the strength of his arms around her. She turned and pressed against him. And right there, in front of everyone, she gave him her heart in a kiss.

His mouth opened to her, and his hands slid down her back and cupped her ass. He was letting her in all the way, opening to her, and she almost couldn't stand so much happiness.

When the kiss deepened, when the thread of decency frayed, he lifted her and carried her into the laundry room. The door slammed with a kick of his boot. She landed on the washing machine, Calix's body stepping between her legs, his fingers pushing her hair back from her face.

His mouth claimed hers. Tongue seeking, stroking, rendering her mindless. She was nothing but a wash of electric heat.

Something deep within started wriggling free, working its way to the surface, forcing her mind to wake up and take notice.

And then it emerged, easing the tight knot of worry and fear lodged deep inside her chest.

I love him.

I love *him.*

God, she loved Calix Bourbon so much.

And tonight he'd given her hope.

He'd taken one step away from his guilt and toward her.

CHAPTER SEVENTEEN

Without the hay bales, the barn was much larger than Mimi had realized. She, Jo, and Lee had hung slender tree branches from the rafters and draped them with tiny white lights. Pastel-colored Chinese paper lanterns dangled at different heights and a massive garland of wildflowers bordered the perimeter of the ceiling. Thick satin ribbons in lavender, pale blue, pink, and creamy yellow trailed down, rippling from the fans they'd placed in the corners of the room.

Pale pink rose petals splashed across each table, and the centerpiece consisted of a miniature copper water trough overflowing with beach roses and baby's breath.

"Where do you want these?"

The guys came into the barn carrying the funky desserts, and Mimi showed them the folding table draped with white tulle.

"This is so cool, Meems," Cooper said, "Thanks."

"You know what we forgot?" Lee came in wearing leggings, a white T-shirt, and a black vest. "The birds." She looked relieved when she saw the guys. "Oh, yay. Can you guys help me unload the truck?"

"Lee, you're not even dressed," Mimi said. "Forget about the birds."

"No way. Why have the branches without the wildlife? Besides, the guys'll help us put the birds up. Right, guys?"

"I'll help you." Ben's strangely serious tone had everyone stopping what they were doing to turn and look.

Lee beamed up at him. "Thanks."

Color washed across Ben's cheeks, and he rushed out of the barn. When he noticed no one had followed, he turned back. "Guys, let's go."

Mimi caught the smiles between them as they took off after Ben and Lee.

A warm breeze stirred the tulle petals of Violet's dress and blew back the long wavy strands of her dark hair. They'd all decided to go with beach waves for this casual affair.

Mimi had wrapped her friend's bouquet of camellias with white, pink, and lavender satin ribbon, which fluttered and danced. In her hair, she wore a wreath of pale pink beach roses.

She looked radiant.

Bracketed by Mimi and Slater, Violet and Derek faced each other, the guests filling the newly built white gazebo. The sweet, earthy scent of wildflowers swirled around them. It couldn't have been more lovely—well, unless the Bourbons had decided to attend. They hadn't wanted to intrude on the intimate affair. But they'd promised to come to the reception.

Mimi's beautiful and elegant mom, Francesca, acting as officiant, spoke quietly to the guests. "The bride and groom had one request. Not a lot of *blah blah blah*."

Everyone smiled.

"Typical," Coop said.

Francesca continued. "So, to get to the heart of the matter, I thought I'd share my own well-earned lessons with you." She turned to the groom with a soft smile. "Derek, your love for Violet shines through everything you do and say. But never take it for granted. Nurture it. Court her, Derek. No matter how much life heaps on you, never stop courting your wife. Every day find one kind, true thing to say to her. Let her know whether in word or gesture that you love her and are thinking about her. Every day of your marriage, give one hundred percent of yourself. Don't hold back, waiting for her to give you what you want—give *her* what you want to receive. I guarantee you'll get it back tenfold. Every gesture of kindness, of consideration, of love you make toward one another forges a deeper bond. And that bond is the one on which your family will be built."

Tenderness softened her mom's features as she faced the bride. "Violet, my sweet girl, open your heart to Derek every day. Let his love sink in so deeply it infuses your every fiber. Praise him for the good things he's done and don't hoard the bad ones. Every day is a fresh start, so toss out the score cards. And . . . this one's important, okay?" She looked between them. "Wake up every morning with one thought in mind: What can I do to make my love feel special today? In the chaos that life will bring, take time to be with each other. To hold hands, to hug, to share a quiet moment. And always, always remember to say 'I love you.' Do you think you can do that?"

She looked to Derek, who nodded, and then to Violet, who whispered, "Yes," as she wiped a tear from her cheek.

"Then I know you'll be as in love in fifty years as you are today. Now, I know you want to exchange vows privately," Francesca said after a pause. "So I'll skip right to the forever part. Derek, do you have the—"

"Wait." Violet gazed up at her groom with fierce determination. "I do want to say something." She reached for Derek's hand.

Swiftly, he caught her fingers, bringing her palm to his mouth. He gave her a magnificent smile.

Violet drew a shaky breath. "Sometimes, out of the blue, I get this jolt. And it's because I remember how I almost didn't get to be with you." She drew a shaky breath. "Before I met you, I was fine. I had a great job. I had Francesca and Mimi and my farm. I was growing a business I loved. And I thought I'd really lucked out because I was finally safe. That's all I'd ever aspired to. Just . . . to be safe." Tears glittered in her eyes. "I would've settled for safe." The words came out a whisper.

"I would have. But then you came along and brought me something I hadn't even contemplated. Hadn't even *considered*. And I ran. I ran from all the passion and . . . and radiance that you offered me."

"And that's no metaphor," Cooper said. "I mean, she *ran*. All the way to Japan."

Ben elbowed him.

"What?" Cooper said. "It's true."

"Shut up," Ben said.

A few people laughed, but Violet's gaze never wavered. "I almost lost you. I almost didn't get *this*." Her incredulous tone made Mimi want to pull her friend into a hug.

All along Derek had remained placid, smiling peacefully, a contrast to Violet's awe. And then he took the bouquet from her, passed it to Mimi, and reached for Violet's other hand. "You were always gonna get this. Not a chance was I gonna let you go. Nothing, V, *nothing* would've kept me away from you." He leaned down and pressed a tender kiss to her mouth. "No worries, sweet V. We got this, okay?"

"Okay." She beamed a smile at him. "I love you."

"You're the love of my life. Forever."

"Forever." She tilted toward him again, and they kissed.

"Got a ring burning a hole in my pocket here, guys," Slater said.

Everyone burst out laughing, and Derek held his hand out behind him, never breaking the kiss. Slater deposited the ring in his palm, and Derek stopped kissing long enough to place it on her finger.

"I'm guessing you take Violet Davis to be your lawfully wedded wife?" Francesca said with a smile in her voice.

Derek straightened, kissing the tip of her nose. "I do."

"I do, too," Violet said.

More laughter, as Mimi reached for Violet's hand, uncurled her fingers, and pressed the ring in it. Violet smiled sheepishly. "Sorry, go on."

"And you take Derek Valencia to be your lawfully wedded husband?"

"Yes, yes, yes."

Derek lunged for her, lifting her off her feet. "Fuck, yeah."

"You sexy beast," Cooper said.

"Would you shut up?" Ben said. "It's a fuckin' wedding."

"Right, because it's *so* traditional."

Francesca gave the guys a look that said, *You done?* And Ben pushed his palms out toward her in a gesture that said, *Please, go ahead.*

"Ladies and gentlemen, I present to you Derek and Violet Valencia."

Pressed to her husband's body, Violet turned to the group and beamed a shy and deeply satisfied smile.

Just then Slater pushed through the small crowd to claim his woman. He backed her against the ledge, one big hand caressing her belly. Emmie tilted her head back, luminous with so much love, Mimi had to look away.

Would she ever have that with Calix? The moments of intimacy they had were transcendent. But as close as they'd gotten, he still held himself back. After a few hours of incredible passion, he left. He always left.

That was weird, right? That they'd never had a whole night together? It was.

He was getting better, but would he ever totally be hers?

Slater and Derek loved their women with abandon. They put their women first. After what he'd gone through, could Calix ever do that? Or would he forever punish himself for losing sight of Hopper?

If he never fully recovered . . . what did that mean for her?

As the group slowly made its way out of the gazebo, across the wildflower fields and to the barn, Mimi reconsidered her promise to bear with him. If he didn't have a whole heart to give, she'd have to compromise her needs.

And she just wouldn't do that. Not for anybody.

Mimi checked the tables and dance floor but didn't see any of the Bourbons. She was determined to be completely present for Violet's wedding, though, so she didn't text Calix to find out when—or if—they were coming.

As she rearranged a tiered cupcake stand, arms went around her waist. "I love this so much."

She straightened and turned into Violet's embrace. "I'm so glad." Mimi breathed in her friend's unique wildflower-scented perfume. "I wanted this day to be perfect for you."

"It is. And you know why? Because it's all us. It's on our farm, in the barn where the music's made. It's our wildflower ice tea, and your incredible food. And these decorations? It's . . . God, Mimi. Look at this. Who wouldn't want to be in this room? You should open your own restaurant."

Mimi had too much exposure to the restaurant business to ever want to own one. "I don't know about that, but this would make a pretty cute bakery." She loved the mason jars with watermelon-colored punch and striped straws, the vintage pedestal cake stands holding a wild assortment of desserts.

A flash of light caught her attention—sun glinting off metal. Several trucks pulled haphazardly onto the grass and doors flew open. What the hell? She wouldn't let anything ruin Violet's reception, so Mimi excused herself and hurried outside, closing the barn doors.

As she made her way toward the fracas, she couldn't miss Terrence's huge body as he leaned inside the driver's side window of a battered Toyota. He pulled out a keychain. Calix had his arms wide open, blocking a woman.

Gus jumped out of his truck. "Dammit, Laney."

"Get the fuck out of my way." The drunken woman could barely get the words out as she struggled to get past Calix.

"What the hell are you doing here?" Gus cut in front of his brother and got hold of her. She started whaling on him, fists pounding. "Cut it out." He grabbed her arms and jerked them behind her back.

The woman's dress, bandeaux style with a wraparound bodice, was askew, nearly exposing her breast. Mimi attempted to get closer, to try and cover her, but Laney was kicking and twisting.

Calix pulled her away. "Sorry we're late, Meems. One of her friends called to tip us off."

Gus wound up behind the woman, her hands at the small of her back, and Mimi took the opportunity to step forward and pull the material up.

In thanks, Laney spit, her legs kicking out.

"That's enough," Terrence snapped in his scary, gravelly voice. "Laney, get in the truck."

The woman stopped fighting, her features going slack. "You fuckin' fuckers. I hate you. I hate you all so much."

Gus murmured in her ear, voice hard and threatening, and Laney calmed down some, looking almost embarrassed. "I'm gonna get her home."

Laney lurched wildly, pulling out of Gus's hold. "Yeah, that's right. Take me home and fuck me. Isn't that why you like me? 'Cause I fuck so good?"

He caught her easily, banding his arms around her. "Jesus, would you shut up?"

"What're you gonna do to get me to shut me up?"

Gus looked mortified.

And then Jo stepped forward. "Look, girl, you got two choices."

Laney quieted, lank hair in her face.

"You either let my son take you to your people, or I call the police. Way I understand it, he ended things with you, so he's got no more ties. Gettin' the police to haul your ass off this property makes good sense to me. Your call."

Laney wavered, looking like she was trying to work through what Jo had said and weigh the options in her alcohol-saturated brain. Finally, with hate turning her eyes hard, she went limp in Gus's arms. "I don't want to be around you losers anyhow. Take me home."

"Sorry about this, Mimi." Exchanging keys with his dad, Gus force-walked Laney to her car and helped her inside. Then he jogged around to the driver's side, turned the ignition, and drove off.

"How's he gonna get home?" Terrence said.

Mimi shot a look to Calix, knowing he'd take responsibility for his brother.

And that meant he wouldn't be with her.

Again.

But Calix didn't answer right away. He watched his mom, patiently, quietly, and then he reached for Mimi's hand. "You got this, Dad?"

Terrence marshaled his look of surprise, but he didn't contain the slight curl at the side of his mouth. He clapped Calix on the back. "Yeah, we got this. I'll text him. See where he's at."

And then Terrence started for the car, stopping when he realized his wife hadn't followed.

With her eyes on the barn, she said, "I want to see how it all turned out."

When no one responded, Jo said, "What? I worked on the damn thing."

"Looks like Gus'll be taking a cab," Terrence said.

Calix gripped Mimi's hand tightly, and then the four of them headed into the reception.

Waking with a start, Calix checked the time. Two in the morning. He should probably get going. But the moment he shifted away, Mimi snuggled up tighter to him.

He smiled. Her hand swept down his chest, coming to rest over his belly button. Her breasts pressed into his rib cage, and her leg lifted over his thighs.

She couldn't get closer if she tried. And he liked it. Liked sleeping with her, her body wrapped around him.

But his pulse kicked up when he realized he was doing it again. Getting carried away. Only this time not in his band but with a woman. He wasn't some reckless kid anymore.

He should probably get going, but he didn't want to wake her. She had her final taping that afternoon and needed her rest. Moonlight shone on her soft auburn curls, making them glow like embers in a smoldering fire. He sifted his fingers through them at her temple.

She stirred. "You leaving?"

"In a minute."

She sat up with a furrowed brow. "Will you ever spend the night with me?"

He pulled his arm out of the covers, adjusted his bracelets. "Of course."

"Whatever." She gave a gentle shake of her head. "It's

all right." She settled back down, rolling onto her side away from him.

He didn't like that. Grabbing her with both hands, he dragged her closer to him. "Want you draped all over me."

"Hey." She laughed but settled in next to him, curving her body with his. "How'm I supposed to look out for my heart when you're always doing things like this?"

Heart pounding, chest tightening, he pressed his palm to her stomach and drew her even closer. He couldn't lose himself, but he also couldn't be careless with her feelings. Hard to strike the right balance—especially when his impulse was to sink all the way into her. "I love your heart, Mimi."

Did he love her? *Love?* That word had once fit easily into his vocabulary. But now its shape had become so distorted, it didn't fit anywhere.

But he loved so many things about her, and she needed to know them. "I love your smile. It's like . . ." How could he describe the way it thrilled him every time? It was like pulling an aerial. "When your surfboard leaves the lip of the wave and you take off and flip? That's how your smile makes me feel."

"You and my mouth."

But he wasn't in a teasing mood. "And your hair. I love it spread out over my pillow. I love your ass, especially how it looks in my hands when I'm fucking you from behind. I love your expression when you're cooking, all focused and peaceful. I love the way you and Lee huddle together and talk about shit. I can't even hear what you're saying, but watching you two together like that makes me happy." And it was the first time he realized that Mimi fit in. She fit in with his family and with his life.

Oh, shit.

"What?" Both hands swept across his cheeks. "Tell me."

"You're in." He took her hand and pressed it to his heart. "You're in here."

Her hand slipped out of his, smoothed up his chest, and wrapped around his neck.

When she sighed, he leaned in and kissed that lush mouth. Jesus, she made him feel so crazy with need. Every time he touched her, he poured himself all over her. "Mimi." Pressing her back, he stretched out over her. Her legs wrapped around his hips, and her hands slid under his shirt to ride up his back.

Fuck, she split him wide open. Made him out of control.

He wanted her—all of her—and it terrified him to understand he could have all of her—she gave herself to him freely. He just had to find it in him to give himself back—or he wouldn't get to keep her.

Pulling away, he jacked up on his knees and tore his shirt off. Her warm hands went right to his pecs, caressing down his stomach until they wrapped around his cock, guiding it to the tight, hot core of her.

He licked into that sexy mouth, gliding his cock through her slick folds. Her back arched, giving him more of that pale, creamy skin, those bouncing breasts, and the glowing auburn curls. She was fucking gorgeous, and when she reached for him, he was a goner. Her hands gripped his ass at the same time her hips rose, trapping his cock between them. And then she thrust, sending shockwaves of sensation through him.

Something in him broke just then, that last barrier guarding his heart. She was his. In the most fundamental way, he just got it. It was a tiny shift, like some small thing had been blocking the light that shone on this piece of his heart. The heart that Mimi owned.

He wanted to show her how he felt, since he didn't have the words. Wanted to savor her. Sitting back on his heels, he lifted her leg and kissed her ankle. He licked a path up her smooth calf, kissing the back of her knee, and then flicking his tongue over the sensitive skin.

She sighed, eyes glazed with lust, breasts trembling with each shaky intake of breath.

His mouth traveled up her thigh until he found the string of red hearts, and he kissed each one. More kisses across her stomach, and then he caressed her breasts, drew them together, and sucked a nipple deep into his mouth, flicking his tongue over it.

She arched under him, her back bowing off the bed,

fingers driving into his hair, scraping his scalp. "More. Give me more."

"I'll give you fucking everything." He knelt before her, hands sliding under her ass to lift her, and he kissed between her legs, deep, wet tongue kisses, just like he gave her mouth. And then he licked the wet, hot length of her, and she arched off the mattress.

"God, Calix. *God.*"

Giving in to the urgent thrust of her hips, the pull of her hands, and the heightened pitch of her cries, he fluttered his tongue over her nub. Her passion fueled his hunger.

And then her body bucked, her hips pinned to his mouth, and she cried out his name. When she settled, her body stretched first one way, then the other, and she gave him a satisfied grin.

"Come here." She reached for him.

He rose over her, mindless with the need to be inside her. Sliding his hands under her back, he gripped her shoulders and pushed inside her slick, hot channel.

"Yes. *God.*" Her legs tightened around him, the soles of her feet digging into his ass.

He wanted that mouth, but he was thrusting too hard, too fast, to latch on to it, so he buried his face in her neck, his body a live wire. And then a shower of electric impulses traveled down his spine, gathering at the base. She lifted her hips, grinding against him, gasping and pulling on his hair, and that was it. He threw his head back as sensation coiled, focused, and then exploded. "Jesus Christ." He pumped his release into her with quick, brutal thrusts.

Collapsing on top of her, he rested his ear against her heart. And then he exhaled roughly. "Yeah, sweet pants. I'll spend the night with you."

With four bodies jamming in the studio, the heat got oppressive.

Sweat dripped down Calix's face, and he hunched a shoulder to wipe it out of his eyes. Dak hadn't let them play together all that often, but Calix's dad thought they sounded better that way, more authentic. And there was no mistaking the energy when they did. No question about it, his dad had returned them to their sound.

Movement in the control room caught his attention, and he looked up. Gus jumped out of a chair and ran out of the room.

Calix faltered, causing his dad to look up from the control board. Everyone stopped. "What—" His dad whipped around toward the open door, threw off his headphones, and flew out of the room.

Calix bolted.

"What's going on?" Cooper said.

Bursting out of the studio, Calix heard shouts, and then a piercing scream filled the air.

A punch of adrenaline propelled him down the driveway to find two cars in the middle of the street, one perpendicular to the other. His dad stabbed buttons on his phone as he crouched over a body.

When he recognized the battered black boots, Calix roared forward. "Gus!" *What the hell?*

As his dad gave Slater and Emmie's address to the 911 operator, Calix crouched next to his brother. He didn't see blood anywhere, but Gus was unconscious. His wrist—oh, Jesus, it shouldn't be twisted at that angle. He pressed two fingers to Gus's carotid artery. "Strong pulse."

His dad gave a terse jerk of his head.

It was only then that he noticed the activity around him. A stranger helped a drunken Laney out of her car, led her to the grass, and sat her down. The nymph wailed, clutching the back of her neck.

Calix glanced at the other driver . . . the one Laney had hit . . . found the band huddled around the driver's door.

Until Slater barked for everyone to get back. The crowd cleared, revealing Slater crouching beside Emmie, barely visible behind a deployed airbag.

The baby.

Jesus Christ.

The baby.

CHAPTER EIGHTEEN

As the train neared Westbury, Mimi's phone vibrated. She loved the support, but she really needed to block everything out and go to her Zen place. Her mom, her friends, her dad, Irwin, everyone had checked in with her. Even Emmie had texted on her way out of the doctor's office.

She'd done everything she could to prepare for today's competition—well, within the boundaries of one short week—so she went in knowing she'd given it her best shot.

Eleanor, though, her final competitor, was good. While her résumé didn't include formal culinary training, she'd been cooking all her life.

Her phone vibrated again. *Okay, something's up.* She glanced at the screen. Violet.

Trying to reach you. Call me.

Immediately, she hit Violet's speed dial.

"Mimi. Hey."

Oh, God. Her body went into high alert from Violet's tone. Her friend, always calm and in control, sounded unnerved. "What's wrong?"

"There's been an accident."

A sickening feeling crashed through her.

"Emmie, Gus, and Laney are headed to Eastern Long Island Hospital right now."

"Oh, my God. Are they all right?" Grabbing her messenger bag, slinging the strap around her neck, she got up, mouthing *Excuse me* to the businessman beside her. Instead of getting up, he turned his knees to the side, accomplishing nothing. She couldn't help banging her bag into him as she edged out of the seat. "Sorry," she whispered.

"It's hard to say for sure at this point. All we know is that Laney came by the studio drunk. She must've texted Gus, because Calix saw him running out of the control room. From the police report, it looks like she backed out crazy fast and smashed into Emmie. She was just coming home from her OB-GYN appointment."

Mimi made her way to the exit and reached for the handrail. "Is she okay?" And then she whispered. "The baby?"

"I don't know anything. I wasn't sure if I should call—it's not like there's anything you can do—but it didn't feel right not telling you."

"Of course you have to tell me." They were her family. She loved them. God, Emmie's *baby*. "How's Slater?"

She was quiet for a moment. "I've never seen him like this."

"Are they okay? God, you have to tell me *something*."

"I wish I could. The guys are hoping the airbag just knocked the wind out of her. She's being seen right now. But Slater's crazy, Meems. They wouldn't let him go in with her, and he was shouting, demanding to see his wife and baby. It killed us to see him like that."

She couldn't even imagine. "I can't believe this."

"Yeah, so, we're all in the ER waiting to hear. What do you want to do?"

"I'm getting off at the next stop. I'll catch a cab and meet you there. V, if you hear anything—anything at all, let me know."

"What about the show?"

"I can't think about the show right now. I mean, Emmie . . ." The *baby*. "And Gus. Tell me you'll let me know."

"You know I will."

As the train neared the station, her thoughts went to Calix. He hadn't been the one to call or text.

And that scared her.

As the cab turned into the hospital parking lot, Mimi leaned forward. "Can you drop me at the emergency room, please?"

The driver nodded. She sat back in her seat and sent texts to Calix and Violet. Here.

She couldn't quell the anxiety. Imagine if something was terribly wrong with Gus. It just wouldn't be fair. How would the Bourbons handle the loss of another child?

They wouldn't have to. Mimi refused to imagine worst-case scenarios. She would think positive thoughts only. Anything else was a waste of energy.

But God, she couldn't bear it if this family had to endure another tragedy.

The driver stopped. "Here you go."

"Great, thank you." She pulled some bills out of her wallet and handed them to her.

Racing into the building, she nearly slammed into Laney, cuffed and with a neck brace, being led out the automatic doors by two cops. As they passed by, the woman tilted her chin, giving Mimi a challenging look.

Mimi held her gaze. *What have you done?* And then she continued on to find her friends.

Against pale green walls people sat in chairs—so many people for early afternoon on a weekday. She found the band together in a corner. Everyone but Slater.

On the other side of the room, Jo Bourbon stood like a pillar looking out the window, arms crossed over her stomach, hands cupping her elbows. Terrence and Calix's muscular, imposing bodies surrounded her and Lee like a bulwark. All of them had their backs to the room.

And Shay was there. Shay and that tall, lean guy she always saw around Calix. Bones?

Shay. Which meant someone had told her.

And how else would she have found out if not from Calix?

She put a stop to that petty line of thinking. *This isn't about me.*

First, she had to make sure Emmie and the baby were okay. She headed to her friends. Coop slumped low, eyes closed, and Ben sat forward, elbows on his knees, texting. Derek stood, back against the wall, arms around Violet. The moment her friend saw her, she stepped forward.

"Hey." Violet wrapped Mimi in a hug.

"What do we know?"

"The baby's okay."

"Oh, thank God."

"They did an ultrasound. But they're keeping Emmie overnight just to be sure. Once they assign her a room, we'll head up there."

"And Emmie?"

Violet smiled. "She's fine. Slater's with her right now."

Mimi tipped her head toward the Bourbons. "Any word?"

"They haven't acknowledged us, so we don't know anything."

Heart aching for them, she headed in their direction. She needed to be there for Calix.

She loved him. She loved him so much. And his whole family . . . God, all they'd done for her with the competition and the wedding. This insular, grieving family had dropped their linked arms to let her in.

The moment she approached, she set her hand on Calix's back. "Hey."

He flinched like she was some stranger groping him in a dark alley.

Shay immediately stepped between them. "Hey." Her voice was soft and sexy. "Mimi, right?"

She nodded, but she didn't want to talk to this woman. She wanted to talk to Calix.

With a hand at the small of Mimi's back, Shay started to lead her away.

Mimi spun away from her. "Calix?" She said it softly but insistently.

When he turned to her, she expected to see conflict, pain—those emotions would've made sense. But she didn't expect Mr. Stoic. Shay gave him a look like, *What can I do? She's just impossible.*

With a terse nod from Calix—*I'll take care of it*—Shay shrugged and moved back to the formidable block of Bourbons.

Mimi reached out to touch his arm, but he stiffened, so she pulled back. "How is he?"

His features tightened, and he shot a glance to his family. Clearly, he didn't want to leave them. As if, in stepping away from them, the foundation would collapse, and they'd be reduced to a puddle of bones and skin on the floor.

She understood how concerned he was about Gus. Of course he was. But he didn't have to shut her out. "I've been worried out of my mind since Violet called me. Are you all right? Have you heard anything about Gus?"

Walking her out of the family's hearing range, he said. "We don't know anything." Spoken quickly, dismissively. He wanted her gone. Or more to the point, he wanted to get back to his family. But why couldn't she be there *with* them?

Wait—oh, God—did they blame her? She was the one who'd gotten Gus the job in the studio. He never would've met Laney had it not been for her. Should she leave? She wanted to do what was best for them, so if having her around upset them, she'd go. But she was worried about Calix. The accident had likely sent him back into default mode—making him feel singularly responsible for the welfare of his family.

No, no. She was overreacting. He'd done the same thing when Gus had called from jail. He'd fully intended on going alone, but she'd insisted on coming with him. He'd been relieved.

She gave him a warm smile that told him he wasn't alone, but when she touched his arm, he took a step back.

"I can't deal with this right now, Mimi. I need to be with my family."

Deal with *this*? What exactly was *this*?

He could barely stand to look at her, his entire body primed to get back where he so obviously wanted to be. "I'm here with you."

The hard line of his mouth scared her. "Not now. I'll talk to you later."

God, he was so cold. Treating her like an unwelcome stranger. But he needed her. She knew he did. "Can you just tell me what happened?" Hours ago, this man had been inside her, his hands caressing, gripping, possessing her. Dirty words in her ear, sweat-slicked bodies writhing together.

A matter of *hours* ago.

She had to get through. "Calix."

"I said not now."

This wasn't at all like the night they'd picked up Gus from jail. He actually didn't want her around. She didn't comfort him—she *agitated* him. "What can I do?"

"You can go. That's the only thing I need. For you to go." The only thing keeping him with her at the moment was the last remnant of civility he possessed. He didn't want her.

"God, Calix, I—"

He probably moved only a few inches, but he towered over her, his intention to intimidate clear. "My brother's in the fucking emergency room." He shot a look to his mom. "I have to get back to my family, and I'm asking you to go."

"Will you text me? Let me know how he's doing?"

Barely suppressing his impatience, he flexed his hands. The muscle in his jaw popped. "Yeah, sure."

Stunned, Mimi looked deeper into his eyes, waiting for him to break, to reach out for her. But he stalked off.

She watched him go, shaken and confused. What had just happened?

"Hey, sweetie." Violet took her arm and led her away. "They're taking Emmie to a room right now, so we can go up and see her. Okay?"

She tried to blink back tears, but she couldn't stop them. They burned a track down her cheeks. What the hell had just happened?

"Come on, Meems." With an arm wrapped around her, Violet led her back to the others.

In a daze, Mimi followed the band to Emmie's room.

They gathered in the doorway, the scene in Emmie's room too private to breach.

Slater lay on the narrow hospital bed facing his wife, one hand on her tiny baby bump, the other on top of her head. "I fucking love you," he whispered.

"I fucking love you, too," she whispered back.

"Yo, can we come in?" Coop said.

"Gotta get eyes on you, woman," Ben said.

Looking exhausted, Emmie smiled. Slater got up, giving them all a hard look. "She's fine. Baby's fine. Thanks for coming."

"Jonny," Emmie said quietly. Only she called Slater by his real name. "It's all right. They can stay."

Everyone crowded around her, and Mimi could feel the absolute love and devotion. It was humbling, and it was beautiful.

Emmie peered around the guys and smiled warmly. She lifted her arms. "Meems."

Mimi eased gently into Emmie's arms. "You okay?"

"It was scary, but yeah. We're okay."

Mimi sat on the edge of the bed. "What happened?"

"Laney was coming out of the driveway like a bat out of hell, and she rammed into me."

"Luckily she only hit the front left wheel well," Slater said. "Missed the door by a foot."

Emmie reached for his hand. "But the worst part was Gus. He came running down the driveway, trying to stop her. I don't know what he thought he could do. So, after she hit me, she reversed and floored it. Went straight at him."

"Oh, my God." No wonder his family was freaking out. "She hit him with her car?"

"It can't be that bad," Ben said. "Not like she could build up any speed. He was right in front of her when she punched the accelerator."

"He hit the windshield," Coop said. "Rolled off."

Emmie's features crumpled in fear and worry, and Slater was at her side. "Hey, angel, it's okay. He's okay."

"Is he?" Mimi asked.

"Dude's gonna be bruised up pretty bad," Coop said.

"But the baby's all right?" Mimi asked Emmie. "Everything's good?"

"Looks good," Emmie began, but Slater interrupted. "He's awesome. But they're going to keep her overnight to make sure."

Violet leaned in. "Hey, you're missing your show."

Mimi waved a hand dismissively. "I don't care."

"No, she's not." Derek pulled out his phone and checked the time. "Doesn't start taping till three. You can still make it."

"You totally can," Violet said.

Should she? Everything in her screamed to go back to Calix. But he didn't want her. Truly, seriously, did not want her.

Emmie was all right, and if she left right now, she could make the show just in time.

She looked to Emmie, who made a shooing motion. "Go. Are you kidding? I'm fine. The baby's fine. Go."

Slater gave her a chin nod. "Check on the Bourbons on your way out. Let us know what's going on."

She got up. "He doesn't . . . he doesn't want to talk to me."

The room went quiet, everyone watching her.

"What?" Emmie said. "Why?"

"I'm not sure. Maybe he blames me." What else could it be?

"For Laney? You don't even know her."

"For getting Gus the job. For suggesting Terrence produce your album. I stuck my nose in where it didn't belong. He kept telling me to mind my own business, and I just kept pushing." Why hadn't she listened to him?

"He's upset," Derek said. "He'll be fine tomorrow."

Cooper nodded toward the door. "Come on. I'll give you a ride to the train station."

"You sure?"

"You bet. Fuckin' hate hospitals."

Her friends surrounded her with hugs and good wishes, and then she took off in a race into the city.

"With thirty minutes on the clock," Verna Bloom said. "Eleanor and Mimi, let's see what kind of dessert you can make with a box of macaroni and cheese, a papaya, Indonesian cassia sticks, and an ostrich egg. Ready ladies? Go."

Fear ticked like a bomb inside Mimi's chest.

But damn it all to hell, she had to sweep the negativity out and focus.

Head in the game.

With the four ingredients placed on the counter before her, she saw only the stiff backs of the Bourbon family in the ER. She couldn't stop thinking about the look passed between Calix and Shay, his silent request to keep Mimi away.

Her friends thought he'd get over it, wake up tomorrow after he'd calmed down and come back to her. But they hadn't looked into those cold eyes.

Was it over? Even though Gus was fine—Violet had texted to let her know he'd come out with only a broken wrist and some pretty bad scrapes and bruises—Calix hadn't contacted her. So it wasn't fear for his brother's life that had him pushing her away. No, it had to be anger that she'd dragged his family back into the world that threatened his mom.

When Eleanor raced past her to get to the refrigerator, Mimi snapped out of her thoughts.

Get your head in the damn game.

Macaroni and cheese . . . turn this into a dessert? Papaya. Cassia sticks—that was basically cinnamon. And the egg was good. *This single ingredient will bind, leaven, emulsify, thicken, clarify, and coat.*

Thank you, Jo.

She could do this. She'd spent the whole week working on desserts. Why couldn't she get her mind to engage? Because she hadn't lost some guy she'd been dating. She'd lost a man she truly, deeply, and thoroughly loved.

She'd gotten so close with Lee. Jo, too. Did Lee blame her, too? Did they *all* blame her? A sickening feeling passed over her.

Stop it.

She looked up. Took in the studio audience, the judges—and found Zoe staring at her.

And it flipped a switch. Snapped her right out of it.

Okay, macaroni and cheese. She tore open the box, ripped

open the packet of noodles, and dumped them in the food processor. She pulsed those suckers into powder.

She'd add some flour to it.

And then images started flooding in. Ricotta cheese. Lemon. Orange zest. She headed for the refrigerator, grabbed some milk, the cheese, and club soda. She'd purée the papaya, use it as a sauce. She could picture the brilliant orange-yellow color against the white plate and knew she'd use it as a drizzle, too. Beautiful. She'd get that syrup going right now.

"Twenty minutes on the clock, ladies. Twenty minutes."

Oh, crap. She'd lost ten minutes. Mimi got out a skillet, dropped a few pats of butter in it, and reached for a bowl. She'd make three small *crespelles* and then deep-fry them. But the moment she realized she was making *cannoli*, fear plucked her spine. Nothing Italian, dammit. Screw it. She'd already lost too much time. Had to do something she could pull off. Maybe she'd lose points for innovation, but she'd blow the judges away with presentation and quick thinking. And it would taste awesome.

She beat the egg, added milk, salt, and melted butter. Then, she added the flour. Not knowing what would happen if she didn't let the batter stand, she decided to go for it anyhow and quickly poured it into the heated skillet. Too runny. *Keep going.*

After grinding the cassia sticks, she grabbed a bowl and mixed the ricotta, vanilla, some milk, sugar, a squeeze of lemon, and some orange zest. She beat the egg and added it.

While flipping the crepes, she thought about the forms. What could she use that would withstand the heat yet pull easily out of the *cannolis*? She really couldn't think of anything other than foil. But it had to be heavy-duty or it wouldn't hold its shape.

Turning back to the papaya, she cut it in half, scraped out the seeds, and pureed it. Quickly straining it, she added it to a sauce pan with sugar and a squeeze of lemon. Very low flame. It couldn't burn while she tended to something else.

Removing the *crespelle* from the skillet—*too thin*—she wrapped each one around the foil dowel. As she set them into the deep fryer, she knew Jo would be disappointed that she'd gone with something Italian, but it couldn't be helped. She'd wasted precious time worrying about Calix.

Thank God Emmie and the baby were okay. Thank God Gus had nothing worse than a broken wrist.

And . . . wait a damn minute. What exactly had she done that was so bad? The accident happened because he'd hooked up with—and moved in with—a freaking nymph.

Mimi had gotten him a *job*. She'd given him an *opportunity*. One he'd desperately wanted.

Screw Calix. She knew how upset he'd been—worst fears realized. She understood that. But rejecting her? *Blaming* her?

Of course, she didn't know what he was thinking since he wouldn't talk to her. *Dick.*

"Ten minutes, ladies," Verna said. "Ten minutes on the clock."

Oh, crap. She'd lost her focus again. *I can do this.* Pulling out three white plates, she found confectioner's sugar and looked around for something green. Mint, perfect.

No, wait, dammit. She couldn't do a drizzle and sprig again. Think, *think*. Glancing across Verna's kitchen, her gaze caught on a huge bouquet of deep red roses on a countertop. The image of those petals against the brilliant orange-yellow of the papaya fired in her mind.

Dashing away from her station, she snatched one stem from the vase, pulled a spray of baby's breath, and hurried back. Verna said something, the audience laughed, but Mimi shut it out.

Crap. How long had the *crespelle* been in the deep fryer? They looked nicely browned, so she pulled them out. Time to remove the dowels . . . but the crepes were so thin.

Please don't break, please don't—

A shell cracked. Damn shaking hands. *Forget it. Put the cracked side down on the plate.* She spooned the filling into each one, poured papaya sauce in two pools on each plate and arranged the rose petals on it. Gorgeous. Setting the *cannoli* in the center, she dusted each one with confectioner's sugar.

Something was still missing. Green. She set a floret of mint in the center of the petals, and she was done.

"Time's up, ladies," Verna said. "Hands off."

Mimi stepped back. Her clothes stuck to her with perspiration, and her whole body trembled. But she'd done it.

Holy crap, that had been close.

And now to face the firing squad.

"**Chef** Alonso?" Verna said.

Even as Mimi cursed herself for forgetting the sweet Marsala, she reminded herself that the judges had deemed Eleanor's gorgeous dessert tasteless, so she still had a chance.

"I think I've tasted heaven," the chef said. "This filling is divine. Absolutely divine. I'm going to give you a four for quick thinking, because even though you were a little slow off the mark, you managed to pull together a lovely dish. A five, as always, for your gorgeous presentation. And a five for innovation because you took a box of macaroni and turned it into a scrumptious *cannoli*."

Relief swept through her so hard, her knees went weak. "Thank you so much."

"Mr. Simmons?" Verna said. "Who, I just want to point out, basically licked the plate clean."

"It was quite tasty." The man gave a boyish grin.

The audience laughed.

"Well, I thought this was terrific. The orange zest in the filling, the perfect crunch to the shell, I'm giving you fives across the board because, Mimi Romano, you dazzle me."

Maybe it was Calix's stunning rejection, or maybe just the crash after the race to perform, but tears blurred her vision. "Thank you." She could barely get the words out. She wanted to walk into that man's arms and sag against him.

If only her dad were so easily dazzled.

Was he watching right now? Was his team? At least she hadn't made a fool out of herself. But she had to win the competition and score the apprenticeship or she'd have no hope of working with him.

"Chef Zoe?"

Mimi held her breath. This woman would determine her

fate. With the high scores she'd gotten from the men, she could afford a few of Zoe's low ones. She just didn't know how tough this judge would be on her.

She only knew failure wouldn't get her a job at Dino Romano and Associates.

"The best thing I can say about this dish is the presentation. You finally moved beyond a drizzle and a sprig. But you basically shoved warm ricotta into a hot shell." Zoe stuck fork tines in the flat filling. "The taste might be excellent, but the texture's like baby food." She sighed, shaking her head. "A *cannoli*? I have to say I'm disappointed. I wanted to see you venture outside your comfort zone, but you didn't. You gave me exactly what I expected. I'm going to give you a one for innovation. I'm also going to give you a one for quick thinking, and I'll tell you why. You froze. I saw it—we all saw it. And in a fast-paced kitchen, there's no room for that. You zone out and someone gets hurt. And a four for presentation." She held Mimi's gaze. "You finally impressed me. It's beautiful."

Her blood turned cold. One point less than Eleanor. Everything in her yearned to find Calix in the audience, seek out the confidence and support he'd always given her. But he wasn't there.

She'd lost him, and she'd lost the competition.

"Thank you, Chef Zoe." She looked to the other judges and then Verna Bloom. "Thank you for the opportunity."

And with that, Mimi walked off the stage.

"I lost, Mom." Mimi's feet ached as she made her way down Avenue of the Americas. Her body felt so sluggish, she wanted to curl up in the vestibule of a bank's ATM station.

"I'm sorry, sweetheart. You gave it your very best shot. You just couldn't get around that one judge."

"She was right." And that hurt the most. "I knew not to make something Italian, but I did it anyway."

"Across the board, the judges loved the taste of your food. Isn't that what matters?"

"No, Mom. That's not what matters at all. I *lost*." Which

meant she either went to Miami or she tried something different.

But this competition *was* trying something different, and she'd failed. So trying again would put off getting a real job even longer. *Enough already.* She'd graduated business school over a year ago. "I'm taking the job."

"What job?"

"In Miami."

"Maybe this isn't the best time to be making important decisions. Give yourself a break."

"That's what I've been doing. I took a really long break, and now it's time to get back to work." And funny enough, she was ready. After going hard her whole life, she'd needed this time cooking and goofing off on a wildflower farm on the tip of Long Island. She'd had a great time. But she was ready to get back on track. Have a real purpose.

"What about Calix? If you go to Miami, you'll lose him."

A stab of pain punctured her brief moment of resolution. "I already lost him." Mimi faltered, looking for a bench, anywhere to sit for just a moment. She couldn't bear all she'd lost.

"I wouldn't write him off so soon."

"You weren't there. You didn't see the way he looked at me."

"I'm not sure he *was* seeing you. From what you've told me, I'm quite sure he was seeing his brother get hit by a car and then seeing his mother's reaction to another son's life in jeopardy. You might want to give him a moment to settle down."

"Okay, but Gus is fine, and I still haven't heard from him." Passing a homeless man parked on a cardboard mat against the filthy stone wall of a high-rise, Mimi reached into her pocket and handed him a twenty-dollar bill. The smell of hot dogs from a street vendor filled the air. She looked at the street sign to see how far she'd gone. She was miles from home.

"You said something interesting not long ago. You said if he takes his eyes off his family and something goes wrong, he'll never forgive himself."

"Right."

"Did he take his eyes off his family to spend time with you?"

Fear slammed her, and she lost her rhythm, nearly stumbling. "Yes. He spent the night with me. He's never done that before. He always goes home to make sure his mom gets something to eat before she goes to bed. Last night he stayed over."

"So, he doesn't blame *you*. He blames himself for spending so much time with you."

She sucked in a breath. "Mom." *Oh, God.*

"What?"

"He thinks the reason Hopper died is because he got selfishly carried away with his band. Hopper wasn't going to grow up and be the independent man Calix was, and he felt so much guilt about that. So right when he was about to get a record contract and truly separate from his family, Hopper died."

"And this time he selfishly got carried away with you. He took his eyes off his family."

Oh, fuck a dozen daisies. "It's too much, Mom. The guilt he carries, it's too much. But he doesn't understand. What he calls getting carried away is really just passion. And that's a good thing. A great thing. He can't see that because he thinks it cost him his brother." Energy flooded in. She had to talk to him. Make him understand. "Mom, I have to go." Racing into the street, she hailed a cab.

"Hang on, sweetheart. You're not going to see him now, are you?"

"I have to. I have to make him understand."

"Mimi, darling. Give him some time. He might not be ready to see you yet."

"But he's hurting, Mom. I have to—"

"You have to give him time."

But she loved him, and he was hurting. And it wasn't in her nature to sit back and wait. "I don't know what to do. I have to talk to him." *I miss him.*

"It just happened today. His family's still reeling from the accident."

The rational part of her agreed with her mom. But the scared, vulnerable side feared time would cement his resolve to stay away from her.

But it wasn't about her. It was about him. What was best for him in this situation.

So she'd leave him be.

For as long as she could stand it.

CHAPTER NINETEEN

She lasted two days.

In a borrowed truck, Mimi pulled into the Bourbons' driveway. While Gus's injuries turned out to be minor, the experience had to have hit the family pretty hard. She hoped Jo hadn't retreated into her cave.

Calix, though . . . she couldn't stand it if he blamed himself. She had to talk to him.

Getting out of the truck, she took a fortifying breath. From the outside, this property looked like paradise. The lush gardens, the vineyard and orchard, the patch of healthy green grass in front of the house. Everything outside thrived thanks to Terrence's loving care. He'd diverted all the energy from music, his true passion, into the land.

She thought of Jo giving new life to discarded objects. They'd done their best to survive a tragedy, and Mimi had carelessly inserted herself, thinking she knew better. She wished she'd minded her own business.

Dragging her damp palms down her shorts, she walked on shaky legs to the door and rang the bell.

No one answered.

But she could hear the thump of bass, punctuated by

squeals of laughter. Sounded like they were on the patio. Maybe she should text him, ask him to come out front so they could talk privately. No, she wanted to talk to all of them. Give them hugs and let them know how happy she was that Gus was all right.

The noises grew louder as she headed around the side of the house. Maybe Calix was all right. His brother had a broken wrist and some bruises, so maybe they were just regrouping as a family. Calix would be glad to see her. She could see his features softening the way they did, apologizing for pushing her away so coldly.

He hadn't meant it.

He couldn't have.

She found Terrence on his knees in his glorious garden, surrounded by plants of every texture and height under the sun.

"Hey, Terrence."

The giant of a man sat back on his heels, wiping a gloved hand across his sweaty brow. He shot a quick look over his shoulder. "Mimi." Standing up on knees that cracked, he reached for her. Brushed a kiss across her cheek.

"How is everyone?"

Terrence gave her a gentle smile, but he lacked his usual spark of energy. "Gus is just fine."

"And Jo? How's she doing?"

"Ah." He looked away. "Still a little rattled."

"I'm scared because I've grown so close to all of you, and I'm afraid you blame me for what happened."

"No, Mimi." He shook his head. "Not at all." He reached out and patted her shoulder. "Real sorry about the competition."

"I'm disappointed, but ..." She batted a hand dismissively. "I'll find another opportunity." And she would. But the only thing on her mind at the moment was making things right with Calix. It killed her thinking about the guilt he suffered, the blame he shouldered.

"What's next for you?" he asked.

She didn't want to talk about her career. She wanted to flat-out ask about Calix, but she couldn't put Terrence in the middle. "I might take that job in Miami."

"Miami?"

Somebody squealed, and then laughter rang out. Mimi looked past Terrence to the patio. Stretched out on a chaise, caramel-colored skin warming in the sun, Calix flashed a devilish smile.

He was *laughing*.

He looked relaxed, happy. She started toward him. While she'd been devastated—God, he'd discarded her like a fresh turd—*and* she'd lost the competition—he'd been hanging out with his friends.

What an *asshole*.

"Mimi." Terrence's warning tone only irritated her. Nothing would stop her from confronting the man who'd played her so carelessly.

She made it to the edge of the patio when she saw Shay pulling off her T-shirt and shorts, wearing nothing but a tiny bikini and tossing them both at Calix. He swatted them away, smiling up at his ex-girlfriend.

Mimi recognized his friends from the beach.

Anger—God, so much wild, unrestrained anger—burst out of her core. "Calix."

Everyone turned to her. Calix's smile slowly died. But he didn't move.

Fury burned a path through her body, making perspiration pop out under her arms and over her lip. She couldn't breathe, couldn't think. "We need to talk."

Looking completely put out, Calix got up. The jerk took his time getting to her.

How the hell had she ever thought she'd broken down his barriers and gotten in? She'd thought they'd had something so special he'd fought his way through all his fears just to hang on to it.

But she was a fool. He'd only taken what she'd freely given.

Calix towered over her. "What's up?"

"What's *up*?" She was so angry, she shook. "Ever since you kicked me out of the emergency room, I've been beside myself with worry. I can barely sleep. You had to know I'd worry, but I haven't heard a word from you. So I came here to make sure you're all right. But you're not upset, you're not freaking out. You're having a great time with your friends. I don't even know what to say to you."

"I'm not having a great time. I'm doing anything but having a great time. My mom's back in the goddamn guest bedroom. Nothing's okay."

"And let me guess. You blame yourself for it. So you've gone right back to making her omelets at midnight." She shook her head in exasperation. "And I thought *I* was a wind-up toy banging into the wall over and over again."

He held up a hand. "Not talking about it with you."

"No, of course not. Because I tell you the truth. Your pesky little problem of getting carried away with the things you enjoy? It's called *passion*. And it's what makes you such an amazing man. It's why girls want to sleep with you and men want to be you. And for you to try and shut it down . . . Well, guess what, buddy? You can't. Because it's *who you are*. And it's beautiful. Gus didn't get hurt because you like spending time with me. It happened because he's been so sheltered. He hasn't had the kinds of experiences that teach him that running off with an unstable groupie leads to bad things. But he's learning that now, just like we all learn from life's lessons. I'll bet he won't get involved with crazy nymphs again no matter how great the sex."

All the while she'd unleashed her thoughts, he'd grown harder and angrier. But when his lip curled back, she shut her mouth.

"Are you out of your fucking mind? You're blaming my *mom* for what happened to Gus?" He stepped even closer to her, a dark shadow blocking the sun. "You know what? I do blame myself. I told you from the start it wasn't the right time for me to get involved, and I was right. I fucked up. You don't know. You've never lost a sibling. You don't know what it does to a family. I never should've listened to your bullshit."

"Okay, I'm done. You don't *want* to get it. You want to roll around in your guilt and live right here in the stuck zone. Have at it. I'm out." She started to go, but he caught her arm.

"You don't know what you're talking about. My mom's not

eating, she's not sleeping, and she's back in the fucking guest bedroom. That's all I can think about right now."

"Yes, Calix. You've made it perfectly clear you don't think about me. Thank you for killing any last shred of hope I might've had for us." She yanked out of his hold and strode off. But she only got a few steps away before she swung back around. She'd never be close enough to talk to him like this again, so she'd damn well say it now. "I loved you, and you screwed up by letting your guilt over what happened with Hopper keep you from living your life. Shame on you. Shame on you for letting Hopper down so badly. He would hate the man you've become. I know I do."

She turned and somehow made it back to the truck. When she sat down, the seat so hot it burned her legs, her hands shook, making it hard to fit the key into the ignition.

But she got the hell out of there.

She was moving on.

The smell of espresso filled her dad's apartment. In her Columbia sweats and Cornell T-shirt, Mimi shuffled into the kitchen. She wanted to curl up on the couch and fall back asleep.

"There she is. *Mia bella*." Her dad leaned against the counter, cell phone in his hand, glasses low on the bridge of his nose. "You want me to cook or do you want to go out for lunch?"

Mimi glanced at the clock on the microwave. God, it was *noon*. She'd had a terrible, restless night. "I'm not hungry."

She didn't know who she hated more—herself or Calix. She'd thought he'd broken through his barriers, gotten back down to his molten hot core. But then one thing had gone wrong, and he'd washed his hands of her.

Oh, God. The pain cut so deep she nearly doubled over. She needed to lie down.

Why had she fallen for someone so clearly incapable of loving her back?

Well, no more. No more emotionally unavailable men. It

wasn't like she hadn't known from the start—she'd just chosen to fight for his attention.

Which, of course, was the most familiar battle in the world for her.

Her dad set his phone down. "You have to eat something."

"Well, I'm not going out. I'm not even showering."

"Ah, Melie. You're killing me."

"It's fine. Everyone gets her heart broken."

Her dad tipped her chin. "I don't care about everyone. I care about my daughter."

But not enough to spend time with her. *Got it.* She turned away from him. God, she wanted to collapse in a heap. Since the band was taking a few days off so Slater could tend to Emmie and Terrence could deal with his family, she didn't have to cook for them until Monday.

"Mimi, come." He sounded worried about her. "We'll make fettuccine."

"Dad, just let me be a mess for a few days, okay?" In the city. Away from the farm and Calix Bourbon.

Oh, God. She'd lost him. Was there anything more potent than loss? Its inherent powerlessness? There was simply nothing she could do to make someone want her. She just had to accept it.

She let out a shuddery breath. "I'm sad—no, I'm heartbroken—and I'm incredibly bummed that I lost that competition. So I'm giving myself a couple days to just feel miserable. But I'll bounce back. You know I will. And I'll fall in love again, blah, blah, blah." It was just . . . she'd thought she'd found . . . what? The one?

She'd thought they'd had something special. Something real. She'd thought he'd seen into the heart of her and fallen in love.

Stupid, stupid girl.

"So." He clapped his hands. "The competition is done."

"Yup."

"You did a great job, Melie."

"You watched?"

"My daughter's on national television. Of course I watched."

"It was fun." She'd loved it. She really had.

"You were a dynamo."

"I was?"

"You were. So, now we need to talk about what's next."

"That's the last thing I want to talk about. Like I said, I'm going to curl up in the fetal position and feel sorry for myself until Sunday night when I'll take a shower and head back to the farm. And then I'll figure it out."

"You have an opportunity waiting for you."

She was well aware. "I'll consider it. But don't get your hopes up. Moving to Miami is for when I hit rock bottom." *Wait, this isn't rock bottom?* It scared the crap out of her to think there was a lower level to fall. *This one sucks donkey balls.*

"I don't know why you're being so close-minded about this. It's the best possible path to working with me. Five years with that kind of experience under your belt, and no one would challenge your position in my office."

"Oh, is it five years now? Way to keep moving the bar."

"What does that mean?"

"You said a year or two."

"I said to close a few deals. It takes time to do that."

"Okay, whatever."

"One significant deal, and then no one will care that you're my daughter."

"God, Dad. I'll earn their respect on the job like I would anywhere else. But you know what? I'm not talking about this anymore. I'm done jumping through hoops for you." She headed out of the kitchen, calling to him over her shoulder, "And now that you've gotten me all stirred up, we might as well go out to eat. Let me grab a shower first."

"That's my girl."

She needed a walk more than she needed food, so she and her dad set off from his Upper East Side co-op toward Avenue of the Americas.

Every week after the taping, she'd pass the same bakery on her walk home, but with the extra weight she was carrying from a year living on the farm, she'd never gone inside. Today, though, she'd get whatever the hell she wanted. An almond croissant and a latte would hit the spot.

As they neared the bakery, her heart gave a little jump. "This is it." She peered through the window at the gorgeous display of cakes and pastries. And she couldn't help superimposing Violet's wedding reception, with the fairy lights, the striped paper straws, and the polka dot–frosted cupcakes.

"What're you doing, *amore mio*? Are we going in or dreaming about it?"

"Hold your horses," she said with a grin. "Anticipation is the best part." Cupcakes with swirls of chocolate frosting, thick slices of strawberry cream cake, mounds of *biscotti* . . . it all made her mouth water.

"Look at you. You should own a bakery."

"I don't want to make the same things every day of my life."

A thought had been brewing in the back of her mind for a while now, but since her dad invested in and developed high-end restaurants, she'd never bothered to pitch it.

But as she stood there, she realized she had nothing to lose. "Dad." Confidence spread through her. "I have an idea for you."

Her almond croissant sat untouched on her plate, and her latte had cooled.

Hands in motion, Mimi described her concept. "Small spaces—large enough to hold a galley-style kitchen, a display case, and maybe two or three café tables. Low-cost start-up, small commitment, and fast turnaround. But each bakery would look like a fairyland—it would catch the attention of anyone passing by."

It was not lost on her that her dad's phone had been lighting up constantly since they'd taken a table near the refrigerator of soft drinks. But he hadn't answered once. He'd given her his full, rapt attention.

So, she continued. "Do you remember Pedro and his grilled cheese truck from the first episode?"

"I do."

"Same idea. A grilled cheese franchise. Like the bakery, it would just be a storefront. Customers on their way to or from work could order a grilled cheese and take it to go. He should offer breakfast sandwiches, too, so people could grab one on their way to work. But they'd be everywhere. Right outside subway stations. Right in the heart of office plazas. What do you think?"

"I think it's got tremendous possibility." Her father smiled broadly.

"What?"

He set his coffee down. "I want to capture this moment."

"Because I'm thinking outside the box?" He liked her business plan. *Yay!*

"No, because when you talk about this idea, you come alive."

"It's a great idea, right? I mean, sure, the city's got bakeries everywhere, but these would be small, with low overhead. You could grab an espresso to go with your cupcake, but mostly you'd grab a box of cookies on your way home to bring to your kids. We'd start out with a supplier, but if this takes off, we could set up our own baking facility. And the grilled cheese shops? That's a no-brainer, right?"

"We will see. If you're serious about this, then put together a presentation. Cost analysis, real estate, everything, and then present it to us at the Monday meeting."

The Monday meeting? "Does that mean—"

A shout of laughter came out of him. "Yes. It means you're hired."

Petals unfurled in her chest. She'd done it. She'd earned her way into his business. "I'll work on it this week."

But before the happiness could spread, reality cut it off cold. This good news—finally working for her dad—meant an end to anything with Calix. She wouldn't run into him on the farm or in the kitchen at Slater and Emmie's house.

And the only reason she could be so painfully disappointed

was because she'd held on to one tiny shard of hope that they'd get back together. That seeing each other every day would make him realize how much he missed her and had to have her.

And now that wouldn't happen.

It was truly over.

CHAPTER TWENTY

As Calix shoved the last bite of toast into his mouth, his dad entered the kitchen.

"What's your rush?"

He brought his plate to the sink. "I'm heading over now."

His dad studied him a few moments. "Well, hang on. Let me grab something to eat first."

"I'll meet you there. I want my own ride anyway." Then, when they took a break for lunch, he could come home. Spend some time with his mom.

His dad pulled the orange juice out of the refrigerator. "You got somewhere to be?"

He did. The way he'd blown off Mimi . . . shitty thing to do. Figured he'd talk to her before work. Make it right. He turned on the faucet, rinsed his plate and knife. "Just want to get there early."

"This about Mimi?"

His dad caught everything. First day back at work, first time seeing her since he'd blown her off on the patio, he guessed it wasn't too hard to figure out. "It's mostly about having my own wheels." He'd handle it right this time. That way he could go back to the way he used to do things—showing up in time to do his job, and then leaving right after.

Until the band hired someone new.

And then he'd be out of her life for good.

Fuck. He grabbed the edge of the counter. Mimi. Out of his life.

"Good, because you know she's gone, right?"

Shock speared through him. "What do you mean, *gone*?"

"She took a job."

He hit the faucet and faced his dad. "Where?" Had she gone to Miami?

"She's working for her dad in the city. Full time, starting today."

The way his stomach plummeted, he may as well have dropped through a trapdoor in the floor. *Gone?*

"She offered to stay on until they found a new chef, but the guys told her not to worry about it."

He'd ended it with her, so why was it so hard to hear she wouldn't be around? *Isn't this what you wanted?*

A hand clapped his shoulder. "You okay?"

"Of course." He reached for a towel to dry his hands. "Good for her. She got what she wanted." He moved too quickly around his dad, slamming into him. "Sorry."

Where were his keys? He patted his pockets. Not there. He cut across the kitchen to find mail piled high on the built-in desk. He pushed around a few stacks, but they only toppled over, creating more of a mess.

Where the hell were his keys?

"She's just in the city," his dad said. "You can see her anytime."

"Have you seen my keys?"

His dad gestured to the island. Where he'd tossed them when he'd started making his breakfast. *Get your head out of your ass.* He grabbed them.

"Still need to go in early?"

"I'm just gonna ride." *Gone.* He needed to get on his bike. Maybe ride to Montauk. *Dammit.* He felt like he'd downed a case of energy drinks.

"Don't know why you cut her loose. Not sure I've ever seen you that way around a girl."

"We were dating, Dad. Now we're not."

"I saw you at the wedding. The way you looked at her . . ." He unfolded his arms, took a few steps toward him. "She thinks we blame her. I told her we didn't, but I'm not sure she believed me."

"It's not her I blame."

His dad cocked his head. "What're you saying?" And then understanding lit his features. "Wait, you blame *yourself*?"

Heat flushed through him, and he had to look away.

But his dad stepped closer. Got right in his face. "You blame yourself for what happened to Hopper." But he didn't wait for a response. Or more likely, Calix's expression was answer enough. His dad tipped his head back and scrubbed his jaw. And then he straightened with a look of astonishment. "Wait, *this* is why you're not joining the band?" He shook his head. "No, son. You got it wrong."

Pulling on his scruff, his dad let out a slow breath. "You were such a sensitive kid. Took everything so deep." He gave Calix's shoulder a squeeze. "You saw how hard it was for Hopper. How frustrated he got that his brothers were growing up and away from him. I think you internalized it. Yeah, Hopper had a hard time lettin' you go, but that's because he was developmentally disabled. Sucked, but you had to grow up and live your life. It hurt him, not denying it, but it had to happen. You couldn't give up your life to stay back with him. You were doing the right thing, living your life, becoming the man you're meant to be, and being the best big brother to him that you could."

"I wasn't good to him."

His dad gave him a shake, pulled him closer. "Yeah, son, you were."

"That's bullshit." Emotion broke through and shattered him. "I wanted him to leave me alone. I didn't want . . ." His mind spun so fast he got dizzy. "I was a selfish prick. He hung on me all the time, and I just wanted to be free. But . . . I loved him." Oh, Jesus, a wave of regret knocked him full-force in the chest. Tears blurred his vision, and he had a hard time taking in a full breath. "I loved him."

"You sure as hell did. You loved him good, too. You were a damn good brother."

"I was a shit brother. I treated him like shit." Pain sliced him, ripping open the old wound. He turned away from his dad, not wanting to be seen like this. "I want him back, Dad. I want to do it better. Be better to him." He couldn't stop them. The tears. They burned a path down his cheeks.

His dad grabbed him and pulled him against his big, burly chest. Brawny arms wrapped around him. "He loved you, son. Hopper loved you like nobody's business. You were his favorite, you know that, right?"

Of course he knew that. That's why he couldn't live with how badly he'd treated him.

His dad tightened his hold. "You're only remembering the times you pushed him away, but you did good by him." Holding on to Calix's shoulders, his dad looked intently into his eyes. "I remember everything. You were good and kind. And Hopper could be a huge pain in the ass. Loved that boy with all my heart, but he tried my patience. He tried all of ours. But especially yours because he wanted you the most. And you did a great job balancing it. Giving him what he needed, while living your own life. You did better than I did. I can't tell you how many times I said that to myself. That I wished I'd had your patience with him."

His dad wiped the back of his hand across his damp cheek. "Listen to me, kid. You were a great brother. You didn't do a damn thing wrong." He gripped his chin, tipped it. "You get to have Mimi." His dad's arms trembled. "You get to be in a band. Blue Fire or not, you get to live the life you want. Anything less and who wins? Does Hopper win?" He practically shook an answer out of him, but Calix gave nothing. "Do you win? Answer me, son. Does any good come out of you not living your life?"

"No. Nothing good comes out of it. Not for anyone." It made sense. Everything his dad said made sense. The idea that he could have Mimi. It made him feel fierce.

"Take it, son. Take everything you can out of this life. And for God's sake, go get your woman."

Before heading inside the house, Calix leaned against his bike, sun hot on his head, and sent Mimi another text.

Coming into the city to see you. What's a good time?

She hadn't answered any of his others. But he knew she wouldn't check her phone at work. Not with the job she'd waited a hell of a long time to get.

And, of course, she hated him.

Hardest words he'd ever had to hear.

So instead of making inane comments, he needed to get to the point. Just like Mimi would do.

Keep remembering your expression in the ER.
Killing me.

Worse, how I treated you when you came to see me.

Wind chimes pealed and clanged around him, and a breeze rustled through the trees. He scratched the whiskers on his chin. Had to go deeper to make it real.

Feel like shit.

Need to see you. Apologize in person.

He had only an hour left on this break from recording, so he needed to get inside, see how his mom was doing. He pocketed the phone and headed in.

The moment it vibrated against his ass, hope tore through him. He pulled it out. *Mimi.* Thank Christ.

I've gotten all your texts, and I accept your apology.
No need to meet up. Best to you and your family.

He smiled. One of the things he loved about her—*wait, loved?* Standing under the shade of the copper beech tree, he let it spread through him. For the first time in a hell of a long time, he could smell the rich earth, the freshly cut grass, and the hint of salty air. He noticed the bright blue of the sky and the deep copper leaves on the enormous sheltering tree. Same color as Mimi's hair.

He smiled wider. Because, yeah, he loved her.

And because her love had changed him.

And just as quickly as the feeling spread through him, it burned to a crisp when he realized how he'd treated her. She'd given him all her beauty, and he'd turned his back on it.

Need to see you, sweet pants.

He stopped himself before he hit Send. He didn't want to send attitude. He wanted to send a piece of his heart. He deleted the comment.

I miss you.

That wasn't even close. Need to see you. Need to fix what I fucked up. Please?

Holding on to his phone, he stepped onto the porch. When his hand closed around the doorknob, his cell vibrated again.

Let me alleviate at least one of your sources of guilt: I forgive you. Now let's just make a clean break. No matter how sorry you are to have hurt my feelings, I'm going to guess nothing has really changed. You tried hard to give me as much of yourself as you were able, but the one thing you could never give me was a future. Not even a glimpse. So, there's really no reason for us to see each other because my time of living in the moment is over. Let's leave it as it is. A clean break.

A clean break? Sure as hell didn't feel like one. Not with edges sharp enough to cut.

He'd talk to her later. This is not over.

At this hour he figured his mom would just be getting up, and since she didn't expect him to be around, he called out, "Ma? I'm home."

The house was eerily quiet. As he made his way down the hallway, a sickly cold sensation crept over his skin. "Mom?" *Stop it.* Nothing was wrong. He'd likely find her in the kitchen having lunch. Or in the studio.

His mom was fine.

"Mom? Lee?" He hadn't seen his sister's pink MINI Cooper out front, so he didn't expect her to be home.

He checked one empty room after another, the absolute stillness kicking up his anxiety. The kitchen showed no signs anyone had used it since he'd left that morning.

She was probably in the studio. His pace picked up as he headed outside, jogging past the cooing chickens.

Throwing the door open, he found it empty. The emptiness sent a chill through him.

He ran back into the house, shouting, "Mom?" Dammit. Where the hell was she?

Calm your ass down. She's probably in the shower. Or taking a walk.

He made his way down the hall, anxiety breaking out on his skin like a rash. Passing the master bedroom, he peered through the open door. It was a total mess, just as his dad would've left it. He continued on to the guest room, where she'd returned so she wouldn't keep her husband up with her insomnia. The one room he dreaded checking.

That image of his mom lying in bed unconscious took up the screen of his mind. What would it take for him to get rid of it once and for all?

He rapped on the closed door. "Ma?" No answer. *Jesus fuck, do not let her be in that bed.* With a damp palm, he turned the knob. "Mom?" Pushed it wide open.

Mother fucking hell. In the race to her bedside, he took in the prescription bottle of pills, the glass of water, half full.

His mom lay on her back, features perfectly slack. More peaceful than he'd seen her in three years. Pale as the white sheets.

"Mom? *Mom*." Ice-cold fear rushed through his veins.

As he whipped out his phone, hitting 911, he touched his fingers to her carotid artery. She had a pulse. Thank fuck. She was still alive.

"Nine-one-one. What's your emergency?"

"My mom's overdosed on pills." He grabbed the bottle. "Ambien." And then he lowered his ear to her nose. Felt the soft brush of warm breath. "She's breathing. But barely." He gave his address and tossed the phone onto the bed. Vaguely, he was aware of the operator's voice.

Grabbing her shoulders, he shook her. "Mom? Mom." Her limp body drooped like a rag doll. He patted her cheeks. "Mom. *Mom*."

The operator's voice grew louder, more insistent.

"Jesus, Mom. What have you done? What the hell have you done?" Both hands on her shoulders, he lifted her. Her head flopped back.

And then her eyelids fluttered, and a look of confusion took hold of her features. "What . . ."

Calix grabbed his phone. "She's alive. She's waking up."

"Sir, *stay with me*. Can you find out how many pills she took?"

"Calix? What's . . ." With effort, his mom dragged herself up to a sitting position. She blinked, looking around her, clearly disoriented. "What's going on?"

"Mom, listen to me. I need to know how many pills you took." And then into the phone, he said, "Are the paramedics on their way? We've got to get her stomach pumped right now."

"I don't need my damn stomach pumped. Are you crazy?" His mom pushed him away, her hand going to her forehead. She winced as if she had a headache.

"Mom, how many pills did you take?" He was trying to keep his shit together, trying not to freak her out, but she needed her stomach pumped *right the fuck now*. Needed the paramedics to get their asses out there.

"One." She smacked him on the arm. "I took one Ambien so I could get some sleep." She held up the bottle, shook it.

He tried to grab it from her, but she snatched it back. "Doc prescribed ten pills. Count 'em. There're nine in there."

He didn't need to count. He could see. With a rough exhalation, he turned to the phone. "She's all right. My mom's fine. I apologize."

"Do you still need us to send someone out there?"

"No. She took one prescribed sleeping pill. I misinterpreted what I saw. I'm sorry."

He set his phone on the nightstand and scrubbed a hand over his face. His body thrummed with anxiety.

"What the hell, Calix?" But she didn't sound worked up anymore. "What just happened?"

His impulse was to shield her, but this shit had to stop. He was done being careful with her. "I've been waiting, Ma. For this. This exact moment."

"What moment? To walk in on me . . ." Her body locked up. Color crept into her cheeks.

He looked her right in the eye. "Exactly."

She reared back. "Wh—why?"

"I think about what happened all the time. What I walked in on."

His mom looked horrified. "You think I'm gonna off myself?"

"Yeah. I do. And I've got to ask you. Do you think about it? Taking pills?"

She reached behind her, stacked up some pillows. "Well, shit. That's why you watch me like a hawk? Feed me like a toddler?" And then awareness slammed home. "*That's* why you're all living at home?"

He nodded.

"I thought you were just being a pain in the ass because you wanted me to go back to being the kind of mom I was." She pushed him aside and got out of bed. Found a pair of pajama bottoms on the chair by the window and stepped into them. "Damn, Calix. I didn't know." She turned to him, hands on her hips. "I'm *not* gonna kill myself. Do I think about it? I mean, sometimes, yeah. On my bad days. But not seriously. I'm not gonna do it."

"But you've tried it before." And that scared the shit out of him. "And if I hadn't come home that day, you wouldn't be here."

She looked so damn weary. "Well, yeah. Those first few

months . . . it was unbearable. I couldn't live without my boy. It tore my heart out."

"I know, Ma. And I'm sorry. I'm so fucking sorry." Goddammit. Why couldn't he have kept a hand on Hopper? Why hadn't he paid attention? Noticed the moment his brother had wandered off?

She shot him a look. "What does that mean?"

He rubbed the leather band between two fingers. "I never should've taken my eyes off him. If I hadn't gotten so fucking carried away—"

"Wait. Stop. Stop, stop, stop." She came closer. "What're you talking about?"

"I was right there. Right fucking there. If I'd just—"

"Hey," she snapped. "Don't you do that. Don't you dare. It is *not* your fault."

"I should have been watching him."

She set her hand on top of his, stopping him from rubbing. "No, you shouldn't have. You had a gig that day. Jason was watching him. And it's not Jason's fault either." She swiped her palms across her cheeks. "Look at us. You know why Jason's not around anymore? Because he blames himself. Can't stand to be near us. And I don't have the energy to convince him otherwise. Got my own demons to slay."

"What're you talking about? You were onstage. You had nothing to do with it."

"I'm not talking about that day." She yanked open the curtain, letting daylight flood in. "I'm talking about the whole first half of my life. Trust me when I tell you, I was *not* a good person. And I can't help thinking I earned what I got."

What the hell? "Are you talking about karma? You led a fast life in the music industry, so you deserve to lose your son?"

"Well, when you put it that way, it does sound pretty lame." She gave a bitter laugh. "But it's more than that. I was a shitty daughter. You didn't know my parents, but they were hard-asses. Not even religious, just strange, uptight people. And I was nothing but trouble. Ran off when I was sixteen and never talked to them again." She lowered her head. When she lifted it again, pain filled her eyes. "Who does that? They weren't bad people. They didn't beat me. They just didn't know how to raise a kid like me. I was foul-mouthed, drank too much, and ditched my classes. They couldn't control me."

"You were a kid."

"No excuse for how I treated them. I knew just which buttons to push. It's just . . . when they couldn't control me, they ignored me. Which only made me act out more. I remember once—what was I? Twelve, thirteen? No, I was thirteen, because my friends were having their confirmation parties. I had a crush on this kid, Marco, and I wanted a new dress. My folks didn't spend money on fancy clothes, so I borrowed my friend's. And my mom snatched that thing out of my hands, walked me over to my friend's house, and made me return it. I wore the damn dress anyway, and she found out because I spilled red punch on it and shoved it under the bed. She didn't talk to me for seven months. Seven months my mother ignored me. Didn't set a place for me at the table, didn't do my laundry. She acted like I didn't exist."

"That's messed up."

"Thing is, looking back, I think, why'd I have to provoke her like that?" She looked down at her hands, scarred with burn marks from the hot metal pieces she worked with. "I only got worse when I met your dad. The things we did . . ."

"Ma, you're not that kid anymore. I've known you twenty-six years, and everything I know about being a good person I learned from you."

"You don't get away scot-free from a life of bad choices."

"So you *do* think Hopper died because you led a wild life."

"I don't know. In a way I guess I do."

"That's bullshit. Everyone's got regrets, Ma, but how many people actually change? And look at the life you've built. Look what you've got."

"You guys are pretty great."

"I don't mean how we turned out. I mean our lives. You did this. You gave us everything you didn't have as a kid. You gave us the best childhoods." He tipped her chin. "Ma, you didn't cause his death."

"Well, you didn't either."

"No, I know. It's not about *blaming* myself. It's that I was right there. If I hadn't been getting my ass kissed by those Voltage guys—"

"They weren't kissing your ass. Calix, you were talented. Like, beyond talented. And you didn't have just one label after you." His mom took a step back, reeling. Tears welled, and she clapped a hand over her mouth.

What just happened?

"You're so damn talented." She turned fierce. "You've got ten times the talent your dad and I ever had, and I've held you back. I've held all of you back. I didn't . . . I didn't get it. I got lost in my own head. I didn't even get that you guys're living at home 'cause you think I'm gonna off myself." Tears spilled down her cheeks. "Is this why you're not joining Blue Fire?"

He didn't need to answer.

"Oh, hell." She tipped her head back, blinking. "Talk about a wake-up call. I'm sorry. I'm so sorry. Listen, no more of this shit. I'm gonna get my head out of my ass." She drew in a breath. "I've been thinking about this for a while, but I'm gonna get some help. I was just gonna go to a doctor about the insomnia, but . . . I think I know what I've got to do. Calix, I'm okay. I promise. You're a good kid, a good guy. I'm so damn sorry for holding you back."

"I think we'll stop with the blame game starting right now, okay?"

"Yeah, okay." She wiped the tears off her face, blinking as she looked at Calix's wrist. She touched the braided leather band, stroked it slowly, reverently. And then her brows pulled together. "Hopper's."

"Yeah."

She gazed up at him as if trying to put the pieces together in her mind.

"I took it off your wrist in the hospital." He watched her for signs that she remembered. "They were gonna cut it off you."

"Yeah." His mom held his gaze a moment, before slowly drawing in a breath. "You mind if I take it back now?"

The moment Mimi entered the lobby, her doorman gave her a chin nod and then gestured across the room.

On the other side of the marble foyer, an imposing, striking man sat on a bench.

Never taking his eyes off her, Calix Bourbon slid his hands down his thickly-muscled thighs and slowly stood.

Her heart leapt into her throat, and her spirits soared. Her muscles readied to run right at him.

And then she remembered.

She'd moved on.

And just like that she settled down. She nodded to her doorman and then met Calix halfway.

"Calix."

"Sweet pants." Those dark eyes studied her, filled with equal parts worry and hope.

"What're you doing here?"

"I gave Lee my cottage, and I'm wondering how attached you are to this building."

Was he . . . holy crap, was he talking about moving in with her? Her excitement died the moment she imagined how many nights she'd be alone, waiting for him, while he was back on Long Island with his family. His brother would have trouble with the next girlfriend or his sister would need help making a decision about the business.

He'd need to make his mom an omelet at midnight.

All sweet. But not for her.

But, boy, did he look gorgeous and genuine and intense and . . . hers.

She'd *missed* him.

But she wasn't going backward. "You know what? It's been an exhausting couple of days, and all I want to do is put on my sweats and curl up in bed with a good book." She moved to get around him. "I'll be out at the farm this weekend, so maybe we can catch up then."

"No."

"Excuse me?" She stopped, turned back to him.

"I was an ass, and I'm sorry." And then he went soft, almost desperate. "I'm *sorry*."

A million thoughts flittered through her head. Why was he in the city? Oh, God, was something wrong? She turned fully toward him. "Is everyone all right?"

"Everyone's great. Except us. But I'm going to fix that. First, I need to know how important this apartment is to you because I'm not sure my instruments and amps will fit. I think we'll need a second bedroom. But if you're attached to it, I'll deal."

Mimi glanced down at the shiny white marble floor, taking a moment to quiet her aching, pounding heart and gather her thoughts. "I would've loved to hear you talk like this when we were together." Her pulse picked up at the very idea of rejecting the man she loved so freaking hard. Every muscle in her body strained to reach out to him, wrap around him.

But she couldn't do it. "It's too late. I believe that you care about me, but I know your family will always come first. That's how you were raised. And I'm just not a peripheral kind of girl. Do I miss you? Oh, yeah. Especially at night when I remember those couple of hours you used to give me." He flinched, but she carried on. She drew in a breath. "I'm sure I'll see you around."

Unlikely, actually. Once she got this project off the ground, she'd be working through weekends. She'd probably have to hire a couple people to help her. She smiled at the thought.

But as she moved around him, he caught her arm. "Things've changed. My mom's seeing a therapist. Lee's applying to FIT. You did that, Mimi. You did that for us."

For *us*. Always that separation. "I'm glad things are better. I truly care about your family, but like I said, I'm done. I wish you well, Calix."

"We're not done."

She'd have given anything to hear these words two weeks ago. "You say that because things are going well. But when something else happens, you're going to push me away again. I'm not going to fall deeper for you when you've shown me your true heart. It isn't mine."

"You own it. My heart. I love you, Mimi." And this was the Calix she'd had in her bed. He was back.

He *loved* her. *God.*

But she just couldn't go through it again—give him her whole heart only to have him push her away again.

He reached for her. "Mimi, you turned the music back on. You turned on all the lights and threw open the windows. There's no going back. I love you. I'm *in love with you*."

Okay, he wanted to get real? She'd get real. "I cried myself to sleep every night for a week. I wanted to hear these words from you . . . You have no idea. But something changed for me. I've changed. I've spent my entire life trying to get my dad to spend time with me. Working so hard for something that was elusive—and not because my dad doesn't like me, but because he's incapable of giving me the kind of love I need. And guess what? Just like my dad will always put his work first, you'll always put your family first. And I'm not going there ever again."

"Give me a chance to show you. I—"

She put up a hand. She didn't want to hear it. "The next man I fall for is going to love me so much he can't help but put me first."

"That man is me. And I'll spend my life proving it to you."

"Let me ask you something. Did you join the band?"

"No."

God, that broke her heart. He'd always be a peripheral guy. "Good night, Calix."

Her Google Alert chimed, and Mimi pulled her phone out of her bag.

Pedro 10 AM 4 Wall Street.

In her brief conversation with him, Pedro hadn't seemed all that interested in her proposition. But she'd do a better job talking to him in person with the architectural drawings she'd had drawn up to give him a visual of how his grilled cheese shops would look.

"Morning, Mimi."

"Morning." As she strode across the lobby, her heels clicking on the shiny marble floor, she gave her doorman a wave. "If I don't see you before you leave today, have a great vacation."

"Thanks."

Shoving her phone into her bag, she pushed through the revolving door and spilled out onto the sidewalk. Before her meeting she needed to head into the office to get the real estate projections—*Oh*.

Calix leaned against the side of her building, long legs stretched out in front of him, crossed at the ankle. His worn black T-shirt pulled taut across the hard muscles of his shoulders, and she couldn't help noticing his tan, muscular forearm as he held out a coffee to her.

"Latte. Two sugars, sprinkle of cinnamon."

In the week since she'd last seen him, he'd continued to send texts and cute, brief e-mails. He wasn't giving up. "What're you doing here?"

With his other hand, he gestured across the street to one of the elegant brownstones. "Renting a place. Well, renting with an option to own. I know you like the neighborhood, and the place is big enough for us and all my equipment. Plenty of bedrooms for when our friends want to crash."

I love you. I'm in love with you. With all her heart she wanted to believe him. And maybe one day he really would be ready. But right then? She had to get to work.

Accepting the coffee, she breezed past him, fighting a smile. "See you around, Calix."

The sweetest sense of familiarity rushed through her as Mimi watched her friends heading toward the house. Warm water hit her fingers as she rinsed the beaters in the sink, and her heart squeezed with how much she'd enjoyed her weekend on the farm.

In the two weeks she'd been working for her dad's firm, she'd come out here both weekends, but that would end soon. Once her project got greenlighted, she wouldn't have time anymore.

She'd miss this. She'd miss *them*.

With a bang of the screen door, Violet and Derek entered the kitchen.

"How's it going?" Over the past several weeks, the band had auditioned over twenty keyboard players.

"All right, I guess." Derek grabbed a cookie sandwich off the platter. "How come you never made these for us?" He took a bite.

"Yeah, Meems." Ben and Cooper slammed into the kitchen and snatched a couple cookies each.

"This is great," Coop said with a mouthful.

"What I want to know is *why* you're making them." Violet pulled the lemonade pitcher out of the refrigerator. "You're supposed to be relaxing. You've got a ton of work to do this week to get your project off the ground."

"This *is* relaxing." She smiled at the quiet realization.

"What're you working on, Meems?" Ben kicked a chair out with his foot and sat down. "And how come we can't be your project?"

"Life's not the same without you," Coop said.

"Tell me about the project," Derek said.

"I'm going to offer small business loans to low-overhead restaurants. The first contestant to get kicked off the show—"

"The grilled cheese dude?" Ben asked.

Mimi set the bowl down to face him. "How did you remember that?"

"We watched." Cooper seemed surprised she'd ask.

Back in the city, in her dad's office, she felt like a stick figure plodding through life. But here? She came alive. This was her family. Right here. These people she'd spent every day with for a year. Funny how hard she'd tried to be part of her dad's world when she'd already become part of this one.

"I miss you guys."

"So come back," Ben said.

"Somehow I don't see her giving up her big-time job with her dad to bake you cookie sandwiches." Violet carried an armful of glasses to the table.

"But these are good," Coop said. "Like, unbelievably good. You should open up a bakery or something."

"Hey, V, would that fit with your products?" Ben asked. "Selling baked shit?"

"She makes tea, ya dope," Coop said.

"So make it a teahouse," Derek said.

Mimi shot a look to Violet. Their gazes connected in a shower of sparks.

"That'd be pretty cool," Coop said. "You could sell all your shit out of that shop. Your tea bags, soaps, potpourri. All that crap."

"That would make a lot of sense, actually," Derek said.

Ideas started popping in Mimi's mind. "I think it's a great idea, V."

"Me, too," Violet said.

She could see it so clearly. "You can design it like we did your reception. With the tree branches and little white lights. A big bay window and pie chests filled with your products. And then you'd have this display case of all the desserts your customers could choose from." She picked up a sandwich cookie. She'd made dark chocolate brownie cookies and filled them with pastel-colored cream. Then, she'd dotted the frosting with sprinkles.

The more she thought about it, the sadder she got that she couldn't be a part of it.

Or could she?

Imagine running a teahouse on the farm. Living out here permanently. The very idea sent a rush of joy corkscrewing through her.

What about working with her dad, though? Could she really give up everything she'd worked so hard to build?

And, most important, when would she see him if she moved out here permanently?

Clarity struck with the snap of a wrist. She'd spent twenty-four years chasing after her dad, begging for his attention. Wasn't it time to stop? Let him come to her?

"Would you do this with me?" Violet asked, her voice filled with so much hope.

"I want to." Images rained down over her like confetti. "Whitewashed wood floors and antique china plates. Vintage cake platters. All those pretty desserts."

"It would fit perfectly here. Meems, we could be like the Serendipity of Eden's Landing. We'd be advertised in all the tourist guides. Can you imagine? Our wildflower tea and your desserts? We'd design it just how you envision it."

"I love it. I just don't think I can." Give up everything she worked so hard for to run a teahouse?

"Of course you can," Derek said. "You can do anything you want."

"What about my job?"

"This would be your job," Violet said. "We'd do it together."

Derek's phone buzzed, and he whipped it out of his pocket. "Another guy's coming for an audition."

"When? Now?" Ben said.

"I thought we were done for the day," Cooper said.

"Terrence just texted." Derek pocketed the phone with a strange grin. "Said the guy's coming by right now."

"Fuck that," Ben said. "I'm hungry. What's for dinner, Meems?"

"She's not cooking you dinner," Derek said. "She's out here for a visit. You cook *her* dinner."

"Sorry, guys. I've got a train to catch. I have to get to work early tomorrow."

"Mimi," Violet said. "Hang on. All that work you're going to put in so other people can realize their restaurant dreams . . . why not realize your own?"

"I don't have restaurant dreams."

"You think about that bakery idea all the time. Why not make it happen? Besides, it wouldn't be like a bakery. You wouldn't make the same things every day. And once we got going, we could hire people so you could continue to cater events for the band."

"Why just the band?" Ben asked. "Irwin would hire her for all his events."

"Hell," Cooper said, sounding excited. "*Amoeba* would."

A rumble of energy got her pulse spiking. Oh, now that sounded really good.

Would she really give up her job to do this?

"Slater's on his way." Derek tipped his chin, indicating they look out the kitchen window.

Slater and Emmie swung hands as they walked down the

road. Emmie threw her head back and laughed, and Slater
tugged on her so that her body collided with his, and he
buried his face in her neck.

"What do you want, Mimi?" Violet asked. "In your heart,
what do you want?"

If she took out wanting to be with her dad, what would she
want to do with her life?

The image of the teahouse—*her* teahouse—hers and
Violet's—sparkled like a glossy ad in a magazine.

It was a no-brainer.

"Why's everyone coming here to audition another guy?"
Ben asked.

The doorbell rang.

"We're about to find out." Derek headed off to answer it.

"Well, I can tell you already he's not gonna work," Coop
said. "Thinks he's too good for an actual audition? I don't
care if he's Keith Emerson, he's gonna have to play for us."

"Oh, Christ, just what we need," Ben said. "Another Dak.
Like we give a shit about his fuckin' résumé."

"He's gotta fit," Coop said. "He's got to smoke those keys,
and he's gotta fit in with us."

"All right, I'm out of here." Mimi made sure she'd turned
off the oven. "Ach. I'm leaving you with a sink full of dishes."

"We got it, Meems," Ben said.

"Thanks, guys."

"I'll get my keys." Violet headed out of the kitchen while
Ben and Coop scooped Mimi into their arms for bear hugs.

"Miss you, Meems," Cooper said.

"Kick some ass out there," Ben said.

And then voices. One voice in particular. Deep, raspy,
incredibly sexy.

The voice that made her heart jump into her throat.

Why would he come by when they were auditioning
someone to replace him?

And then he was in the kitchen. His easy demeanor turned
tense when he saw the guys touching her. He didn't need to say
a word for Coop and Ben to quickly take their hands off her.

"Dude. What're you doing here?" Ben gave him a man hug.

Calix never took his gaze off hers.

"He's auditioning," Derek said.

He was joining the band? Committing to them. What did this mean? What the hell did this mean? But she knew from the way he looked at her that he was all in.

The guys kept talking—*You serious, man? You're in? Fuck, yeah*—as Calix slowly walked toward her.

"Meems, you ready?" Violet hitched her purse over her shoulder, keys in hand.

Her body went hot, and her cheeks flamed. And then Calix was right in front of her. Knees bent, arms banding around her hips.

And then she was in the air.

"Calix?" Violet said. "Oh."

The guys, the kitchen, the living room, everything was a blur around her. Her heart beat painfully, and she could barely take a breath. He swept her up the stairs, kicked open the door to her bedroom, and dropped her on the bed.

He towered over her with an expression that brooked no argument. Those warm, dark eyes, so intense, so demanding, told her everything.

She had a hard time catching her breath. "We should . . . talk."

"Said what I had to say." With a snap, he tore open the buttons of his jeans.

"Yeah, but—"

He lunged for her, covering her mouth with his. And he took her, claimed her, kissing her senseless. "I love you, Mimi, and if you think for one fuckin' second I'm gonna let you get away, you're outta your mind."

"But if—"

"No buts, sweet pants." He pulled back, sitting on the edge of the bed to dump his boots on the floor, then toss his jeans. "This past week sucked. It hurt to breathe without you. Nothing tasted right." In black boxer briefs, he stretched out alongside her, his hand sweeping a slow path up her rib cage. "I love you. I'm sorry if I hurt you, but it's not gonna happen again."

"Yeah?" Hard to concentrate when his thumb stroked the underside of her breast.

"I got stuck in my own head. I couldn't see beyond my own guilt. Turns out my mom had guilt of her own. And instead of helping each other, we were keeping each other stuck. You unstuck me."

"Well, I'm happy for you, and you can send me a nice gift card if that'll make you feel better, but as for us—"

"Spitfire." He gently tugged on her earlobe with his teeth. "I love you, Amelia Romano. I love you because you're the strongest person I know. I love your spirit. We're a stubborn bunch of bastards, my family, and we don't let many people in, but you broke through. I love your passion. I need it. Because it matches mine, and I shut mine down. But you brought it back out. You brought me out. And I'm not letting you go. I'm not."

"But I . . ."

"You love me?"

It flooded her. Rushed her so hard she lost her breath. "Yes."

"You gonna let me spend the rest of my life making you as happy as you make me?"

"The idea has a certain appeal." She reached for him, clasping the back of his head and bringing him in for a kiss. "But you're gonna have to get a move on it. I've got a train to catch."

His smile bloomed deliciously across his handsome face. And then his big, warm hand covered her breast, and he leaned in to lick her nipple. "Fuck the train. You're stayin' here with me."

Happiness spread through her, thick and warm. "No place I'd rather be."

CHAPTER TWENTY-ONE

"I thought this was a teahouse?"

The older woman peered up at Mimi with a confused expression, teacup halfway to her coral-colored lips.

"It is, Mrs. Mahoney." On the round table covered with a crisp white linen tablecloth, the tea service included a china pot with mismatched plates and antique silverware. A tiered pewter dessert stand held tea sandwiches in egg salad, ham, brie and apple, salmon cucumber, and steak *au poivre*.

"But this is a brownie. Brownies aren't served at a tea."

Violet breezed by with a large crate. "It's actually *torta Barozzi*, Mrs. Mahoney. Try it. You'll think you've gone to heaven." She set the box down in front of the pie chest and began stocking the shelves with her wildflower-based products.

"But I wanted scones."

"Then you'll have scones." Mimi shot Violet a quick smile. She didn't bother reminding the woman she'd chosen her own desserts from the display case.

"And clotted cream." The woman looked genuinely upset.

Mimi gently nudged the ramekin toward her. "This is the clotted cream." The grand opening for Four O'Clock Farm's

Tea Party didn't start for another two hours, but they'd invited their elderly neighbor in early, since she'd stopped by every day for the past several months to check on the progress. Few new businesses opened this far out on Long Island, and fewer still were associated with rock bands.

Okay, none were. Just this one.

"Oh." Mrs. Mahoney brought the container to her nose and sniffed. "I thought it was butter."

Mimi smiled. "Is there anything else I can get you?" As she reached for the cake to take it away, the woman's eyebrows shot up and her hand made a grab for the plate.

"Well, hold on. I want some heaven."

"Then you'll have it, Mrs. Mahoney." Finished stocking, Violet turned to take in the room. She and Mimi shared a smile. They'd created a magical, whimsical teahouse. Everything she'd envisioned they'd brought to life.

Mimi smiled warmly at her elderly neighbor. "You can have heaven *and* scones. We have—" But before she could describe the scone selection, the woman bit into the deep chocolate tart and her eyelids fluttered closed, a look of rapture softening her features.

"Oh. Oh, my. Oh, my Lord." Her eyelids popped open. "This is *divine*."

Someone rapped at the door. "Excuse me." Mimi stepped out onto the porch to find a group of teenage girls. "Hey, ladies. Did you come for the grand opening? Because we're not open just yet, and we're solidly booked for the next several weeks." Reaching inside to the hostess stand, she grabbed a postcard-sized menu. "Give us a call, and we'll reserve a table for you."

"We don't want tea." One girl stepped forward. "Is Blue Fire here?"

Mimi held back a laugh. "They're actually on tour." Her heart pinched, missing Calix and wishing so much he could've been home for the opening. Of course, she had more help than she could possibly need, but still. She hated when they weren't together.

"When will Slater be here?" one of the girls at the back of the group asked.

"They'll be away for several months." And once the teahouse was on solid ground, Mimi and Violet would join their men off and on throughout the six-month tour. "You know, they won't really come here all that often." She noticed the T-shirts and posters they carried. "But if you want to leave those, I can have them sign them when they come back to town."

One of the girls perked up, readily handing over her items, but the leader scowled. "No, thank you. We want them to sign in person. We'll come back."

"Okay, then." Mimi went back inside the restaurant just as the kitchen door swung open.

"Amelia." Her dad raced out in a white apron that said, *I don't need a recipe, I'm Italian.* "For God's sake, we're out of ricotta."

"Of course we're not." How could they be? They hadn't even opened their doors. "We have more than enough."

"Look in the refrigerator. Look. There is no more ricotta. How can I make my *cannoli*?"

"What're you shouting about?" her mom asked, coming out of the kitchen with a stack of sky blue cake boxes and peach satin ribbon.

"Ricotta." Her dad sounded affronted. "How can we open for tea without the *cannoli*?"

"We're not out, Dino."

Mimi loved her mom's soothing tone. It was great seeing her parents in a whole new relationship. After the divorce, Francesca had cut herself off from her ex as she sought to find her true self. Mimi knew her dad had missed his wife terribly, and it was good to see them becoming friends. History enabled them to know just how to comfort and support each other. And since Irwin knew he had Francesca's whole heart, he didn't mind.

Well, not much anyway.

"You ordered too much to fit in this refrigerator, so I stocked it in the in-law house. I'll go get some." Her mom set the supplies down. "How many do you need?"

A strange *thwap thwap thwap* sounded overhead. At that same moment Calix's mom came in the back door of the kitchen, carrying the notebook they used for the event planning side of the business. The record label was throwing a huge party for Blue Fire's recent Grammy win, and Sweet Cheeks Event Planners had scored the job. Lee was kicking herself for not getting to participate, but she'd just started at FIT for the spring semester and couldn't afford to miss anything. It was hard enough for her to get back into the groove of school after so many years.

A thunderous sound had all of them racing outside to see what was happening.

"Why's a helicopter landing on your property?" Mimi asked as they all lined up to watch.

A huge green and white chopper set down in the middle of the wildflower field. Her dad stood with his arms at his sides, looking like a gunslinger from the Wild West, ready to draw.

The rotors slowed, the door opened, and the stairs came down.

Out walked Slater-fucking-Vaughn with a pink baby carrier strapped to his chest. The big, muscular man had a hand on his little girl's bottom and another on the back of her head as he leaned low to clear the blades. Once on the ground, he turned to wait for Emmie, and the two of them held hands as they headed toward the teahouse.

Mimi leaned into Violet. "What the hell?"

"I have no idea."

"They have a show in Columbus tonight."

Violet turned to her in alarm. "Maybe something's wrong with the baby?"

"No, we'd have heard."

They both turned back, waiting for Slater and Emmie to reach them.

Violet looked concerned. "Derek didn't tell me a thing."

And then the doorway of the aircraft filled with Calix's big, hard body. His gaze sought and found hers instantly, and Mimi took off. By the time he hit the ground, she was flying into his arms.

He caught her, held a hand on top of her head as he hustled her away from the now-still rotors. She breathed in his familiar scent and kissed his neck. "What're you *doing* here?"

"Not gonna miss my girl's opening." She loved that deep, sexy voice in her ear.

"But you're on tour. You've got sound check at three."

"Sound check's covered. Besides, the flight's just over an hour."

"Calix."

"You happy to see me?"

She gave him a teasing smile. "Well, I was kind of in the middle of something."

His smile widened. "Yeah, well, you're about to be in the middle of something else." Cupping her ass and lifting her legs around his waist, he stalked toward the in-law house they shared while their new house was being renovated about half a mile down the road.

"You hardly need to carry me." She rubbed her nose against his scruffy cheek, breathing in his familiar masculine scent. "I'm pretty willing, if you know what I mean."

"I've only got you for a few hours. Not gonna let you go."

She wrapped her arms around his neck and hugged him tightly. "Don't want you to let me go."

"Never, sweet pants."

She kissed the corner of his mouth. "I love you so much, Calix Bourbon."

"I love you more."

Cupping his cheek, she whispered, "Show me."

He kissed her, right there in the middle of the wildflowers, the bright sun shining down on them. "Count on it." He nuzzled her ear. "Every single day for the rest of your life."

Keep reading for an excerpt from the first
Rock Star Romance novel by Erika Kelly

YOU REALLY GOT ME

Now available from Berkley Sensation

"Oh, bollocks, *Emmie*!"

Emmie Valencia's boss hollered so loudly her teeth rattled. And there was a *wall* between them. She pressed the button on her intercom and said, "Be right there." He could be such a baby.

Seconds later, the office came alive with excited voices and laughter. Her coworkers hurried down the hall, heading for the foyer.

Frontierland was back from their tour. Which meant . . . *Alex.*

Her gut twisted hard. Briefly, she imagined ducking under her desk, maybe dashing to the mail room. But, of course, she wouldn't do that. She could face him. No big deal.

In fact, that's exactly what she *should* do. Talk to him as casually as she did the rest of the guys. She hated the way people looked at her whenever he came into the office. Besides, they'd ended it months ago.

One of the interns popped breathlessly into her office. "They're here." Her features flushed, she mouthed, "Flash," and pretended to fan herself. Then she darted down the hall.

Emmie smiled and shook her head. Even though they

worked with bands for a living, everyone got all goofy and fawning when the artists came in.

Except Emmie, of course. She'd grown up around musicians. She saw beneath the glitter to their tortured, attention-craving, twisted souls. Everyone wanted a piece of them, to be the one to get in, breach the barrier. To win their hearts. But she knew better. They didn't let anyone in. Not really. They drew people in with their dazzling charisma and then pushed them back when they got too close. Loving an artist *hurt*.

Obviously, she'd thought Alex would be different. They'd grown up together. Their parents were best friends. Silly girl. Musicians were musicians. She'd *known* that.

As she pulled papers from the printer, she heard, "Emmie!" in a far more upbeat tone than her boss's. She spun around to find the boys from Frontierland crowding into her office.

Crap, was Alex there?

She'd keep her cool. Treat him exactly the way she treated the other guys. No big deal. Because *he* was no big deal. Not after what he'd done to her. Lifelong friendship be damned.

"Great job, you guys," she said, as the drummer pulled her to him. They played an outrageous mix of rockabilly, country, and country rock, so they dressed like badass banditos in leather, vests, and straw cowboy hats. "Have you read the reviews yet?"

"Brenda doesn't make those fuckin' scrapbooks like you do, man." The keyboardist pushed through the others to give her a hug. He smelled of whiskey and patchouli.

"Why couldn't we score Irwin as our A&R guy?" another one asked.

She winced. Her boss wouldn't sign them because she'd been dating their bass player.

As the next guy leaned in for a hug, Emmie made a quick scan of their faces. No Alex. *Good*. But right when the rhythm guitarist belted his arms around her and lifted her off the floor, Emmie caught sight of him.

Alex Paulson, clad in black leather pants and a stretched-out white T-shirt, flirted with the new receptionist across the hallway. Emmie hated that he'd do it right in front of her, of course, but mostly she couldn't believe he thought so little of their relationship that he actually felt *comfortable* doing it. Like their time together hadn't really counted.

It had to her.

Flash, the lead singer, yanked her out of the other guy's arms and said, "There's my girl." Gorgeous in a rough way, Flash had gotten his nickname because in the middle of every show he asked the girls in the audience to "flash me your tits" so he could take a photo on his phone and post it on the band's website. Classy. "You gonna marry me yet?"

"I think I'd rather marry your fiancée. She's hot."

Just as his hand skimmed down her back heading for forbidden territory, she jerked her hips and pulled out of his embrace.

"You're no fun, Emmie Valencia."

A sharp pain sliced into her heart. Her gaze flicked over his shoulder to the office where Alex and the receptionist shared a quiet laugh. "So I've heard."

"Hey." Tilting his head, he gave her a concerned look. "I'm just playing with you."

"I know." She smiled, hoping to brush away the uncomfortable moment. God, she had to get ahold of herself.

"But if I can't get you to marry me, then can you at least get me one of those bags you got Irwin's kid?"

"You want me to score you the latest Hermès purse?"

"For my fiancée."

Emmie let out an exaggerated sigh. "What did you do this time?" She whipped her hand up. "Never mind. I don't want to hear. And you don't need me to do it—just get yourself on the list. Make a call like I did."

"Oh, come on. We're stuck with Brenda. She doesn't do shit for us. Besides, I don't have your connections. You make shit happen."

"Yes, for Irwin. And I don't *have* connections. I make them when I need to."

"I could make shit happen for you."

Their gazes caught. Behind his incessantly flirtatious vibe lived a shark of a businessman. "You offering me a job, Flash?"

A slow smile ate up his ruggedly handsome features. "Fuck, yeah."

"What kind of job?"

"What kind of job you want?"

Wasn't that just the question? She didn't want just a *job*. She wanted *inside*. Eight years on the periphery of the music industry as Irwin Ledger's personal assistant was enough. She needed to take that next obvious step to A&R coordinator—discovering bands, working with talent—and Flash couldn't help her with that. Only Irwin could.

"Flash?" his bandmate called. "Leave Em alone and get in here. Bob's waiting."

"We'll finish this convo later." Flash started to go.

"Hey, can you close the door behind you?" She didn't need to watch Alex flirting.

Unfortunately, Flash followed her gaze, got an eyeful of Alex and the receptionist, and then looked back at her with a hint of pity. He pointed a finger at her. "Golden rule, baby. Never get involved with the talent."

She smirked. "So we're *not* getting married?" So much for her resolve not to make people uncomfortable. "You know what? Leave it open. I haven't said hello to Alex yet."

He gave her an appreciative smile before taking off.

"Oh, for fuck's sake," her boss shouted. "Emmie?"

"Coming," she said into the intercom box.

"I can't imagine what's taking you so bloody long. I have a crisis, Emmie. Cri-sis."

She pressed the button. "Crisis as in you scuffed your favorite Bruno Magli chocolate suede loafers and they don't make them anymore so you need me to call the designer himself and get a pair custom-made? Or crisis as in the drummer from Wicked Beast fell off the wagon again and can't make the show tonight so I need to get to the hotel and get him sobered up?"

"You mock me. I count on you, and you mock me."

She smiled. "Two seconds." Grabbing her iPad, she spun around to the door . . . only to catch the receptionist pressing her body against Alex.

Oh, hell.

Memories slammed her. His hard chest, the spicy scent of his soap, the creak of his leather. How many times had she held him just like that?

Alex's hand wrapped around the woman's waist, pulling her tight against him. That moment of intimacy, the way Val conformed her body to his, the way her hands cupped the back of his neck, her features soft—it struck Emmie right in her core.

It was so intimate, so sensual. And it hurt. God, it hurt. Because she wasn't sexy like Val. She just . . . wasn't.

Tucking the iPad to her chest, she leaned back against the wall, out of sight. Why did she let him affect her? It wasn't like she missed him or even wanted him. He'd cheated on her.

The sex is fine. It's just not . . . you're not wild, you know? You service *me.*

She cringed remembering his words.

A guy wants more than that.

Oh, God. She couldn't bear the memories. She charged out of her office. Just as she turned into the hallway, she saw Alex capture Val's leg, his hand cupping her thigh, as he murmured against her mouth. Val curled around him, her expression sultry.

God. Emmie had never held him like that. Not with that kind of total abandon.

"Emmie?" Irwin shouted.

"I'm coming." Seeing Val be the woman Alex had wanted *her* to be, the kind of woman who melted around a man, who lost herself in sensation, well, it just made it hard to breathe.

The worst thing was that she'd never felt that kind of passion, that urgency. Not for any guy.

She stood there a moment longer, contemplating barging in and greeting Alex, letting the whole office know she was cool with him. Letting *him* know he didn't affect her anymore.

But then she realized something. She *wasn't* cool with him. She wasn't unaffected at all.

Because he flirted right under her nose with the receptionist.

And that was just a lousy thing to do.

Taking a deep breath, Emmie pushed off the wall and

strode out into the hallway. She didn't even spare Alex a glance as she hurried into Irwin's office.

She came to a halt when she saw her boss's expression.

Lips drawn into a taut line, he held the phone to his ear. She walked right up to his ultramodern chair, which hung from the ceiling like a hammock, and he looked at her with utter relief. Immediately, his features turned slack, and he thrust the phone at her.

Placing it to her ear, she had about two seconds to get up to speed, not having the slightest idea who was on the line.

"He wants me to be there, Daddy. I'm, like, his muse. He said he for sure can't do his best work unless I'm there. Do you want this track to suck?"

"Caroline," Emmie said. "Who're we talking about?"

The girl exhaled roughly. "James. He wants me in the studio with him."

Honestly, Emmie did not have time to deal with this nonsense. "James is a drug addict, Caroline. Your dad had to drop him from the label because he couldn't fulfill his contract. Do you see why your dad wouldn't want you hanging out with James while he's out of the country?"

"So, what, I'm supposed to be all locked up because my dad's out of town? I'm an *adult*."

"Not when your dad's paying your bills, including the lawyer he keeps on retainer for your *indiscretions*."

"Oh, my God—"

"Last weekend the sound engineer got you so drunk you blacked out. Your dad and I spent seven hours racing around the city, out of our minds, trying to find you. You can't blame him if he's not comfortable giving you the run of Manhattan when he's not around."

"You don't even know what you're talking about. Rory didn't *get* me drunk. I thought I was drinking iced tea. I didn't know they were *Long Island* Iced Teas. That's not his fault. We were just hanging out. Besides, it's not like I'm going to be *alone*. You'll be here."

Tipping her head back, she blew out a breath. "Caroline. You know I'm going with your dad. Look, hanging out with

James the drug addict is obviously out of the question, but let's come up with a few—"

"No, you're not."

"I'm not what?"

"Going with my dad."

"Of course I'm going with him." She glanced to Irwin, found him examining his cell phone, swinging in his chair. He didn't have a formal office, the kind with the big oak desk facing two guest chairs, a potted plant, and a filing cabinet. Why would he need a desk? No, he had a plush couch, a world-class sound system, a pinball machine, a dartboard, and a Picasso hanging on the wall.

Movement from the corner of her eye made her turn to the door. Alex stood in the threshold, a hint of remorse on his face. Her heart pounded, and her nerves tingled. But before he could take one step into the office, Irwin flew out of his chair, stalked to the door, and slammed it in her ex's face.

Emmie smiled.

Irwin stalked back to the chair, gripping the metal arm, and set it off rocking again.

"I'm not talking to either of you anymore," Caroline said. "I'm going into the studio with James because I'm his muse and he needs me. And if my dad doesn't like it, then you can just come with us and hang out in the lounge."

"I won't be able to come with you because I *am going to Australia.*"

Irwin got up, leaving the leather and chrome chair swinging. He went to the built-in media center that took up one wall and got busy shuffling through his CDs.

"You're not going to Australia! Dad said. God, why are you being such a bitch?"

Emmie closed her eyes, taking a moment before responding. "And so end my efforts to help you. Here's your dad." With that, she handed the phone back to Irwin. "Hold your ground. She shouldn't be anywhere near James Beckman."

He put the phone back to his ear. "What did you say that made your auntie Emmie hand me back the phone?" His gaze kicked up to Emmie's. "Nothing? Are you sure? She's usually so indulgent with us." His brow furrowed. "A bitch? Ah, well, then. I'm afraid you're on your own on this one, darling. Must go, my love. Kiss, kiss." He hung up on her. "Wretched child, isn't she?"

Emmie smiled, knowing how he adored his only kid. But the smile quickly faded. "So, Australia?"

"Yes, right. Slight change of plans." He ran his hand through his messy, floppy hair. Only the silver streaking through his dark hair made him look anything close to his forty-nine years.

"We're not going?"

"That would be a *total* change of plans. Slight means only one of us isn't going."

"Irwin. We leave tomorrow."

"Emmie, darling, I'm sorry, but I can't leave Caroline alone for six weeks. I'm going to need you to stay here."

Okay, wait. For months Emmie had planned this trip. Two weeks ago one of the producers had realized his passport had expired. She'd had to wave her wand, cast spells, and rub magic lamps in order to push his renewal through. She'd planned every detail down to the minute of their time there. Down to using MapQuest to find the coffee shops closest to the recording studios. She'd booked reservations, arranged delivery of industry periodicals to his hotels, and spent months researching and contacting up-and-coming bands.

Oh, and hang on. She'd spent last night *packing* for her boss. Yes, that meant handling his black silk boxers.

Not only that, but this trip meant more than assisting Irwin. She'd gotten him to agree to let her go off and discover some bands of her own. So she could finally get that promotion. But now, the day before departure, he was telling her she couldn't go. Because . . .

"Wait a minute. You want me to *babysit*?"

"Don't be ridiculous. Of course not. You're not changing nappies. You just need to look after her."

"You want me to babysit your daughter." She said it dully, lowering herself onto the plush leather couch. "I'm twenty-five years old, I've worked for you for eight years—" She flashed him a look. "Even as a high school intern I did more for you than your own secretary. And your best use for me is babysitting."

"You make it sound so trivial. This is my daughter we're talking about. And you're more like a mother to her than her own mother."

"I'm four years older than her. I'm not like her mother."

"No, you're better than her mother. And something's off with her."

Emmie narrowed her gaze.

"More so than usual. You heard her. She's all screechy." His phone buzzed, and he quickly answered it.

Coward.

She needed to get a handle on this situation. Heading to the window, she glanced out, pressing close to look down to the street twenty-seven floors below. If she focused on the steady stream of pedestrian traffic, the yellow cabs, the exhaust-spewing buses, she could tell herself he really was just looking out for his daughter. But she knew better. It was so much more than that.

Oh, hell, she couldn't hold it back. The unbearable pain of being shut out again rolled in and threatened to just *crush* her. God, it hurt.

She wanted in so badly. Why was it so elusive? All these feelings . . . God, it was her childhood all over again. Being shut out of her dad's world for not being creative enough, for not really *getting* him, had made her too sensitive to these slights. Because, truthfully? Artists didn't have a lock on creativity. She had it, too, just in other ways. The whole reason Irwin valued her as his assistant was for her ability to think outside the box. She'd proven herself an Amoeba a hundred times over. So why did he hold her back? Sure, he needed her in this role as his assistant. But she could do so much more.

She knew she was lucky to work for the top A&R guy in the business. At the best record company in the world. She didn't take it for granted, but she also knew it was time for more. If she actually stayed behind and babysat Caroline, she'd never break out of this role. At some point, she had to take the initiative and actually say no to one of his demands. She had to force him to see her in a more creative role, or she'd never have the chance to explore that side of herself. To unleash it.

Besides—*hello*?—he couldn't function without her, so how could he get through the next six weeks on the other side of the world?

She spun around, pointing a finger at him. "What are you going to do without me?"

He looked alert then. Most of the time he had a dozen very important ideas going on in his head all at once, so it was nearly impossible to gain his full attention.

Those sharp blue eyes pierced her, and she knew she had it then.

"Right," he said to the caller. "Emmie will get back to you later." He stowed his phone in the back pocket of his jeans. "I'm taking Bax with me."

Had she been standing on a trap door? Because the floor gave way, and she was in freefall. Baxter Reynolds had started as an intern five years ago. When Irwin hadn't shown any interest in promoting him, he'd attached himself to Bob, one of the other A&R guys.

And *now* Irwin was showing an interest in him? Instead of Emmie?

She didn't know what to say. "Bax?" How was *Bax* better than her?

His phone buzzed, but he ignored it as he came right up to her, close enough that she could smell the Christian Dior cologne she kept stocked for him. He brushed his hand down her arm. "I'm sorry, Em. As much as I need you with me, I can't leave Caroline alone."

"Where's her mother?"

"Well, that's the point, isn't it? I can't really count on Claire. But I *can* count on you."

See? When he did that, she caved. Irwin loved his daughter, and who else could he trust to look out for her? His entire family lived in England. Flighty, gorgeous, sexy Claire Murphy flitted around the world on a whim, barely touching down long enough to take care of anything but her most immediate and impulsive needs.

But Emmie needed more. She needed *in*. She couldn't stay

his personal assistant forever. So what should she do? Of course, if Caroline were in any danger, Emmie would have to help. But the girl was twenty-one. And, sorry, but Emmie simply wasn't her mother or her big sister.

She didn't want to let Irwin down. But she was continuing to let herself down if she never took the next step—which meant taking charge of her own career.

She needed the promotion. "I'm not going to babysit Caroline, Irwin. You need me in Australia, and I need to go to Australia to see the bands I've been researching."

He let out a deep sigh. "Truth is, you've set everything up perfectly, as you always do. You've got my every moment organized and arranged to the point that I *don't* need you there."

"But you need Bax?"

"You've given me the list of bands to check out, along with the scheduled times to meet them. So, yes, I need Bax."

"I researched those bands."

"From the privacy of your office. Bax *lives* it, Emmie."

"You're saying I'm not good enough to be promoted?" She felt the sting of it, like he'd doused alcohol on a blister. *No, no, no.* That was bullcrap. She *was* good enough.

"I'm saying that I need you right where you are."

"And I need a career. Not just a job."

His phone buzzed again, and this time he checked the caller ID. "I have to take this."

"No. Please, Irwin. Not until we settle this."

"It *is* settled, Em." He said it gently. "I'm taking Bax." He punched the button on his phone. "Yes?"

"Then I quit."

Irwin's eyes flared. His features burned crimson.

She stood there, letting the words settle around her. The only sound was her own breathing, the only movement the wild and erratic beating of her heart.

Had she actually done it? Quit her coveted job?

"Wait, wait, hang on a moment," he said into the phone.

"I'm sorry, Irwin. I can't keep doing this. You have no intention of promoting me." *Standing on the periphery hurts too much.*

"You can't quit." He turned back to the phone. "Let me get back to you." Without waiting for a response, he hung up. "You can't quit." He looked utterly lost and baffled. "Why would you quit?"

"I'll find my replacement." She turned to go.

"Good God, Emmie. You cannot leave me."

"You've given me no choice."

"All right, just stop this. Stop it right now. I can't function without you, and you know that. You're threatening me. That's not a good way to get a promotion."

"It's not a threat. I told you I needed a career, and you told me you needed me right where I am. Fetching your Americanos and cajoling your landlord into letting you keep amphibians in your penthouse apartment isn't a career. I can't be your personal assistant the rest of my life. You get that, right? I've loved working for you, but it's supposed to be a stepping stone. You've just shown me it's a cage. I deserve more."

He had a strange expression, like he was listening to an incoming message from an ethereal source. "It's not right for you."

"What isn't?" He'd punched the accelerator on her pulse, making it rev so fast she went light-headed. *This is not happening.* He was *not* shutting her out of this world.

"A&R."

"I . . ." She found it hard to take a full breath. But he was wrong. Of course it was right for her. She pretty much did the job anyway. Maybe not discovering the bands, but . . . oh, God. She needed to breathe. *Deep breaths.* "That's ridiculous. I've been doing it for eight years."

"Em, look, I have to get to the studio. You simply can't quit. I won't allow it. We'll find a way to compromise, right? I want you to be happy."

"I'm not happy babysitting your daughter."

He winced. "Loud and clear."

"I need to know there's a place for me here other than going through your laundry room and drawers looking for a missing cashmere night sock."

Looking pained, he touched her arm, ignoring his buzzing phone. "Let's both think on it. Come up with a solution."

"Am I going to Australia with you tomorrow?"

"No."

She bit down hard on fear. It was scary as hell, but she had to do this.

"Emmie . . ."

She turned and walked out of the room.

M1641T0215